ISBN 978-0-483-52787-4
PIBN 10757332

FB &c Ltd, Dalton House, 60 Windsor Avenue, London, SW19 2RR.
Company number 08720141. Registered in England and Wales.

For support please visit www.forgottenbooks.com

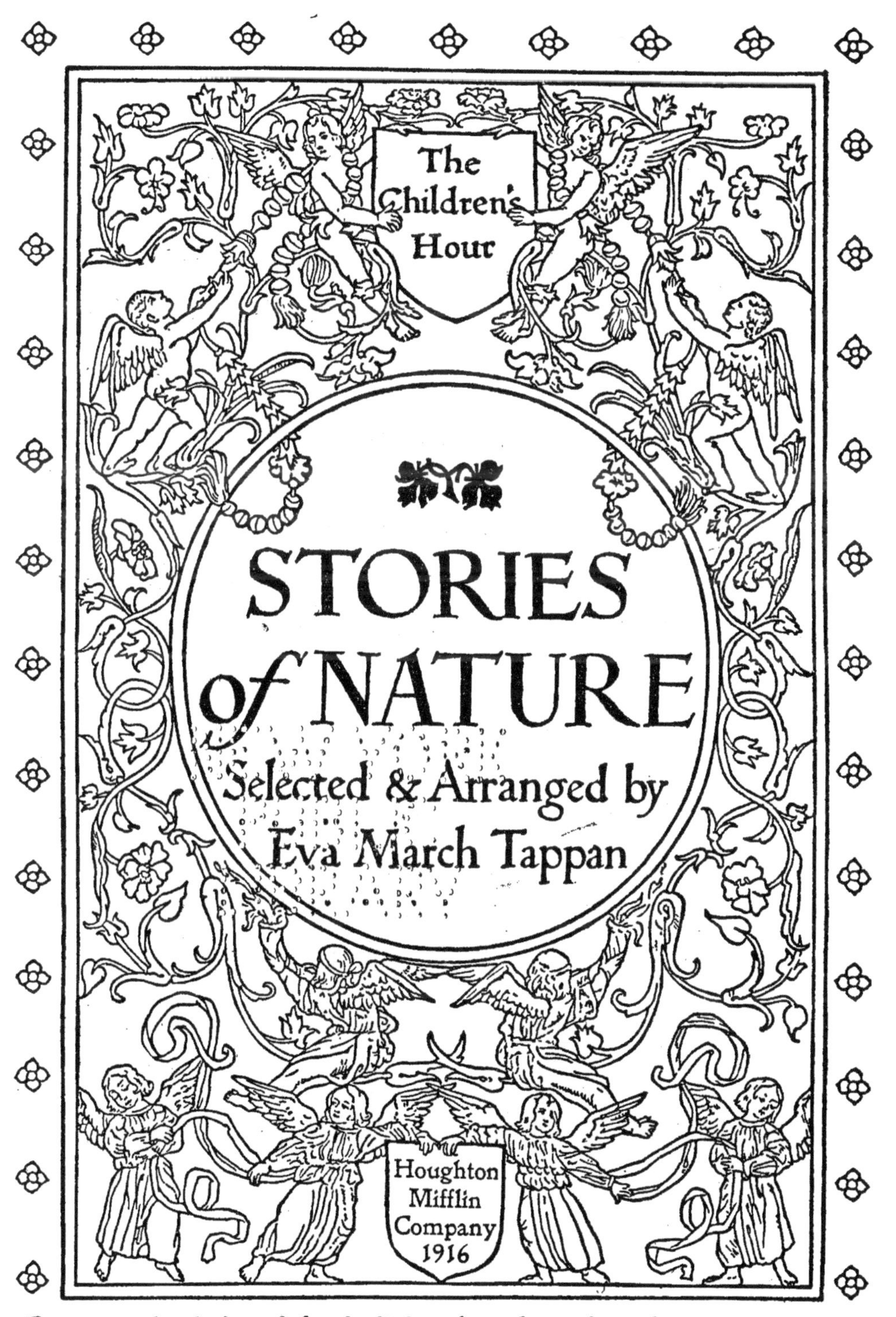

Between the dark and the daylight, when the night is beginning to lower,
Comes a pause in the day's occupations, that is known as the Children's Hour.

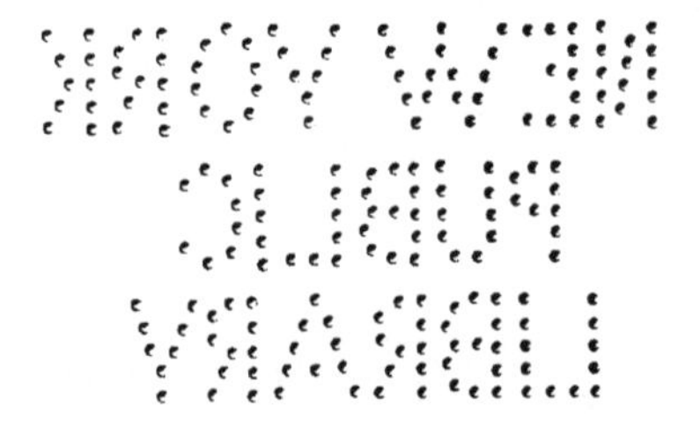

NOTE

ALL rights in stories in this volume are reserved by the holders of the copyrights. The publishers and others named in the subjoined list are the proprietors, either in their own right or as the agents for the authors, of the stories taken from the works enumerated, of which the ownership is hereby acknowledged. The editor takes this opportunity to thank both authors and publishers for the ready generosity with which they have allowed her to include these stories in "The Children's Hour."

"Stickeen," by John Muir; published by Houghton Mifflin Company.

"Wild Life on the Rockies," by Enos A. Mills; published by Houghton Mifflin Company.

"My Summer in a Garden," by Charles Dudley Warner; published by Houghton Mifflin Company.

"Gabriel Conroy, Bohemian Papers," etc., by Bret Harte; published by Houghton Mifflin Company.

"Dixie Kitten," by Eva March Tappan; published by Houghton Mifflin Company.

"The Epworth Herald" ("The Island's Wild Cat," by George Ethelbert Walsh); published by The Methodist Book Concern, Chicago.

"Home Progress" ("Children's Pets," by Alice Perkins Coville; "Wild Life through the Camera," by Dwight Franklin; "Professor Guy A. Bailey and Bird Photography," by David Zukerman; "The Red-breasted Nuthatch," "The Brown Creeper," and "A Brave Little Widower," by Cordelia J. Stanwood; "Woodpeckers as Workmen," "The Busy Bee," and "Snowflakes under a Microscope," by Elizabeth G. Chapin; "The Wisdom of Nature," by Albert H. Pratt; "Weeds: Good, Bad, and Indifferent" and "Our Common Ferns," by E. Thayles Emmons); published by Houghton Mifflin Company.

"Wilderness Pets," by Edward Breck; published by Houghton Mifflin Company.

"The Face of the Fields," by Dallas Lore Sharp; published by Houghton Mifflin Company.

"The Mountains of California," by John Muir; published by The Century Company.

"In Beaver World," by Enos A. Mills; published by Houghton Mifflin Company.

"The Spell of the Rockies," by Enos A. Mills; published by Houghton Mifflin Company.

"My First Summer in the Sierra," by John Muir; published by Houghton Mifflin Company.

"Sinopah, the Indian Boy," by James Willard Schultz; published by Houghton Mifflin Company.

"St. Nicholas" ("Curious Friendships among Animals," by Ellen Velvin); published by The Century Company.

"Winter," by Dallas Lore Sharp; published by Houghton Mifflin Company.

"The Diary of a Goose Girl," by Kate Douglas Wiggin; published by Houghton Mifflin Company.

"Bird Stories from Burroughs," by John Burroughs; published by Houghton Mifflin Company.

NOTE

"The Second Book of Birds," by Olive Thorne Miller; published by Houghton Mifflin Company.

"A Florida Sketch-Book," by Bradford Torrey; published by Houghton Mifflin Company.

"A-Birding on a Bronco," by Florence A. Merriam (Florence Merriam Bailey); published by Houghton Mifflin Company.

"The Foot-Path Way," by Bradford Torrey; published by Houghton Mifflin Company.

"The Clerk of the Woods," by Bradford Torrey; published by Houghton Mifflin Company.

"A Rambler's Lease," by Bradford Torrey; published by Houghton Mifflin Company.

"The Fall of the Year," by Dallas Lore Sharp; published by Houghton Mifflin Company.

"Country Life in America" ("The Story of an Egret Warden," by Oscar E. Baynard); published by Doubleday, Page & Company.

"Where Rolls the Oregon," by Dallas Lore Sharp; published by Houghton Mifflin Company.

"The Spring of the Year," by Dallas Lore Sharp; published by Houghton Mifflin Company.

"The Jonathan Papers," by Elisabeth Woodbridge; published by Houghton Mifflin Company.

"Wasps, Social and Solitary," by George W. and Elizabeth D. Peckham; published by Houghton Mifflin Company.

"The Wild Flower Book for Young People," by Alice Lounsberry; published by Frederick A. Stokes Company.

"Travels in Alaska," by John Muir; published by Houghton Mifflin Company.

NOTE

"Rose o' the River," by Kate Douglas Wiggin; published by Houghton Mifflin Company.

"Among the Isles of Shoals," by Celia Thaxter; published by Houghton Mifflin Company.

"Cape Cod," by Henry D. Thoreau; published by Houghton Mifflin Company.

"The Lure of the Camera," by Charles S. Olcott; published by Houghton Mifflin Company.

"Hours of Exercise in the Alps," by John Tyndall; published by D. Appleton & Company.

"Corona and Coronet," by Mabel Loomis Todd; published by Houghton Mifflin Company.

CONTENTS

CONTENTS

ILLUSTRATIONS

TO THE CHILDREN

THE reason why people are never tired of reading about nature is that no two objects in nature are alike. No two mountains are exactly the same; indeed, any one mountain differs so much at different seasons of the year that it might almost be counted as three or four. No two rivers are alike. Most capes are satisfied to remain in their places, but Cape Cod actually travels. Plants have their own notions and characteristics almost as if they were people. A hollyhock gazes straight into your face, while a columbine looks shyly down at the ground. A morning-glory twists to the right, and it is no easy matter to induce it to take the left-hand turning. Plants insist upon being treated according to their own ideas. The rambler rose thrives best under pruning; but the sweet briar is happiest when it is allowed to grow in its own fashion. Each plant has its time of blooming. The witch-hazel will not blossom until the last moment of autumn, while the snowdrop cannot wait till the snow is gone, and the trailing arbutus is so afraid of being late to the spring opening that she gets her buds ready in the fall.

As for the beasts and birds, every one of them has its own way of living. More than that, each one has little whims and peculiarities just as people have. Even the animals that have learned to live with people are shy about revealing their little ways unless they are sure that people sympathize with them. When they are once convinced that they can trust you, then they show the intelligence and affection that no one who does not love them ever has a chance to see. A caged canary bird that is never petted and talked to and made one of the family will finally make up its mind that there is no use in trying to make friends of people and will become hardly more than a music box. Pet animals manifest in great degree the traits that their masters' treatment and character develop in them. If a dog's master is a thorough gentleman, the dog rarely shows himself to be a vicious cur. A cat likes to be treated gently and never to be rudely surprised. The kitten that is hectored and played with roughly, even if it seems to enjoy the fun, is sure to become a quick-tempered and rather dangerous cat; while the kitten that knows only "gentle words and gentle hands" will become more and more gentle as her days pass on. A stupid person seldom has an intelligent pet; while a person who is intelligent enough to enjoy intelligence in animals rarely has a stupid one.

The following nature stories show how well even the wildest and shyest animals understand kindness and what pleasure there is in becoming acquainted with them and learning their ways. They tell not only about beasts and birds and insects and plants, but about visits to Indians, about holding back a flood, about climbing mountains on foot and descending on avalanches, about walking on glaciers and falling into crevasses, about "jams" and eclipses and volcanoes — and yet they are only a beginning of the delightful and interesting things that have been written about nature.

STORIES OF NATURE

STICKEEN

By John Muir

IN the summer of 1880 I set out from Fort Wrangel in a canoe to continue the exploration of the icy region of southeastern Alaska, begun in the fall of 1879. After the necessary provisions, blankets, etc., had been collected and stowed away, and my Indian crew were in their places ready to start, while a crowd of their relatives and friends on the wharf were bidding them good-bye and good-luck, my companion, the Reverend S. H. Young, for whom we were waiting, at last came aboard, followed by a little black dog, that immediately made himself at home by curling up in a hollow among the baggage. I like dogs, but this one seemed so small and worthless that I objected to his going, and asked the missionary why he was taking him.

"Such a little helpless creature will only be in the way," I said; "you had better pass him up to the Indian boys on the wharf, to be taken home to play with the children. This trip is not likely to be good for toy-dogs. The poor silly thing will be in rain and snow for weeks or months, and will require care like a baby."

But his master assured me that he would be no trouble at all; that he was a perfect wonder of a dog, could endure cold and hunger like a bear, swim like a seal, and was wondrous wise and cunning, etc., making out a list of virtues to show he might be the most interesting member of the party.

Nobody could hope to unravel the lines of his ancestry. In all the wonderfully mixed and varied dog-tribe I never saw any creature very much like him, though in some of his sly, soft, gliding motions and gestures he brought the fox to mind. He was short-legged and bunchy-bodied, and his hair, though smooth, was long and silky and slightly waved, so that when the wind was at his back it ruffled, making him look shaggy. At first sight his only noticeable feature was his fine tail, which was about as airy and shady as a squirrel's, and was carried curling forward almost to his nose. On closer inspection you might notice his thin sensitive ears, and sharp eyes with cunning tan-spots above them. Mr. Young told me that when the little fellow was a pup about the size of a woodrat he was presented to his wife by an Irish prospector at Sitka, and that on his arrival at Fort Wrangel he was adopted with enthusiasm by the Stickeen Indians as a sort of new good-luck totem, was named "Stickeen" for the tribe, and became a universal favorite; petted, protected, and admired wherever he went, and regarded as a mysterious fountain of wisdom.

On our trip he soon proved himself a queer character — odd, concealed, independent, keeping invincibly quiet, and doing many little puzzling things that piqued my curiosity. As we sailed week after week through the long intricate channels and inlets among the innumerable islands and mountains of the coast, he spent most of the dull days in sluggish ease, motionless, and apparently as unobserving as if in deep sleep. But I discovered that somehow he always knew what was going on. When the Indians were about to shoot at ducks or seals, or when anything along the shore was exciting our attention, he would rest his chin on the edge of the canoe and calmly look out like a dreamy-eyed tourist. And when he heard us talking about making a landing, he immediately roused himself to see what sort of a place we were coming to, and made ready to jump overboard and swim ashore as soon as the canoe neared the beach. Then, with a vigorous shake to get rid of the brine in his hair, he ran into the woods to hunt small game. But though always the first out of the canoe, he was always the last to get into it. When we were ready to start he could never be found, and refused to come to our call. We soon found out, however, that though we could not see him at such times, he saw us, and from the cover of the briers and huckleberry bushes in the fringe of the woods was watching the canoe with wary eye. For as soon as we were fairly off he came trotting down the beach, plunged into the surf, and swam after us, knowing well that we would cease rowing and take him in. When the contrary little vagabond came alongside, he was lifted by the neck, held at arm's length a moment to drip, and dropped aboard. We tried to cure him of this trick by compelling him to swim a long way, as if we had a mind to abandon him; but this did no good: the longer the swim the better he seemed to like it.

Though capable of great idleness, he never failed to be ready for all sorts of adventures and excursions. One pitch-dark rainy night we landed about ten o'clock at the mouth of a salmon stream when the water was phosphorescent. The salmon were running, and the myriad fins of the onrushing multitude were churning all the stream into a silvery glow, wonderfully beautiful and impressive in the ebon darkness. To get a good view of the show I set out with one of the Indians and sailed up through the midst of it to the foot of a rapid about half a mile from camp, where the swift current dashing over rocks made the luminous glow most glorions. Happening to look back down the stream, while the Indian was catching a few of the struggling fish, I saw a long spreading fan of light like the tail of a comet, which we thought must be made by some big strange animal that was pursuing us. On it came with its magnificent train, until we imagined we could see the monster's head and eyes; but it was only Stickeen, who, finding I had left the camp, came swimming after me to see what was up.

When we camped early, the best hunter of the crew usually went to the woods for a deer, and Stickeen was sure to be at his heels, provided I had not gone out. For, strange to say, though I never carried a gun, he always followed me, forsaking the hunter and even his master to share my wanderings. The days that were too stormy for sailing I spent in the woods, or on the adjacent mountains, wherever my studies called me; and Stickeen always insisted on going with me, however wild the weather, gliding like a fox through dripping huckleberry bushes and thorny tangles of panax and rubus, scarce stirring their rain-laden leaves; wading and wallowing through snow, swimming icy streams, skipping over logs and rocks and the crevasses of glaciers with the patience and endurance of a determined mountaineer, never tiring or getting discouraged. Once he followed me over a glacier the surface of which was so crusty and rough that it cut his feet until every step was marked with blood; but he trotted on with Indian fortitude until I noticed his red track, and, taking pity on him, made him a set of moccasins out of a handkerchief. However great his troubles he never asked help or made any complaint, as if, like a philosopher, he had learned that without hard work and suffering there could be no pleasure worth having.

Yet none of us was able to make out what Stickeen was really good for. He seemed to meet danger and hardships without anything like reason, insisted on having his own way, never obeyed an order, and the hunter could never set him on anything, or make him fetch the birds he shot. His equanimity was so steady it seemed due to want of feeling; ordinary storms were pleasures to him, and as for mere rain, he flourished in it like a vegetable. No matter what advances you might make, scarce a glance or a tail-wag would you get for your pains. But though he was apparently as cold as a glacier and about as impervious to fun, I tried hard to make his acquaintance, guessing there must be something worth while hidden beneath so much courage, endurance, and love of wild-weathery adventure. No superannuated mastiff or bulldog grown old in office surpassed this fluffy midget in stoic dignity. He sometimes reminded me of a small, squat, unshakable desert cactus. For he never displayed a single trace of the merry, tricksy, elfish fun of the terriers and collies that we all know, nor of their touching affection and devotion. Like children, most small dogs beg to be loved and allowed to love; but Stickeen seemed a very Diogenes, asking only to be let alone: a true child of the wilderness, holding the even tenor of his hidden life with the silence and serenity of nature. His strength of character lay in his eyes. They looked as old as the hills, and as young, and as wild. I never tired of looking into them: it was like looking into a landscape; but they were small and rather deep-set, and had no explaining lines around them to give out particulars. I was accustomed to look into the faces of plants and animals, and I watched the little sphinx more and more keenly as an interesting study. But there is no estimating the wit and wisdom concealed and latent in our lower fellow mortals until made manifest by profound experiences; for it is through suffering that dogs as well as saints are developed and made perfect.

After we had explored the Sumdum and Tahkoo fiords and their glaciers, we sailed through Stephen's Passage into Lynn Canal and thence through Icy Strait into Cross Sound, searching for unexplored inlets leading toward the great fountain ice-fields of the Fairweather Range. Here, while the tide was in our favor, we were accompanied by a fleet of icebergs drifting out to the ocean from Glacier Bay. Slowly we paddled around Vancouver's Point Wimbledon, our frail canoe tossed like a feather on the massive heaving swells coming in past Cape Spenser. For miles the sound is bounded by precipitous mural cliffs, which, lashed with wave-spray and their heads hidden in clouds, looked terribly threatening and stern. Had our canoe been crushed or upset we could have made no landing here, for the cliffs, as high as those of Yosemite, sink sheer into deep water. Eagerly we scanned the wall on the north side for the first sign of an opening fiord or harbor, all of us anxious except Stickeen, who dozed in peace or gazed dreamily at the tremendous precipices when he heard us talking about them. At length we made the joyful discovery of the mouth of the inlet now called "Taylor Bay," and about five o'clock reached the head of it and encamped in a spruce grove near the front of a large glacier.

While camp was being made, Joe the hunter climbed the mountain wall on the east side of the fiord in pursuit of wild goats, while Mr. Young and I went to the glacier. We found that it is separated from the waters of the inlet by a tide-washed moraine, and extends, an abrupt barrier, all the way across from wall to wall of the inlet, a distance of about three miles. But our most interesting discovery was that it had recently advanced, though again slightly receding. A portion of the terminal moraine had been plowed up and shoved forward, uprooting and overwhelming the woods on the east side. Many of the trees were down and buried, or nearly so, others were leaning away from the ice-cliffs, ready to fall, and some stood erect, with the bottom of the ice plow still beneath their roots and its lofty crystal spires towering high above their tops. The spectacle presented by these century-old trees standing close beside a spiry wall of ice, with their branches almost touching it, was most novel and striking. And when I climbed around the front, and a little way up the west side of the glacier, I found that it had swelled and increased in height and width in accordance with its advance, and carried away the outer ranks of trees on its bank.

On our way back to camp after these first observations I planned a far-and-wide excursion for the morrow. I awoke early, called not only by the glacier, which had been on my mind all night, but by a grand flood-storm. The wind was blowing a gale from the north and the rain was flying with the clouds in a wide passionate horizontal flood, as if it were all passing over the country instead of falling on it. The main perennial streams were booming high above their banks, and hundreds of new ones, roaring like the sea, almost covered the lofty gray walls of the inlet with white cascades and falls. I had intended making a cup of coffee and getting something like a breakfast before starting, but when I heard the storm and looked out I made haste to join it; for many of Nature's finest lessons are to be found in her storms, and if careful to keep in right relations with them, we may go safely abroad with them, rejoicing in the grandeur and beauty of their works and ways, and chanting with the old Norsemen, "The blast of the tempest aids our oars, the hurricane is our servant and drives us whither we wish to go." So, omitting breakfast, I put a piece of bread in my pocket and hurried away.

Mr. Young and the Indians were asleep, and so, I hoped, was Stickeen; but I had not gone a dozen rods before he left his bed in the tent and came boring through the blast after me. That a man should welcome storms for their exhilarating music and motion, and go forth to see God making landscapes, is reasonable enough; but what fascination could there be in such tremendous weather for a dog? Surely nothing akin to human enthusiasm for scenery or geology. Anyhow, on he came, breakfastless, through the choking blast. I stopped and did my best to turn him back. "Now don't," I said, shouting to make myself heard in the storm, "now don't, Stickeen. What has got into your queer noddle now? You must be daft. This wild day has nothing for you. There is no game abroad, nothing but weather. Go back to camp and keep warm, get a good breakfast with your master, and be sensible for once. I can't carry you all day or feed you, and this storm will kill you."

But Nature, it seems, was at the bottom of the affair, and she gains her ends with dogs as well as with men, making us do as she likes, shoving and pulling us along her ways, however rough, all but killing us at times in getting her lessons driven hard home. After I had stopped again and again, shouting good warning advice, I saw that he was not to be shaken off; as well might the earth try to shake off the moon. I had once led his master into trouble, when he fell on one of the topmost jags of a mountain and dislocated his arm;

now the turn of his humble companion was coming. The pitiful little wanderer just stood there in the wind, drenched and blinking, saying doggedly, "Where thou goest I will go." So at last I told him to come on if he must, and gave him a piece of the bread I had in my pocket; then we struggled on together, and thus began the most memorable of all my wild days.

The level flood, driving hard in our faces, thrashed and washed us wildly until we got into the shelter of a grove on the east side of the glacier near the front, where we stopped awhile for breath and to listen and look out. The exploration of the glacier was my main object, but the wind was too high to allow excursions over its open surface, where one might be dangerously shoved while balancing for a jump on the brink of a crevasse. In the mean time the storm was a fine study. Here the end of the glacier, descending an abrupt swell of resisting rock about five hundred feet high, leans forward and falls in ice cascades. And as the storm came down the glacier from the north, Stickeen and I were beneath the main current of the blast, while favorably located to see and hear it. What a psalm the storm was singing, and how fresh the smell of the washed earth and leaves, and how sweet the still small voices of the storm! Detached wafts and swirls were coming through the woods, with music from the leaves and branches and furrowed boles, and even from the splintered rocks and ice-crags overhead, many of the tones soft and low and flute-like, as if each leaf and tree, crag and spire were a tuned reed. A broad torrent, draining the side of the glacier, now swollen by scores of new streams from the mountains, was rolling boulders along its rocky channel, with thudding, bumping, muffled sounds, rushing towards the bay with tremendous energy, as if in haste to get out of the mountains; the waters above and beneath calling to each other, and all to the ocean, their home.

Looking southward from our shelter, we had this great torrent and the forested mountain wall above it on our left, the spiry ice-crags on our right, and smooth gray gloom ahead. I tried to draw the marvelous scene in my note-book, but the rain blurred the page in spite of all my pains to shelter it, and the sketch was almost worthless. When the wind began to abate, I traced the east side of the glacier. All the trees standing on the edge of the woods were barked and bruised, showing high-ice mark in a very telling way, while tens of thousands of those that had stood for centuries on the bank of the glacier farther out lay crushed and being crushed. In many places I could see down fifty feet or so beneath the margin of the glacier-mill, where trunks from one to two feet in diameter were being ground to pulp against outstanding rock-ribs and bosses of the bank.

About three miles above the front of the glacier I climbed to the surface of it by means of axe-steps made easy for Stickeen. As far as the eye could reach, the level, or nearly level, glacier stretched away indefinitely beneath the gray sky, a seemingly boundless prairie of ice. The rain continued, and grew colder, which I did not mind, but a dim snowy look in the drooping clouds made me hesitate about venturing far from land. No trace of the west shore was visible, and in case the clouds should settle and give snow, or the wind again become violent, I feared getting caught in a tangle of crevasses. Snow-crystals, the flowers of the mountain clouds, are frail, beautiful things, but terrible when flying on storm-winds in darkening, benumbing swarms or when welded together into glaciers full of deadly crevasses. Watching the weather, I sauntered about on the crystal sea. For a mile or two out I found the ice remarkably safe. The marginal crevasses were mostly narrow, while the few wider ones were easily avoided by passing around them, and the clouds began to open here and there.

Thus encouraged, I at last pushed out for the other side; for Nature can make us do anything she likes. At first we made rapid progress, and the sky was not very threatening, while I took bearings occasionally with a pocket compass to enable me to find my way back more surely in case the storm should become blinding; but the structure lines of the glacier were my main guide. Toward the west side we came to a closely crevassed section in which we had to make long, narrow tacks and doublings, tracing the edges of tremendons transverse and longitudinal crevasses, many of which were from twenty to thirty feet wide, and perhaps a thousand feet deep — beautiful and awful. In working a way through them I was severely cautious, but Stickeen came on as unhesitating as the flying clouds. The widest crevasse that I could jump he would leap without so much as halting to take a look at it. The weather was now making quick changes, scattering bits of dazzling brightness through the wintry gloom; at rare intervals, when the sun broke forth wholly free, the glacier was seen from shore to shore with a bright array of encompassing mountains partly revealed, wearing the clouds as garments, while the prairie bloomed and sparkled with irised light from myriads of washed crystals. Then suddenly all the glorious show would be darkened and blotted out.

Stickeen seemed to care for none of these things, bright or dark, nor for the crevasses, wells, moulins, or swift flashing streams into which he might fall. The little adventurer was only about two years old, yet nothing seemed novel to him, nothing daunted him. He showed neither caution nor curiosity, wonder nor fear, but bravely trotted on as if glaciers were playgrounds. His stout, muffled body seemed all one skipping muscle, and it was truly wonderful to see how swiftly and to all appearance heedlessly he flashed across nerve-trying chasms six or eight feet wide. His courage was so unwavering that it seemed to be due to dullness of perception, as if he were only blindly bold; and I kept warning him to be careful. For we had been close companions on so many wilderness trips that I had formed the habit of talking to him as if he were a boy and understood every word.

We gained the west shore in about three hours; the width of the glacier here being about seven miles. Then I pushed northward in order to see as far back as possible into the fountains of the Fairweather Mountains, in case the clouds should rise. The walking was easy along the margin of the forest, which, of course, like that on the other side, had been invaded and crushed by the swollen, overflowing glacier. In an hour or so, after passing a massive headland, we came suddenly on a branch of the glacier, which, in the form of a magnificent ice-cascade two miles wide, was pouring over the rim of the main basin in a westerly direction, its surface broken into wave-shaped blades and shattered blocks, suggesting the wildest updashing, heaving, plunging motion of a great river cataract. Tracing it down three or four miles, I found that it discharged into a lake, filling it with icebergs.

I would gladly have followed the lake outlet to tidewater, but the day was already far spent, and the threatening sky called for haste on the return trip to get off the ice before dark. I decided therefore to go no farther, and, after taking a general view of the wonderful region, turned back, hoping to see it again under more favorable auspices. We made good speed up the cañon of the great ice-torrent, and out on the main glacier until we had left the west shore about two miles behind us. Here we got into a difficult network of crevasses, the gathering clouds began to drop misty fringes, and soon the dreaded snow came flying thick and fast. I now began to feel anxious about finding a way in the blurring storm. Stickeen showed no trace of fear. He was still the same silent, able little hero. I noticed, however, that after the storm-darkness came on he kept close up behind me. The snow urged us to make still greater haste, but at the same time hid our way. I pushed on as best I could, jumping innumerable crevasses, and for every hundred rods or so of direct advance traveling a mile in doubling up and down in the turmoil of chasms and dislocated ice-blocks. After an hour or two of this work we came to a series of longitudinal crevasses of appalling width, and almost straight and regular in trend, like immense furrows. These I traced with firm nerve, excited and strengthened by the danger, making wide jumps, poising cautiously on their dizzy edges after cutting hollows for my feet before making the spring, to avoid possible slipping or any uncertainty on the farther sides, where only one trial is granted — exercise at once frightful and inspiring. Stickeen followed seemingly without effort.

Many a mile we thus traveled, mostly up and down, making but little real headway in crossing, running instead of walking most of the time as the danger of being compelled to spend the night on the glacier became threatening. Stickeen seemed able for anything. Doubtless we could have weathered the storm for one night, dancing on a flat spot to keep from freezing, and I faced the threat without feeling anything like despair; but we were hungry and wet, and the wind from the mountains was still thick with snow and bitterly cold, so of course that night would have seemed a very long one. I could not see far enough through the blurring snow to judge in which general direction the least dangerous route lay, while the few dim, momentary glimpses I caught of mountains through rifts in the flying clouds were far from encouraging either as weather signs or as guides. I had simply to grope my way from crevasse to crevasse, holding a general direction by the ice-structure, which was not to be seen everywhere, and partly by the wind. Again and again I was put to my mettle, but Stickeen followed easily, his nerve apparently growing more unflinching as the danger increased. So it always is with mountaineers when hard beset. Running hard and jumping, holding every minute of the remaining daylight, poor as it was, precious, we doggedly persevered and tried to hope that every difficult crevasse we overcame would prove to be the last of its kind. But on the contrary, as we advanced they became more deadly trying.

At length our way was barred by a very wide and straight crevasse, which I traced rapidly northward a mile or so without finding a crossing or hope of one; then down the glacier about as far, to where it united with another uncrossable crevasse. In all this distance of perhaps two miles there was only one place where I could possibly jump it, but the width of this jump was the utmost I dared attempt, while the danger of slipping on the farther side was so great that I was loath to try it. Furthermore, the side I was on was about a foot higher than the other, and even with this advantage the crevasse seemed dangerously wide. One is liable to underestimate the width of crevasses where the magnitudes in general are great. I therefore stared at this one mighty keenly, estimating its width and the shape of the edge on the farther side, until I thought that I could jump it if necessary, but that in case I should be compelled to jump back from the lower side I might fail. Now, a cautious mountaineer seldom takes a step on unknown ground which seems at all dangerous that he cannot retrace in case he should be stopped by unseen obstacles ahead. This is the rule of mountaineers who live long, and, though in haste, I compelled myself to sit down and calmly deliberate before I broke it.

Retracing my devious path in imagination as if it were drawn on a chart, I saw that I was recrossing the glacier a mile or two farther up stream than the course pursued in the morning, and that I was now entangled in a section I had not before seen. Should I risk this dangerous jump, or try to regain the woods on the west shore, make a fire, and have only hunger to endure while waiting for a new day? I had already crossed so broad a stretch of dangerous ice that I saw it would be difficult to get back to the woods through the storm, before dark, and the attempt would most likely result in a dismal night-dance on the glacier; while just beyond the present barrier the surface seemed more promising, and the east shore was now perhaps about as near as the west. I was therefore eager to go on. But this wide jump was a dreadful obstacle.

At length, because of the dangers already behind me, I determined to venture against those that might be ahead, jumped and landed well, but with so little to spare that I more than ever dreaded being compelled to take that jump back from the lower side. Stickeen followed, making nothing of it, and we ran eagerly forward, hoping we were leaving all our troubles behind. But within the distance of a few hundred yards we were stopped by the widest crevasse yet encountered. Of course I made haste to explore it, hoping all might yet be remedied by finding a bridge or a way around either end. About three-fourths of a mile upstream I found that it united with the one we had just crossed, as I feared it would. Then, tracing it down, I found it joined the same crevasse at the lower end also, maintaining throughout its whole course a width of forty to fifty feet. Thus to my dismay I discovered that we were on a narrow island about two miles long, with two barely possible ways of escape: one back by the way we came, the other ahead by an almost inaccessible sliver-bridge that crossed the great crevasse from near the middle of it!

After this nerve-trying discovery I ran back to the sliver-bridge and cautiously examined it. Crevasses, caused by strains from variations in the rate of motion of different parts of the glacier and convexities in the channel, are mere cracks when they first open, so narrow as hardly to admit the blade of a pocket-knife, and gradually widen according to the extent of the strain and the depth of the glacier. Now some of these cracks are interrupted, like the cracks in wood, and in opening, the strip of ice between overlapping ends is dragged out, and may maintain a continuous connection between the sides, just as the two sides of a slivered crack in wood that is being split are connected. Some crevasses remain open for months or even years, and by the melting of their sides continue to increase in width long after the opening strain has ceased; while the sliver-bridges, level on top at first and perfectly safe, are at length melted to thin, vertical, knife-edged blades, the upper portion being most exposed to the weather;

and since the exposure is greatest in the middle, they at length curve downward like the cables of suspension bridges. This one was evidently very old, for it had been weathered and wasted until it was the most dangerons and inaccessible that ever lay in my way. The width of the crevasse was here about fifty feet, and the sliver crossing diagonally was about seventy feet long; its thin knife-edge near the middle was depressed twenty-five or thirty feet below the level of the glacier, and the upcurving ends were attached to the sides eight or ten feet below the brink. Getting down the nearly vertical wall to the end of the sliver and up the other side were the main difficulties, and they seemed all but insurmountable. Of the many perils encountered in my years of wandering on mountains and glaciers none seemed so plain and stern and merciless as this. And it was presented when we were wet to the skin and hungry, the sky dark with quick driving snow, and the night near. But we were forced to face it. It was a tremendous necessity.

Beginning, not immediately above the sunken end of the bridge, but a little to one side, I cut a deep hollow on the brink for my knees to rest in. Then leaning over with my short-handled axe I cut a step sixteen or eighteen inches below, which on account of the sheerness of the wall was necessarily shallow. That step, however, was well made; its floor sloped slightly inward and formed a good hold for my heels. Then, slipping cautiously upon it, and crouching as low as possible, with my left side toward the wall, I steadied myself against the wind with my left hand in a slight notch while with the right I cut other similar steps and notches in succession, guarding against losing balance by glinting of the axe, or by wind-gusts, for life and death were in every stroke and in the niceness of finish of every foothold.

After the end of the bridge was reached I chipped it down until I had made a level platform six or eight inches wide, and it was a trying thing to poise on this little slippery platform while bending over to get safely astride of the sliver. Crossing was then comparatively easy by chipping off the sharp edge with short, careful strokes, and hitching forward an inch or two at a time, keeping my balance with my knees pressed against the sides. The tremendous abyss on either hand I studiously ignored. To me the edge of that blue sliver was then all the world. But the most trying part of the adventure, after working my way across inch by inch and chipping another small platform, was to rise from the safe position astride and to cut a step-ladder in the nearly vertical face of the wall, — chipping, climbing, holding on with feet and fingers in mere notches. At such times one's whole body is eye, and common skill and fortitude are replaced by power beyond our call or knowledge. Never before had I been so long under deadly strain. How I got up that cliff I never could tell. The thing seemed to have been done by somebody else. I never have held death in contempt, though in the course of my explorations I have oftentimes felt that to meet one's fate on a noble mountain, or in the heart of a glacier, would be blessed as compared with death from disease, or from some shabby lowland accident. But the best death, quick and crystal-pure, set so glaringly open before us, is hard enough to face, even though we feel gratefully sure that we have already had happiness enough for a dozen lives.

But poor Stickeen, the wee, hairy, sleekit beastie, think of him! When I had decided to dare the bridge, and while I was on my knees chipping a hollow on the rounded brow above it, he came behind me, pushed his head past my shoulder, looked down and across, scanned the sliver and its approaches with his mysterious eyes, then looked me in the face with a startled air of surprise and concern, and began to mutter and whine; saying as plainly as if speaking with words, "Surely, you are not going into that awful place." This was the first time I had seen him gaze deliberately into a crevasse, or into my face with an eager, speaking, troubled look. That he should have recognized and appreciated the danger at the first glance showed wonderful sagacity. Never before had the daring midget seemed to know that ice was slippery or that there was any such thing as danger anywhere. His looks and tones of voice when he began to complain and speak his fears were so human that I unconsciously talked to him in sympathy as I would to a frightened boy, and in trying to calm his fears perhaps in some measure moderated my own. "Hush your fears, my boy," I said, "we will get across safe, though it is not going to be easy. No right way is easy in this rough world. We must risk our lives to save them. At the worst we can only slip, and then how grand a grave we will have, and by and by our nice bones will do good in the terminal moraine."

But my sermon was far from reassuring him: he began to cry, and after taking another piercing look at the tremendous gulf, ran away in desperate excitement, seeking some other crossing. By the time he got back, baffled of course, I had made a step or two. I dared not look back, but he made himself heard; and when he saw that I was certainly bent on crossing he cried aloud in despair. The danger was enough to daunt anybody, but it seems wonderful that he should have been able to weigh and appreciate it so justly. No mountaineer could have seen it more quickly or judged it more wisely, discriminating between real and apparent peril.

When I gained the other side, he screamed louder than ever, and after running back and forth in vain search for a way of escape, he would return to the brink of the crevasse above the bridge, moaning and wailing as it in the bitterness of death. Could this be the silent, philosophic Stickeen? I shouted encouragement, telling him the bridge was not so bad as it looked, that I had left it flat and safe for his feet, and he could walk it easily. But he was afraid to try. Strange so small an animal should be capable of such big, wise fears. I called again and again in a reassuring tone to come on and fear nothing; that he could come if he would only try. He would hush for a moment, look down again at the bridge, and shout his unshakable conviction that he could never, never come that way; then lie back in despair, as if howling, "O-o-oh! what a place! No-o-o, I can never go-o-o down there!" His natural composure and courage had vanished utterly in a tumultuous storm of fear. Had the danger been less, his distress would have seemed ridiculons. But in this dismal, merciless abyss lay the shadow of death, and his heartrending cries might well have called Heaven to his help. Perhaps they did. So hidden before, he was now transparent, and one could see the workings of his heart and mind like the movements of a clock out of its case. His voice and gestures, hopes and fears, were so perfectly human that none could mistake them; while he seemed to understand every word of mine. I was troubled at the thought of having to leave him out all night, and of the danger of not finding him in the morning. It seemed impossible to get him to venture. To compel him to try through fear of being abandoned, I started off as if leaving him to his fate, and disappeared back of a hummock; but this did no good; he only lay down and moaned in utter hopeless misery. So, after hiding a few minutes, I went back to the brink of the crevasse and in a severe tone of voice shouted across to him that now I must certainly leave him, I could wait no longer, and that, if he would not come, all I could promise was that I would return to seek him next day. I warned him that if he went back to the woods the wolves would kill him, and finished by urging him once more by words and gestures to come on, come on.

He knew very well what I meant, and at last, with the courage of despair, hushed and breathless, he crouched down on the brink in the hollow I had made for my knees, pressed his body against the ice as if trying to get the advantage of the friction of every hair, gazed into the first step, put his little feet together and slid them slowly, slowly over the edge and down into it, bunching all four in it and almost standing on his head. Then, without lifting his feet, as well as I could see through the snow, he slowly worked them over the edge of the step and down into the next and the next in succession in the same way, and gained the end of the bridge. Then, lifting his feet with the regularity and slowness of the vibrations of a seconds pendulum, as if counting and measuring *one-two-three*, holding himself steady against the gusty wind, and giving separate attention to each little step, he gained the foot of the cliff, while I was on my knees leaning over to give him a lift should he succeed in getting within reach of my arm. Here he halted in dead silence, and it was here I feared he might fail, for dogs are poor climbers. I had no cord. If I had had one, I would have dropped a noose over his head and hauled him up. But while I was thinking whether an available cord might be made out of clothing, he was looking keenly into the series of notched steps and finger-holds I had made, as if counting them, and fixing the position of each one of them in his mind. Then suddenly up he came in a springy rush, hooking his paws into the steps and notches so quickly that I could not see how it was done, and whizzed past my head, safe at last!

And now came a scene! "Well done, well done, little

boy! Brave boy!" I cried, trying to catch and caress him; but he would not be caught. Never before or since have I seen anything like so passionate a revulsion from the depths of despair to exultant, triumphant, uncontrollable joy. He flashed and darted hither and thither as if fairly demented, screaming and shouting, swirling round and round in giddy loops and circles like a leaf in a whirlwind, lying down, and rolling over and over, sidewise and heels over head, and pouring forth a tumultuous flood of hysterical cries and sobs and gasping mutterings. When I ran up to him to shake him, fearing he might die of joy, he flashed off two or three hundred yards, his feet in a mist of motion; then, turning suddenly, came back in a wild rush and launched himself at my face, almost knocking me down, all the time screeching and screaming and shouting as if saying, "Saved! saved! saved!" Then away again, dropping suddenly at times with his feet in the air, trembling and fairly sobbing. Such passionate emotion was enough to kill him. Moses' stately song of triumph after escaping the Egyptians and the Red Sea was nothing to it. Who could have guessed the capacity of the dull, enduring little fellow for all that most stirs this mortal frame? Nobody could have helped crying with him!

But there is nothing like work for toning down excessive fear or joy. So I ran ahead, calling him in as gruff a voice as I could command to come on and stop his nonsense, for we had far to go and it would soon be dark. Neither of us feared another trial like this. Heaven would surely count one enough for a lifetime.

The ice ahead was gashed by thousands of crevasses, but they were common ones. The joy of deliverance burned in us like fire, and we ran without fatigue, every muscle with immense rebound glorying in its strength. Stickeen flew across everything in his way, and not till dark did he settle into his normal fox-like trot. At last the cloudy mountains came in sight, and we soon felt the solid rock beneath our feet, and were safe. Then came weakness. Danger had vanished, and so had our strength. We tottered down the lateral moraine in the dark, over boulders and tree trunks, through the bushes and devil-club thickets of the grove where we had sheltered ourselves in the morning, and across the level mud-slope of the terminal moraine. We reached camp about ten o'clock, and found a big fire and a big supper. A party of Hoona Indians had visited Mr. Young, bringing a gift of porpoise meat and wild strawberries, and Hunter Joe had brought in a wild goat. But we lay down, too tired to eat much, and soon fell into a troubled sleep. The man who said, "The harder the toil, the sweeter the rest," never was profoundly tired. Stickeen kept springing up and muttering in his sleep, no doubt dreaming that he was still on the brink of the crevasse; and so did I, that night and many others long afterward, when I was overtired.

Thereafter Stickeen was a changed dog. During the rest of the trip, instead of holding aloof, he always lay by my side, tried to keep me constantly in sight, and would hardly accept a morsel of food, however tempting, from any hand but mine. At night, when all was quiet about the camp-fire, he would come to me and rest his head on my knee with a look of devotion as if I were his god. And often as he caught my eye he seemed to be trying to say, "Was n't that an awful time we had together on the glacier?"

Nothing in after years has dimmed that Alaska storm-day. As I write it all comes rushing and roaring to mind as if I were again in the heart of it. Again I see the gray flying clouds with their rain-floods and snow, the ice-cliffs towering above the shrinking forest, the majestic ice-cascade, the vast glacier outspread before its white mountain fountains, and in the heart of it the tremendous crevasse, — emblem of the valley of the shadow of death, — low clouds trailing over it, the snow falling into it; and on its brink I see little Stickeen, and I hear his cries for help and his shouts of joy. I have known many dogs, and many a story I could tell of their wisdom and devotion; but to none do I owe so much as to Stickeen. At first the least promising and least known of my dog-friends, he suddenly became the best known of them all. Our storm-battle for life brought him to light, and through him as through a window I have ever since been looking with deeper sympathy into all my fellow mortals.

None of Stickeen's friends knows what finally became of him. After my work for the season was done I departed for California, and I never saw the dear little fellow again. In reply to anxious inquiries his master wrote me that in the summer of 1883 he was stolen by a tourist at Fort Wrangel and taken away on a steamer. His fate is wrapped in mystery. Doubtless he has left this world — crossed the last crevasse — and gone to another. But he will not be forgotten. To me Stickeen is immortal.

FAITHFUL SCOTCH

By Enos A. Mills

I CARRIED little Scotch all day long in my overcoat pocket as I rode through the mountains on the way to my cabin. His cheerful, cunning face, his good behavior, and the clever way in which he poked his head out of my pocket, licked my hand, and looked at the scenery, completely won my heart before I had ridden an hour. That night he showed so strikingly the strong, faithful characteristics for which collies are noted that I resolved never to part with him. Since then we have had great years together. We have been hungry and happy together, and together we have played by the cabin, faced danger in the wilds, slept peacefully among the flowers, followed the trails by starlight, and cuddled down in winter's drifting snow.

On my way home through the mountains with puppy Scotch, I stopped for a night near a deserted ranch-house and shut him up in a small abandoned cabin. He at once objected and set up a terrible barking and howling, gnawing fiercely at the crack beneath the door and trying to tear his way out. Fearing he would break his little puppy teeth, or possibly die from frantic and persistent efforts to be free, I concluded to release him from the cabin. My fears that he would run away if left free were groundless. He made his way to my saddle, which lay on the ground near by, crawled under it, turned round beneath it, and thrust his little head from beneath the arch of the horn and lay down with a look of contentment, and also with an air which said, "I'll take care of this saddle. I'd like to see any one touch it."

And watch it he did. At midnight a cowboy came to my camp-fire. He had been thrown from his bronco and was making back to his outfit on foot. In approaching the fire his path lay close to my saddle, beneath which Scotch was lying. Tiny Scotch flew at him ferociously; never have I seen such faithful ferociousness in a dog so small and young. I took him in my hands and assured him that the visitor was welcome, and in a moment little Scotch and the cowboy were side by side gazing at the fire.

I suppose his bravery and watchful spirit may be instinct inherited from his famous forbears who lived so long and so cheerfully on Scotland's heaths and moors. But, with all due respect for inherited qualities, he also has a brain that does a little thinking and meets emergencies promptly and ably.

He took serious objection to the coyotes which howled, serenaded, and made merry in the edge of the meadow about a quarter of a mile from my cabin. Just back of their howling-ground was a thick forest of pines, in which were scores of broken rocky crags. Into the tangled forest the coyotes always retreated when Scotch gave chase, and into this retreat he dared not pursue them. So long as the coyotes sunned themselves, kept quiet, and played, Scotch simply watched

FAITHFUL SCOTCH

them contentedly from afar; but the instant they began to howl and yelp, he at once raced over and chased them into the woods. They often yelped and taunted him from their safe retreat, but Scotch always took pains to lie down on the edge of the open and remain there until they became quiet or went away.

During the second winter that Scotch was with me and before he was two years of age, one of the wily coyotes showed a tantalizing spirit and some interesting cunning which put Scotch on his metal. One day when Scotch was busy driving the main pack into the woods, one that trotted lame with the right fore leg emerged from behind a rocky crag at the edge of the open and less than fifty yards from Scotch. Hurrying to a willow clump about fifty yards in Scotch's rear, he set up a broken chorus of yelps and howls, seemingly with delight and to the great annoyance of Scotch, who at once raced back and chased the noisy taunter into the woods.

The very next time that Scotch was chasing the pack away, the crippled coyote again sneaked from behind the crag, took refuge behind the willow clump, and began delivering a perfect shower of broken yelps. Scotch at once turned back and gave chase. Immediately the entire pack wheeled from retreat and took up defiant attitudes in the open, but this did not seem to trouble Scotch; he flung himself upon them with great ferocity, and finally drove them all back into the woods. However, the third time that the cunning coyote had come to his rear, the entire pack stopped in the edge of the open and, for a time, defied him.

He came back from this chase panting and tired and carrying every expression of worry. It seemed to prey upon him to such an extent that I became a little anxious about him.

One day, just after this affair, I went for the mail, and allowed Scotch to go with me. I usually left him at the cabin, and he stayed unchained and was faithful, though it was always evident that he was anxious to go with me and also that he was exceedingly lonely when left behind. But on this occasion he showed such eagerness to go that I allowed him the pleasure.

At the post-office he paid but little attention to the dogs which, with their masters, were assembled there, and held himself aloof from them, squatting on the ground with head erect and almost an air of contempt for them, but it was evident that he was watching their every move. When I started homeward, he showed great satisfaction by leaping and barking.

That night was wildly stormy, and I concluded to go out and enjoy the storm on some wind-swept crags. Scotch was missing and I called him, but he did not appear, so I went alone. After being tossed by the wind for more than an hour, I returned to the cabin, but Scotch was still away. This had never occurred before, so I concluded not to go to bed until he returned. He came home after daylight, and was accompanied by another dog, — a collie, which belonged to a rancher who lived about fifteen miles away. I remembered to have seen this dog at the post-office the day before. My first thought was to send the dog home, but I finally concluded to allow him to remain, to see what would come of his presence, for it was apparent that Scotch had gone for him. He appropriated Scotch's bed in the tub, to the evident satisfaction of Scotch. During the morning the two played together in the happiest possible manner for more than an hour. At noon I fed them together.

In the afternoon, while I was writing, I heard the varied voices of the coyote pack, and went out with my glass to watch proceedings, wondering how the visiting collie would play his part. There went Scotch, as I supposed, racing for the yelping pack, but the visiting collie was not to be seen. The pack beat the usual sullen, scattering retreat, and while the dog, which I supposed to be Scotch, was chasing the last slow tormenter into the woods, from behind the crag came the big limping coyote, hurrying toward the willow clump from behind which he was accustomed to yelp triumphantly in Scotch's rear. I raised the glass for a better look, all the time wondering where the visiting collie was keeping himself. I was unable to see him, yet I recollected he was with Scotch less than an hour before.

The lame coyote came round the willow clump as usual, and threw up his head as though to bay at the moon. Then the unexpected happened. On the instant, Scotch leaped into the air out of the willow clump, and came down upon the coyote's back! They rolled about for some time, when the coyote finally shook himself free and started at a lively limping pace for the woods, only to be grabbed again by the visiting collie, which had been chasing the pack, and which I had mistaken for Scotch. The pack beat a swift retreat. For a time both dogs fought the coyote fiercely, but he at last tore himself free, and escaped into the pines, badly wounded and bleeding. I never saw him again. That night the visiting collie went home. As Scotch was missing that night for a time, I think he may have accompanied him at least a part of the way.

One day a young lady from Michigan came along and wanted to climb Long's Peak all alone, without a guide. I agreed to consent to this if first she would climb one of the lesser peaks unaided, on a stormy day. This the young lady did, and by so doing convinced me that she had a keen sense of direction and an abundance of strength, for the day on which she climbed was a stormy one, and the peak was completely befogged with clouds. After this, there was nothing for me to do but allow her to climb Long's Peak alone.

Just as she was starting, that cool September morning, I thought to provide for an emergency by sending Scotch with her. He knew the trail well and would, of course, lead her the right way, providing she lost the trail. "Scotch," said I, "go with this young lady, take good care of her, and stay with her till she returns. Don't you desert her." He gave a few barks of satisfaction and started with her up the trail, carrying himself in a manner which indicated that he was both honored and pleased. I felt that the strength and alertness of the young lady, when combined with the faithfulness and watchfulness of Scotch, would make the journey a success, so I went about my affairs as usual. When darkness came on that evening, the young lady had not returned.

She climbed swiftly until she reached the rocky alpine moorlands above timber-line. Here she lingered long to enjoy the magnificent scenery and the brilliant flowers. It was late in the afternoon when she arrived at the summit of the peak. After she had spent a little time there resting and absorbing the beauty and grandeur of the scene, she started to return. She had not proceeded far when clouds and darkness came on, and on a slope of slide-rock she lost the trail.

Scotch had minded his own affairs and enjoyed himself in his own way all day long. Most of the time he followed her closely, apparently indifferent to what happened, but when she, in the darkness, left the trail and started off in the wrong direction, he at once came forward, and took the lead with an alert, aggressive air. The way in which he did this should have suggested to the young lady that he knew what he was about, but she did not appreciate this fact. She thought he had become weary and wanted to run away from her, so she called him back. Again she started in the wrong direction; this time Scotch got in front of her and refused to move. She pushed him out of the way. Once more he started off in the right direction, and this time she scolded him and reminded him that his master had told him not to desert her. Scotch dropped his ears and sheepishly fell in behind her and followed meekly along. He had obeyed orders.

After traveling a short distance, the young lady realized that she had lost her way, but it never occurred to her that she had only to trust Scotch and he would lead her directly home. However, she had the good sense to stop where she was, and there, among the crags, by the stained remnants of winter's snow, thirteen thousand feet above sea-level, she was to spend the night. The cold wind blew a gale, roaring and booming among the crags, the alpine brooklet turned to ice, while, in the lee of the crag, shivering with cold, hugging shaggy Scotch in her arms, she lay down for the night.

I had given my word not to go in search of her if she failed to return. However, I sent out four guides to look for her. They suffered much from cold as they vainly searched among the crags through the dark hours of the windy night. Just at sunrise one of them found her, almost exhausted, but, with slightly frost-bitten fingers, still hugging Scotch in her arms. He gave her food and drink and additional wraps, and without delay started with her down the trail. As soon as she was taken in charge by the guide, patient Scotch left her and hurried home. He had saved her life.

Scotch's hair is long and silky, black with a touch of tawny about the head and a little bar of white on the nose. He has the most expressive and pleasing dog's face I have ever seen. There is nothing he enjoys so well as to have some one kick the football for him. For an hour at a time he will chase it and try to get hold of it, giving an occasional eager, happy bark. He has good eyes, and these, with his willingness to be of service, have occasionally made him useful to me in finding articles which I, or some one else, had forgotten or lost on the trail. Generally it is difficult to make him understand just what has been lost or where he is to look for it, but when once he understands, he keeps up the search, sometimes for hours if he does not find the article before. He is always faithful in guarding any object that I ask him to take care of. I have but to throw down a coat and point at it, and he will at once lie down near by, there to remain until I come to dismiss him. He will allow no one else to touch it. His attitude never fails to convey the impression that he would die in defense of the thing intrusted to him, but desert it or give it up, never!

One February day I took Scotch and started up Long's Peak, hoping to gain its wintry summit. Scotch easily followed in my snowshoe tracks. At an altitude of thirteen thousand feet on the wind-swept steeps there was but little snow, and it was necessary to leave snowshoes behind. After climbing a short distance on these icy slopes, I became alarmed for the safety of Scotch. By and by I had to cut steps in the ice. This made the climb too perilous for him, as he could not realize the danger he was in should he miss a step. There were places where slipping from these steps meant death, so I told Scotch to go back. I did not, however, tell him to watch my snowshoes, for so dangerons was the climb that I did not know that I should ever get back to them myself. However, he went to the snowshoes, and with them he remained for eight cold hours until I came back by the light of the stars.

On a few occasions I allowed Scotch to go with me

on short winter excursions. He enjoyed these immensely, although he had a hard time of it and but very little to eat. When we camped among the spruces in the snow, he seemed to enjoy sitting by my side and silently watching the evening fire, and he contentedly cuddled with me to keep warm at night.

One cold day we were returning from a four days' excursion when, a little above timber-line, I stopped to take some photographs. To do this it was necessary for me to take off my sheepskin mittens, which I placed in my coat-pocket, but not securely, as it proved. From time to time, as I climbed to the summit of the Continental Divide, I stopped to take photographs, but on the summit the cold pierced my silk gloves and I felt for my mittens, to find that one of them was lost. I stooped, put an arm around Scotch, and told him I had lost a mitten, and that I wanted him to go down for it to save me the trouble. "It won't take you very long, but it will be a hard trip for me. Go and fetch it to me." Instead of starting off hurriedly, willingly, as he had invariably done before in obedience to my commands, he stood still. His alert, eager ears drooped, but no other move did he make. I repeated the command in my most kindly tones. At this, instead of starting down the mountain for the mitten, he slunk slowly away toward home. It was clear that he did not want to climb down the steep icy slope of a mile to timber-line, more than a thousand feet below. I thought he had misunderstood me, so I called him back, patted him, and then, pointing down the slope, said, "Go for the mitten, Scotch; I will wait here for you." He started for it, but went unwillingly. He had always served me so cheerfully that I could not understand, and it was not until late the next afternoon that I realized that he had not understood me, but that he had loyally, and at the risk of his life, tried to obey me.

The summit of the Continental Divide, where I stood when I sent him back, was a very rough and lonely region. On every hand were broken snowy peaks and rugged cañons. My cabin, eighteen miles away, was the nearest house to it, and the region was utterly wild. I waited a reasonable time for Scotch to return, but he did not come back. Thinking he might have gone by without my seeing him, I walked some distance along the summit, first in one direction and then in the other, but, seeing neither him nor his tracks, I knew that he had not yet come back. As it was late in the afternoon, and growing colder, I decided to go slowly on toward my cabin. I started along a route that I felt sure he would follow, and I reasoned that he would overtake me. Darkness came on and still no Scotch, but I kept going forward. For the remainder of the way I told myself that he might have got by me in the darkness.

When, at midnight, I arrived at the cabin, I expected to be greeted by him, but he was not there. I felt that something was wrong and feared that he had met with an accident. I slept two hours and rose, but still he was missing, so I concluded to tie on my snowshoes and go to meet him. The thermometer showed fourteen below zero.

I started at three o'clock in the morning, feeling that I should meet him without going far. I kept going on and on, and when, at noon, I arrived at the place on the summit from which I had sent him back, Scotch was not there to cheer the wintry, silent scene.

I slowly made my way down the slope, and at two in the afternoon, twenty-four hours after I had sent Scotch back, I paused on a crag and looked below. There in the snowy world of white he lay by the mitten in the snow. He had misunderstood me, and had gone back to guard the mitten instead of to get it. He could hardly contain himself for joy when he saw me. He leaped into the air, barked, jumped, rolled over, licked my hand, whined, grabbed the mitten, raced round and round me, and did everything that an alert, affectionate, faithful dog could do to show that he appreciated my appreciation of his supremely faithful services.

After waiting for him to eat a luncheon, we started merrily towards home, where we arrived at one o'clock in the morning. Had I not returned, I suppose Scotch would have died beside the mitten. In a region cold, cheerless, oppressive, without food, and perhaps to die, he lay down by the mitten because he understood that I had told him to. In the annals of dog heroism, I know of no greater deed.

CALVIN: A CAT

By Charles Dudley Warner

CALVIN is dead. His life, long to him, but short for the rest of us, was not marked by startling adventures, but his character was so uncommon and his qualities were so worthy of imitation that I have been asked by those who personally knew him to set down my recollections of his career.

His origin and ancestry were shrouded in mystery; even his age was a matter of pure conjecture. Although he was of the Maltese race, I have reason to suppose that he was American by birth, as he certainly was in sympathy. Calvin was given to me eight years ago by Mrs. Stowe, but she knew nothing of his age or origin. He walked into her house one day, out of the great unknown, and became at once at home, as if he had been always a friend of the family. He appeared to have artistic and literary tastes, and it was as if he had inquired at the door if that was the residence of the author of "Uncle Tom's Cabin," and, upon being assured that it was, had decided to dwell there. This is, of course, fanciful, for his antecedents were wholly unknown; but in his time he could hardly have been in any household where he would not have heard "Uncle Tom's Cabin" talked about. When he came to Mrs. Stowe he was as large as he ever was, and apparently as old as he ever became. Yet there was in him no appearance of age; he was in the happy maturity of all his powers, and you would rather have said that in that maturity he had found the secret of perpetual youth. And it was as difficult to believe that he would ever be aged as it was to imagine that he had ever been in immature youth. There was in him a mysterious perpetuity.

After some years when Mrs. Stowe made her winter home in Florida, Calvin came to live with us. From the first moment he fell into the ways of the house and assumed a recognized position in the family, — I say recognized, because after he became known he was always inquired for by visitors, and in the letters to the other members of the family he always received a message. Although the least obtrusive of beings, his individuality always made itself felt.

His personal appearance had much to do with this, for he was of royal mould, and had an air of high breeding. He was large, but he had nothing of the fat grossness of the celebrated Angora family; though powerful, he was exquisitely proportioned, and as graceful in every movement as a young leopard. When he stood up to open a door — he opened all the doors with old-fashioned latches — he was portentously tall, and when stretched on the rug before the fire he seemed too long for this world, — as indeed he was. His coat was the finest and softest I have ever seen, a shade of quiet Maltese; and from his throat downward, underneath, to the white tips of his feet, he wore the whitest and most delicate ermine; and no person was ever more fastidiously neat. In his finely formed head you saw something of his aristocratic character; the ears were small and cleanly cut, there was a tinge of pink in the nostrils, his face was handsome, and the expression of his countenance exceedingly intelligent, — I should call it even a sweet expression, if the term were not inconsistent with his look of alertness and sagacity.

It is difficult to convey a just idea of his gayety in connection with his dignity and gravity, which his name expressed. As we know nothing of his family, of course it will be understood that Calvin was his Christian name. He had times of relaxation into utter playfulness, delighting in a ball of yarn, catching sportively at stray ribbons when his mistress was at her toilet, and pursuing his own tail with hilarity, for lack of anything better. He could amuse himself by the hour, and he did not care for children; perhaps something in his past was present to his memory. He had absolutely no bad habits, and his disposition was perfect. I never saw him exactly angry, though I have seen his tail grow to an enormous size when a strange cat appeared upon his lawn. He disliked cats, evidently regarding them as feline and treacherous, and he had no association with them. Occasionally there would be heard a night concert in the shrubbery. Calvin would ask to have the door opened, and then you would hear a rush and a "pestzt" and the concert would explode, and Calvin would quietly come in and resume his seat on the hearth. There was no trace of anger in his manner, but he would n't have any of that about the house. He had the rare virtue of magnanimity. Although he had fixed notions about his own rights, and extraordinary persistency in getting them, he never showed temper at a repulse; he simply and firmly persisted till he had what he wanted. His diet was one point; his idea was that of the scholars about dictionaries, — to "get the best." He knew as well as any one what was in the house, and would refuse beef if turkey was to be had; and if there were oysters, he would wait over the turkey to see if the oysters would not be forthcoming. And yet he was not a gross gourmand; he would eat bread if he saw me eating it, and thought he was not being imposed on. His habits of feeding, also, were refined; he never used a knife, and he would put up his hand and draw the fork down to his mouth as gracefully as a grown person. Unless necessity compelled, he would not eat in the kitchen, but insisted upon his meals in the dining-room, and would wait patiently, unless a stranger were present; and then he was sure to importune the visitor, hoping that the latter was ignorant of the rule of the house, and would give him something. They used to say that he preferred as his table-cloth on the floor a certain well-known church journal; but this was said by an Episcopalian. So far as I know, he had no religious prejudices, except that he did not like the association with Romanists. He tolerated the servants, because they belonged to the house, and would sometimes linger by the kitchen stove; but the moment visitors came in, he arose, opened the door, and marched into the drawing-room. Yet he enjoyed the company of his equals, and never withdrew, no matter how many callers — whom he recognized as of his society — might come into the drawing-room. Calvin was fond of company, but he wanted to choose it; and I have no doubt that his was an aristocratic fastidiousness rather than one of faith. It is so with most people.

The intelligence of Calvin was something phenomenal, in his rank of life. He established a method of communicating his wants and even some of his sentiments; and he could help himself in many things. There was a furnace register in a retired room, where he used to go when he wished to be alone, that he always opened when he desired more heat; but never shut it, any more than he shut the door after himself. He could do almost everything but speak; and you would declare sometimes that you could see a pathetic longing to do that in his intelligent face. I have no desire to overdraw his qualities, but if there was one thing in him more noticeable than another, it was his fondness for nature. He could content himself for hours at a low window, looking into the ravine and at the great trees, noting the smallest stir there; he delighted, above all things, to accompany me walking about the garden, hearing the birds, getting the smell of the fresh earth, and rejoicing in the sunshine. He followed me and gambolled like a dog, rolling over on the turf and exhibiting his delight in a hundred ways. If I worked, he sat and watched me, or looked off over the bank, and kept his ear open to the twitter in the cherry-trees. When it stormed, he was sure to sit at the window, keenly watching the rain or the snow, glancing up and down at its falling; and a winter tempest always delighted him. I thing he was genuinely fond of birds, but, so far as I know, he usually confined himself to one a day; he never killed, as some sportsmen do, for the sake of killing, but only as civilized people do, — from necessity. He was intimate with the flying-squirrels who dwell in the chestnut-trees, — too intimate, for almost every day in the summer he would bring in one, until he nearly discouraged them. He was, indeed, a superb hunter, and would have been a devastating one, if his bump of destructiveness had not been offest by a bump of moderation. There was very little of the brutality of the lower animals about him; I don't think he enjoyed rats for themselves, but he knew his business, and for the first few months of his residence with us he waged an awful campaign against the horde, and after that his simple presence was sufficient to deter them from coming on the premises. Mice amused him, but he usually considered them too small game to be taken seriously; I have see him play for an hour with a mouse, and then let him go with a royal condescension. In this whole matter of "getting a living," Calvin was a great contrast to the rapacity of the age in which he lived.

I hesitate a little to speak of his capacity for friendship and the affectionateness of his nature, for I know from his own reserve that he would not care to have it much talked about. We understood each other perfectly, but we never made any fuss about it: when I spoke his name and snapped my fingers he came to me; when I returned home at night he was pretty sure to be waiting for me near the gate, and would rise and saunter along the walk, as if his being there were purely accidental, — so shy was he commonly of showing feeling; and when I opened the door he never rushed in, like a cat, but loitered and lounged, as if he had had no intention of going in, but would condescend to. And yet the fact was, he knew dinner was ready, and he was bound to be there. He kept the run of dinner-time. It happened sometimes, during our absence in the summer, that dinner would be early, and Calvin, walking about the grounds, missed it and came in late. But he never made a mistake the second day. There was one thing he never did, — he never rushed through an open doorway. He never forgot his dignity. If he had asked to have the door opened, and was eager to go out, he always went deliberately; I can see him now, standing on the sill, looking about at the sky as if he was thinking whether it were worth while to take an umbrella, until he was near having his tail shut in.

His friendship was rather constant than demonstrative. When we returned from an absence of nearly two years, Calvin welcomed us with evident pleasure, but showed his satisfaction, rather by tranquil happiness than by fuming about. He had the faculty of making us glad to get home. It was his constancy that was so attractive. He liked companionship, but he would n't be petted, or fussed over, or sit in any one's lap a moment; he always extricated himself from such familiarity with dignity and with no show of temper. If there was any petting to be done, however, he chose to do it. Often he would sit looking at me, and then, moved by a delicate affection, come and pull at my coat and sleeve until he could touch my face with his nose, and then go away contented. He had a habit of coming to my study in the morning, sitting quietly by my side or on the table for hours, watching the pen run over the paper, occasionally swinging his tail round for a blotter, and then going to sleep among the papers by the inkstand. Or, more rarely, he would watch the writing from a perch on my shoulder. Writing always interested him, and, until he understood it, he wanted to hold the pen.

He always held himself in a kind of reserve with his friend, as if he had said, "Let us respect our personality, and not make a 'mess' of friendship." He saw, with Emerson, the risk of degrading it to trivial conveniency. "Why insist on rash personal relations with your friend?" "Leave this touching and clawing." Yet I would not give an unfair notion of his aloofness, his fine sense of the sacredness of the me and the not-me. And, at the risk of not being believed, I will relate an incident, which was often repeated. Calvin had the practice of passing a portion of the night in the contemplation of its beauties, and would come into our chamber over the roof of the conservatory through the open window, summer and winter, and go to sleep on the foot of my bed. He would do this always exactly in this way; he never was content to stay in the chamber if we compelled him to go upstairs and through the door. He had the obstinacy of General Grant. But this is by the way. In the morning, he performed his toilet and went down to breakfast with the rest of the family. Now, when the mistress was absent from home, and at no other time, Calvin would come in the morning, when the bell rang, to the head of the bed, put up his feet and look into my face, follow me about when I rose, "assist" at the dressing, and in many purring ways show his fondness, as if he had plainly said, "I know that she has gone away, but I am here." Such was Calvin in rare moments.

He had his limitations. Whatever passion he had for nature, he had no conception of art. There was sent to him once a fine and very expressive cat's head in bronze, by Frémiet. I placed it on the floor. He regarded it intently, approached it cautiously and crouchingly, touched it with his nose, perceived the fraud, turned away abruptly, and never would notice it afterward. On the whole, his life was not only a successful one, but a happy one. He never had but one fear, so far as I know: he had a mortal and a reasonable terror of plumbers. He would never stay in the house when they were here. No coaxing could quiet him. Of course he did n't share our fear about their charges, but he must have had some dreadful experience with them in that portion of his life which is unknown to us. A plumber was to him the devil, and I have no doubt that, in his scheme, plumbers were foreordained to do him mischief.

In speaking of his worth, it has never occurred to me to estimate Calvin by the worldly standard. I know that it is customary now, when any one dies, to ask how much he was worth, and that no obituary in the newspapers is considered complete without such an estimate. The plumbers in our house were one day overheard to say that "they say that *she* says that *he* says that he would n't take a hundred dollars for him." It is unnecessary to say that I never made such a remark, and that, so far as Calvin was concerned, there was no purchase in money.

As I look back upon it, Calvin's life seems to me a fortunate one, for it was natural and unforced. He ate when he was hungry, slept when he was sleepy, and enjoyed existence to the very tips of his toes and the end of his expressive and slow-moving tail. He delighted to roam about the garden and stroll among the trees, and to lie on the green grass and luxuriate in all the sweet influences of summer. You could never accuse him of idleness, and yet he knew the secret of repose. The poet who wrote so prettily of him that his little life was rounded with a sleep understated his felicity; it was rounded with a good many. His conscience never seemed to interfere with his slumbers. In fact, he had good habits and a contented mind. I can see him now walk in at the study door, sit down by my chair, bring his tail artistically about his feet, and look up at me with unspeakable happiness in his handsome face. I often thought that he felt the dumb limitation which denied him the power of language. But since he was denied speech, he scorned the inarticulate mouthings of the lower animals. The vulgar mewing and yowling of the cat species was beneath him; he sometimes uttered a sort of articulate and well-bred ejaculation, when he wished to call attention to something that he considered remarkable, or to some want of his, but he never went whining about. He would sit for hours at a closed window, when he desired to enter, without a murmur, and when it was opened he never admitted that he had been impatient by "bolting" in. Though speech he had not, and the unpleasant kind of utterance given to his race he would not use, he had a mighty power of purr to express his measureless content with congenial society. There was in him a musical organ with stops of varied power and expression, upon which I have no doubt he could have performed Scarlatti's celebrated cat's-fugue.

Whether Calvin died of old age, or was carried off by one of the diseases incident to youth, it is impossible to say; for his departure was as quiet as his advent was mysterious. I only know that he appeared to us in this world in his perfect stature and beauty, and that after a time, like Lohengrin, he withdrew. In his illness there was nothing more to be regretted than in all his blameless life. I suppose there never was an illness that had more of dignity and sweetness and resignation in it. It came on gradually, in a kind of listlessness and want of appetite. An alarming symptom was his preference for the warmth of a furnace-register to the lively sparkle of the open wood-fire. Whatever pain he suffered, he bore it in silence, and seemed only anxious not to obtrude his malady. We tempted him with the delicacies of the season, but it soon became impossible for him to eat, and for two weeks he ate or drank scarcely anything. Sometimes he made an effort to take something, but it was evident that he made the effort to please us. The neighbors — and I am convinced that the advice of neighbors is never good for anything — suggested catnip. He would n't even smell it. We had the attendance of an amateur practitioner of medicine, whose real office was the cure of souls, but nothing touched his case. He took what was offered, but it was with the air of one to whom the time for pellets was passed. He sat or lay day after day almost motionless, never once making a display of those vulgar convulsions or contortions of pain which are so disagreeable to society. His favorite place was on the brightest spot of a Smyrna rug by the conservatory, where the sunlight fell and he could hear the fountain play. If we went to him and exhibited our interest in his condition, he always purred in recognition of our sympathy. And when I spoke his name, he looked up with an expression that said, "I understand it, old fellow, but it 's no use." He was to all who came to visit him a model of calmness and patience in affliction.

I was absent from home at the last, but heard by daily postal-card of his failing condition, and never again saw him alive. One sunny morning, he rose from his rug, went into the conservatory (he was very thin then), walked around it deliberately, looking at all the plants he knew, and then went to the bay-window in the dining-room, and stood a long time looking out upon the little field, now brown and sere, and toward the garden, where perhaps the happiest hours of his life had been spent. It was a last look. He turned and walked away, laid himself down upon the bright spot in the rug, and quietly died.

It is not too much to say that a little shock went through the neighborhood when it was known that Calvin was dead, so marked was his individuality; and his friends, one after another, came in to see him. There was no sentimental nonsense about his obsequies; it was felt that any parade would have been distasteful to him. John, who acted as undertaker, prepared a candle-box for him, and I believe assumed a professional decorum; but there may have been the usual levity underneath, for I heard that he remarked in the kitchen that it was the "dryest wake he ever attended." Everybody, however, felt a fondness for Calvin, and regarded him with a certain respect. Between him and Bertha there existed a great friendship, and she apprehended his nature: she used to say that sometimes she was afraid of him, he looked at her so intelligently; she was never certain that he was what he appeared to be.

When I returned they had laid Calvin on a table in an upper chamber by an open window. It was February. He reposed in a candle-box, lined about the edge with evergreen, and at his head stood a little wineglass with flowers. He lay with his head tucked down in his arms, — a favorite position of his before the fire, — as if asleep in the comfort of his soft and exquisite fur. It was the involuntary exclamation of those who saw him, "How natural he looks!" As for myself, I said nothing. John buried him under the twin hawthorn-trees, — one white and the other pink,

— in a spot where Calvin was fond of lying and listening to the hum of summer insects and the twitter of birds.

Perhaps I have failed to make appear the individuality of character that was so evident to those who knew him. At any rate, I have set down nothing concerning him but the literal truth. He was always a mystery. I did not known whence he came; I do not know whither he has gone. I would not weave one spray of falsehood in the wreath I lay upon his grave.

HOW BOBBIE CAME BACK

From the Boston Herald

A CABLEGRAM has just gone oversea to Rome announcing to a friend of George H. Mifflin glad tidings with Cæsarlike brevity. It reads: "Bobbie back." That, by the way, might make an excellent title for a mystery story, if Mr. Mifflin were in the habit of publishing fiction of the type. At any rate, it marks the ending, if not the solution, of a mystery in which he and scores of his acquaintances have been interested for the past ten months.

There is no need of emphasizing the quality of "suspense," and it may be stated here at the very outset that Bobbie is a Boston terrier. The pith of this relation lies in his being "back." How he came to be "back" nobody knows exactly. Where he was when he was not "back" is sufficiently puzzling for any detective. Why he should go anywhere to come "back" from, probably will never be explained.

The full circumstances of the Odyssey of Bobbie cannot be learned, for Bobbie's best manner of conversation, the wagging of a stump of a tail, is not particularly lucid. Of the disappearance of Bobbie, of the tireless search for him and of his final return, a nonchalant prodigal, the details are known and are here published for the first time.

This, then, is the tale, a tale with few rivals in strangeness in all the tales of dogs.

To begin with, Bobbie came to Mr. Mifflin out of the everywhere into here. In a word, he was found, a waif of the streets, taken to the Animal Rescue League, and there through his winning personality so endeared himself to Mr. Mifflin that he became a member of the latter's household in Marlboro street.

There was a certain affectionate reserve about Bobbie, coupled with a dash of the hunting spirit and a willingness to debate any question with other dogs of high or low degree and of all sizes and weights, that commanded respect and sympathy. He became well beloved in the Mifflin household and in the offices of Houghton Mifflin Company on Park Street, whither he accompanied his master every day, keeping regular business hours.

To all outward appearances he was a model of dogs. He seemed delighted with his home and with the litcrary atmosphere of his days. Then the wanderlust, or something, entered the canine heart. One night, ten months ago, Mr. Mifflin opened his door at eleven o'clock to give Bobbie a whiff of air, and out went Bobbie, unmindful of all summonses. Bobbie had gone back to the everywhere.

Such behavior on the part of his pet puzzled his owner, and although it was then late, Mr. Mifflin called up the Union Club to learn that a terrier much like Bobbie in appearance had been seen sniffing at the staid portals of that organization. Believing that Bobbie might have gone to the office again, Mr. Mifflin

BOBBIE

donned hat and coat and journeyed to Park Street. There was no Bobbie.

It was then that the search began. It was then that the police, dog fanciers, possible dog thieves and all Mr. Mifflin's friends took up the hunt for Bobbie without avail. Mr. Mifflin knows the value of advertising, and he sought the services of the "Herald." He offered a reward; he stated the points of his dog; he solicited coöperation.

Strange to say, there were few answers. Mr. Mifflin wondered, and finally consulted an expert. Said the expert: —

"If you wish to appeal to dog thieves, you must seek a medium which appeals to dog thieves. Dog thieves do not read the 'Herald.'"

The advice seemed good, and his advertisement was placed elsewhere, where it would meet the eye of the sort of persons he wished to interest.

Letters began to flow into the office of Mr. Mifflin. His days and nights were full of futile journeys. He sought out dark places which his correspondents indicated. He entered devious byways, obscure tenements and back alleys. He saw many dogs of the Boston terrier persuasion, but no Bobbie.

One letter postmarked Taunton came to him printed as by the hand of a conspirator. It gave the address as that of a private box in the Taunton Post-office. Taunton-ward Mr. Mifflin fared with a detective. They found the box, only to discover that it was the property of the Taunton insane asylum.

Odd voices called Mr. Mifflin on the telephone.

One insisted that Bobbie was found. There was no doubt of it, said the owner of the voice. The markings were the same. The only out about it was that the foundling was distinctly feminine. Mr. Mifflin asserted the undoubted masculinity of Bobbie.

"What difference does that make?" shouted the voice. "This is your dog."

The seeker hung up the receiver disconsolately.

The reward was marked up to fifty dollars, but there were no results. Every dog fancier in the city was visited. The police were notified. Mr. Mifflin's friends became a band of amateur detectives.

Nobody was sure of escaping suspicion. One lady informed Mr. Mifflin that she was convinced that Bobbie was in the possession of a distinguished clergyman. She did not wish to reflect on anybody's reputation, but facts were facts. She whispered and others whispered, and the story only found rest when Mr. Mifflin made it plain that the dog of the divine was not Bobbie.

A Boston terrier was killed in the Fenway by an automobile. From two distinct sources Mr. Mifflin was informed of the accident. He jumped into his automobile, located the remains in the midst of a group of curious boys, after scrambling down an embankment. It was n't Bobbie.

Thus month after month passed and Mr. Mifflin gave up hope of ever seeing Bobbie alive. Then the miracle happened — Bobbie returned; returned as if nothing had happened; returned and took up the threads of his career where he left them without even a casual reference to aphasia.

The way of it was remarkable. For some time it has been the practice of Houghton Mifflin Company to send one of the boys to the post-office for the firm's mail, and it chanced that one of the newer employes was chosen for the task. The bag for the mail, however, was the same that had always been used.

As the boy made his way along the crowded sidewalks of Washington Street he noticed a little brown terrier with white markings sniffing curiously at the bag. He felt a tug at the leg of his trousers at the heel, and then another. The dog stopped, wagged his tail, and then followed. Up Bromfield Street, across Tremont and into Park went the boy, the mail bag, and the dog.

At the door of Houghton Mifflin Company the boy paused, shooed his chance friend away, and closed the door in his face. The visitor would not be rebuffed. He stood on the steps, balanced characteristically on three legs and waited.

Somebody else came along, opened the door again, and in darted the terrier. Up the stairs he went and waited again. The inner door opened and again the dog went in. There may be ninety and nine or ninety times nine Boston terriers in and about the business district, but to the employees of Houghton Mifflin Company there is only one Bobbie.

He was no stranger to them. No other dog had his pleasant manners. To be sure, he was somewhat travel-stained, but still the same. No prodigal ever received a warmer welcome as he moved sedately through the outer offices to the sanctum of Mr. Mifflin. There he paused, looked up at his master, and flourished the stump of tail. Bobbie was back — that expresses it.

Now you may see him any day taking his ease on a cushion in front of the large fireplace in Mr. Mifflin's office, wagging his ears and looking wise. What have been his wanderings he alone knows.

There are many things that still puzzle Mr. Mifflin: Why his collar was changed; why those who had him did not return him to the address on his old collar; why he returned when he did, and a lot of other whys. It's all a mystery, no doubt; but, then, there is rejoicing in the Mifflin household, and it is enough that — Bobbie's back.

BOONDER

By Bret Harte

I NEVER knew how the subject of this memoir came to attach himself so closely to the affections of my family. He was not a prepossessing dog. He was not a dog of even average birth and breeding. His pedigree was involved in the deepest obscurity. He may have had brothers and sisters, but in the whole range of my canine acquaintance (a pretty extensive one), I never detected any of Boonder's peculiarities in any other of his species. His body was long, and his fore legs and hind legs were very wide apart, as though Nature originally intended to put an extra pair between them, but had unwisely allowed herself to be persuaded out of it. This peculiarity was annoying on cold nights, as it always prolonged the interval of keeping the door open for Boonder's ingress long enough to allow two or three dogs of a reasonable length to enter. Boonder's feet were decided; his toes turned out considerably, and in repose his favorite attitude was the first position of dancing. Add to a pair of bright eyes ears that seemed to belong to some other dog, and a symmetrically pointed nose that fitted all apertures like a pass-key, and you have Boonder as we knew him.

I am inclined to think that his popularity was mainly

due to his quiet impudence. His advent in the family was that of an old member who had been absent for a short time, but had returned to familiar haunts and associations. In a Pythagorean point of view this might have been the case, but I cannot recall any deceased member of the family who was in life partial to bone-burying, and this was Boonder's great weakness. He was at first discovered coiled up on a rug in an upper chamber, and was the least disconcerted of the entire household. From that moment Boonder became one of its recognized members, and privileges often denied the most intelligent and valuable of his species were quietly taken by him and submitted to by us. Thus, if he were found coiled up in a clothes-basket, or any article of clothing assumed locomotion on its own account, we only said, "Oh, it's Boonder!" with a feeling of relief that it was nothing worse.

I have spoken of his fondness for bone-burying. It could not be called an economical faculty, for he invariably forgot the locality of his treasure, and covered the garden with purposeless holes; but although the violets and daisies were not improved by Boonder's gardening, no one ever thought of punishing him. He became a synonym for Fate; a Boonder to be grumbled at, to be accepted philosophically, — but never to be averted. But although he was not an intelligent dog, nor an ornamental dog, he possessed some gentlemanly instincts. When he performed his only feat, — begging upon his hind legs (and looking remarkably like a penguin), — ignorant strangers would offer him crackers or cake, which he did n't like, as a reward of merit. Boonder always made a great show of accepting the proffered dainties, and even made hypocritical contortions as if swallowing, but always deposited the morsel when he was unobserved in the first convenient receptacle, — usually the visitor's overshoes.

In matters that did not involve courtesy, Boonder was sincere in his likes and dislikes. He was instinctively opposed to the railroad. When the track was laid through our street, Boonder maintained a defiant attitude toward every rail as it went down, and resisted the cars shortly after to the fullest extent of his lungs. I have a vivid recollection of seeing him, on the day of the trial trip, come down the street in front of the car, barking himself out of all shape, and thrown back several feet by the recoil of each bark. But Boonder was not the only one who has resisted innovations, or has lived to see the innovation prosper and even crush. But I am anticipating. Boonder had previously resisted the gas, but although he spent one whole day in angry altercation with the workmen, — leaving his bones unburied and bleaching in the sun, — somehow the gas went in. The Spring Valley water was likewise unsuccessfully opposed, and the grading of an adjoining lot was for a long time a personal matter between Boonder and the contractor.

These peculiarities seemed to evince some decided character and embody some idea. A prolonged debate in the family upon this topic resulted in an addition to his name, — we called him "Boonder the Conservative," with a faint acknowledgment of his fateful power.

But, although Boonder had his own way, his path was not entirely of roses. Thorns sometimes pricked his sensibilities. When certain minor chords were struck on the piano, Boonder was always painfully affected and howled a remonstrance. If he were removed for company's sake to the back yard, at the recurrence of the provocation he would go his whole length (which was something) to improvise a howl that should reach the performer. But we got accustomed to Boonder, and as we were fond of music, the playing went on.

One morning Boonder left the house in good spirits with his regular bone in his mouth, and apparently the usual intention of burying it. The next day he was picked up lifeless on the track, — run over apparently by the first car that went out of the depot.

DIXIE KITTEN IN HER NEW HOME

By Eva March Tappan

POOR little Dixie was roaming about in the gloom, alone and miserable, and too wretched even to run away. Lady put her hand upon her, and she was grieved to feel how thin the little cat had grown. Her silky fur was rough and harsh, and she did not seem half so large as she had been before. "You poor little Dixie kitten," said Lady, tenderly, "I shall have to frighten you for a little while, but I think you will be happy afterwards." She held the kitten firmly and put her into the rattan case. Mistress shut down the cover in a twinkling, and in half a minute the straps were fastened and Dixie was a prisoner. Of course she cried, for she was terribly alarmed; but Lady talked to her and soothed her, and before they were in the car she was quiet.

It was not long before the car stopped at the Road where the new house was. Lady got out and carried the extension-case to the door and into the house. A Caller was there, for Somebody Else had told her that Lady had gone to get Dixie, and she had waited to see how the kitten would behave. "Though I don't believe Lady will be able to catch her," she had said. "Cats care nothing for people. They are selfish little creatures, and all they want is to be comfortable. Probably this one has forgotten all about her by this time."

When Lady came in, the Caller said, "You'd better open the case in the kitchen. The cat will probably be as crazy as a loon, and she may dash about and tear things and do a great deal of damage." So the Caller and Lady and Somebody Else and the case with the kitten all went to the kitchen; and Lady began very slowly and gently to loosen the straps. It was all so quiet in the case that she wondered whether it could have been so close that the poor little cat was half smothered, and she pulled the last strap off in a great hurry. "You'd better be careful," said the Caller, "and not have your face too near. You never can trust a cat, and no one can tell what she will do. She may spring right at you." Lady did not believe Dixie would do any such thing, and she took the cover off in a twinkling. Dixie stepped quietly out of the case and looked around her. She saw Lady and Somebody Else, and she saw the Mother standing in the doorway. They talked to her, and patted her, and told her they were glad to see her. Dixie forgot the lonely days at the old house when she thought Lady had abandoned her. It was all past; Lady had remembered her and had brought her home, and now she was going to live with Lady and be really her own little cat. Never was a cat so happy before, and she purred so, she could be heard far into the dining-room. As Lady bent over her, she stretched up and tried to rub her face against Lady's. She ran about the room and touched with her keen little nose the stove hearth, the chairs, the rugs, the table cover, one familiar thing after another; and every minute or two she ran back to Lady to tell her how glad she was to be with her.

"Dixie dear, how miserable you must have been," said Lady, with tears in her eyes.

"I never knew that just a cat could be either so happy or so unhappy," said the Caller, with tears in her eyes, too. As for Somebody Else, she had long been wiping her own eyes when she thought no one was looking; so it was really quite a tearful time. By and by Dixie discovered in a corner a little dish heaped full of the canned salmon that she especially liked, for on the way home Lady had stopped a minute to go into a store to buy it to celebrate the homecoming. Close beside the salmon was a half-open package that smelled wonderfully good. Even Dixie's small black nose would not go into it, but it was too tempting to leave, for it was catnip. At length she pushed in her little paw, curled it up, and brought out a mouthful, which she held up and ate just as a boy would eat a piece of candy.

It was pretty late in the evening by this time. The Caller went home, and Lady called Dixie to go to bed. There was a good soft bed all made ready for her in the cellar. It was in a barrel of shavings, for cats like to sleep high up from the floor. Near the barrel was a saucer of milk, for fear she might be thirsty in the night. It was all very comfortable, but I do not believe that Dixie went to sleep at once. Cats like to know all about a place that is new to them, and I have no doubt that she examined every corner of the cellar before she curled herself up to rest. I am almost sure, too, that she purred herself to sleep, and that she had happy dreams all night long.

When the Caller went away, she said, "I never knew that a cat could behave like that. She acts as if she really loved you as much as a person could do. Still, they say cats care for places rather than people; and if I were you, I would shut her up for two or three days till she gets used to the house, and then she will not try to run away.

"But if she wants to run away," replied Lady, "I do not want to keep her here."

And Somebody Else said softly to herself, "Run away? You could n't drag her away."

When morning came, a very happy and curious little cat stepped up from the cellar and began to look about the house. There were only a few things in it that she had not seen before, but they were all in new places; and so she found a great deal to examine. Instead of carpets, however, she found many rugs. She was not sure that she liked this, for sometimes she slipped a little on the hardwood floors. The stairs did not go straight up, but made a turn. This was a delightful change, for she could run up part way, then turn and look back through the balusters. After a while she came to the study. Here she found a new bookcase. It was far better than the tall ones, she thought, for it was much lower, and she felt sure that the top of it would be an excellent place for a kitten to take a nap. Two or three mirrors were now either hung low, or were over tables, so she could jump up and look into them, and Somebody Else declared that the kitten would surely become vain if these were not changed, for she liked so much to sit in front of them and gaze at her own little self. The windows she liked especially, for they were so low that even a little cat could stretch up and rest her forepaws on the sills and see all that was going on out of doors. Better still, at one of the windows Lady had put a plush-covered foot-rest, and here Dixie could sit comfortably in the sunshine and watch the People going by.

After a while Dixie began to wonder what was out of doors, and she let Somebody Else know that she wished the door opened. Somebody Else had not forgotten that the Caller had said the cat would run away; but evidently such an idea never entered Dixie's pretty little head. She walked slowly around the house. There was a piazza at the back; and that suited her; but she was still more pleased with the front piazza. It was reached by five or six steps, and there was a high railing where a cat could sit; and no dog would dare to come near her. There were shrubs on either side of the walk, with fine cool places to sleep, or to lie awake and watch everything that was going on. There was plenty of grass, there were two gnarled apple-trees behind the house, and beyond them there was a fine old stone wall that had stood ever since the days when no one had dreamed of turning the great Baldwin orchard into house-lots. Some of the rough stones were covered with green moss, and they cast soft gray shadows. Here and there a bit of white quartz flashed in the sunshine. Bright orange nasturtiums ran over the wall, and some tall hollyhocks stood close beside it in neighborly fashion. It was a beautiful old wall. Dixie thought so, too; but the reason she liked it was because she was sure that in some one of those shadowy places she would certainly find a field mouse.

It took Dixie the whole forenoon to look at everything around the house and smell of it. Moreover, in the course of the morning she had a caller. It was not exactly a friendly call, for this Next-Door Cat had been in the habit of coming to see the People who used to live in the house, and she was not pleased to see another cat making herself at home there. She came through the little barberry hedge and said "Meow!" in a surprised and aggrieved fashion. I suppose it meant, "Who are you and what are you here for?" but Dixie did not deign to answer. She jumped upon the piazza railing and looked straight at the Next-Door Cat. The Next-Door Cat ran up the nearest apple-tree and looked straight at her. After a while, the Next-Door Cat said "Meow-ow-ow!" and came down from the apple-tree. She gave one more look over her shoulder at Dixie, but Dixie was opening and shutting her mouth as fast as ever she could, as if she meant to devour everything in sight. The Next-Door Cat marched straight to the gap in the low barberry hedge and went home. This was Dixie's first caller.

So it was that the wild little barn cat became a house cat. She had come to live with busy people, and I fancy she thought that she was as busy as they. In the morning, as soon as she heard the steps of Somebody Else, she ran to the top of the stairs to be ready to come out the moment that the door was opened. The next thing to do was to go up to Lady's room. The door was almost always closed, but Dixie sat down beside it and waited patiently until she heard some little sounds within. Then she rubbed on the door with the little pads on the bottom of her paw, — very softly, to be sure, but Lady always heard her and opened it. Once in a while Dixie went out of doors when she first came up from the cellar, and occasionally it happened that she could not get in again at once. That did not trouble her, for she had another way of reaching Lady's room that she liked fully as well as going by the hall and the stairs. Not far from the front piazza there grew an apple-tree. Dixie could run up this tree, walk carefully out on a slender branch, and jump to the piazza roof. A little way beyond the farther end of the roof was one of the windows of Lady's room. The blind nearest this roof was usually closed, and there was not room enough on the sill to hold even a kitten; but Dixie would go to the very edge of the roof and scratch. "Is that you, Dixie?" Lady would ask. "Meow," Dixie would reply, and any one would know that this meant "Yes." Then Lady would go into the little room that opened on the roof and let her in. So it was that every morning the kitten made sure that Lady was safe and sound, and came to purr to her while she was dressing.

After Lady and Dixie had both eaten breakfast, Lady took a few minutes for the morning paper. Of course it was a great help to her to have a small black cat lie on her lap; and I am sure I do not know how she could have set her room in order unless the same little cat had sat on the window-sill watching her. When Lady went to the study, Dixie always went with her to stay by her while she wrote. This study was an excellent place for a nap. Sometimes Dixie lay on top of the low bookcase, where Lady had put a cushion for her benefit; sometimes she stretched herself out on the carpet in the sunshine; and sometimes she had a comfortable little snooze on a corner of the big library table. If she did not care to sleep, there were various things that a kitten could do in the study to amuse herself. She could sit at the window and watch the birds in the apple-trees, or sometimes a dog hurrying home across lots. She could run over the typewriter keys if she chose, and even across the big table. Indeed, she soon learned that the surest way to make Lady pay attention to her was to walk slowly over the paper on which she was writing, or even to sit down upon it and begin to take a bath. Once she sat down upon a loose pile of books and papers, and a moment later books, papers, and Dixie slid to the floor together, with a great thump. She turned and gazed at them with surprise and wrath, but not the least bit of fear. She was afraid of sudden noises elsewhere, however. While a carpenter was at work in the kitchen, she utterly refused to eat her meals in the room unless Lady stood beside her. She seemed to feel convinced that Somebody Else was to blame for all that hammering, and for several days after it ceased she refused to have anything to do with her while in the kitchen, though she was friendly enough in other places. In Lady's study she felt safe, and apparently she had come to the conclusion that in that room nothing could ever hurt kittens.

Whenever Dixie was in trouble she always ran to the study for comfort. One day she dashed into the room and sat down in front of Lady and gazed at her so earnestly and with such an air of wanting to tell something that Lady called to Somebody Else and asked if anything had happened to Dixie. "Sure, there has," replied Somebody Else. "Now that the screens are in, the window-sill is not wide enough to hold her, and when she jumped from the railing to the window, she fell down. She would n't stop for a bit of dinner, but ran upstairs as fast as ever she could go." Once when Lady had been away for a month, she missed the kitten after the first greeting. Some time later she went to the study, and there sat Dixie in the dark, patiently waiting for her to appear.

In some ways Dixie was remarkably obedient. If she was in the street and Lady knocked on the window, she would come running home as promptly as the best of children. If she was upstairs and Lady called her to come down, you could hear on the instant the jump of a little cat — often from a down quilt on a bed or from some other forbidden place, I am sorry to say — to the floor; and in half a minute she was hurrying downstairs to see what was wanted. One morning Lady called, but Dixie did not come. Some ten minutes later she burst into the kitchen like a little football rush with a long "Meow-yow-yow-yow!" which sounded so angry and indignant that Somebody Else called Lady and declared that something had surely gone wrong with Dixie. When Lady went upstairs, she saw what had happened. The heavy door had blown to, and it was plain that the kitten had been working at it with her soft little paws until she had pushed it back far enough to let her squeeze through.

Part of Dixie's work was to drive away the stray cats and dogs that ventured on her lawn or under her apple-trees. Sometimes she herself played dog, and did her best to guard the house. One dark night there was a strange clanking sound in the backyard. Lady started for the door; but before she could reach it, the little cat had crouched all ready to make a spring as soon as the door should be opened. The noise proved to have been made by a hungry dog at a garbage can; and he ran away as fast as ever he could; but I think Dixie would have enjoyed chasing him.

Evidently Dixie felt that her first duty was to keep watch of Lady; and this was no easy matter when Lady was busy about the house. She hurried "upstairs and downstairs and in my lady's chamber"; but wherever she went, a little black cat followed her like a shadow. This shadow behaved somewhat unlike other shadows, however, for it had a way of catching at the hem of her dress in the hope of a frolic, or suddenly dashing around corners at her to surprise her, in a fashion which no properly behaved shadow would ever dream of following.

Another of Dixie's duties was to entertain the

Mother. The Mother had always been afraid of cats, and she had never liked them, but she could not help liking Dixie. The kitten often went to her room and lay on a small high table in the sunshine while the Mother sat in her big easy-chair and talked to her. Dixie purred back, and they were very comfortable together, and the best of friends.

When callers came, Dixie was not altogether pleased. Sometimes she would turn her back on them, march straight upstairs, and not come down again until she heard the front door close; but generally she thought it better to keep pretty close watch of them. She was inclined to think that Lady paid them too much attention; therefore she would often jump into Lady's lap and insist upon remaining there until they were ready to start for home.

Another one of Dixie's responsibilities was the telephone, and she always ran to it at the first ring. Her care of it was a great convenience to Lady, for the telephone bell and the doorbell sounded so nearly alike that before Dixie came, she had often made mistakes, and had hurried to the telephone when the doorbell rang. Dixie never made a mistake, however, and when Lady saw her running to the telephone, she did not have to guess which bell had rung. The telephone was as much of a mystery to Dixie as it is to some other folk. She would jump up on the table to listen, and would put her head on one side with a puzzled look. One day she stretched out her soft little paw and touched Lady's lips to see if she could not find out where those strange sounds came from. Once Lady asked the friend with whom she was talking to call "Dixie!" Then the kitten was puzzled indeed. She looked at the receiver from all sides and even tried to get her head into it. At last she left it and jumped down from the table; for most certainly she had come upon something that no kitten could understand.

THE ISLAND'S WILD CAT

By George Ethelbert Walsh

IT was right up here on one of these islands in the St. Lawrence that a family came one summer from New York to spend a few months, bringing along with them several dogs and pet cats.

They left the island early in September, and, when the house was closed up, the place was entirely deserted. I passed the island late one afternoon, and decided to land for a few moments.

The sides of the island were bluff and rocky, and I scrambled up with some difficulty. When I reached the summit, I heard the deep baying of my hound. I whistled, and in response to it he came tearing toward me from the thicket.

But what a sight he presented! Riding on his back and tearing mercilessly at his neck and head was the strangest looking creature I ever saw. It was so gaunt that it looked more like a starved wolf than a cat.

No wonder the hound was frightened. The half-starved cat was fighting fiercely, and actually enjoying the taste of fresh blood which its claws drew from the hound's warm body. The creature had been a pet house cat the summer before, but its lonely, desperate life on the island had made it fiercer and wilder than its primitive ancestors.

I examined the island hastily, and found that the cat had taken possession of an old dog-kennel for its lonely home. There it had gathered the few bones left behind and gnawed them half up. A few birds had apparently been caught and eaten, and the bones of a squirrel and several rats were also scattered around. The bark of the trees was nibbled as if the poor thing had in desperation tried to satisfy its hunger with green things.

It had broken through the shutters of one window and entered the closed house, but there was nothing to eat there. An old fur blanket that had been left behind was chewed half up, and an old shoe was also nibbled and chewed. The marks of the cat's teeth were on nearly everything which promised a mite of nutriment.

The cat's tracks were found in the snow and on the ice to the very edge of the frozen surface. It had contemplated escaping on the ice, but the channel was too swift and deep for it.

I tried to make friends with the creature, calling it by pet names and trying to coax it toward me. Wherever I went the baleful eyes watched me, but always at a safe distance.

I had only a single biscuit with me, but I threw this to the starving animal. It would not approach near enough to touch it, but when I moved away it leaped for the biscuit and swallowed it at one gulp.

The next day I returned to the island with an ample supply of fresh milk, bread, and meat. These I spread out on the snow and called "Kitty! kitty!" in my most alluring voice. But the cat would n't come a step nearer. It backed away and disappeared in the thicket. I hunted around for it, but could n't find it anywhere on the island. I was disappointed, and finally returned to my boat.

Imagine my surprise when I reached the place where I had landed to see the cat perched in the stern of the canoe. It glared at me, and, when I attempted to step into the craft it spit and hissed in a threatening manner. It had taken possession of the boat, and had no intention of leaving it.

Again I tried to make friends with it, throwing bits of meat toward it, but these it ignored, still facing me and hissing. Finally I tipped the canoe suddenly and nearly dropped the creature into the icy water. It touched the water with its tail, and then with a snarl and hiss leaped toward me. I ducked just in time. It went over my head, but before it landed on the rocks it gave me such a dig with one of its claws that the blood spurted out in a tiny stream.

Such a reception was n't encouraging, and I felt a little squeamish about returning the next day; but I did, and took more food. This time I placed the food on the rocks and pushed off. At a safe distance I could see the cat come out of the underbrush and crawl up to the food. What a ravenous appetite it had! It bolted the pieces of meat and bread and lapped up the milk with marvelous rapidity. It licked its chops and smelled around for more. Its appetite seemed insatiable.

For three days I made regular trips to the island to

feed pussy. By the third the cat was tame enough to eat the food in my presence, although I had to stay at a safe distance. Then gradually by degrees it permitted me to approach closer. A sudden spit and hiss always informed me how far I could come.

A cold wave came up one night and froze the river so quickly that the channel was closed. When I finally dared to venture out on the ice, I made straight for pussy's island.

When I reached it, I heard a dismal howling and barking. I hurried up the rocks, and found the cat treed, with four dogs howling anxiously at the foot of the tree.

I had to use a good deal of violent persuasion to drive the dogs away. They were loath to leave the island with pussy on it.

I tried to coax the cat down from the tree with food, but only succeeded after two hours of patient endeavor. Then I was surprised and not a little frightened, when it suddenly dropped down on my shoulders. I expected to feel its claws in my head and neck, but instead it snatched the meat from my hand and swallowed it. I fed it all I had. I was wondering what next to do, with the cat on my shoulder, when a gentle purring noise startled me. It was soft and low at first, and then louder and more rhythmic. I felt the furry head pressed against my cheek in a rub that made me happier than if I had found a small fortune.

I had won the cat's trust and affections, and she was now showing it unmistakably. I put up a hand and rubbed the purring head. It licked the hand and then permitted me to hold it on my shoulder as I walked away.

Pussy and I scrambled down the rocks to the ice. I must have talked and crooned to pussy all the way home, for I was fearful all the time it would get frightened and leave me. When I got it home, I made a comfortable bed for it in the kitchen and there it sleeps every night. I don't think I 'd part with the cat for any amount of money, and I know pussy is satisfied with me.

It 's a pretty, sleek, fat cat to-day, and the most affectionate pet you ever saw; but, when I think of my first sight of it on that deserted island, I feel very much like saying some hard things about the people who left it on the island without any thought of what might happen to it.

CHILDREN'S PETS

By Alice Perkins Coville

IF Dr. Montessori and modern pedagogy are correct in deciding that the child who comes to his heritage is to have an option on the form his play shall take, then every mother knows her child will demand as his right the companionship of animals and pets of his own, — house pets, door-yard pets, anything he can acquire. It may be only a caterpillar spinning his cocoon in a pasteboard box, or a pollywog growing legs in a pail; or it may be a bench dog and a thoroughbred pony. From each he will gain, as did the "barefoot boy," a knowledge never learned of schools.

It is quite possible Mary's lamb would make the children laugh and play to-day as of old, but it is not probable that the teacher would turn him out if he followed her to school only *one* day. The teacher realizes, as never before, that there is in the lamb a something more than its meekness and docility which makes appeal to the Marys of all times; and she welcomes every opportunity to increase the love of a child for, and foster an appreciative interest in, the animals which help or feed or amuse us. In every flock of sheep I seem to see a pet lamb I once had; and still I can hear the clatter of its hard pursuing little hoofs on the village street, and the tinkle of a tiny bell it always wore.

In no way can grown-ups come into closer contact with children than at the many points of genuine common interest in pets. Last Sunday I chanced to hear a kindergartner getting acquainted with her new class. "Who has a canary at home?" she asked. No child in the large circle had one; and a mother, who was looking on, said to me, "Mothers who have children have no time for canaries!" The words teased me unknowingly, as I came up the long hill, wondering; — and recalling with marvelous distinctness the canary of my childhood home, who always seemed ever the happiest member of our large household, and who paid in full with song and cheer the price of his care. I remembered how he flew away one time, when some of the children had let him out in the room, as they often did; and how he came back the next day, and flew into the cage that hung in the pine tree by the dining room window. Best of all, I remembered how glad we all were, — little mother gladdest of all! Could it be that *she* ever thought Dicky a nuisance?

In that same long ago, a parrot lived next door to us. He had a remarkable memory, and to me he was very intelligent, — not at all the "brainless chatterer" the lady-with-the-side-puffs, who lived on his other side, considered him. She took a nap, — or tried to, — every afternoon, and Poll was the one subject upon which she and I could come to no sort of agreement. She could not comprehend my happy, quiet sittings on the doorstep, over which hung Poll's spacious cage.

This bird took a great interest in the members of his household, and would have shared his social humor even with the puff-lady had she noticed him. In front of the house was a "thank-you-marm," which invited the driver of an occasional heavy load to rest his horses a moment on the hill. If he tarried too long, Poll would give the signal, perfectly, for the horses to start. But there was little "hauling" on the street; and waits were sometimes too prolonged, so we children taught Poll to holler "Whoa!" to any team that passed. Ere the driver had time to recover from his surprise, Poll would send the horses on their way with a blink of satisfaction to us on the doorstep. To the "rectory goat," with his over-load of laughing youngsters, Poll could never be persuaded to say "Whoa!" though we drove the long-suffering animal up and down, with such persuading and firmness as are demanded by goat nature; nor could we ever guess Poll's reason why, — we never doubted that he had one. No child believes his pets do not talk because they have nothing to say.

A small boy at whose country home I visited this summer had a hen and five chickens, which were his first thought in the morning and his last at night. I had scarcely arrived when I was promised the next egg for my breakfast. Each morning one sturdy chick was found outside the wire inclosure, and her secret way of escape could not be discovered. "If she thinks it's nicer outside, why does n't she tell the others how to get out?" asked the astonished young keeper. To see the mother hen control and manage the family, when she took them abroad for bugs, was a lesson in efficiency that seemed greatly to impress him.

Was there ever a real boy who did not achieve rabbits? A rabbit's makeshift to appeal to our sympathy, and her sense of social service, are the admiration of every child. With her faithful hind feet pounding an incredibly loud warning of approaching danger, I saw my boy's rabbit stand, forgetful of self, until every other rabbit was safe in the hut, and the disturbing dog had fled. Rabbits are so cheap to keep, and so indifferent as to what they eat (their own carrots or a neighbor's pansies) that a boy, if he is conscientious, can acquire some financial gain, as well as valuable experience, in breeding rabbits.

Children are intensely interested in the remarkable friendships arising between animals from temporary association. To find a kitten asleep with Bob in the kennel established an entirely new standard of brotherhood in the mind of a small boy, who had had the world very distinctly classified by species.

Society, in self-defense, is providing playgrounds as a sort of safety-valve for the accumulated animal and savage instincts of hiding, seeking, and raiding in the child, whose only outlets are play or crime. Mayor Gaynor would have liked to have a zoo, containing domestic as well as wild animals, in every recreation center. The psychologists tell us the play of animals is identical with that of children, only within the same "limitations to a ready-made circle of associations, which characterize animal life." But it is n't how nor what the cat plays, that matters to a child. It is the fact that she *does* play. Stealthily creeping to spring upon the child's trailing string, the kitten stirs within him a kindred impulse inherited from some animal ancestor who delighted to pounce upon its prey. Her gluttony amazes him; but her unbelievable patience in watching a mouse can teach him the same lesson the spider taught to "Scotland's future king." He likes the feel of her coat, and the sound of her soft purr. Does a child ever forget the first sight of a basket of blind kittens — their mother's watchful care and their funny clumsy tumbles? It tells with perfect directness of the beginnings of human social life. The very way in which a cat slips off all by her lone instinct, without a clew to where she is going, interests a child. He too hears — very faintly — the call of the wild, and if he dared he'd follow. But he knows that if he has not pulled her talkative fascinating tail too hard, she will return, and play with him the games that please her. Even though the cat catches no mouse, the mother feels, when she hears her child laugh as he plays with her, that the cat does her a service as well as the child.

In one of the "Just So Stories," Mr. Kipling tells how the dog sniffed the mutton out in the wet wild woods, and for its sake made the first compact with the Woman in the Cave, to hunt and to protect, and to help her possess the world. That compact he has surely kept faithfully unto this day, — often without the mutton. Every child who has pets may experience the joy of seeing a look of fear and dread in an animal change to trust and love, as did the Cave woman.

"It is funny; but no one can ever seem to make me afraid of a dog," said a small boy to his mother, when some one warned him against a St. Bernard he was caressing. The mother's reassuring smile showed no trace of anxiety. The strange dog would know the child was a friend of all dogs, for a dog had been brother to him ever since one sniffed about his baby basket the morning it was first occupied.

This "true first friend" will play anything the child chooses. He guards with equal fidelity his little master's clothes at the swimming-hole, or his mistress' silver. He bears no grudge and wishes only to please you. That friendly nipping (which should have been stopped at the beginning) started out as affectionate liking (taught him as a puppy by his master), and easily leads to friendly biting, which is so disastrous to dog character; although, like a play fight, it is only a ruse — the psychologist says — to review pleasurable memories of a real fight. "Yours is the only dog I ever saw that had manners," I heard a lady say to her friend. That particular dog with manners, I happened to know, has never been allowed to disobey. Every infraction is punished at once, with words, or by shutting him away by himself; but encouragement and praise have been the key to success. His neatness and consideration for chairs and sofas is attributed to a pillow of his own, on which a fresh slip is more frequently tied than is customary in dogdom. His runaway habit, which was acquired under a former preoccupied master, has been absolutely cured by regular feeding and by deliberate intent of each member of the family to give him cordial welcome and recognition each time he comes home. In fact it would be quite impossible now to ignore him, so expectant is he in his attitude even toward a casual guest. "I've heard all about you," said a stranger from afar, bearing a letter of introduction, as he stooped to pat "the dog-with-manners," just as his mistress appeared. The letter seemed quite superfluous. The stranger did not even present it. The dog had given him the countersign.

Dogs will take the tone of the household, and are capable of much development, though they may not all have a genealogical tree of "seven couples of pure blood," which is as desirable for dogs as for humans; and though, like the "slum cat," they seem sometimes to have a disgusting preference for "unsterilized eatables." Any boy can fill a volume with the everyday doings of his dog.

My boy insists that one of his earliest recollections is a jolly race down a grassy terrace with his bull-terrier, whose collar, hanging on the playroom wall to-day, is more tenderly dusted than any valuable vase. The reporter to whom I refused data for Beta's obituary notice argued that the dog had more friends than most people; and he wrote the story (out of his head and heart), without the desired details. It was copied by many papers; and from San Francisco, New Orleans, and a dozen smaller towns came clippings from students who had known Beta while in college, and remembered his faithful devotion to a child. The insistent reporter knew the world likes to hear of the good in dogs or men.

We often blame our pets, and let our children blame them, for a seeming lack of obedience, which is not the animal's fault, but our own, due to forgetfulness, or ignorance of the law of association or habit by which the animal brain is bound. Reluctant to leave a crackling fire in the dining-room the other evening, we pushed the table against the wall, to make room for our chairs before the fireplace. Gyp, the worthy grandson of Beta, joined us immediately; and our boy soon began amusing us by telling him to "Close the door," "Sneeze," "Be sleepy dog," "Show big tongue," and so on, but when he gave the perfectly familiar order to "Go out in the kitchen," the dog seemed completely dazed; he hastened to roll over, and do other things, but not the one asked. "Step to the spot where your chair usually stands," suggested the boy's father. The boy did so, and Gyp, standing in the familiar location, by some process of association, found himself at once, and eagerly obeyed the command without confusion the first time it was given.

"You must ride alone to-day?" I asked a girl friend whose companion was away. "O, I never feel alone when I'm on Buster," she replied quickly. "He 's so human. He seems to understand every word I say to him, and he likes to do the very same things I like." As she rehearsed with pride the pony's tricks, I recalled a remark of her father's, that he had never spent any money to better advantage than that with which he bought his daughter's pony, for it had "kept her a little girl," — a feat not easily accomplished in this age of precocity, — although it had made her fearless and more self-reliant.

It did not concern this girl that the psychologist has decided to his satisfaction that Buster is but a creature of habit. His "smartness" bridges for her the chasm between "simple associated processes and appreciative intellectual operations," on whose brink the ages have stood bewildered, but across which our "little brothers" never call to willingly deaf ears, if attuned in childhood by intimate and faithful fellowship with pets.

POMPEY AND HIS KINDRED

By Edward Breck

JUST off the mouth of Elder Brook in Eleven-Mile Lake is a famous place for trout, and one day, as Uncle Ned was working the canoe slowly toward it, so that the girls might cast their flies in the right spot, a dark object was seen in the water, swimming toward the shore. The girls could not make out whether it was a mink, a muskrat, an otter, or even a beaver, — for it was quite large enough for the last animal. But, as he made no attempt to dive, and swam on very deliberately, they were quite nonplussed. Great was their astonishment when Uncle Ned pronounced it a porcupine.

"Gracious!" exclaimed Madge, "I did n't know porcupines could swim!"

"Swim? Guess they can," said Uncle Ned; "and so can any animal that lives in the woods when it has to. Why, I've seen wildcats in the water more than once, and foxes too! See how cheeky that beggar is! He does n't even change his course to get farther away from the canoe. I have a great mind to knock him on the head."

"Oh, no Uncle Ned! You could n't be so cruel!" said Nell.

"Well, I hope I'm not cruel exactly, but we woodsmen have our own ideas about porkies. Well, I guess we'll let this one go. I like 'em all right 'xcept for their killin' the trees."

The porcupine meanwhile landed on the beach and lumbered heavily into the second-growth timber, where the party presently heard a series of funny snarls and grunts.

"Hm," mused Uncle Ned. "Guess she's got young ones."

At this the girls were wild to go ashore and get one of the little ones for a pet; but the old guide put them off with a promise to hunt for one later; so that they finally returned to camp with only a fine string of trout as trophies. It happened, however, the very next day that the girls were out in a canoe with Farish Owen, a friend who had come to visit Jack, when they discovered a young porcupine sitting disconsolately on a big rock called by the natives Pompey.

"Aha, my lad, you're my meat!" cried Farish; and, working the canoe up to the rock without alarming the animal, he landed carefully, and then, with a spring, threw his coat over Mr. Porky, who in a jiffy was stowed in the bow of the canoe and taken to camp in triumph. With due ceremonies he was presented to Uncle Ned, who unwrapped him and let him go free on the cabin veranda. At first Pompey, for so he was immediately dubbed, backed off a bit, and then spent a moment in scrutinizing the company. He seemed very little put out, but finally turned tail and tried to amble off the veranda. Mr. Buckshaw headed him off, and Pompey sat down and gazed sleepily at his captor. Uncle Ned touched his nose, whereupon Pompey drew back with a nervous jerk, but made no effort to run away.

"Curious," remarked Uncle Ned; "he don't even turn his back and get his tail in commission. They mostly do that."

But Pompey proved to be a remarkable porcupine in many ways, and seemed to have left all his wildness behind him on the rock where he was taken. Not once in the whole course of his career did he offer to strike with his tail, his principal weapon of attack as well as of defense, and in this Uncle Ned declared him to be a remarkable and in fact unique exception from all his kind. His tameness from the very start was surprising; and it is a fact that within two hours after his capture he was sitting contentedly on Uncle Ned's lap, gnawing at a biscuit.

Camp Buckshaw had entertained porcupines before, and there was a large wire-netted pen built round a small poplar beside the cabin all ready for occupancy. Here Pompey was kept nights, and whenever there was nobody left about the cabin to look after the wants of the pets; for it was Uncle Ned's custom to confine his pets when first taken, for so long a time as was sufficient for them to get accustomed to Camp Buckshaw and look upon it as their home. After that they were always allowed to run free.

The North-American porcupine, especially in its younger years, is so covered with long, black hairs that its quills, of which, except on nose and belly, it has enough and to spare, are partly, and often wholly, concealed. In Pompey's case, all the very long quills, those most apt to show, seemed to have been pulled out when he was captured; for Farish's coat, in which he had wrapped his captive, was stuck through with scores of sharp spines, and it was a long time before he succeeded in extracting them all. As it was, good old Uncle John McLeod, in using the coat one day for a pillow as he took his afternoon snooze on the sofa, got a small quill so firmly embedded in his nose that he was forced to post off to town and have it taken out by a physician.

A queer, uncanny thing is a porcupine quill, and a very dangerous one. It is tipped with minute barbs that offer no resistance when penetrating, but a good deal when being pulled out. It therefore happens that, if left in the flesh, every movement tends to force it farther in; so that quills have been known to run all over a beast's body, often coming at last in contact with a vital organ, resulting in the animal's death. Therefore, the only safe course, when a quill has become deeply embedded, is to have it taken out at once. It is said, that by thrusting the quill a little farther in and then withdrawing it, all in one quick movement, the barbs will remain unopened and the quill can thus be pulled out with ease. The movement must be a twisting one.

Let those who come in contact with porky try the experiment. This was always Uncle Ned's suggestion when he was asked as to the value of certain ancient crotchets. Once he set Alan rubbing two sticks of soft dry pine together in order to produce fire, as the

Indians were said to have done. After rubbing until his hands were ready to drop off, Alan gave up the experiment and declared that he would in future stick to flint and steel or to the burning-glass in case that despised thing, a good match, was not to be had.

"But," he added, "those sticks were real hot, anyway!"

The fact that Pompey's principal quills were left in Farish's jacket proves how very loosely these weapons of defense are attached to the skin; so loosely, in fact, that they are often flirted out with some violent movement on the part of the animal, — a happening which, no doubt, gave rise to the tradition that porcupines could throw their quills.

However all this may be, it is certain that, so far as appearance is concerned, Pompey was a very hairy but not a spiny individual; though you had but to handle him carelessly to discover that he was really an animated pincushion. Uncle Ned was the only one who cared to take him up, and this he usually did by lifting him by the two front paws, and then being cautious in stroking him the "right way." Yankee rather chummed up with Pompey, but she kept him well at paw's length all the same, for she had had experiences of porcupines before, and once, when she and her twin sister, Bluenose of sacred memory, were skylarking up a tree with another spiny pet of Uncle Ned's, she had slipped and landed full on Mr. Porky, with direful results.

It must not be supposed that all porcupines are outwardly as quill-less as was Pompey. Some, especially the old "bucks," bear on their backs a miniature jungle of brownish-black and white quills, and on their powerful tails also. This last appendage may be called the porcupine's one weapon of offense, though, strictly speaking, it never actually attacks any animate object. Most naturalists say that it curls up in a ball when attacked itself by a wildcat or bear. In most cases, however, it probably acts as it nearly always does when molested by man. It does not curl up, but endeavors to get its head and forepart of the body in some crevice of rock or under a log, crouching close to the ground and holding its tail ready for action, This, of course, only when it has no chance to make off; for its natural line of retreat is up a tree or into some den in the rocks. Uncle Ned once touched the back of a porcupine with the cork handle of a fishing-rod while the animal was in this position of defense, and then picked twenty-eight quills from it as the result of one blow! No wonder the beasts of the forest give Mr. "Erethizon Dorsatus," as the wise men call him, a very wide berth, though wildcats are said sometimes to kill him by taking him at a disadvantage, when his quill-less belly is exposed, and ripping that up with a blow of a paw. It is likely that only the young and inexperienced of the panther, wildcat, fisher, and wolverine tribes ever attack the porcupine. It is the same with domestic dogs, nearly every one of which will throw itself furiously at a porky the first time it sees one; but only a "fool-dog" will repeat the experiment after being once subjected to the process of having a dozen or two quills jerked out of its mouth and skin with tweezers.

Mr. Manly Hardy of Bangor, Maine, who has probably personally handled more fur-bearing animals than any other man of the north, once assured Uncle Ned that, while most wild animals that meddle with the porcupine are very apt to lose their lives through the quills, there was one that attacked and ate it with impunity. This is the fisher, or black-cat, which Mr. Hardy says he has never known to be killed by the quills, though he has found hundreds of them lying harmless under the skins of fishers. This is passing strange if true, and Mr. Hardy is a man of truth and great experience.

Porcupines have very strong incisor teeth, which are busy half the animal's lifetime gnawing the bark off trees; and long, powerful claws, though they are plantigrades (flat-footed animals), like the bear and raccoon. They will eat pretty much everything that comes in their way, from cast-off antlers to the verandas of woodland camps; but their staple food is the bark of trees, particularly hemlocks. Pompey's favorite dishes, strange to say, were milk and the dry biscuit called in New England "crackers." He would, however, put up with almost anything set before him. Like all his kind, he spent most of his time eating and sleeping, and was in a fair way to cultivate a genuine Daniel-Lambert stomach.

Pompey had been an inmate of Camp Buckshaw for a week or more when Lou Harlow, the mighty Indian hunter, brought Uncle Ned a companion in the shape of a diminutive porcupine which he had come by under very peculiar circumstances. The mother had been shot, and in the course of cutting her up this little, as yet unborn, creature was found. It was a most curious example of the pure power of birth instinct, or heredity, that the first act of the little fellow, which was quite lively, was to strike out sidewise with its puny tail. It did not have to go to the "school of the woods" to learn to recognize danger, or to put in action the weapon Nature had given it. From the circumstances of its premature birth Pompey's new friend was christened Julius Cæsar, and perhaps Julius would have thriven and waxed if he had been left only to Pompey's tender mercies, for Pompey was a gentle, friendly soul. But in an evil hour came Brutus, also a present to Uncle Ned. Now Brutus was the very opposite of Pompey, being much older and larger, and of a sour, resentful character. No amount of coaxing and cajoling would soften his heart, and his one and invariable answer to all such approaches was a prompt turning of his back and the assumption of that attitude of tail-readiness which plainly looked for trouble. With his fellow porcupines he was, however, more than familiar, and within two or three days lorded it over them like a tyrant. No bowl of milk or toothsome cracker or tender twig of birch or hemlock that he did not do his best to keep for himself alone, and, though Pompey succeeded, after a good deal of trouble, in winning his fair share, poor little Julius Cæsar got very poor pickings indeed. Not only that, but Brutus seemed to take pleasure in bullying the little animal between meals. After giving Brutus a fair trial of ten days, and seeing that he was apparently as untamed and defiant as ever, and bade fair to be the death of poor Julius, Uncle Ned one fine day disposed of him. History does not say what became of Brutus, but he was heard of no more.

Soon after his disappearance Uncle Ned opened the pen door and allowed the other porcupines to roam about at will. At first they spent all their time in trees near the cabin, though Uncle Ned was forever pulling them down out of some favorite tree of his. By degrees they wandered farther and farther away, until at last, toward the end of the summer, their relations with the camp were confined to one visit each day, and that was invariably between half-past one and half-past two in the afternoon. About then, anybody watching could hear a faint swishing among the leaves and then see a black head poked up above some log. If all appeared serene, Pompey, followed usually by Julius Cæsar, would amble sedately up the steps and across the veranda to the cabin door, where he would pause and peek in cautiously. If strangers were present, or if he heard any unwonted noises, he would turn away and go back into the woods; but if he heard Uncle Ned's voice, gently urging him to come in and make himself at home, he would cross the threshold and move slowly over the floor to the hearth, where he knew he would find a pan of milk and some crackers. In his wake, but always a minute or two later, would come Julius Cæsar, who never got to be as tame and confiding as Pompey, and the least alarm would send him scurrying out of the cabin; whereas Pompey, once in full enjoyment of his daily "civilized" meal, was quite fearless and at home. It was droll to see him sit quite upright, with a cracker in one paw, or both, just like a dignified ape.

"Ain't he an amusin' little cuss?" Uncle Ned would say. "Just look at him sittin' there, nothin' but a feedin' machine. I can't help feelin' a kind o' sneakin' fondness for porkipines, they 're so sort o' homelike an' comf'table an' outrageous peculiar. But between you an' me they 're about the pure opposite o' what anything or anybody ought 'o be. They 're sure an awful example, that 's what. Look at 'em — they do nothin' but feed, feed, feed, and then sleep. They 're just as we 'd be if our streets and squares were all piled up with steaks and murphies and pie, and all we had to do was just to reach out and grab some. Nothin' but trees all round 'em and all of 'em good to eat. No, they don't even fight, — that 's it, boys. I tell you, look all through natur' and all through hist'ry, and you 'll find ev'ry time that the race o' people or the race o' animals that stops fightin' ain't worth shucks! When they don't have to fight any more for their bread an' butter they get fat an' lazy an' good for nothin', that's what they do. Just look at those gulls — beautiful, sleek, strong, quick, — an' why? Because they live a life o' scrappin'! Don't you take no stock in those folks that talk about eternal peace an' that kind o' drivel. Peace don't mean alone throwin' away cannons and bayonets. There's war in gettin' to the office first, in beatin' the ball to first base, in gettin' a big order placed ahead o' the other feller. But that kind o' war ain't enough to keep the human race keen an' strong for its best work. It needs man-to-man fightin', whether with rifles an' intrenchin'-tools or in a canoe-race. I tell you, boys, life is a fight, first, last, an' all the time; an' when you go out into the world to cut your swaths in it, — just you fight — fight like demons — but fight fair!"

Uncle Ned rubbed his face, which was quite hot with the effort of such undue eloquence, in which he seldom indulged, though he had his own strong convictions on most subjects.

"As to those porkies," he continued, in a more subdued voice, "they show their uselessness; and where the fightin' gulls help the world a lot by cleanin' up and such, those lazy cusses do nothin' that I can think of 'xcept chew up the trees. So you'll see that old chap Darwin was right. The porkies will disappear and we'll all help 'em do so. Let the sentimental people talk as much as they like, the amount of good timber destroyed by Pomp an' his friends is somethin' awful. Their liver's pretty fine though, that's a fact, but I could live without it, same's I can without ice cream."

Uncle Ned was not called upon to tell his young friends anything about porcupine meat, for they had eaten of it many times in the woods and in his cabin. They voted the liver of a young "piggypine," roasted with a strip of bacon over it, *the* tidbit of the forest, though Uncle Ned persisted that beaver-tail was better. But beavers had been protected for some years, and the young folks had not had a chance to taste it. On one occasion, Louis the Indian prepared a real Micmac dish at Camp Buckshaw. It consisted of the entire skin of a young porcupine, cleaned and scraped of all hair and quills, so that it looked, as Nell said, for all the world like a baby's winter undershirt, soft and white and thick. This was boiled in a pot and eaten with seasoning. Lou and Uncle Ned and Sam pronounced it "darn good"; but the others, after tasting of it, declared that they were too generous to deprive the guides of such a dainty. Sam roasted the rest of the porcupine on a kind of frame before the fire. That was good, but rather tough.

Pompey was one of the last pets to stand by the cabin, in spite of Uncle Ned's poor opinion of him and his kindred. But he unfortunately fell a victim to his constitutional gluttony. Not only did he take a fancy to Mr. Thomas's apple-trees, causing murmurs and even remarks, but one fine morning, on entering the pantry, always sacred to the perfect housewife, Mrs. Thomas saw before her astonished and indignant eyes that same Pompey sitting squarely in the middle of a big squash-pie!

This was Pompey's undoing!

THE SCARCITY OF SKUNKS

By Dallas Lore Sharp

THE ragged quilt of snow had slipped from the shoulders of the slopes, the gray face of the maple swamp showed a flush of warmth, and the air, out of the south to-day, breathed life, the life of buds and catkins, of sappy bark, oozing gum, and running water — the life of spring; and through the faintly blending breaths, as a faster breeze ran down the hills, I caught a new and unmistakable odor, single, pointed, penetrating, the sign to me of an open door in the wood-lot, to me, indeed, the Open Sesame of spring.

"When does the spring come? And who brings it?" asks the watcher in the woods. "To me spring begins when the catkins on the alders and the pussy-willows begin to swell," writes Mr. Burroughs, "when the ice breaks up on the river and the first sea-gulls come prospecting northward." So I have written, also; written verses even to the pussy-willow, to the bluebird, and to the hepatica, as spring's harbingers; but never a line yet to celebrate this first forerunner of them all, the gentle early skunk. For it is his presence, blown far across the February snow, that always ends my New England winter and brings the spring. Of course there are difficulties, poetically, with the wood-pussy. I don't remember that even Whitman tried the theme. But, perhaps, the good gray poet never met a spring skunk in the streets of Camden. The animal is comparatively rare in the densely populated cities of New Jersey.

It is rare enough here in Massachusetts; at least, it used to be; though I think, from my observations, that the skunk is quietly on the increase in New England. I feel very sure of this as regards the neighborhood immediate to my farm.

This is an encouraging fact, but hard to be believed, no doubt. I, myself, was three or four years coming to the conviction, often fearing that this little creature, like so many others of our thinning woods, was doomed to disappear. But that was before I turned to keeping hens. I am writing these words as a naturalist and nature-lover, and I am speaking also with the authority of one who keeps hens. Though a man give his life to the study of the skunk, and have not hens, he is nothing. You cannot say, "Go to, I will write an essay about my skunks." There is no such anomaly as professional nature-loving, as vocational nature-writing. You cannot go into your woods and count your skunks. Not until you have kept hens can you know, can you even have the will to believe, the number of skunks that den in the dark on the purlieus of your farm.

That your neighbors keep hens is not enough. My neighbors' hens were from the first a stone of stumbling to me. That is a peculiarity of next-door hens. It would have been better, I thought, if my neighbors had had no hens. I had moved in among these half-farmer folk, and while I found them intelligent enough, I immediately saw that their attitude toward nature was wholly wrong. They seemed to have no conception of the beauty of nature. Their feeling for the skunk was typical: they hated the skunk with a perfect hatred, a hatred implacable, illogical, and unpoetical, it seemed to me, for it was born of their chicken-breeding.

Here were these people in the lap of nature, babes in nature's arms, knowing only to draw at her breasts and gurgle, or, the milk failing, to kick and cry. Mother Nature! She was only a bottle and rubber nipple, only turnips and hay and hens to them. Nature a mother? a spirit? a soul? fragrance? harmony? beauty? Only when she cackled like a hen.

Now there is something in the cackle of a hen, a very great deal, indeed, if it is the cackle of your own hen. But the morning stars did not cackle together, and there is still a solemn music in the universe, a music that is neither an anvil nor a barnyard chorus. Life ought to mean more than turnips, more than hay, more than hens to these rural people. It ought, and it must. I had come among them. And what else was my coming but a divine providence, a high and holy mission? I had been sent unto this people to preach the gospel of the beauty of nature. And I determined that my first text should be the skunk.

All of this, likewise, was previous to the period of my hens.

It was now, as I have said, my second February upon the farm, when the telltale wind brought down this poignant message from the wood-lot. The first spring skunk was out! I knew the very stump out of which he had come — the stump of his winter den. Yes, and the day before, I had actually met the creature in the woods, for he had been abroad now something like a week. He was rooting among the exposed leaves in a sunny dip, and I approached to within five feet of him, where I stood watching while he grubbed in the thawing earth. Buried to the shoulders in the leaves, he was so intent upon his labor that he got no warning of my presence. My neighbors would have knocked him over with a club, — would have done it eagerly, piously, as unto the Lord. What did the Almighty make such vermin for, anyway? No one will phrase an answer; but everyone will act promptly, as by command and revelation.

I stood several minutes watching, before the little wood-pussy paused and pulled out his head in order to try the wind. How shocked he was! He had been caught off his guard, and instantly snapped himself into a startled hump, for the whiff he got on the wind said *danger!* — and nigh at hand! Throwing his pointed nose straight into the air, and swinging it quickly to the four quarters, he fixed my direction, and turning his back upon me, tumbled off in a dreadful hurry for home.

This interesting, though somewhat tame, experience, would have worn the complexion of an adventure for my neighbors, a bare escape, — a ruined Sunday suit, or, at least, a lost jumper or overalls. I had never lost so much as a roundabout in all my life. My neighbors had had innumerable passages with this ramping beast, most of them on the edge of the dark, and many of them verging hard upon the tragic. I had small patience with it all. I wished the whole neighborhood were with me, that I might take this harmless little wood-pussy up in my arms and teach them again the first lesson of the Kingdom of Heaven, and of this earthly Paradise, too, and incidentally put an end forever to these tales of Sunday clothes and nights of banishment in the barn.

As nobody was present to see, of course I did not pick the wood-pussy up. I did not need to prove to myself the baselessness of these wild misgivings; nor did I wish, without good cause, further to frighten the innocent creature. I had met many a skunk before this, and nothing of note ever had happened. Here was one, taken suddenly and unawares, and what did he do? He merely winked and blinked vacantly at me over the snow, trying vainly to adjust his eyes to the hard white daylight, and then timidly made off as fast as his pathetic legs would carry him, fetching a compass far around toward his den.

I accompanied him, partly to see him safely home, but more to study him on the way, for my neighbors would demand something else than theory and poetry of my new gospel: they would require facts. Facts they should have.

I had been a long time coming to my mind concerning the skunk. I had been thinking years about him; and during the previous summer (my second here on the farm) I had made a careful study of the creature's habits, so that even now I had in hand material of considerable bulk and importance, showing the very great usefulness of the animal. Indeed, I was about ready to embody my beliefs and observations in a monograph, setting forth the need of national protection — of a Committee of One Hundred, say, of continental scope, to look after the preservation and further introduction of the skunk as the friend and ally of man, as the most useful of all our insectivorous creatures, bird or beast.

What, may I ask, was this one of mine doing here on the edge of the February woods? He was grubbing. He had been driven out of his winter bed by hunger, and he had been driven out into the open snowy sunshine by the cold, because the nights (he is nocturnal) were still so chill that the soil would freeze at night past his plowing. Thus it chanced, at high noon, that I came upon him, grubbing among my soft, wet leaves, and grubbing for nothing less than obnoxious insects!

My heart warmed to him. He was ragged and thin, he was even weak, I thought, by the way he staggered as he made off. It had been a hard winter for men and for skunks, particularly hard for skunks on account of the unbroken succession of deep snows. This skunk had been frozen into his den, to my certain knowledge, since the last of November.

Nature is a severe mother. The hunger of this starved creature! To be put to bed without even the broth, and to be locked in, half awake, for nearly three months. Poor little beastie! Perhaps he had n't intelligence enough to know that those gnawings within him were pain. Perhaps our sympathy is all agley. Perhaps. But we are bound to feel it when we watch him satisfying his pangs with the pestiferous insects of our own wood-lot.

I saw him safely home, and then returned to examine the long furrows he had plowed out among the leaves. I found nothing to show what species of insects he had eaten, but it was enough to know that he had been bent on bugs — gypsy-moth eggs, maybe, on the underside of some stick or stone, where they had escaped the keen eye of the tree-warden. We are greatly exercised over this ghastly caterpillar. But is it entomologists, and national appropriations, and imported parasites that we need to check the ravaging plague? These things might help, doubtless; but I was intending to show in my monograph that it is only skunks we need; it is the scarcity of skunks that is the whole trouble — and the abundance of cats.

My heart warmed, I say, as I watched my one frail skunk here by the snowy woodside, and it thrilled as I pledged him protection, as I acknowledged his right to the earth, his right to share life and liberty and the pursuit of happiness with me. He could have only a small part in my life, doubtless, but I could enter largely into his, and we could live in amity together — in amity here on *this* bit of the divine earth, anyhow, if nowhere else under heaven.

This was along in February, and I was beginning to set my hens.

A few days later, in passing through the wood-lot, I was surprised and delighted to see three skunks in the near vicinity of the den, — residents evidently of the stump! "Think!" I exclaimed to myself, "think of the wild flavor to this tame patch of woods! And the creatures so rare, too, and beneficial! They multiply rapidly, though," I thought, "and I ought to have a fine lot of them by fall. I shall stock the farm with them."

This was no momentary enthusiasm. In a book that I had published some years before I had stoutly championed the skunk. "Like every predatory creature," I wrote, "the skunk more than balances his debt for corn and chickens by his destruction of obnoxious vermin. He feeds upon insects and mice, destroying great numbers of the latter by digging out the nests and eating the young. But we forget our debt when the chickens disappear, no matter how few we lose. Shall we ever learn to say, when the red-tail swoops among the pigeons, when the rabbits get into the cabbage, when the robins rifle the cherry trees, and when the skunk helps himself to a hen for his Thanksgiving dinner — shall we ever learn to love and understand the fitness of things out-of-doors enough to say, 'But then, poor beastie, thou maun live'?"

Since writing those warm lines I had made further studies upon the skunk, all establishing the more firmly my belief that there is a big balance to the credit of the animal. Meantime, too, I had bought this small farm, with a mowing field and an eight-acre wood-lot on it; with certain liens and attachments on it, also, due to human mismanagement and to interference with the course of Nature in the past. Into the orchard, for instance, had come the San José scale; into the wood-lot had crawled the gypsy-moth — human blunders! Under the sod of the mowing land had burrowed the white grub of the June-bugs. On the whole fourteen acres rested the black shadow of an insect plague. Nature had been interfered with and thwarted. Man had taken things into his own clumsy hands. It should be so no longer on these fourteen acres. I held the deed to these, not for myself, nor for my heirs, but for Nature. Over these few acres the winds of heaven should blow free, the birds should sing, the flowers should grow, and through the gloaming, unharmed and unaffrighted, the useful skunk should take his own sweet way.

The preceding summer had been a season remarkable for the ravages of the June-bug. The turf in my mowing went all brown and dead suddenly in spite of frequent rains. No cause for the trouble showed on the surface of the field. You could start and with your hands roll up the tough sod by the yard, as if a clean-cutting knife had been run under it about an inch below the crowns. It peeled off under your feet in great flakes. An examination of the soil brought to light the big fat grubs of the June-bugs, millions of the ghastly monsters! They had gone under the grass, eating off the roots so evenly and so thoroughly that not a square foot of green remained in the whole field.

It was here that the skunk did his good work (I say "the skunk," for there was only one on the farm that summer, I think). I would go into the field morning after morning to count the holes he had made during the night in his hunt for the grubs. One morning I got over a hundred holes, all of them dug since last sundown, and each hole representing certainly one grub, possibly more; for the skunk would hear or smell his prey at work in the soil before attempting to dig.

A hundred grubs for one night, by one skunk! It took me only a little while to figure out the enormous number of grubs that a fair-sized family of skunks would destroy in a summer. A family of skunks would rid my farm of the pest in a single summer and make inroads on the grubs of the entire community.

Ah! the community! the ignorant, short-sighted, nature-hating community! What chance had a family of skunks in this community? And the fire of my mission burned hot within me.

And so did my desire for more skunks. My hay crop was short, was *nil*, in fact, for the hayfield was as barren of green as the hen-yard. I had to have it plowed and laid down again to grass. And all because of this scarcity of skunks.

Now, as the green of the springing blades began to show through the melting snow, it was with immense satisfaction that I thought of the three skunks under the stump. That evening I went across to my neighbor's, the milkman's, and had a talk with him over the desirability, the necessity indeed, of encouraging the skunks about us, I told him a good many things about these harmless and useful animals that, with all his farming and chicken-raising, he had never known.

But these rural folk are quite difficult. It is hard

to teach them anything worth while, so hopelessly surrounded are they with things — common things. If I could only get them into a college class-room — removed some way from hens and hoes — I might, at least, put them into a receptive attitude. But that cannot be. Perhaps, indeed, I demand too much of them. For, after all, it takes a naturalist, a lover of the out-of-doors, to appreciate the beautiful adjustments in nature. A mere farmer can hardly do it. One needs a keen eye, but a certain aloofness of soul also, for the deeper meaning and poetry of nature. One needs to spend a vacation, at least, in the wilderness and solitary place, where no other human being has ever come, and there, where the animals know man only as a brother, go to the school of the woods and study the wild folk, one by one, until he discovers them personally, temperamentally, all their likes and dislikes, their little whimseys, freaks, and fancies — all of this, there far removed from the cankering cares of hens and chickens, for the sake of the right attitude toward nature.

My nearest neighbor had never been to the wilderness. He lacked imagination, too, and a ready pen. Yet he promised not to kill my three skunks in the stump; a rather doubtful pledge, perhaps, but at least a beginning toward the new earth I hoped to see.

Now it was perfectly well known to me that skunks will eat chickens if they have to. But I had had chickens — a few hens — and had never been bothered by skunks. I kept my hens shut up, of course, in a pen — the only place for a hen outside of a pie. I knew, too, that skunks like honey, that they had even tampered with my hives, reaching in at night through the wide summer entrances and tearing out the brood combs. But I never lost much by these depredations. What I felt more was the destruction of the wild bees and wasps and ground-nesting birds, by the skunks.

But these were trifles! What were a few chickens, bees, yellow-jackets, and even the occasional bird's-nest, against the hay-devouring grubs of the June-bug! And as for the characteristic odor which drifted in now and again with the evening breeze, that had come to have a pleasant quality for me, floating down across my two wide acres of mowing.

February passed gently into March, and my chickens began to hatch. Every man must raise chickens at some period of his life, and I was starting in for my turn now. Hay had been my specialty heretofore, making two blades grow where there had been one very thin one. But once your two acres are laid down, and you have a stump full of skunks, near by, against the ravages of the June-bugs, then there is nothing for you but chickens or something, while you wait. I got Rhode Island Reds, fancy exhibition stock, — for what is the use of chickens if you cannot take them to the show?

The chickens began to hatch, little downy balls of yellow, with their pedigrees showing right through the fuzz. How the sixty of them grew! I never lost one. And now the second batch of sitters would soon be ready to come off.

Then one day, at the morning count, five of one hen's

brood were gone! I counted again. I counted all the other broods. Five were gone!

My nearest neighbor had cats, mere barn cats, as many as ten, at the least. I had been suspicious of those cats from the first. So I got a gun. Then more of my chickens disappeared. I could count only forty-seven.

I shifted the coop, wired it in, and stretched a wire net over the top of the run. Nothing could get in, nor could a chicken get out. All the time I was waiting for the cat.

A few nights after the moving of the coop a big hole was dug under the wire fence of the run, another hole under the coop, and the entire brood of Rhode Island Reds was taken.

Then I took the gun and cut across the pasture to my neighbor's.

"Hard luck," he said. "It 's a big skunk. Here, you take these traps, and you 'll catch him; anybody can catch a skunk."

And I did catch him. I killed him, too, in spite of the great scarcity of the creatures. Yet I was sorry, and, perhaps, too hasty; for catching him near the coop was no proof. He might have wandered this way by chance. I should have put him in a bag and carried him down to Valley Swamp and liberated him.

That day, while my neighbor was gone with his milk wagon, I slipped through the back pasture and hung the two traps up on their nail in the can-house.

I went anxiously to the chicken-yard the next morning. All forty came out to be counted. It must have been the skunk, I was thinking, as I went on into the brooding-house, where six hens were still sitting.

One of the hens was off her nest and acting queerly. Her nest was empty! Not a chick, not a bit of shell! I lifted up the second hen in the row, and of her thirteen eggs, only three were left. The hen next to her had five eggs; the fourth hen had four. Forty chickens gone (counting them before they were hatched), all in one night.

I hitched up the horse and drove thoughtfully to the village, where I bought six skunk-traps.

"Goin' skunkin' some, this spring," the store man remarked, as he got me the traps, adding, "Well, they 's some on 'em. I 've seen a scaac'ty of a good many commodities, but I never yet see a scaac'ty o' skunks."

I did n't stop to discuss the matter, being a trifle uncertain just then as to my own mind, but hurried home with my six traps. Six, I thought, would do to begin with, though I really had no conception of the number of cats (or skunks) it had taken to dispose of the three and one third dozens of eggs (at three dollars a dozen!) in a single night.

Early that afternoon I covered each sitting hen so that even a mouse could not get at her, and fixing the traps, I distributed them about the brooding-house floor; then, as evening came on, I pushed a shell into each barrel of the gun, took a comfortable perch upon a keg in the corner of the house, and waited.

I had come to stay. Something was going to happen. And something did happen, away on in the small hours of the morning, namely — one little skunk. He walked into a trap while I was dozing. He seemed pretty small hunting then, but he looms larger now, for I have learned several more things about skunks than I knew when I had the talk with my neighbor: I have learned, for one thing, that forty eggs, soon to hatch, are just an average meal for the average half-grown skunk.

The catching of these two thieves put an end to the depredations, and I began again to exhibit in my dreams when one night, while sound asleep, I heard a frightful commotion among the hens. I did the hundred-yard dash to the chicken-house in my unforgotten college form, but just in time to see the skunk cross the moon-lit line into the black woods ahead of me.

He had wrought dreadful havoc among the thoroughbreds. What devastation a skunk, single-handed, can achieve in a pen of young chickens beggars all description.

I was glad that it was dead of night, that the world was home and asleep in its bed. I wanted no sympathy. I wished only to be alone, alone in the cool, the calm, the quiet of this serene and beautiful midnight. Even the call of a whippoorwill in the adjoining pasture worried me. I desired to meditate, yet clear, consecutive thinking seemed strangely difficult. I felt like one disturbed. I was out of harmony with this peaceful environment. Perhaps I had hurried too hard, or I was too thinly clothed, or perhaps my feet were cold and wet. I only know, as I stooped to untwist a long and briery runner from about my ankle, that there was great confusion in my mind, and in my spirit there was chaos. I felt myself going to pieces, —

I, the nature-lover! Had I not advocated the raising of a few extra hens just for the sake of keeping the screaming hawk in air and the wild fox astir in our scanty picnic groves? And had I not said as much for the skunk? Why, then, at one in the morning should I, nor clothed, nor in my right mind, be picking my bare-foot way among the tangled dewberry vines behind the barn, swearing by the tranquil stars to blow the white-striped carcass of that skunk into ten million atoms if I had to sit up all the next night to do it?

One o'clock in the morning was the fiend's hour. There could be no unusual risk in leaving the farm for a little while in the early evening, merely to go to the bean supper over at the chapel at the Corner. So we were dressed and ready to start, when I spied one of my hens outside the yard, trying to get in.

Hurrying down, I caught her, and was turning back to the barn, when I heard a slow, faint rustling among the bushes behind the hen-house. I listened! Something was moving cautiously through the dead leaves! Tiptoeing softly around, I surprised a large skunk making his way slowly toward the hen-yard fence.

I grabbed a stone and hurled it, jumping, as I let it drive, for another. The flying missile hit within an inch of the creature's nose, hard upon a large flat rock over which he was crawling. The impact was stunning, and before the old rascal could get to his groggy feet, I had fallen upon him — literally — and done for him.

But I was very sorry. I hope that I shall never get so excited as to fall upon another skunk, — never!

I was picking myself up, when I caught a low cry from the direction of the house — half scream, half shout. It was a woman's voice, the voice of my wife, I thought. Was something the matter?

"Hurry!" I heard. But how could I hurry? My breath was gone, and so were my spectacles, and other more important things besides, while all about me poured a choking blinding smother. I fought my way out.

"Oh, hurry!"

I was on the jump; I was already rounding the barn, when a series of terrified shrieks issued from the front of the house. An instant more and I had come. But none too soon, for there stood the dear girl, backed into a corner of the porch, her dainty robes drawn close about her, and a skunk, a wee baby of a skunk, climbing confidently up the steps toward her.

"Why *are* you so slow!" she gasped. "I 've been yelling here for an hour! — Oh! do — don't kill that little thing, but shoo it away, quick!"

She certainly had not been yelling an hour, nor anything like it. But there was no time for argument now, and as for shooing little skunks, I was past that. I don't know exactly what I did say, though I am positive that it was n't "shoo." I was clutching a great stone, that I had run with all the way from behind the henyard, and letting it fly, I knocked the little creature into a harmless bunch of fur. The family went over to the bean supper and left me all alone on the farm. But I was calm now, with a strange, cold calmness born of extremity. Nothing more could happen to me; I was beyond further harm. So I took up the bodies of the two creatures, and carried them, together with some of my late clothing, over beyond the ridge for burial. Then I returned by way of my neighbor's, where I borrowed two sticks of blasting-powder and a big cannon fire-cracker. I had watched my neighbor use these explosives on the stumps in a new piece of meadow. The next morning, with an axe, a crowbar, shovel, gun, blasting-powder, and the cannon-cracker, I started for the stump in the wood-lot. I wished the cannon-cracker had been a keg of powder. I could tamp a keg of powder so snugly into the hole of those skunks!

It was a beautiful summer morning, tender with the half-light of breaking dawn, and fresh with dew. Leaving my kit at the mouth of the skunks' den, I sat down on the stump to wait a moment, for the loveliness and wonder of the opening day came swift upon me. From the top of a sapling, close by, a chewink sent his simple, earnest song ringing down the wooded slope, and, soft as an echo, floated up from the swampy tangle of wild grape and azalea the pure notes of a wood thrush, mellow and globed, and almost fragrant of the thicket where the white honeysuckle was in bloom. Voices never heard at other hours of the day were vocal now; odors and essences that vanish with the dew hung faint in the air; shapes and shadows and intimations of things that slip to cover from the common light, stirred close about me. It was very near — the gleam! the vision splendid! How close to a revelation seems every dawn! And this early summer dawn, how near a return of that

> time when meadow, grove, and stream,
> The earth and every common sight
> To me did seem
> Apparelled in celestial light.

From the crest of my ridge I looked out over the tree-tops far away to the Blue Hills still slumbering in the purple west. How huge and prone they lie! How like their own constant azure does the spirit of rest seem to wrap them round! On their distant slopes it is never common day, never more than dawn, for the shadows always sleep among their hollows, and a haze of changing blues, their own peculiar beauty, hangs, even at high noon, like a veil upon them, shrouding them with largeness and mystery.

A rustle in the dead leaves down the slope recalled me. I reached instinctively for the gun, but stayed my hand. Slowly nosing his way up the ridge, came a full-grown skunk, his tail a-drag, his head swinging close to the ground. He was coming home to the den, coming leisurely, contentedly, carelessly, as if he had a right to live. I sat very still. On he came, scarcely checking himself as he winded me. How like the dawn he seemed! — the black of night with the white of day — the furtive dawn slipping into its den! He sniffed at the gun and cannon-cracker, made his way over them, brushed past me, and calmly disappeared beneath the stump.

The chewink still sang from the top of the sapling, but the tame broad day had come. I stayed a little while, looking off still at the distant hills. We had sat thus, my six-year-old and I, only a few days before, looking away at these same hills, when the little fellow, half questioningly, half pensively asked, "Father, how can the Blue Hills be so beautiful and have rattlesnakes?"

I gathered up the kit, gun and cannon-cracker, and started back toward home, turning the question of hills and snakes and skunks over and over as I went along. Over and over the question still turns: How can the Blue Hills be so beautiful? The case of my small wood-lot is easier: beautiful it must ever be, but its native spirit, the untamed spirit of the original wilderness, the free wild spirit of the primeval forest, shall flee it, and vanish forever, with this last den of the skunks.

THE DOUGLAS SQUIRREL

By John Muir

ALL the true squirrels are more or less birdlike in speech and movements; but the Douglas is preëminently so, possessing as he does, every attribute peculiarly squirrelish enthusiastically concentrated. He is the squirrel of squirrels, flashing from branch to branch of his favorite evergreens crisp and glossy and undiseased as a sunbeam. Give him wings and he would outfly any bird in the woods. His big gray cousin is a looser animal, seemingly light enough to float on the wind; yet when leaping from limb to limb, or out of one tree-top to another, he sometimes halts to gather strength, as if making efforts concerning the upshot of which he does not always feel exactly confident. But the Douglas, with his denser body, leaps and glides in hidden strength, seemingly as independent of common muscles as a mountain stream. He threads the tasseled branches of the pines, stirring their needles like a rustling breeze; now shooting across openings in arrowy lines; now launching in curves, glinting deftly from side to side in sudden zigzags, and swirling in giddy loops and spirals around the knotty trunks; getting into what seem to be the most impossible situations without sense of danger; now on his haunches, now on his head; yet ever graceful, and punctuating his most irrepressible outbursts of energy with little dots and dashes of perfect repose. He is, without exception, the wildest animal I ever saw, — a fiery, sputtering little bolt of life, luxuriating in quick oxygen and the woods' best juices. One can hardly think of such a creature being dependent, like the rest of us, on climate and food. But, after all, it requires no long acquaintance to learn he is human, for he works for a living. His busiest time is in the Indian summer. Then he gathers burs and hazel-nuts like a plodding farmer, working continuously every day for hours; saying not a word; cutting off the ripe cones at the top of his speed, as if employed by the job, and examining every branch in regular order, as if careful that not one should escape him; then, descending, he stores them away beneath logs and stumps, in anticipation of the pinching hunger days of winter. He seems himself a kind of coniferous fruit, — both fruit and flower. The resiny essences of the pines pervade every pore of his body, and eating his flesh is like chewing gum.

One never tires of this bright chip of nature, — this brave little voice crying in the wilderness, — of observing his many works and ways, and listening to his curious language. His musical, piny gossip is as savory to the ear as balsam to the palate; and though he has not exactly the gift of song, some of his notes are as sweet as those of a linnet — almost flute-like in softness, while others prick and tingle like thistles. He is the mocking-bird of squirrels, pouring forth mixed chatter and song like a perennial fountain; barking like a dog, screaming like a hawk, chirping like a blackbird or a sparrow; while in bluff, audacious noisiness he is a very jay.

In descending the trunk of a tree with the intention of alighting on the ground, he preserves a cautious silence, mindful, perhaps, of foxes and wildcats; but while rocking safely at home in the pine-tops there is no end to his capers and noise; and woe to the gray squirrel or chipmunk that ventures to set foot on his favorite tree! No matter how slyly they trace the furrows of the bark, they are speedily discovered, and kicked downstairs with comic vehemence, while a torrent of angry notes comes rushing from his whiskered lips that sounds remarkably like swearing. He will even attempt at times to drive away dogs and men, especially if he has had no previous knowledge of them. Seeing a man for the first time, he approaches nearer and nearer, until within a few feet; then, with an angry outburst, he makes a sudden rush, all teeth and eyes, as if about to eat you up. But, finding that the big, forked animal does n't scare, he prudently beats a retreat, and sets himself up to reconnoiter on some overhanging branch, scrutinizing every movement you make with ludicrous solemnity. Gathering courage, he ventures down the trunk again, churring and chirping, and jerking nervously up and down in curious loops, eyeing you all the time, as if showing off and demanding your admiration. Finally, growing calmer, he settles down in a comfortable posture on some horizontal branch commanding a good view, and beats time with his tail to a steady "Chee-up! chee-up!" or when somewhat less excited, "Pee-ah!" with the first syllable keenly accented, and the second drawn out like the scream of a hawk, — repeating this slowly and more emphatically at first, then gradually faster, until a rate of about 150 words a minute is reached; usually sitting all the time on his haunches, with paws resting on his breast, which pulses visibly with each word. It is remarkable, too, that, though articulating distinctly, he keeps his mouth shut most of the time, and speaks through his nose. I have occasionally observed him even eating Sequoia seeds and nibbling a troublesome flea, without ceasing or in any way confusing his "Pee-ah! pee-ah!" for a single moment.

While ascending trees all his claws come into play, but in descending the weight of his body is sustained chiefly by those of the hind feet; still in neither case do his movements suggest effort, though if you are near enough you may see the bulging strength of his short, bear-like arms, and note his sinewy fists clinched in the bark.

Whether going up or down, he carries his tail extended at full length in line with his body, unless it be required for gestures. But while running along horizontal limbs or fallen trunks, it is frequently folded forward over the back, with the airy tip daintily upcurled. In cool weather it keeps him warm. Then, after he has finished his meal, you may see him crouched close on some level limb with his tail-robe neatly spread and reaching forward to his ears, the electric, outstanding hairs quivering in the breeze like pine needles. But in wet or very cold weather he stays in his nest, and while curled up there his comforter is long enough to come forward around his nose. It is seldom so cold, however, as to prevent his going out to his stores when hungry.

Once as I lay storm-bound on the upper edge of the timber line on Mount Shasta, the thermometer nearly at zero and the sky thick with driving snow, a Douglas came bravely out several times from one of the lower hollows of a Dwarf Pine near my camp, faced the wind without seeming to feel it much, frisked lightly about over the mealy snow, and dug his way down to some hidden seeds with wonderful precision, as if to his eyes the thick snow-covering were glass.

No other of the Sierra animals of my acquaintance is better fed, not even the deer, amid abundance of sweet herbs and shrubs, or the mountain sheep, or omnivorous bears. His food consists of grass-seeds, berries, hazel-nuts, chinquapins, and the nuts and seeds of all the coniferous trees without exception, — Pine, Fir, Spruce, Libocedrus, Juniper, and Sequoia, — he is fond of them all, and they all agree with him, green or ripe. No cone is too large for him to manage, none so small as to be beneath his notice. The smaller ones, such as those of the Hemlock, and the Douglas Spruce, and the Two-leaved Pine, he cuts off and eats on a branch of the tree, without allowing them to fall; beginning at the bottom of the cone and cutting away the scales to expose the seeds; not gnawing by guess, like a bear, but turning them around and round in regular order, in compliance with their spiral arrangement.

When thus employed, his location in the tree is

betrayed by a dribble of scales, shells, and seed-wings, and, every few minutes, by the fall of the stripped axis of the cone. Then of course he is ready for another, and if you are watching you may catch a glimpse of him as he glides silently out to the end of a branch and see him examining the cone-clusters until he finds one to his mind; then, leaning over, pull back the springy needles out of his way, grasp the cone with his paws to prevent its falling, snip it off in an incredibly short time, seize it with jaws grotesquely stretched, and return to his chosen seat near the trunk. But the immense size of the cones of the Sugar Pine — from fifteen to twenty inches in length — and those of the Jeffrey variety of the Yellow Pine compel him to adopt a quite different method. He cuts them off without attempting to hold them, then goes down and drags them from where they have chanced to fall up to the bare, swelling ground around the instep of the tree, where he demolishes them in the same methodical way, beginning at the bottom and following the scale-spirals to the top.

From a single Sugar Pine cone he gets from two to four hundred seeds about half the size of a hazel-nut, so that in a few minutes he can procure enough to last a week. He seems, however, to prefer those of the two Silver Firs above all others; perhaps because they are most easily obtained, as the scales drop off when ripe without needing to be cut. Both species are filled with an exceedingly pungent, aromatic oil, which spices all his flesh, and is of itself sufficient to account for his lightning energy.

You may easily know this little workman by his chips. On sunny hillsides around the principal trees they lie in big piles, — bushels and basketfuls of them, all fresh and clean, making the most beautiful kitchen-middens imaginable. The brown and yellow scales and nut-shells are as abundant and as delicately penciled and tinted as the shells along the sea-shore; while the beautiful red and purple seed-wings mingled with them would lead one to fancy that innumerable butterflies had there met their fate.

He feasts on all the species long before they are ripe, but is wise enough to wait until they are matured before he gathers them into his barns. This is in October and November, which with him are the two busiest months of the year. All kinds of burs, big and little, are cut off and showered down alike, and the ground is speedily covered with them. A constant thudding and bumping is kept up; some of the larger cones chancing to fall on old logs make the forest reëcho with the sound. Other nut-eaters less industrious know well what is going on, and hasten to carry away the cones as they fall. But however busy the harvester may be, he is not slow to descry the pilferers below, and instantly leaves his work to drive them away. The little striped Tamias is a thorn in the flesh, stealing persistently, punish him as he may. The large Gray Squirrel gives trouble also, although the Douglas has been accused of stealing from him. Generally, however, just the opposite is the case.

The excellence of the Sierra evergreens is well known to nurserymen throughout the world, consequently there is considerable demand for the seeds. The greater portion of the supply has hitherto been procured by chopping down the trees in the more accessible sections of the forest alongside of bridle-paths that cross the range. Sequoia seeds at first brought from twenty to thirty dollars per pound, and therefore were eagerly sought after. Some of the smaller fruitful trees were cut down in the groves not protected by government, especially those of Fresno and King's River. Most of the Sequoias, however, are of so gigantic a size that the seedmen have to look for the greater portion of their supplies to the Douglas, who soon learns he is no match for these freebooters. He is wise enough, however, to cease working the instant he perceives them, and never fails to embrace every opportunity to recover his burs whenever they happen to be stored in any place accessible to him, and the busy seedsman often finds on returning to camp that the little Douglas has exhaustively spoiled the spoiler. I know one seed-gatherer who, whenever he robs the squirrels, scatters wheat or barley beneath the trees as conscience-money.

The want of appreciable life remarked by so many travelers in the Sierra forests is never felt at this time of year. Banish all the humming insects and the birds and quadrupeds, leaving only Sir Douglas, and the most solitary of our so-called solitudes would still throb with ardent life. But if you should go impatiently even into the most populous of the groves on purpose to meet him, and walk about looking up among the branches, you would see very little of him. But lie down at the foot of one of the trees and straightway he will come. For, in the midst of the ordinary forest sounds, the falling of burs, piping of quails, the screaming of the Clark Crow, and the rustling of deer and bears among the chaparral, he is quick to detect your strange footsteps, and will hasten to make a good, close inspection of you as soon as you are still. First, you may hear him sounding a few notes of curious inquiry, but more likely the first intimation of his approach will be the prickly sounds of his feet as he descends the tree overhead, just before he makes his savage onrush to frighten you and proclaim your presence to every squirrel and bird in the neighborhood. If you remain perfectly motionless, he will come nearer and nearer, and probably set your flesh a-tingle by frisking across your body. Once, while I was seated at the foot of a Hemlock Spruce in one of the most inaccessible of the San Joaquin yosemites engaged in sketching, a reckless fellow came up behind me, passed under my bended arm, and jumped on my paper. And one warm afternoon, while an old friend of mine was reading out in the shade of his cabin, one of his Douglas neighbors jumped from the gable upon his head, and then with admirable assurance ran down over his shoulder and on to the book he held in his hand.

Our Douglas enjoys a large social circle; for, besides his numerous relatives, Sciurus fossor, Tamias quadrivitatus, T. Townsendii, Spermophilus Beecheyi, S. Douglasii, he maintains intimate relations with the nut-eating birds, particularly the Clark Crow (Picicorvus columbianus) and the numerous woodpeckers and jays. The two spermophiles are astonishingly abundant in the lowlands and lower foot-hills, but more and more sparingly distributed up through the Douglas domains, — seldom venturing higher than six or seven thousand feet above the level of the sea. The gray Sciurus ranges but little higher than this. The little striped Tamias alone is associated with him everywhere. In the lower and middle zones, where they all meet, they are tolerably harmonious—a happy family, though very amusing skirmishes may occasionally be witnessed. Wherever the ancient glaciers have spread forest soil there you find our wee hero, most abundant where depth of soil and genial climate have given rise to a corresponding luxuriance in the trees, but following every kind of growth up the curving moraines to the highest glacial fountains.

Though I cannot of course expect all my readers to sympathize fully in my admiration of this little animal, few, I hope, will think this sketch of his life too long. I cannot begin to tell here how much he has cheered my lonely wanderings during all the years I have been pursuing my studies in these glorious wilds; or how much unmistakable humanity I have found in him. Take this for example: One calm, creamy Indian summer morning, when the nuts were ripe, I was camped in the upper pine-woods of the south fork of the San Joaquin, where the squirrels seemed to be about as plentiful as the ripe burs. They were taking an early breakfast before going to their regular harvest-work. While I was busy with my own breakfast I heard the thudding fall of two or three heavy cones from a Yellow Pine near me. I stole noiselessly forward within about twenty feet of the base of it to observe. In a few moments down came the Douglas. The breakfast-burs he had cut off had rolled on the gently sloping ground into a clump of ceanothus bushes, but he seemed to know exactly where they were, for he found them at once, apparently without searching for them. They were more than twice as heavy as himself, but after turning them into the right position for getting a good hold with his long sickle-teeth he managed to drag them up to the foot of the tree from which he had cut them, moving backward. Then seating himself comfortably, he held them on end, bottom up, and demolished them at his ease. A good deal of nibbling had to be done before he got anything to eat, because the lower scales are barren, but when he had patiently worked his way up to the fertile ones he found two sweet nuts at the base of each, shaped like trimmed hams, and spotted purple like bird's eggs. And notwithstanding these cones were dripping with soft balsam, and covered with prickles, and so strongly put together that a boy would be puzzled to cut them open with a jack-knife, he accomplished his meal with easy dignity and cleanliness, making less effort apparently than a man would in eating soft cookery from a plate.

Breakfast done, I whistled a tune for him before he went to work, curious to see how he would be affected by it. He had not seen me all this while; but the instant I began to whistle he darted up the tree nearest to him, and came out on a small dead limb opposite me, and composed himself to listen. I sang and whistled more than a dozen airs, and as the music changed his eyes sparkled, and he turned his head quickly from side to side, but made no other response. Other squirrels, hearing the strange sounds, came around on all sides, also chipmunks and birds. One of the birds, a handsome, speckle-breasted thrush, seemed even more interested than the squirrels. After listening for a while on one of the lower dead sprays of a pine, he came swooping forward within a few feet of my face, and remained fluttering in the air for half a minute or so, sustaining himself with whirring wing-beats, like a humming-bird in front of a flower, while I could look into his eyes and see his innocent wonder.

By this time my performance must have lasted nearly half an hour. I sang or whistled "Bonnie Doon," "Lass o' Gowrie," "O'er the Water to Charlie," "Bonnie Woods o' Craigie Lee," etc., all of which seemed to be listened to with bright interest, my first Douglas sitting patiently through it all, with his telling eyes fixed upon me until I ventured to give the "Old Hundredth," when he screamed his Indian name, Pillillooeet, turned tail, and darted with ludicrous haste up the tree out of sight, his voice and actions in the case leaving a somewhat profane impression, as if he had said "I 'll be hanged if you get me to hear anything so solemn and unpiny." This acted as a signal for the general dispersal of the whole hairy tribe, though the birds seemed willing to wait further developments, music being naturally more in their line.

What there can be in that grand old church-tune that is so offensive to birds and squirrels I can't imagine. A year or two after this High Sierra concert, I was sitting one fine day on a hill in the Coast Range where the common Ground Squirrels were abundant. They were very shy on account of being hunted so much; but after I had been silent and motionless for half an hour or so they began to venture out of their holes and to feed on the seeds of the grasses and thistles around me as if I were no more to be feared than a tree-stump. Then it occurred to me that this was a good opportunity to find out whether they also disliked "Old Hundredth." Therefore I began to whistle as nearly as I could remember the same familiar airs that had pleased the mountaineers of the Sierra. They at once stopped eating, stood erect, and listened patiently until I came to "Old Hundredth," when with ludicrous haste every one of them rushed to their holes and bolted in, their feet twinkling in the air for a moment as they vanished.

No one who makes the acquaintance of our forester will fail to admire him; but he is far too self-reliant and warlike ever to be taken for a darling.

How long the life of a Douglas Squirrel may be, I don't know. The young seem to sprout from knot-holes, perfect from the first, and as enduring as their own trees. It is difficult, indeed, to realize that so condensed a piece of sun-fire should ever become dim or die at all. He is seldom killed by hunters, for he is too small to encourage much of their attention, and when pursued in settled regions becomes excessively shy, and keeps close in the furrows of the highest trunks, many of which are of the same color as himself. Indian boys, however, lie in wait with unbounded patience to shoot them with arrows. In the lower and middle zones a few fall a prey to rattlesnakes. Occasionally he is pursued by hawks and wildcats, etc. But, upon the whole, he dwells safely in the deep bosom of the woods, the most highly favored of all his happy tribe. May his tribe increase!

HOW THE BEAVERS SAVED THEIR HOME

By Enos A. Mills

BEAVERS become strongly attached to localities and especially to their homes. It is difficult to drive them away from these, but the exhaustion of the food-supply sometimes compels an entire colony to abandon the old home-site, migrate, and found a new colony. Some of the beavers' most audacious engineering works are undertaken for the purpose of maintaining the food-supply of the colony. It occasionally happens that the food trees near the water by an old colony become scarce through excessive cutting, fires, or tree diseases. In cases of this kind the colonists must go a long distance for their supplies, or move. They prefer to stay at the old place, and will work for weeks and brave dangers to be able to do this. They will build a dam, dig a new canal, clear a difficult right-of-way to a grove of food saplings, and then drag the harvest a long distance to the water; and now and then do all these for just one more harvest, one more year in the old home.

The Moraine Colony had lost its former greatness. Instead of the several ponds and the eight houses of which it had consisted twenty years before, only one house and a single pond remained. The house was in the deep water of the pond, about twenty feet above the dam. A vigorous brook from Chasm Lake, three thousand feet above, ran through the pond and poured over the dam near the house. The colony was on a delta tongue of a moraine. Here it had been established for generations. It was embowered in a young pine forest and had ragged areas of willows around it. A fire and excessive cutting by beavers had left but few aspens near the water. These could furnish food for no more than two autumn harvests, and perhaps for only one. Other colonies had met similar conditions. How would the Moraine Colony handle theirs?

The Moraine colonists mastered the situation in their place with the most audacious piece of work I have ever known beavers to plan and accomplish. About one hundred and thirty feet south of the old pond was a grove of aspens. Between these and the pond was a small bowldery flat that had a scattering of dead and standing spruces and young lodge-pole pines. A number of fallen spruces lay broken among the partly exposed bowlders of the flat. One day I was astonished to find that a dam was being built across this flat, and still more astonished to discover that this dam was being made of heavy sections of fire-killed trees. Under necessity only will beavers gnaw dead wood, and then only to a limited extent. Such had been my observations for years; but here they were cutting dead, fire-hardened logs in a wholesale manner. Why were they cutting this dead wood, and why a dam across a rocky flat, — a place across which water never flowed? A dam of dead timber across a dry flat appeared to be a marked combination of animal stupidity, — but the beavers knew what they were doing. After watching their activities and the progress of the dam daily for a month, I realized that they were doing development work, with the intention of procuring a food-supply. They completed a dam of dead timber.

At least two accidents happened to the builders of this dead-wood dam. One of these occurred when a tree which the beavers had gnawed off pinned the beaver that had cut it between its end and another tree immediately behind the animal. The other accident was caused by a tree falling in an unexpected direction. This tree was leaning against a fallen one that was held several feet above the earth by a bowlder. When cut off, instead of falling directly to the earth it slid alongside the log against which it had been leaning and was shunted off to one side, falling upon and instantly killing two of the logging beavers.

The dam, when completed, was eighty-five feet long. It was about fifty feet below the main pond and sixty feet distant from the south side of it. Fifty feet of the new dam ran north and south, parallel to the old one; then, forming a right angle, it extended thirty-five feet in height, being made almost entirely of large chunks, dead-tree cuttings from six to fifteen inches in diameter, and from two to twelve feet long. It appeared a crude windrow of dead-timber wreckage.

The day it was completed the builders shifted the scene of activity to the brook, a short distance below the point where it emerged from the main pond. Here they placed a small dam across it and commenced work on a canal, through which they endeavored to lead a part of the waters of the brook into the reservoir which their dead-wood dam had formed.

There was a swell or slight rise in the earth of about eighteen inches between the reservoir and the head of the canal that was to carry water into it. The swell, I suppose, was not considered by the beavers. At any rate, they completed about half the length of the canal, then apparently discovered that water would not flow through it in the direction desired. Other canal-builders have made similar errors. The beavers were almost human. This part of the canal was abandoned and a new start made. The beavers now apparently tried to overcome the swell in the earth by an artificial work.

A pondlet was formed immediately below the old pond by building a sixty-foot bow-like dam, the ends of which were attached to the old dam. The brook pouring from the old pond quickly filled this new narrow, sixty-foot-long reservoir. The outlet of this was made over the bow dam at the point nearest to the waiting reservoir of the dead-wood dam. The water, where it poured over the outlet of the bow dam, failed to flow toward the waiting reservoir, but was shed off to one side by the earth-swell before it. Instead of flowing southward, it flowed eastward. The beavers remedied this and directed the flow by building a wing dam, which extended southward from the bow dam at the point where the water overpoured. This earth-

A BEAVER CANAL

work was about fifteen feet long, four feet wide, and two high. Along the upper side of this the water flowed, and from its end a canal was dug to the reservoir.

About half of the brook was diverted, and this amount of water covered the flat and formed a pond to the height of the dead-wood dam in less than three days. Most of the leaky openings in this dam early became clogged with leaves, trash, and sediment that were carried in by the water, but here and there were large openings which the beavers mudded themselves. The new pond was a little more than one hundred feet long and from forty to fifty feet wide. Its southerly shore flooded into the edge of the aspen grove which the beavers were planning to harvest.

The canal was from four to five feet wide and from eight to twenty inches deep. The actual distance that lay between the brook and the shore of the new pond was ninety feet. Though the diverting of the water was a task, it required less labor than the building of the dam.

With dead timber and the canal, the beavers had labored two seasons for the purpose of getting more supplies without abandoning the colony. If in building the canal they had used the green, easily cut aspens, they would have greatly reduced the available food-supply. It would have required most of these aspens to build the dam. The only conclusion I can reach is that the beavers not only had the forethought to begin work to obtain a food-supply that would be needed two years after, but also, at the expense of much labor, actually saved the scanty near-by food-supply of aspens by making their dam with the hard, fire-killed trees.

A large harvest of aspen and willow was gathered for winter. Daily visits to the scene of the harvest enabled me to understand many of the methods and much of the work that otherwise would have gone on unknown to me. Early in the harvest an aspen cluster far downstream was cut. Every tree in this cluster and every near-by aspen was felled, dragged to the brook, and in this, with wrestling, pushing, and pulling, taken up stream through shallow water, — for most mountain streams are low during the autumn. In the midst of this work the entrance or inlet of the canal was blocked and the bow dam was cut. The water in the brook was almost doubled in volume by the closing of the canal, thereby making the transportation of aspens upstream less laborious.

When the downstream aspens at last reposed in a pile beside the house, harvesting was briskly begun in the aspens along the shore of the new pond. Then came another surprise. The bow dam was repaired, and the canal not only opened, but enlarged so that almost all the water in the brook was diverted into the canal, through which it flowed into the new pond.

The aspens cut on the shore of the new pond were floated across it, then dragged up the canal into the old pond. Evidently the beavers not only had again turned the water into the canal that they might use it in transportation, but also had increased the original volume of water simply to make this transportation of the aspens as easy as possible.

Their new works enabled the colonists to procure nearly five hundred aspens for the winter. All these were taken up the new canal, dragged over the bow and the main dams, and piled in the water by the house. In addition to these, the aspens brought from downstream made the total of the harvest seven hundred and thirty-two trees; and with these went several hundred small willows. Altogether these made a large green brush-pile that measured more than a hundred feet in circumference, and after it settled averaged four feet in depth. This was the food-supply for the oncoming winter.

LITTLE BOY GRIZZLY

By Enos A. Mills

ONE day, while wandering in the pine woods on the slope of Mount Meeker, I came upon two young grizzly bears. Though they dodged about as lively as chickens, I at last cornered them in a penlike pocket of fallen trees.

Getting them into a sack was one of the liveliest experiences I ever had. Though small and almost starved, these little orphans proceeded to "chew me up" after the manner of big grizzlies, as is told of them in books. After an exciting chase and tussle, I would catch one and thrust him into the sack. In resisting, he would insert his claws into my clothes, or thrust them through the side of the sack; then, while I was trying to tear him loose, or to thrust him forcibly in, he would lay hold of a finger, or take a bite in my leg. Whenever he bit, I at once dropped him, and then all began over again.

Their mother had been killed a few days before I found them; so, of course, they were famished and in need of a home; but so bitterly did they resist my efforts that I barely succeeded in taking them. Though hardly so large as a collie when he is at his prettiest, they were nimble athletes.

At last I started home, the sack over my shoulder,

with these lively *Ursi horribiles* in the bottom of it. Their final demonstration was not needed to convince me of the extraordinary power of their jaws. Nevertheless, while going down a steep slope, one managed to bite into my back through sack and clothes, so effectively that I responded with a yell. Then I fastened the sack at the end of a long pole, which I carried across my shoulder, and I was able to travel the remainder of the distance to my cabin without another attack in the rear.

Of course the youngsters did not need to be taught to eat. I simply pushed their noses down into a basin of milk, and the little red tongues at once began to ply; then raw eggs and bread were dropped into the basin. There was no hesitation between courses; they simply gobbled the food as long as I kept it before them.

Jenny and Johnny were pets before sundown. Though both were alert, Johnny was the wiser and the most cheerful of the two. He took training as readily as a collie or shepherd-dog, and I have never seen any dog more playful. All bears are keen of wit, but he was the brightest one of the wild folk that I have ever known. He grew rapidly, and ate me almost out of supplies. We were intimate friends in less than a month, and I spent much time playing and talking with him. One of the first things I taught him was, when hungry, to stand erect with arms extended almost horizontally, with palms forward. I also taught him to greet me in this manner.

One day, after two weeks with me, he climbed to the top of a pole fence to which he was chained. Up there he had a great time; he perched, gazed here and there, pranced back and forth, and finally fell off. His chain tangled and caught. For a few seconds he dangled in the air by the neck, then slipped through his collar and galloped off up the mountainside and quickly disappeared in the woods. I supposed he was gone for good. Although I followed for several hours, I did not even catch sight of him.

This little boy had three days of runaway life, and then concluded to return. Hunger drove him back. I saw him coming and went to meet him; but kept out of sight until he was within twenty feet, then stepped into view. Apparently a confused or entangled mental condition followed my appearance. His first impulse was to let me know that he was hungry by standing erect and outstretching his arms; this he started hastily to do.

In the midst of this performance, it occurred to him that if he wanted anything to eat he must hurry to me; so he interrupted his first action, and started to carry his second into instant effect. These incomplete proceedings interrupted and tripped one another three or four times in rapid succession. Though he tumbled about in comic confusion while trying to do two things at once, it was apparent through all that his central idea was to get something to eat.

And this, as with all boys, was his central idea much of the time. I did not find anything that he would not eat. He simply gobbled scraps from the table, — mountain sage, rhubarb, dandelion, and apples. Of course, being a boy, he liked apples best of all.

JOHNNY AND JENNY

If I approached him with meat and honey upon a plate and with an apple in my pocket, he would smell the apple and begin to dance before me, ignoring the eatables in sight. Instantly, on permission, he would clasp me with both fore paws and thrust his nose into the apple pocket. Often, standing between him and Jenny, I alternately fed each a bit. A few times I broke the regular order and gave Jenny two bits in succession. At this Johnny raged, and usually ended by striking desperately at me; I never flinched, and the wise little rogue made it a point each time to miss me by an inch or two. A few other people tried this irritating experiment with him, but he hit them every time. However, I early tried to prevent anything being done that teased or irritated him. Visitors did occasionally tease him, and frequently they fed the two on bad-temper-producing knickknacks.

Occasionally the two quarreled, but not more frequently than two ordinary children; and these were largely traceable to fight-producing food mixtures. Anyway, bears will maintain a better disposition with a diet of putrid meat, snakes, mice, and weeds than upon desserts of human concoction.

Naturally bears are fun-loving and cheerful; they like to romp and play. Johnny played by the hour. Most of the time he was chained to a low, small shed that was built for his accommodation. Scores of times each day he covered all the territory that could be traversed while he was fastened with a twelve-foot chain. Often he skipped back and forth in a straight line for an hour or more. These were not the restless, aimless movements of the caged tiger, but those of playful, happy activity. It was a pleasure to watch this eager play; in it he would gallop to the outer limit of his chain, then, reversing his legs without turning his body, go backward with a queer, lively hippety-hop to the other end, then gallop forward again. He knew the length of his chain to an inch. No matter how wildly he rushed after some bone-stealing dog, he was never jerked off his feet by forgetting his limitations.

He and Scotch, my collie, were good friends and jolly playmates. In their favorite play Scotch tried to take a bone which Johnny guarded; this brought out from both a lively lot of feinting, dodging, grabbing, and striking. Occasionally they clinched, and when this ended, Johnny usually tried for a good bite or two on Scotch's shaggy tail. Scotch appeared always to have in mind that the end of Johnny's nose was sensitive, and he landed many a good slap on this spot.

Apparently, Johnny early appreciated the fact that I would not tease him, and also that I was a master who must be obeyed. One day, however, he met with a little mishap, misjudged things, and endeavored to make it lively for me. I had just got him to the point where he enjoyed a rocking-chair. In this chair he sat up like a little man. Sometimes his fore paws lay awkwardly in his lap, but more often each rested on an arm of the big chair. He found rocking such a delight that it was not long until he learned to rock himself. This brought on the mishap. He had grown over-confident, and one day was rocking with great enthusiasm. Suddenly, the big rocker, little man and all, went over backward. Though standing by, I was unable to save him, and did not move. Seeing his angry look when he struck the floor, and guessing his next move, I leaped upon the table. Up he sprang, and delivered a vicious blow that barely missed, but which knocked a piece out of my trousers.

Apparently no other large animal has such intense curiosity as the grizzly. An object in the distance, a scent, a sound, or a trail, may arouse this, and for a time overcome his intense and wary vigilance. In satisfying this curiosity he will do unexpected and apparently bold things. But the instant the mystery is solved he is himself again, and may run for dear life from some situation into which his curiosity has unwittingly drawn him. An unusual noise behind Johnny's shed would bring him out with a rush, to determine what it was. If not at once satisfied as to the cause, he would put his fore paws on the top of the shed and peer over in the most eager and inquiring manner imaginable. Like a scout, he spied mysterious and dim objects afar. If a man, a dog, or a horse, appeared in the distance, he quickly discovered the object, and at once stood erect, with fore paws drawn up, until he had a good look at it. The instant he made out what it was, he lost interest in it. At all times he was vigilant to know what was going on about him.

He was like a boy in his fondness for water. Usually, when unchained and given the freedom of the place, he would spend much of the time in the brook, rolling, playing, and wading. He and I had a few foot-races, and usually, in order to give me a better chance, we ran down hill. In a two-hundred-yard dash he usually paused three or four times and waited for me to catch up, and I was not a slow biped, either.

The grizzly, though apparently awkward and lumbering, is really one of the most agile of beasts. I constantly marveled at Johhny's lightness of touch, or the deftness of movement of his fore paws. With but one claw touching it, he could slide a coin back and forth on the floor more rapidly and lightly than I could. He would slide an eggshell swiftly along without breaking it. Yet by using but one paw, he could, without apparent effort, overturn rocks that were heavier than himself.

One day, while he slept in the yard, outstretched in the sun, I opened a large umbrella and put it over him, and waited near for him to wake up. By and by the sleepy eyes half opened, but without a move he closed them and slept again. Presently he was wide awake, making a quiet study of the strange thing over him, but except to roll his eyes, not a move did he make. Then a puff of wind gave sudden movement to the umbrella, rolling it over a point or two. At this he leaped to his feet, terribly frightened, and made a dash to escape this mysterious monster. But, as he jumped, the wind whirled the umbrella, and plump into it he landed. An instant of desperate clawing, and he shook off the wrecked umbrella and fled in terror. A minute or two later I found him standing behind the house, still frightened and trembling. When I came up and spoke to him, he made three or four lively attempts to bite my ankles. Plainly, he felt that I had played a mean and uncalled-for trick upon him. I talked to him for some time and endeavored to explain the matter to him.

A sudden movement of a new or mysterious object will usually frighten any animal. On more than one occasion people have taken advantage of this characteristic of wild beasts, and prevented an attack upon themselves. In one instance I unconsciously used it to my advantage. In the woods, one day, as I have related elsewhere, two wolves and myself unexpectedly met. With bared teeth they stood ready to leap upon me. Needing something to keep up my courage and divert my thoughts, it occurred to me to snap a picture of them. This effectively broke the spell, for when the kodak door flew open they wheeled and fled.

Autumn came, and I was to leave for a forestry tour. The only man that I could persuade to stay at my place for the winter was one who neither understood nor sympathized with my wide-awake and aggressive young grizzly. Realizing that the man and the bear would surely clash, and perhaps to the man's disadvantage, I settled things once and for all by sending Johnny to the Denver Zoo.

He was seven months old when we parted, and apparently as much attached to me as any dog to a master. I frequently had news of him, but let two years go by before I allowed myself the pleasure of visiting him. He was lying on the ground asleep when I called, while around him a number of other bears were walking about. He was no longer a boy bear, but a big fellow. In my eagerness to see him I forgot to be cautious and, climbing to the top of the picket fence, leaped into the pen, calling, "Hello, Johnny!" as I leaped, and repeating this greeting as I landed on the ground beside him. He jumped up, fully awake, and at once recognized me. Instantly, he stood erect, with both arms extended, and gave a few happy grunts of joy and by way of greeting.

I talked to him for a little while and patted him as I talked. Then I caught a fore paw in my hand and we hopped and pranced about as in old times. A yell from the outside brought me to my senses. Instinctively I glanced about for a way of escape, though I really did not feel that I was in danger. We were, however, the observed of all observers, and I do not know which throng was staring with greater interest and astonishment, — the bears in the pen or the spectators on the outside.

THE NATURALIST VISITS THE BEAR

By John Muir

JULY 21, [1869][1] . . . . Saw a common house fly and a grasshopper and a brown bear. The fly and grasshopper paid me a merry visit on the top of the Dome, and I paid a visit to the bear in the middle of a small garden meadow between the Dome and the camp where he was standing alert among the flowers as if willing to be seen to advantage. I had not gone more than half a mile from camp this morning, when Carlo, who was trotting a few yards ahead of me, came to a sudden, cautious standstill. Down went tail and ears, and forward went his knowing nose, while he seemed to be saying, "Ha, what 's this? A bear, I guess." Then a cautious advance of a few steps, setting his feet down softly like a hunting cat, and questioning the air as to the scent he had caught until all doubt vanished. Then he came back to me, looked me in the face, and with his speaking eyes reported a bear near by; then led on softly, careful, like an experienced hunter, not to make the slightest noise, and frequently looking back as if whispering, "Yes, it 's a bear, come and I 'll show you." Presently we came to where the sunbeams

[1] From John Muir's Journal.

were streaming through between the purple shafts of the firs, which showed that we were nearing an open spot, and here Carlo came behind me, evidently sure that the bear was very near. So I crept to a low ridge of moraine boulders on the edge of a narrow garden meadow, and in this meadow I felt pretty sure the bear must be. I was anxious to get a good look at him; so drawing myself up noiselessly back of one of the largest of the trees I peered past its bulging buttresses, exposing only a part of my head, and there stood neighbor Bruin within a stone's throw, his hips covered by tall grass and flowers, and his front feet on the trunk of a fir that had fallen out into the meadow, which raised his head so high that he seemed to be standing erect. He had not yet seen me, but was looking and listening attentively, showing that in some way he was aware of our approach. I watched his gestures and tried to make the most of my opportunity to learn what I could about him, fearing he would catch sight of me and run away. For I had been told that this sort of bear, the cinnamon, always ran from his bad brother man, never showing fight unless wounded or in defense of young. He made a telling picture standing alert in the sunny forest garden. How well he played his part, harmonizing in bulk and color and shaggy hair with the trunks of the trees and lush vegetation, as natural a feature as any other in the landscape.

After examining at leisure, noting the sharp muzzle thrust inquiringly forward, the long shaggy hair on his broad chest, the stiff erect ears nearly buried in hair, and the slow, heavy way he moved his head, I thought I should like to see his gait in running, so I made a sudden rush at him, shouting and swinging my hat to frighten him, expecting to see him make haste to get away. But to my dismay he did not run or show any sign of running. On the contrary, he stood his ground ready to fight and defend himself, lowered his head, thrust it forward, and looked sharply and fiercely at me. Then I suddenly began to fear that upon me would fall the work of running; but I was afraid to run, and therefore, like the bear, held my ground. We stood staring at each other in solemn silence within a dozen yards or thereabouts, while I fervently hoped that the power of the human eye over wild beasts would prove as great as it is said to be. How long our awfully strenuous interview lasted, I don't know; but at length in the slow fullness of time he pulled his huge paws down off the log, and with magnificent deliberation turned and walked leisurely up the meadow, stopping frequently to look back over his shoulder to see whether I was pursuing him, then moving on again, evidently neither fearing me very much nor trusting me. He was probably about five hundred pounds in weight, a broad rusty bundle of ungovernable wildness, a happy fellow whose lines have fallen in pleasant places. The flowery glade in which I saw him so well, framed like a picture, is one of the best of all I have yet discovered, a conservatory of Nature's precious plant people. Tall lilies were swinging their bells over that bear's back, with geraniums, larkspurs, columbines, and daisies brushing against his sides. A place for angels, one would say, instead of bears.

In the great cañons Bruin reigns supreme. Happy fellow, whom no famine can reach while one of his thousand kinds of food is spared him. His bread is sure at all seasons, ranged on the mountain shelves like stores in a pantry. From one to the other, up or down he climbs, tasting and enjoying each in turn in different climates, as if he had journeyed thousands of miles to other countries north or south to enjoy their varied productions. I should like to know my hairy brothers better, — though after this particular Yosemite bear, my very neighbor, had sauntered out of sight this morning, I reluctantly went back to camp for the Don's rifle to shoot him, if necessary, in defense of the flock. Fortunately I could n't find him, and after tracking him a mile or two toward Mount Hoffman I bade him Godspeed and gladly returned to my work on the Yosemite Dome.

BESIEGED BY BEARS

By Enos A. Mills

TWO old prospectors, Sullivan and Jason, once took me in for the night, and after suppér they related a number of interesting experiences. Among these tales was one of the best best stories I have ever heard. The story was told in the graphic, earnest, realistic style so often possessed by those who have lived strong, stirring lives among crags and pines. Although twenty years had gone by, these prospectors still had a vivid recollection of that lively night when they were besieged by three bears, and in recounting the experience they mingled many good word-pictures of bear behavior with their exciting and amusing story. "This happened to us," said Sullivan, "in spite of the fact that we were minding our own business and had never hunted bears."

The siege occurred at their log cabin during the spring of 1884. They were prospecting in Geneva Park, where they had been all winter, driving a tunnel. They were so nearly out of supplies that they could not wait for snowdrifts to melt out of the trail. Provisions must be had, and Sullivan thought that, by allowing twice the usual time, he could make his way down through the drifts and get back to the cabin with them. So one morning, after telling Jason that he would be back the next evening, he took their burro and set off down the mountain. On the way home next day Sullivan had much difficulty in getting the loaded burro through the snowdrifts, and when within a mile of the cabin, they stuck fast. Sullivan unpacked and rolled the burro out of the snow, and was busily repacking, when the animal's uneasiness made him look round.

In the edge of the woods, only a short distance away, were three bears, apparently a mother and her two well-grown children. They were sniffing the air eagerly and appeared somewhat excited. The old bear would rise on her hind paws, sniff the air, then drop back to the ground. She kept her nose pointed toward Sullivan, but did not appear to look at him. The smaller bears moved restlessly about; they would walk a few steps in advance, stand erect, draw their fore paws close to their breasts, and sniff, sniff, sniff the air, upward and in all directions before them. Then they would slowly back up to the old bear. They all seemed very good-natured.

When Sullivan was unpacking the burro, the wrapping had come off two hams which were among the supplies, and the wind had carried the delicious aroma to the bears, who were just out of their winter dens after weeks of fasting. Of course, sugar-cured hams smelled good to them. Sullivan repacked the burro and went on. The bears quietly eyed him for some distance. At a turn in the trail he looked back and saw the bears clawing and smelling the snow on which the provisions had lain while he was getting the burro out of the snowdrift. He went on to the cabin, had supper, and forgot the bears.

The log cabin in which he and Jason lived was a small one; it had a door in the side and a small window in one end. The roof was made of a layer of poles thickly covered with earth. A large shepherd-dog often shared the cabin with the prospectors. He was a playful fellow, and Sullivan often romped with him. Near their cabin were some vacant cabins of other prospectors, who had "gone out for the winter" and were not yet back for summer prospecting.

The evening was mild, and as soon as supper was over Sullivan filled his pipe, opened the door, and sat down on the edge of the bed for a smoke, while Jason washed the dishes. He had taken only a few pulls at his pipe when there was a rattling at the window. Thinking the dog was outside, Sullivan called, "Why don't you go round to the door?" This invitation was followed by a momentary silence, then smash! a piece of sash and fragments of window glass flew past Sullivan and rattled on the floor. He jumped to his feet. In the dim candlelight he saw a bear's head coming in through the window. He threw his pipe of burning tobacco into the bear's face and eyes, and then grabbed for some steel drills which lay in the corner on the floor. The earth roof had leaked, and the drills were ice-covered and frozen fast to the floor.

While Sullivan was dislodging the drills, Jason began to bombard the bear vigorously with plates from the table. The bear backed out; she was looking for food, not clean plates. However, the instant she was outside, she accepted Sullivan's invitation and went round to the door! And she came for it with a rush! Both Sullivan and Jason jumped to close the door. They were not quick enough, and instead of one bear there were three! The entire family had accepted the invitation, and all were trying to come in at once!

When Sullivan and Jason threw their weight against the door it slammed against the big bear's nose, — a very sensitive spot. She gave a savage growl. Apparently she blamed the other two bears either for hurting her nose or for being in the way. At any rate, a row started; halfway in the door the bears began to fight; for a few seconds it seemed as if all the bears would roll inside. Sullivan and Jason pushed against the door with all their might, trying to close it. During the struggle the bears rolled outside and the door went shut with a bang. The heavy securing crossbar was quickly put into place; but not a moment too soon, for an instant later the old bear gave a furious growl and flung herself against the door, making it fairly crack; it seemed as if the door would be broken in. Sullivan and Jason hurriedly knocked their slab bed to pieces and used the slats and heavy sides to prop and strengthen the door. The bears kept surging and clawing at the door, and while the prospectors were spiking the braces against it and giving their entire attention to it, they suddenly felt the cabin shake and heard the logs strain and give. They started back, to see the big bear struggling in the window. Only the smallness of the window had prevented the bear from getting in unnoticed, and surprising them while they were bracing the door. The window was so small that the bear in trying to get in had almost wedged fast. With hind paws on the ground, fore paws on the windowsill, and shoulders against the log over the window, the big bear was in a position to exert all her enormous strength. Her efforts to get in sprung the logs and gave the cabin the shake which warned.

Sullivan grabbed one of the steel drills and dealt the bear a terrible blow on the head. She gave a growl of mingled pain and fury as she freed herself from the window. Outside she backed off growling.

For a little while things were calmer. Sullivan and Jason, drills in hand, stood guard at the window. After some snarling in front of the window the bears went round to the door. They clawed the door a few times and then began to dig under it. "They are tunneling in for us," said Sullivan. "They want those hams; but they won't get them."

After a time the bears quit digging and started away, occasionally stopping to look hesitatingly back. It was almost eleven o'clock, and the full moon shone splendidly through the pines. The prospectors hoped that the bears were gone for good. There was an old rifle in the cabin, but there were no cartridges, for Sullivan and Jason never hunted and rarely had occasion to fire a gun. But, fearing that the animals might return, Sullivan concluded to go to one of the vacant cabins for a loaded Winchester which he knew to be there.

As soon as the bears disappeared, he crawled out of the window and looked cautiously around; then he made a run for the vacant cabin. The bears heard him running, and when he had nearly reached the cabin, they came around the corner of it to see what was the matter. He was up a pine tree in an instant. After a few growls the bears moved off and disappeared behind a vacant cabin. As they had gone behind the cabin which contained the loaded gun, Sullivan thought it would be dangerous to try to make the cabin, for if the door should be swelled fast, the bears would surely get him. Waiting until he thought it safe to return, he dropped to the ground and made a dash for his own cabin. The bears heard him and again gave chase, with the evident intention of getting even for all their annoyances. It was only a short distance to his cabin, but the bears were at his heels when he dived in through the broken window.

A bundle of old newspapers was then set on fire and thrown among the bears, to scare them away. There was some snarling, until one of the young bears with a stroke of a fore paw scattered the blazing papers in all directions; then the bears walked round the cabin-corner out of sight and remained quiet for several minutes.

Just as Jason was saying, "I hope they are gone for good," there came a thump on the roof which told the prospectors that the bears were still intent on the hams. The bears began to claw the earth off the roof. If they were allowed to continue, they would soon clear off the earth and would then have a chance to tear out the poles. With a few poles torn out, the bears would tumble into the cabin, or perhaps their combined weight might cause the roof to give way and drop them into the cabin. Something had to be done to stop their clawing and if possible get them off the roof. Bundles of hay were taken out of the bed mattress. From time to time Sullivan would set fire to one of these bundles, lean far out through the window, and throw the blazing hay upon the roof among the bears. So long as he kept these fireworks going, the bears did not dig; but they stayed on the roof and became furiously angry. The supply of hay did not last long, and as soon as the annoyance from the bundles of fire ceased, the bears attacked the roof again with renewed vigor.

Then it was decided to prod the bears with red-hot drills thrust up between the poles of the roof. As there was no firewood in the cabin, and as fuel was necessary in order to heat the drills, a part of the floor was torn up for that purpose.

The young bears soon found hot drills too warm for them and scrambled or fell off the roof. But the old one persisted. In a little while she had clawed off a large patch of earth and was tearing the poles with her teeth.

The hams had been hung up on the wall in the end of the cabin; the old bear was tearing just above them. Jason threw the hams on the floor and wanted to throw them out of the window. He thought that the bears would leave contented if they had them. Sullivan thought differently; he said that it would take six hams apiece to satisfy the bears, and that two hams would be only a taste which would make the bears more reckless than ever. The hams stayed in the cabin.

The old bear had torn some of the poles in two and was madly tearing and biting at others. Sullivan was short and so were the drills. To get within easier reach, he placed the table almost under the gnawing bear, sprang upon it, and called to Jason for a red-hot drill. Jason was about to hand him one when he noticed a small bear climbing in at the window, and, taking the drill with him, he sprang over to beat the bear back. Sullivan jumped down to the fire for a drill, and in climbing back on the table he looked up at the gnawed hole and received a shower of dirt in his face and eyes. This made him flinch and he lost his balance and upset the table. He quickly straightened the table and sprang upon it, drill in hand. The old bear had a paw and arm thrust down through the hole between the poles. With a blind stroke she struck the drill and flung it and Sullivan from the table. He shouted to Jason for help, but Jason, with both young bears trying to get in at the window at once, was striking right and left. He had bears and troubles of his own and did not heed Sullivan's call. The old bear thrust her head down through the hole and seemed about to fall in, when Sullivan in desperation grabbed both hams and threw them out the window.

The young bears at once set up a row over the hams, and the old bear, hearing the fight, jumped off the roof and soon had a ham in her mouth.

While the bears were fighting and eating, Sullivan and Jason tore up the remainder of the floor and barricaded the window. With both door and window closed, they could give their attention to the roof. All the drills were heated, and both stood ready to make it hot for the bears when they should again climb on the roof. But the bears did not return to the roof. After eating the last morsel of the hams they walked round to the cabin door, scratched it gently, and then became quiet. They had lain down by the door.

It was two o'clock in the morning. The inside of the cabin was in utter confusion. The floor was strewn with wreckage; bedding, drills, broken boards, broken plates, and hay were scattered about. Sullivan gazed at the chaos and remarked that it looked like poor housekeeping. But he was tired, and, asking Jason to keep watch for a while, he lay down on the blankets and was soon asleep.

Toward daylight the bears got up and walked a few times round the cabin. On each round they clawed at the door, as though to tell Sullivan that they were there, ready for his hospitality. They whined a little, half good-naturedly, but no one admitted them, and finally, just before sunrise, they took their departure and went leisurely smelling their way down the trail.

THE KODAK AND THE WOLVES

By Enos A. Mills

HAD I encountered the two gray wolves during my first unarmed camping-trip into the wilds, the experience would hardly have suggested to me that going without firearms is the best way to enjoy wild nature. But I had made many unarmed excursions beyond the trail before I had that adventure, and the habit of going without a gun was so firmly fixed and so satisfactory that even a perilous wolf encounter did not arouse any desire for firearms. The habit continued, and to-day the only way I can enjoy the wilds is to leave guns behind.

On that autumn afternoon I was walking along slowly, reflectively, in a deep forest. Not a breath of air moved, and even the aspen's golden leaves stood still in the sunlight. All was calm and peaceful around and within me, when I came to a little sunny frost-tanned grass-plot surrounded by tall, crowding pines. I felt drawn to its warmth and repose and stepped joyfully into it. Suddenly two gray wolves sprang from almost beneath my feet and faced me defiantly. At a few feet distance they made an impressive show of ferocity, standing ready apparently to hurl themselves upon me.

Now the gray wolf is a powerful, savage beast, and directing his strong jaws, tireless muscles, keen scent, and all-seeing eyes are exceedingly nimble wits. He is well equipped to make the severe struggle for existence which his present environment compels. In many Western localities, despite the high price offered for his scalp, he has managed not only to live, but to increase and multiply. I had seen gray wolves pull down big game. On one occasion I had seen a vigorous long-horned steer fall after a desperate struggle with two of these fearfully fanged animals. Many times I had come across scattered bones which told of their triumph; and altogether I was so impressed with their deadliness that a glimpse of one of them usually gave me over to a temporary dread.

The two wolves facing me seemed to have been asleep in the sun when I disturbed them. I realized the danger and was alarmed, of course, but my faculties were under control, were stimulated, indeed, to unusual alertness, and I kept a bold front and faced them without flinching. Their expression was one of mingled surprise and anger, together with the apparent determination to sell their lives as dearly as possible. I gave them all the attention which their appearance and their reputation demanded. Not once did I take my eyes off them. I held them at bay with my eyes. I still have a vivid picture of terribly gleaming teeth, bristling backs, and bulging muscles in savage readiness.

They made no move to attack. I was afraid to attack and I dared not run away. I remembered that some trees I could almost reach behind me had limbs that stretched out toward me, yet I felt that to wheel, spring for a limb, and swing up beyond their reach could not be done quickly enough to escape those fierce jaws.

Both sides were of the same mind, ready to fight, but not at all eager to do so. Under these conditions our nearness was embarrassing, and we faced each other for what seemed, to me at least, a long time. My mind working like lightning, I thought of several possible ways of escaping. I considered each at length, found it faulty, and dismissed it. Meanwhile, not a sound had been made. I had not moved, but something had to be done. Slowly I worked the small folding axe from its sheath, and with the slowest of movements placed it in my right coat pocket with the handle up, ready for instant use. I did this with studied deliberation, lest a hidden movement should release the springs that held the wolves back. I kept on staring. Statues, almost, we must have appeared to the "camp-bird" whose call from a near-by limb told me we were observed, and whose nearness gave me courage. Then, looking the nearer of the two wolves squarely in the eye, I said to him, "Well, why don't you move?" as though we were playing checkers instead of the game of life. He made no reply, but the spell was broken. I believe that both sides had been bluffing. In attempting to use my kodak while continuing the bluff, I brought matters to a focus. "What a picture you fellows will make," I said aloud, as my right hand slowly worked the kodak out of the case which hung under my left arm. Still keeping up a steady fire of looks, I brought the kodak in front of me ready to focus, and then touched the spring that released the folding front. When the kodak mysteriously, suddenly opened before the wolves, they fled for their lives. In an instant they had cleared the grassy space and vanished into the woods. I did not get their picture.

With a gun, the wolf encounter could not have ended more happily. At any rate, I have not for a moment cared for a gun since I returned enthusiastic from my first delightful trip into the wilds without one. Out in the wilds with nature is one of the safest and most sanitary of places. Bears are not seeking to devour, and the death-list from lions, wolves, snakes, and all other bugbears combined does not equal the death-list from fire, automobiles, street-cars, or banquets. Being afraid of nature or a rainstorm is like being afraid of the dark.

AN INDIAN BUFFALO DRIVE

By James Willard Schultz

THERE had been so much hunting near the river that the game had been driven far out on the plains, and that was the reason the chiefs had decided to move to another camping-ground, where meat could be more quickly and easily killed by the hunters. It was about thirty miles across country to the Hills. For half that distance only a few old buffalo bulls and two or three bands of very wild antelope were seen. But when about ten miles from the middle butte the people could see thousands and thousands of buffalo and other game close to the north, the east, and the west. Most of the men now rode ahead of the columns to hunt. They could be seen chasing different herds of the buffalo on their swift, trained horses, and shooting them with guns and bow and arrows; and where they passed were left many of the big, brown, shaggy-haired animals lying dead on the plain, or standing all humped up on weakening legs, sorely wounded, and soon to tumble down and die. The sight made the hearts of the people glad; there would be plenty of fresh, fat meat, many rich tongues to roast for the evening meal; food for many, many days to come. The old men watched the chase with glistening eyes, and became so excited that many of them pounded their safe, slow horses with heels and quirt, forgetting for the moment that they could not be made to go faster than an ambling trot; and so they fell to talking of what big hunts they had made in their young days.

To the east the hunters who had gone in that direction rode out of sight behind a low ridge on the plain and chased a herd of several thousand buffalo. At first the animals ran eastward; but the wind was from the west, and as they always ran against it, they soon circled and came thundering over the ridge and straight toward the long column of the moving camp. The hunters saw the danger in that, but could not turn them. The women and then the children began to shriek and cry, the old men to shout and try to drive a part of the column forward, the other part back, so as to save them from being gored and trampled by the frightened and wildly rushing herd. It was a terrible sight, that resistless mass of huge and sharp-horned animals coming straight for the center of the columns of traveling people. The leaders of the herd, the swiftest of the cows, had of course by this time smelled the riders, but they were now powerless to stop or turn back, for the closely packed herd behind was pushing them; they had to keep going or be trampled to death.

The old men had now succeeded in dividing the column by a little gap, and were driving the women and children and the pack animals to the north and to the south, crowding them and widening the gap as fast as possible. The confusion increased. The horses squealed and kicked one another, and some of the frightened pack animals ran away, scattering their loads along the plain. A few old women, regardless of danger, rode bawling after them in hope of recovering their little keepsakes and treasures.

When the column was separated by a clear space of several hundred yards, the buffalo began passing through it, on each edge so close to the people that the wind caused by their rush could be felt, and their black, angrily gleaming eyes could be plainly seen. The noise of their thudding and rattling hoofs and clashing horns was terrific.

Sinopah and his mother were right at the north edge of the gap. His little pony, always very gentle before this, now began to get frightened and show signs of running away; and before anyone could prevent it, it bolted straight out toward the passing buffalo.

"Oh, my boy! My little boy! Save him!" his mother shrieked, and madly whipping her horse and without thought of the danger took after him.

Other women shrieked and called for help. The old men there yelled and followed after the mother, resolved to save her and the boy, and half crazed because of the slowness of their horses.

Sinopah never once cried out or looked back. The people watching saw his little mouth tightly shut, saw him gripping the saddle with both hands, and they yelled him to let go; to fall off. And at the same time they knew that it was useless to shout to him, for even a clap of thunder would have been lost in the roar and clatter of the passing herd.

It was only a few yards across the clear space to the edge of the stream of buffalo. As the pony ran he seemed to go faster and faster. The people watching lost all hope, and so did the mother and the old men; but without a thought for themselves they only whipped their horses the harder and pressed on.

The pony now had only a few more jumps to make in order to reach the buffalo, but, excited as he was, still, from force of habit he was watching out for safe footing. So it was that when almost on the point of hitting a badger hole he suddenly jumped sideways to save himself; jumped as quickly as a cat could have done, at a right angle to his course. Sinopah was not prepared for that, he was only bracing himself for straight-ahead running, and so when the pony jumped sideways he was jerked loose from all holds. His little body flew out of the saddle, went spinning through the air, and down he came to the ground on his feet, then fell, and went rolling over and over on the short, thick grass, and almost into the stream of buffalo. The pony kept on. As he came to the herd, the animals shrank and made way for him; he entered the gap and in an instant it closed and he was lost to sight.

Sinopah's mother reached him almost as soon as he stopped rolling. Jumping from her horse, she snatched him up from the ground and ran back as fast as she could go, thinking no more of the horse nor caring what became of it. One of the old men caught the animal and turned it over to her later. Just as she got back to the people the last of the long herd of buffalo passed, and the thunder of their hoofs soon died away. She set Sinopah down on his feet and looked at him, felt of him, all the men and women and children there crowding around. Sinopah was not crying, nor laughing: just then his father came up on a big horse all covered with foam, and he cried out to him: "Nina, awt-sim-o-ta no-tas. Nok-o-twe-in-is." (Father, my horse ran away. Go get him.)

THE STORY OF THE LEOPARD AND THE COW

By Sir Samuel W. Baker

THE depredations of leopards among cattle are no inconsiderable causes of loss. At Newera Ellia hardly a week passes without some casualty among the stock of different proprietors. Here the leopards are particularly daring, and cases have frequently occurred where they have effected their entrance to a cattle shed by scratching a hole through the thatched roof. They then commit a wholesale slaughter among sheep and cattle. Sometimes, however, they catch a Tartar. The native cattle are small, but very active, and the cows are particularly savage when the calf is with them.

About three years ago a leopard took it into his head to try the beefsteaks of a very savage and sharp-horned cow, who with her calf was the property of the blacksmith. It was a dark rainy night, the blacksmith and his wife were in bed, and the cow and her calf were nestled in the warm straw in the cattle shed. The door was locked, and all was apparently secure, when the hungry leopard prowled stealthily round the cow-house sniffing the prey within. The strong smell of the leopard at once alarmed the keen senses of the cow, made doubly acute by her anxiety for her little charge, and she stood ready for the danger, as the leopard, having mounted on the roof, commenced scratching his way through the hatch.

Down he sprang! — but at the same instant, with a spendid charge, the cow pinned him against the wall, and a battle ensued which can easily be imagined. A coolie slept in the corner of the cattle shed, whose wandering senses were completely scattered when he found himself the unwilling umpire of the fight.

He rushed out and shut the door. In a few minutes he succeeded in awakening the blacksmith, who struck a light, and proceeded to load a pistol, the only weapon that he possessed. During the whole of this time the bellowing of the cow, the roars of the leopard, and the thumping, trampling, and shuffling which proceeded from the cattle shed explained the savage nature of the fight.

The blacksmith, who was no sportsman, shortly found himself with a lantern in one hand, a pistol in the other, and no idea what he meant to do. He waited, therefore, at the cattle-shed door, and holding the light so as to shine through the numerous small apertures in the shed, he looked in.

The leopard no longer growled; but the cow was mad with fury. She alternately threw a large dark mass above her head, then quickly pinned it to the ground on its descent, then bored it against the wall, as it crawled helplessly toward a corner of the shed. This was the "beefeater" in reduced circumstances! The gallant little cow had nearly killed him, and was giving him the finishing strokes. The blacksmith perceived the leopard's helpless state, and, boldly opening the door, he discharged his pistol, and the next moment was bolting as hard as he could run with the warlike cow after him! She was regularly "up," and was ready for anything or anybody. However, she was at length pacified, and the dying leopard was put out of his misery.

NATURAL HISTORY IN A GARDEN

By Charles Dudley Warner

I FIND that gardening has unsurpassed advantages for the study of natural history; and some scientific facts have come under my own observation, which cannot fail to interest naturalists and un-naturalists in about the same degree. Much, for instance, has been written about the toad, an animal without which no garden would be complete. But little account has been made of his value: the beauty of his eye alone has been dwelt on; and little has been said of his mouth, and its important function as a fly and bug trap. His habits, and even his origin, have been misunderstood. Why, as an illustration, are toads so plenty after a thundershower? All my life long, no one has been able to answer me that question. Why, after a heavy shower, and in the midst of it, do such multitudes of toads, especially little ones, hop about on the gravel walks? For many years, I believed that they rained down; and I suppose many people think so still. They are so small, and they come in such numbers only in the shower, that the suppositiou is not a violent one. "Thick as toads after a shower" is one of our best proverbs. I asked an explanation of this of a thoughtful woman, — indeed, a leader in the great movement to have all the toads hop in any direction, without any distinction of sex or religion. Her reply was that the toads came out during the shower to get water. This, however, is not the fact. I have discovered that they come out not to get water. I deluged a dry flower-bed, the other night, with pailful after pailful of water. Instantly the toads came out of their holes in the dirt, by tens and twenties and fifties, to escape death by drowning. The big ones fled away in a ridiculous streak of hopping; and the little ones sprang about in the wildest confusion. The toad is just like any other land animal: when his house is full of water, he quits it. These facts, with the drawings of the water and the toads, are at the service of the distinguished scientists of Albany in New York, who were so much impressed by the Cardiff Giant.

The domestic cow is another animal whose ways I have a chance to study, and also to obliterate in the garden. One of my neighbors has a cow, but no land; and he seems desirous to pasture her on the surface of the land of other people, — a very reasonable desire. The man proposed that he should be allowed to cut the grass from my grounds for his cow. I knew the cow, having often had her in my garden; knew her gait and the size of her feet, which struck me as a little large for the size of the body. Having no cow myself, but acquaintance with my neighbor's, I told him that I thought it would be fair for him to have the grass. He was, therefore, to keep the grass nicely cut, and to keep his cow at home. I waited some time after the grass needed cutting; and, as my neighbor did not appear, I hired it cut. No sooner was it done than he promptly appeared, and raked up most of it, and carried it away. He had evidently been waiting that opportunity. When the grass grew again, the neighbor did not appear with his scythe; but one morning I found the cow tethered on the sward, hitched near the clothes-horse, a short distance from the house. This seemed to be the man's idea of the best way to cut the grass. I disliked to have the cow there, because I knew her inclination to pull up the stake, and transfer her field of mowing to the garden, but especially because of her voice. She has the most melancholy "moo" I ever heard. It is like the wail of one un-infallible, excommunicated, and lost. It is a most distressing perpetual reminder of the brevity of life and the shortness of feed. It is unpleasant to the family. We sometimes hear it in the middle of the night, breaking the silence like a suggestion of coming calamity. It is as bad as the howling of a dog at a funeral.

I told the man about it; but he seemed to think that he was not responsible for the cow's voice. I then told him to take her away; and he did, at intervals, shifting her to different parts of the grounds in my absence, so that the desolate voice would startle us from unexpected quarters. If I were to unhitch the cow, and turn her loose, I knew where she would go. If I were to lead her away, the question was, Where? for I did not fancy leading a cow about till I could find somebody who was willing to pasture her. To this dilemma had my excellent neighbor reduced me. But I found him, one Sunday morning, — a day when it would not do to get angry, — tying his cow at the foot of the hill;

the beast all the time going on in that abominable voice. I told the man that I could not have the cow in the grounds. He said, "All right, boss;" but he did not go away. I asked him to clear out. The man, who is a French sympathizer from the Republic of Ireland, kept his temper perfectly. He said he was n't doing anything,—just feeding his cow a bit: he would n't make me the least trouble in the world. I reminded him that he had been told again and again not to come here; that he might have all the grass, but he should not bring his cow upon the premises. The imperturbable man assented to everything that I said, and kept on feeding his cow. Before I got him to go to fresh scenes and pastures new, the Sabbath was almost broken: but it was saved by one thing; it is difficult to be emphatic when no one is emphatic on the other side. The man and his cow have taught me a great lesson, which I shall recall when I keep a cow. I can recommend the cow, if anybody wants one, as a steady boarder, whose keeping will cost the owner little; but if her milk is at all like her voice, those who drink it are on the straight road to lunacy.

I think I have said that we have a game-preserve. We keep quails, or try to, in the thickly wooded, bushed, and brushed ravine. This bird is a great favorite with us, dead or alive, on account of its tasteful plumage, its tender flesh, its domestic virtues, and its pleasant piping. Besides, although I appreciate toads and cows, and all that sort of thing, I like to have a game-preserve more in the English style. And we did. For in July, while the game-law was on, and the young quails were coming on, we were awakened one morning by firing, — musketry-firing, close at hand. My first thought was that war was declared; but, as I should never pay much attention to war declared at that time in the morning, I went to sleep again. But the occurrence was repeated, and not only early in the morning, but at night. There was calling of dogs, breaking down of brush, and firing of guns. It is hardly pleasant to have guns fired in the direction of the house, at your own quails. The hunters could be sometimes seen, but never caught. Their best time was about sunrise; before one could dress and get to the front, they would retire.

One morning, about four o'clock, I heard the battle renewed. I sprang up, but not in arms, and went to a window. Polly (like another "blessed damozel") flew to another window, —

> "The blessed damozel leaned out
> From the gold bar of heaven," —

and reconnoitered from behind the blinds.

> "The wonder was not yet quite gone
> From that still look of hers,"

when an armed man and a legged dog appeared in the opening. I was vigilantly watching him.

> "And now
> She spoke through the still weather."

"Are you afraid to speak to him?" asked Polly. Not exactly,

> "she spoke as when
> The stars sang in their spheres."

Stung by this inquiry, I leaned out of the window till

"The bar *I* leaned on (was) warm,"

and cried, —

"Halloo, there! What are you doing?"

"Look out he don't shoot you," called out Polly from the other window, suddenly going on another tack.

I explained that a sportsman would not be likely to shoot a gentleman in his own house, with bird-shot, so long as quails were to be had.

"You have no business here: what are you after?" I repeated.

"Looking for a lost hen," said the man as he strode away.

The reply was so satisfactory and conclusive that I shut the blinds and went to bed.

But one evening I overhauled one of the poachers. Hearing his dog in the thicket, I rushed through the brush, and came in sight of the hunter as he was retreating down the road. He came to a halt, and we had some conversation in a high key. Of course I threatened to prosecute him. I believe that is the thing to do in such cases; but how I was to do it, when I did not know his name or ancestry, and could n't see his face, never occurred to me. (I remember, now, that a farmer once proposed to prosecute me when I was fishing in a trout brook on his farm, and asked my name for that purpose.) He said he should smile to see me prosecute him.

"You can't do it: there ain't no notice up about

trespassing." This view of the common law impressed me; and I said, —

"But these are private grounds."

"Private h—!" was all his response.

You can't argue much with a man who has a gun in his hands, when you have none. Besides, it might be a needle-gun, for aught I knew. I gave it up, and we separated.

There is this disadvantage about having a game-preserve attached to your garden: it makes life too lively.

CURIOUS FRIENDSHIPS AMONG ANIMALS

By Ellen Velvin, F.Z.S.

IN all the animal world, there is no voluntary recluse, or hermit. No animal, whether wild or domestic, ever likes to be alone for very long at a time. Even the birds, of all kinds and species, hate solitude. Parrots, particularly, and all gregarious birds of the tropics, begin to mope and pine away if kept in solitary captivity.

The well-known American naturalist, Alexander Wilson, tells a pathetic story of a green Carolina parrot of which he made a great pet, and he was so fond of it that he even took it with him at one time when he went to South America. The parrot was very docile and affectionate, but seemed ill at ease and restless whenever birds of its own species flew by. So the naturalist, sympathizing with his pet, got a companion for it, and it was at once perfectly happy and contented.

Unfortunately, the companion was accidentally killed, and the poor green parrot grieved and fretted until its master thought it would die. One day, holding it in his arms, he passed his shaving-glass, and the parrot, seeing its own reflection in the looking-glass, at once called out a welcome to the imaginary parrot, so wonderfully like itself! After this, the naturalist procured a larger looking-glass, and put it on the parrot's table, and here, day after day, the parrot would nestle up to the glass, talk to its own reflection, and seemed delighted with all the movements that the image of itself made in the glass. After this, it was never lonely or depressed, but, I believe, lived to a happy old age.

This liking for society has no doubt been the reason why, in captivity, so many strange friendships have been formed, not only between animals of the same species, but between animals who, in their native state, are antagonistic to one another in every respect.

In one of the mixed groups which Mr. Carl Hagenbeck had trained, there were a tiger, a panther, and a little pert fox-terrier. Curiously enough, these three animals, so entirely different in every way, usually hating and afraid of one another, became the greatest of friends. The panther would lie on its back and even invite the dog to play with him, by rolling on his back, pawing him gently, and then gliding swiftly away, with a little invitation to him to follow; and when the terrier, coming forward with uplifted tail, and barking impudently, would playfully bite him, the puma would pat him on the nose, and then run away. And, occasionally, this would go on for a whole hour at a time.

Meanwhile, the tiger, a particularly fierce Bengal specimen, would watch them with a curious, inscrutable expression, and sometimes get up and roll over on his back—he was never as familiar as the terrier, and never as playful as the panther. But this tiger would actually allow the little terrier to gnaw the same bone that he was gnawing, and when, at one time, the terrier took up a small piece of the tiger's bone and walked off with it to a corner, the huge animal did not attempt to hurt him, not even growling or showing the slightest anger. This is particularly remarkable with the large carnivora, as, even with the most amiable animals, no liberties must be taken with their food.

In the New York Hippodrome a short time ago, a remarkable friendship existed between a baby elephant and a large boar-hound, both belonging to Mr. George Power. The dog was in the habit of going regularly every morning to a butcher's shop close by the Hippodrome, where the butcher would give him a goodly parcel of bones and scraps of meat wrapped in brown paper. The dog would go straight home to the Hippodrome, lay the parcel down in front of the little elephant, and wait patiently until the young animal had turned out the contents on the floor. Not caring for meat, he would blow at it with his little trunk, and then take no further notice of it.

This was the moment when the boar-hound would come forward and take it all up again — bone by bone and scrap by scrap — carry it over to his own kennel and then make a good breakfast at his ease. But he was never once known to attempt to eat it without first offering it to his little friend.

Also, when he had cake or biscuit, the dog would offer it first to the young elephant. But this was a different matter. Not a bit or a scrap did the little elephant give back to his faithful friend. Once or twice, when watching them, I was amused to see that the dog, after waiting patiently and watching the other's enjoyment, would very cautiously put one paw forward as though to take a little bit of the dainty. But at the least sign of such an action, the little elephant would lift up his trunk and his voice, and trumpet his loudest, vastly indignant that the dog should try to get any. And then the funniest thing was to watch the dog's expression!

Such a meek, apologetic, reproachful expression, as though to say, as he licked his lips, "Well, I think you might let me have a *taste!*" He never used strong measures, however; if the baby elephant liked to eat it all, he let him do it without any further remonstrance. But I was pleased when his trainer told me, sometime afterward, that the dog had left off taking all his scraps of cake to his friend. When he had a particularly nice piece, he either ate it at once, or else took it to his kennel, where he ate it without saying anything about it.

A most peculiar friendship has existed for several years between one of the giraffes and a bantam rooster at the Barnum and Bailey circus. The little rooster, self-satisfied and conceited as all bantams are, always stays just outside the giraffes' inclosure, sometimes strutting along on the ground, or else sitting on the railing, crowing at all sorts of times, by day and night. The giraffe will look down on him, watch him crowing, and once in a while try to reach him with his long, black tongue. At other times, the rooster will fly up and sit on the giraffe's back or sloping neck, and crow there! As a general rule, giraffes are terribly nervous, sensitive creatures, and some would be terrified at the unusualness of such a thing, but this giraffe takes it all quietly, turns his head and looks at the bantam with his large, beautiful eyes, puts out his tongue, which the rooster dodges most skilfully, and takes no further notice, no matter how many times he crows, or how many times he tumbles off the giraffe's sloping neck and flies up again — all in the noisy, fussy manner that all bantams have.

In Mr. Frank Bostock's wild animal show, there is a strange trio who, from having been trained and taught to work together, have become the firmest friends. This is Napoleon, the clever little chimpanzee, riding what looks like a diminutive pony. As a matter of fact, the "pony" is a large dog, dressed up with a head- and tail-piece. But between this large dog, the chimpanzee, and the little terrier who follows them around, led by a rope, there is the firmest friendship. On one occasion, when walking around, the little terrier was accidentally kicked by the attendant, and yelped out; the chimpanzee, thinking, I suppose, that he was hurt, looked angrily at the attendant, and told him what he thought of him in many fearful grimaces and sharp chatterings.

But although there is a good deal of love between these three, there is also a great deal of jealousy. One must not be given anything unless the others get something at the same time. Otherwise, there is an uproar and much angry discussion in their own language. And let me explain here, that when an angry chimpanzee screams at the top of his voice, a big dog bays his loudest, and a fox-terrier barks his hardest in his quick, snappy way, the only word which adequately describes this combination of sounds is pandemonium. So care is now always taken to give a little to each, unless they are separated from one another. But these three do not care to be apart for very long. Their friendship is strong and sincere, and they are always happiest when working, playing, or sleeping together.

It is not a usual thing for horses and elephants to become friendly, although there have been several instances of this. In a circus in Australia, there is a full-grown male elephant who performs with two little ponies. At first, there were the usual difficulties in making them even become sufficiently used to one another so that they would not be frightened or hurt. After this came the training; this was followed by one of the firmest friendships that ever existed between animals. The ponies were never happy when away from the elephant; the elephant was never happy when away from the ponies. But the most curious fact was that the two dogs, who performed with them, never made friends with either, but kept coldly aloof, and very much to themselves.

The cubs of wild animals rarely become friendly with one another. As a rule, they fight so fiercely and vindictively that, unless separated, one or the other is eventually killed. But in the Dublin Zoölogical Gardens in Ireland, two little lion cubs and two little tiger cubs are on the most friendly terms, and play together as though they were all of one family. This same sort of thing was found in the Amsterdam Zoölogical Gardens, a short time ago. A tiger cub and a puma cub lived together in the most perfect harmony for months. But when, with increasing age, their natural, fierce instincts asserted themselves and they showed signs of quarreling, to prevent any chance of an accident, they were separated before they had an actual fight.

In the Jardin d'Acclimatation, in Paris, there is an infirmary for sick monkeys. A large baboon, who had been a great care and anxiety to his keepers on account of his vicious and savage disposition, fell ill and was sent to the infirmary. Owing to his reputation, he was put into a large cage by himself. Near by was a little common Mona monkey, very pitiful and pathetic in his illness, and to this little monkey the savage baboon took a great fancy. He showed his preference in such a marked manner, that at last it was decided to put their cages closer together. in order to see what the little monkey thought about it.

But the little monkey appeared to reciprocate the affection, and after a while the two were put together, not without many misgivings on the part of the attendants. And the two were perfectly happy, and became the greatest of friends. The baboon became almost amiable in comparison to what he had been, and when, after a time, they both regained their health and were taken back to their old quarters, they were still allowed to remain together, and this friendship continued until the death of the baboon, when the little monkey was almost inconsolable for a time.

The most wonderful friendship I have ever seen is the friendship of "Baldy," the chimpanzee in the New York Zoölogical Park, for his keeper. The keeper is devoted to him, and has spent many long and tedious nights in sitting up with him when he has been sick. But on Baldy's part the friendship is nothing short of absolute devotion. The minute the keeper goes out of the building, Baldy begins to fret, and keeps an eye on the door in painful expectancy until he reappears, whimpering and moaning all the time. His supreme delight and happiness when Keeper Engleholm is seen coming in the distance is too funny for words. But Baldy is also very jealous, not only of other animals gaining any attention from his keeper, but of human beings. Too much talking in front of his cage is strongly disapproved, and if Baldy's own particular language is taken no notice of, he demands attention by stamping his feet, thumping his knuckles on the floor, and jumping all around his cage, banging the horizontal bars, rattling the doors and little windows, and anything else he can think of to make a noise and attract attention to himself.

A wonderful friendship exists at the present time between a woman lion-trainer, a full-grown Nubian lion, and a little dog, a cross between a shepherd's dog and a Scotch terrier. The lion seems to be extremely fond of the woman and the dog, and the dog just as fond of the woman and the lion; while the trainer herself is so fond of them both, that she said she was never so happy as when she was performing with them. The lion was wonderfully obedient and docile with her, and never gave the least trouble, while the little dog would frisk around, jumping over the lion, playing with his mistress, and taking all sorts of liberties with both. Very often when sitting together at table the lion would put out a paw toward his trainer, very much in the same manner as a dog will when wishing to attract attention.

But I think the most extraordinary friendship — and certainly with the most extraordinary ending — is that of a beautiful full-grown llama and a sacred white donkey in Mr. Bostock's show, at the present time in London. Soon after the purchase of the llama, about three years ago, the white donkey was put into the llama's inclosure while his own was being put in order. To all appearances, at first, the llama resented his intrusion by rudely spitting at him as soon as he entered. But this treatment not affecting the donkey in any way, the llama became interested, and when the donkey was put back into his own inclosure, seemed quite distressed and unhappy.

So, by way of experiment, the donkey was put into his inclosure again, and from that time, these two, so strangely unlike in every way, became the firmest of friends. They were, in fact, inseparable, and it became rather tiresome when it was found impossible to get the llama to move anywhere unless the sacred white donkey went first, when he would follow at once. They were placarded "The Inseparable Friends," and the odd-looking couple provoked much comment and merriment among the onlookers,

But one memorable night last summer, there was

suddenly a terrible noise after all the keepers had gone to bed. Sounds of terrific snorting and scrambling; screams and weird cries, intermixed with violent kicking at the boards of the inclosure in which were kept the llama and the sacred white donkey. Lights were procured hastily, and on going to the llama's inclosure, they found the most terrible fight going on between the llama and the donkey! What started it will never be known, but the llama was hitting out with its fore feet and biting viciously; the sacred donkey, forgetting his sacredness, was also biting and hitting out with his hind legs in the most savage fashion.

In vain, for some time, the men tried to part them. Both animals were in such furious rages that it was difficult to go near them, and prodding and hitting seemed to have no effect whatever. Eventually, after a bite on his shin, the donkey turned his back to his recent friend, and kicked out with all his might, hitting the llama near one eye with his full force. This settled matters, for the pain was so great that the llama sank down and showed no more desire to fight.

The donkey would probably have continued to kick him had not the men been there, but he was forced out at the end of some pronged forks, and put into a place by himself, where he has been kept ever since. As for the poor llama, a surgeon was sent for and did his best to soothe the poor animal's pain. He bandaged up its eye and head, and a very sorry sight he looked! It was thought perhaps that it had simply been a quarrel between the two, and that they would be pleased to be together again. But when they once more found themselves at close quarters, the llama's one eye grew wild and angry, and the sacred donkey at once turned his back and began kicking furiously. So that wonderful friendship is at an end.

WILD LIFE THROUGH THE CAMERA

By Dwight Franklin

A FLASH of wings and the kingfisher had disappeared. But I had her picture.

I had waited an eternity in my camera blind — an umbrella affair draped with green cloth — and, as the month was June, with the midday sun blazing overhead, my sensations were much like those of a man in a Turkish bath. Moreover, I had to wait — in a standing position — for the kingfisher to cross a certain spot only seven feet away and just in front of her tunnel in the sand-bank, on which I had carefully focused my camera.

The shutter was of the most rapid type, set for a 2000th of a second, and as the long minutes crawled by, I was almost afraid that the mother bird would not return.

Common sense, however, assured me that she would; for her several young were impatiently awaiting her home-coming, even as I — though, of course, for a more material motive. Then, too, she had been fishing for a long time.

My hand grew cramped from grasping the shutter release and my patience was suffering sorely; also I was suffocating. At last I heard far away a harsh rolling clatter — the traveling cry of the kingfisher — growing louder and louder as she approached.

Without hesitating she dove into the tunnel, and I had a glimpse of a large fat minnow in her bill. Appreciative though muffled rattles, issuing from the chamber at the end of the burrow, told me that the young "Prince-fishers" were dining.

This little incident is merely one of many likely to happen to anyone going in for nature photography as a recreation.

That day I secured some splendid pictures of kingfishers in flight and felt more than repaid for the temporary discomfort which, after all, is a mere incident when seen in retrospect.

There are many kinds of nature photographers; from the child who snaps the family cat, to the intrepid sportsman who often risks his life for the sake of a picture of some dangerous beast of the jungle. We have heard of one man who faced a charging rhino and took a picture of him at a distance of only fifteen feet, while his companion stood by with a gun ready to turn him, should occasion require, which it certainly did. Generally speaking there are two methods employed in photographing birds and animals — lying-in-wait and stalking.

Each has its good and bad points, and each is thoroughly interesting. Lying-in-wait is often done when photographing birds on their nests, and the umbrella blind is widely used for this purpose. This blind is simply a large green umbrella, with a hole in the top for ventilation, fitting into a telescopic rod, one end of which is sharpened and driven into the ground. It should be high enough to stand under comfortably. Hanging from the umbrella is a green curtain, with a draw-string at the top and an opening on one side, which forms the entrance and exit. There is, sometimes, a hole on the opposite side through which the camera is worked.

This method of lying-in-wait is used when the creature has some definite reason for coming to a certain place. In the case of birds, the nest and young are generally the attraction, although shore birds can often be called, and one enterprising photographer used a dummy fish as a lure for fishhawks with success.

In photographing small mammals excellent pictures have been taken by luring them to a certain place each day by means of food; then, when they have acquired the habit of coming regularly, the camera is focused on the spot and the photographer either works the shutter with a long string (having retired to some distance) or else the umbrella blind is used. A peculiar feature of this green blind is that the wild creatures pay no attention to it; probably mistaking it for a bit of the green environment. In fact, in my own case, I have repeatedly retired into my blind in full view of the bird which shortly afterward returned to the nest unalarmed.

Working in a blind is often tedious; but when the subject is one of great interest, the game develops into one of keen excitement which lasts until the plate has been developed.

Birds vary so much individually, in temperament, that it is unwise to lay down rules as to their timidity.

Only last summer I was fortunate enough to secure some excellent pictures of the least bittern, a little heron quite common in the Middle West. I had heard always that it was an exceedingly shy and retiring bird and one rather difficult to photograph, but this notion was upset by my own experience. I found, that with a little patience, the bird could be approached as close as I wished; and eventually it was difficult to induce either father or mother bird to leave the nest. The parents took turns in brooding the young. They had become so accustomed to my presence, or else were so plucky in their defense of the nest, that it was necessary to lift them from it in order to observe the young birds. Perhaps this case is exceptional, but I am inclined to believe that many of our so-called shy birds may be photographed if one could only devote the necessary time to them. Unless we are professionals, most of us have only a day or two at a time at our disposal, generally week-ends; and while much can be accomplished in two days, it often happens that a week is not long enough in which to win the friendship of some of our mother birds.

Stalking with a camera is another branch of nature photography which is most successfully used with a camera of the reflecting type through which one may see the subject right side up on a ground glass. With other cameras it is difficult to estimate correctly distances under six feet as, with a reflecting camera, one hand is constantly focusing, while the other presses the release to make the exposure. This is a great convenience in working with small mammals and birds, as they often change their positions while being stalked.

The great drawback to these reflecting cameras is their weight and size, most of them being entirely too heavy for a long tramp.

However, it is all in the game; and the enthusiast is not daunted by such trifles — as he constantly proves in his work. As has been said, "A bird on the plate is worth two in the bush."

PROF. GUY A. BAILEY AND BIRD-PHOTOGRAPHY

By David Zukerman

NATURE-LOVERS who have attempted to any extent to substitute the camera for the gun have found themselves handicapped, especially in photographing birds, because of the difficulty of getting near enough to the subject to secure a proper focus. The shyness and timidity of the feathered songsters, frightened as they are by the slightest noise or unusual rustle, make it almost impossible to picture them in natural poses. Hence most studies of birds must be drawings rather than photographs, drawings which can be made only by capable artists who are also naturalists and careful students of natural phenomena.

One nature enthusiast, with an inventive turn of mind, has managed to overcome this difficulty to some extent. His methods will prove interesting, even if it be impracticable for most to follow his example.

The person in question is Prof. Guy A. Bailey, head of the Biology Department of the New York State Normal School, at Geneseo. He is likewise County Bacteriologist; wherefore — as he smilingly said to me — he works twenty-two months a year, and is an exceedingly busy person. Enthusiastic about his work, he manages to impart some of his zeal to the students in his charge, and drags them out, half-grumbling, at four to five o'clock in the morning for observations in the fields.

In addition to all his duties, however, Professor Bailey manages to find or make time to ride his hobby, — bird photography. He gives most of his spare time to it; and has already collected some five thousand photographs on the subject. He makes his own lantern slides and is very much in demand as a popular lecturer on nature study.

Professor Bailey's office, in the extreme left wing of the school, presented a curious sight to the visitor. In one corner was a queer bit of mechanism which looked as though it had once belonged to a clock. There were cogwheels and a pendulum, as well as a complicated arrangement of wires. I afterwards discovered that this was the phonographic arrangement — a counterpart of which was in his bedroom across the street — which Professor Bailey used to announce that a picture had been secured. There was also a cabinet, full of slides and photographs. To the right was a large telescope trained upon a tree a mile away. Near this telescope was an electrical apparatus of switches and coils and fuses, — a wireless arrangement for controlling a camera focused upon a perch in this same tree. Think of photographing an object a mile away, with a camera the same distance away, — a camera you do not handle at the time, nor focus, nor do aught to! Instead, you sit in a room and close for a moment a switch that causes a number of electrical sparks and flashes.

The chief interest of the room, however, was a window immediately ahead. The lower casement was raised slightly, and a board inserted in which were bored seven holes, through each one of which was affixed a small telescope. These were numbered, and underneath each one was an electric push-button to correspond.

A glance cast through these telescopes revealed a scene of amazing beauty. They were trained upon a small funnel-shaped gully, with the narrow end pointing to the left. Within this gully, Professor Bailey has set up several perches, which he baits regularly with suet. About a foot from each perch is another upon which rests a mysterious looking box of medium size.

The mystery ceased to be one when we left the building and entered the gully to examine one of these boxes. Within reposed a camera, loaded, and focused upon the perch. The shutter of the camera was connected with an electro-magnet, which in turn was controlled by the push-button corresponding to the telescope trained upon this particular perch.

One of his perches, Professor Bailey found, was rather hidden by the leaves of the tree whereon it rested, and could not be reached directly; so he set up in the fields near by a mirror at such an angle that, when he trained a telescope upon the mirror, he could get an unobstructed view of the perch. He also arranged a mirror in his window so as to enable him to reflect the sunlight upon the lower portion of the gully, which grew dark too early in the day and too soon in the year.

With his apparatus thus ingeniously set, all he need do is to sit comfortably in a large armchair and keep his eyes glued to the telescopic eye-pieces. He secures an uninterrupted view of at least seven or eight spots to which the birds are sure to come, — attracted by the knowledge that food has been placed there for their special convenience. Confident, pert as ever, unsuspicious of the box near by, which does not seem to interfere with the meal in any manner, birds can thus be photographed in the most natural and attractive poses. There is no movement of the spectator creeping nearer to get his focus, no crackle of twig or dry leaf, nothing other than their ordinary surroundings, nothing to disturb, nothing to hinder their movements. How shall they know that they are watched nevertheless? For all their alertness and keenness of sense, man has again proved his ability to overcome his environment.

Eager, expectant, the watcher above awaits his chance. A bird presents an attractive, suitable pose; it is the work of a moment to press a button, and the snapshot is taken. Truly the click, though slight, was sufficient to frighten the bird away; but what of it? He has served his purpose, and acted his part. Now he is no longer needed. On the sensitive plate is a counterpart of him that can be recalled again and again.

I have described the apparatus thus minutely, because I consider it an extremely important development in nature study, a development that can be used to ascertain more carefully the habits and appearance of shy birds. By the duplication of such an arrangement in suitable localities, and the use of plates that will photograph the objects in their natural colors, we shall have an excellent means of studying the subject with greater ease and exactitude. Such photographs will give us details that ordinarily compel long and continued periods of observation. They will show any extraordinary marking; and the study of a single photograph will be of very great assistance toward the identification of a bird when next seen.

The preliminary labor and cost involved in setting up such apparatus is slight compared with the results. It is to be hoped that Professor Bailey's arrangements will be duplicated many times over.

THE TURKEY DRIVE

By Dallas Lore Sharp

THE situation was serious enough for the two boys. It was not a large fortune, but it was their whole fortune, that straggled along the slushy road in the shape of five hundred weary, hungry turkeys, which were looking for a roosting-place.

But there was no place where they could roost, no safe place, as the boys well knew, for on each side of the old road stretched the forest trees, a dangerous, and in the weakened condition of the turkeys, an impossible roost on such a night as was coming.

For the warm south wind had again veered to the north; the slush was beginning to grow crusty, and a fine sifting of snow was slanting through the open trees. Although it was still early afternoon, the gloom of the night had already settled over the forest, and the turkeys, with empty crops, were peevishly searching the bare trees for a roost.

It was a strange, slow procession that they made, here in the New Brunswick forest — the flock of five hundred turkeys, tolled forward by a boy of eighteen, kept in line by a well-trained shepherd-dog that raced up and down the straggling column, and urged on in the rear by a boy of nineteen, who was followed, in his turn, by an old horse and farm wagon, creeping along behind.

It was growing more difficult all the time to keep the turkeys moving. But they must not be allowed to stop until darkness should put an end to the march. And they must not be allowed to take to the trees at all. Some of them, indeed, were too weak to roost high; but the flock would never move forward again if exposed in the tall trees on such a night as this promised to be.

The thing to do was to keep them stirring. Once allow them to halt, give one of them time to pick out a roosting-limb for himself, and the march would be over for that afternoon. The boys knew their flock. This was not their first drive. They knew from experience that once a turkey gets it into his small head to roost, he is bound to roost. Nothing will stop him. And in this matter the flock acts as a single bird.

In the last village, back along the road, through which they had passed, this very flock took a notion suddenly to go to roost, and to go to roost on a little chapel as the vesper bells were tolling. The bells were tolling, the worshipers were gathering, when, with a loud gobble, one of the turkeys in the flock sailed into the air and lighted upon the ridgepole beside the belfry! Instantly the flock broke ranks, ran wildly round the little building, and with a clamor that drowned the vesper bell, came down on the chapel in a feathered congregation that covered every shingle of the roof. Only the humor and quick wit of the kindly old priest prevented the superstitious of his people from going into a panic. The service had to wait until the birds made themselves comfortable for the night — belfry, roof, windowsills, and porch steps thick with roosting turkeys!

The boys had come to have almost a fear of this mania for roosting, for they never knew when it might break out or what strange turn it might take. They knew now, as the snow and the gray dusk began to thicken in the woods, that the flock must not go to roost. Even the dog understood the signs, — the peevish *quint, quint, quint,* the sudden bolting of some gobbler into the brush, the stretching necks, the lagging steps, — and redoubled his efforts to keep the line from halting.

For two days the flock had been without food. Almost a week's supply of grain, enough to carry them through to the border, had been loaded into the wagon before starting in upon this wild, deserted road through the Black Creek region; but the heavy, day-long snow storm had prevented their moving at all for one day, and had made travel so nearly impossible since then that here they were, facing a blizzard, with night upon them, five hundred starving turkeys straggling wearily before them, and a two days' drive yet to go!

The two brothers had got a short leave from college, and had started their turkey drive in the more settled regions back from the New Brunswick border. They had bought up the turkeys from farm to farm, had herded them in one great flock as they drove them leisurely along, and had moved all the while toward the state line, whence they planned to send them through Maine for the New England market. Upon reaching the railroad, they would rest and feed the birds, and ship them, in a special freight-car ordered in advance, to a Boston commission house, sell the horse and rig for what they could get, and, with their dog, go directly back to college.

More money than they actually possessed had gone into the daring venture. But the drive had been more than successful until the beginning of the Black Creek road. The year before they had gone over the same route, which they had chosen because it was sparsely settled and because the prices were low. This year the farmers were expecting them; the turkeys were plentiful; and the traveling had been good until this early snow had caught them here in the backwoods and held them; and now, with the sudden shift of the wind again to the north, it threatened to delay them farther, past all chance of bringing a single turkey through alive.

But George and Herbert Totman had not worked their way into their junior year at college to sit down by the roadside while there was light to travel by. They were not the kind to let their turkeys go to roost before sundown. It was a slow and solemn procession that moved through the woods, but it moved — toward a goal that they had set for that day's travel.

All day, at long intervals, as they had pushed along the deep forest road, the muffled rumble of distant trains had come to them through the silence; and now, although neither of them had mentioned it, they were determined to get out somewhere near the tracks before the night and the storm should settle down upon them. Their road, hardly more here than a wide trail, must cross the railroad tracks, as they remembered it, not more than two or three miles ahead.

Leaving more and more of the desolate forest behind them with every step, they plodded doggedly on. But there was so much of the same desolate forest still before them! Yet yonder, and not far away, was the narrow path of the iron track through the interminable waste; something human — the very sight of it enough to warm and cheer them. They would camp to-night where they could see a train go by.

The leaden sky lowered closer upon them. The storm had not yet got under full headway, but the fine icy flakes were flying faster, slanting farther, and the wind was beginning to drone through the trees.

Without a halt, the flock moved on through the thickening storm. But the dog was having all that he could do to keep the stragglers in order; and George, in the rear, saw that they must stir the flock, for the birds were gradually falling back into a thick bunch before him.

Hurrying back to the wagon, he got two loaves of bread, and ran ahead with them to Herbert. The famished turkeys seemed to know what he carried, and broke into a run after him. For half a mile they kept up the gait, as both boys, trotting along the road, dropped pieces of bread on the snow.

Then the whole game had to be repeated; for the greater part of the flock, falling hopelessly behind, soon forgot what they were running after, and began to cry, "*Quint! quint! quint!*" — the roosting-cry! So, starting again at the rear with the bread, George carried the last of the flock forward for another good run.

"We should win this game," Herbert panted, "if we only had loaves enough to make a few more touch-downs."

"There's half an hour yet to play," was George's answer.

"But what on?"

"Oh, on our nerve now," the older boy replied grimly.

"That railroad is not far ahead," said Herbert.

"Half an hour ahead. We've got to camp by that track to-night or —"

"Or what?"

But George had turned to help the dog head off some runaways.

Herbert, picking up a lump of frozen leaves and snow, began to break this in front of the flock to toll them on.

He had hardly started the birds again, when a long-legged gobbler brushed past him and went swinging down the road, calling, "*Quint! quint! quint!*" to the flock behind. The call was taken up and passed along the now extended line, which, breaking immediately into double-quick, went streaming after him.

Herbert got out of the way to let them pass, too astonished for a moment to do more than watch them go. It was the roosting-cry! An old gobbler had given it; but as it was taking him, for once, in the right direction, Herbert ordered back the dog that had dashed forward to head him off, and fell in with George to help on the stragglers in the rear.

As the laggards were brought up to a slight rise in

the road, the flock was seen a hundred yards ahead, gathered in a dark mass about a telegraph-pole! It could be nothing else, for through the whirling snow the big cross-arms stood out, dim but unmistakable.

It was this that the gobbler had spied and started for, this sawed and squared piece of timber, that had suggested a barnyard to him, — corn and roost, — as to the boys it meant a human presence in the forest and something like human companionship.

It was after four o'clock now, and the night was hard upon them. The wind was strengthening every minute; the snow was coming finer and swifter. The boys' worst fears about the storm were beginning to be realized.

But the sight of the railroad track heartened them. The strong-armed poles, with their humming wires, reached out hands of hope to them; and getting among the turkeys, they began to hurry them off the track and down the steep embankment, which fortunately offered them here some slight protection from the wind. But as fast as they pushed the birds off, the one-minded things came back on the track. The whole flock, meanwhile, was scattering up and down the iron rails and settling calmly down upon them for the night.

They were going to roost upon the track! The railroad bank shelved down to the woods on each side, and along its whitened peak lay the two black rails like ridgepoles along the length of a long roof. In the thick half-light of the whirling snow, the turkeys seemed suddenly to find themselves at home: and as close together as they could crowd, with their breasts all to the storm, they arranged themselves in two long lines upon the steel rails.

And nothing could move them! As fast as one was tossed down the bank, up he came. Starting down the lines, the boys pushed and shoved to clear the track; but the lines re-formed behind them quickly, evenly, and almost without a sound. As well try to sweep back the waves of the sea! They worked together to collect a small band of the birds and drive them into the edge of the woods; but every time the band dwindled to a single turkey that dodged between their legs toward its place on the roost. The two boys could have kept *two* turkeys off the rails, but not five hundred.

"The game is up, George," said Herbert, as the sickening thought of a train swept over him.

The words were hardly uttered when there came the *tankle, tankle* of the big cow-bell hanging from the collar of the horse, that was just now coming up to the crossing!

George caught his breath and started over to stop the horse, when, above the loud hum of the wires and the sound of the wind in the forest trees, they heard through the storm the muffled whistle of a locomotive.

"Quick! The horse, Herbert! Hitch him to a tree and come!" called George, as he dived into the wagon and pulled out their lantern. "Those birds could wreck the train!" he shouted, and hurried forward along the track with his lighted lantern in his hand.

It was not the thought of the turkeys, but the thought of the people on the flying Montreal express, — if that it was, — that sped him up the track. In his imagination he saw the wreck of a ditched train below him;

the moans of a hundred mangled beings he heard sounding in his ears!

On into the teeth of the blinding storm he raced, while he strained his eyes for a glimpse of the coming train.

The track seemed to lie straightaway in front of him, and he bent his head for a moment before the wind, when, out of the smother of the snow, the flaring headlight leaped almost upon him.

He sprang aside, stumbled, and pitched headlong down the bank, as the engine of a freight, with a roar that dazed him, swept past.

But the engineer had seen him, and there was a screaming of iron brakes, a crashing of cars together, and a long-drawn shrieking of wheels, as the heavy train slid along the slippery rails to a stop.

As the engineer swung down from his cab, he was met, to his great astonishment, by a dozen turkeys clambering up the embankment toward him. He had plowed his way well among the roosting flock and brushed them unhurt from the rails as the engine skidded along to its slow stop.

By this time the conductor and the train-hands had run forward to see what it all meant, and stood looking at the strange obstruction on the track, when Herbert came into the glare of the headlight and joined them. Then George came panting up, and the boys tried to explain the situation. But their explanation only made a case of sheer negligence out of what at first had seemed a mystery to the trainmen. Both the engineer and the conductor were anxious and surly. Their train was already an hour late; there was a through express behind, and the track must be cleared at once.

And they fell at once to clearing it — conductor, fireman, brakemen, and the two boys. Those railroad men had never tried to clear a track of roosting turkeys before. They cleared it, — a little of it, — but it would not stay cleared, for the turkeys slipped through their hands, squeezed between their legs, ducked about their heels, and got back into place. Finally the conductor, putting two men in line on each rail, ordered the engineer to follow slowly, close upon their heels, with the train, as they scattered the birds before them.

The boys had not once thought of themselves. They had had no time to think of anything but the danger and the delay that they had caused. They helped with all their might to get the train through, and as they worked, silently listened to the repeated threats of the conductor.

At last, with a muttered something, the conductor kicked one of the turkeys into a fluttering heap beneath the engine, and, turning, commanded his crew to stand aside and let the engineer finish the rest of the flock.

The men got away from the track. Then, catching Herbert by the arm, George pointed along the train, and bending made a tossing motion toward the top of the cars.

"Quick!" he whispered. "One on every car!" and stepping calmly back in front of the engine, he went down the opposite side of the long train.

As he passed the tender, he seized a big gobbler,

and sent him with a wild throw up to the top of a low coal-car, just as Herbert on his side, sent another fluttering up to the same perch. Both birds landed with a flap and a gobble that were heard by the other turkeys up and down the length of the train.

Instantly came a chorus of answering gobbles as every turkey along the track saw, in the failing light, that real buildings — farmyard buildings — were here to roost on! And into the air they went, helped all along the train by the boys, who were tossing them into the cars, or upon the loads of lumber, as fast as they could pass from car to car.

Luckily, the rails were sleety, and the mighty driving-wheels, spinning on the ice with their long load, which seemed to freeze continually to the track, made head-way so slowly that the whole flock had come to roost upon the cars before the train was fairly moving.

Conductor and brakeman, hurrying back to board the caboose, were midway of the train before they noticed what was happening. *How* it was happening they did not see at all, so hidden were the movements of the two boys in the swirl of the blinding snow.

For just an instant the conductor checked himself. But it was too late to do anything. The train was moving, and he must keep it moving as fast as he could to the freight-yards ahead at the junction — the very yards where, even now, an empty car was waiting for the overdue turkeys.

As he ran on down the track and swung aboard the caboose, two other figures closed in behind the train. One of them seizing the other by the arm, landed him safe upon the steps, and then shouted at him through the storm: —

"Certainly you shall! I'm safe enough! I'll drive on to that old sawmill to-night. Feed 'em in the morning and wait for me! Good-by," and as the wind carried his voice away, George Totman found himself staring after a ghost-white car that had vanished in the storm.

He was alone; but the thought of the great flock speeding on to the town ahead was company enough. Besides, he had too much to do, and to do quickly, to think of himself; for the snow was blocking his road, and the cold was getting at him. But how the wires overhead sang to him! How the sounding forest sang to him as he went back to give the horse a snatch of supper!

He was soon on the road, where the wind at his back and the tall trees gave him protection. The four-wheeled wagon pulled hard through the piling snow, but the horse had had an easy day, and George kept him going until, toward eight o'clock, he drew up behind a lofty pile of slabs and sawdust at the old mill.

A wilder storm never filled the resounding forests of the North. The old mill was far from being proof against the fine, icy snow; but when George rolled himself in his heavy blanket and lay down beside his dog, it was to go to sleep to the comfortable munching of the horse, and with the thought that Herbert and the turkeys were safe.

And they were safe. It was late in the afternoon the next day when George, having left the wagon at the mill, came floundering behind the horse through the unbroken road into the streets of the junction, to find Herbert anxiously waiting for him, and the turkeys, with full crops, trying hard to go to roost inside their double-decked car.

MISS CRIPPLETOES AND HER FRIENDS

By Kate Douglas Wiggin

THERE follows the true story of Sir Muscovy Drake, the Lady Blanche, and Miss Mallardina Crippletoes.

Phœbe's flock consisted at first mostly of Brown Mallards, but a friend gave her a sitting of eggs warranted to produce a most beautiful variety of white ducks. They were hatched in due time, but proved hard to raise, till at length there was only one survivor, of such uncommon grace and beauty that we called her the Lady Blanche. Presently a neighbor sold Phœbe his favorite Muscovy drake, and these two splendid creatures by "natural selection" disdained to notice the rest of the flock, but forming a close friendship, wandered in the pleasant paths of duckdom together, swimming and eating quite apart from the others.

In the brown flock there was one unfortunate, misshapen from the egg, quite lame, and with no smoothness of plumage; but on that very account, apparently, or because she was too weak to resist them, the others treated her cruelly, biting her and pushing her away from the food.

One day it happened that the two ducks — Sir Muscovy and Lady Blanche — had come up from the water before the others, and having taken their repast were sitting together under the shade of a flowering currant bush, when they chanced to see poor Miss Crippletoes very badly used and crowded away from the dish. Sir Muscovy rose to his feet; a few rapid words seemed to pass between him and his mate, and then he fell upon the other drake and the heartless minions who had persecuted the helpless one, drove them far away out of sight, and, returning, went to the corner where the victim was cowering, her face to the wall. He seemed to whisper to her, or in some way to convey to her a sense of protection; for after a few moments she tremblingly went with him to the dish, and hurriedly ate her dinner while he stood by, repulsing the advances of the few brown ducks who remained near and seemed inclined to attack her.

When she had eaten enough Lady Blanche joined them and they went down the hill together to their favorite swimming-place. After that, Miss Crippletoes always followed a little behind her protectors, and thus shielded and fed she grew stronger and well-feathered, though she was always smaller than she should have been and had a lowly manner, keeping a few steps in the rear of her superiors and sitting at some distance from their noon resting-place.

Phœbe noticed after a while that Lady Blanche was seldom to be seen, and Sir Muscovy and Miss Crippletoes often came to their meals without her. The would-be mother refused to inhabit the house Phœbe had given her, and for a long time the place she had chosen for her sitting could not be found. At length the Square

Baby discovered her in a most ideal spot. A large bowlder had dropped years ago into the brook that fills our duck-pond; dropped and split in halves with the two smooth walls leaning away from each other. A grassy bank towered behind, and on either side of the opening, tall bushes made a miniature forest where the romantic mother could brood her treasures while her two guardians enjoyed the water close by her retreat.

All this happened before my coming to Thornycroft Farm, but it was I who named the hero and heroines of the romance when Phœbe had told me all the particulars. Yesterday morning I was sitting by my open window. It was warm, sunny, and still, but in the country sounds travel far, and I could hear fowl conversation in various parts of the poultry yard as in all the outlying bits of territory occupied by our feathered friends. Hens have only three words and a scream in their language, but ducks, having more thoughts to express, converse quite fluently, so fluently, in fact, that it reminds me of dinner at the Hydropathic Hotel. I fancy I have learned to distinguish seven separate sounds, each varied by degrees of intensity, and with upward or downward inflections like the Chinese tongue.

In the distance, then, I heard the faint voice of a duck calling as if breathless and excited. While I wondered what was happening, I saw Miss Crippletoes struggling up the steep bank above the duck-pond. It was the quickest way from the water to the house, but difficult for the little lame webbed feet. When she reached the level grass sward she sank down a moment, exhausted; but when she could speak again she cried out, a sharp staccato call, and ran forward.

Instantly she was answered from a distant knoll, where for some reason Sir Muscovy loved to retire for meditation. The cries grew lower and softer as the birds approached each other, and they met at the corner just under my window. Instantly they put their two bills together and the loud cries changed to confiding murmurs. Evidently some hurried questions and answers passed between them, and then Sir Muscovy waddled rapidly by the quickest path, Miss Crippletoes following him at a slower pace, and both passed out of sight, using their wings to help their feet down the steep declivity. The next morning, when I wakened early, my first thought was to look out, and there on the sunny greensward where they were accustomed to be fed, Sir Muscovy, Lady Blanche, and their humble maid, Mallardina Crippletoes, were scattering their own breakfast before the bills of twelve beautiful golden balls of ducklings. The little creatures could never have climbed the bank, but must have started from their nest at dawn, coming round by the brook to the level at the foot of the garden, and so by slow degrees up to the house.

Judging from what I heard and knew of their habits, I am sure the excitement of the previous morning was occasioned by the hatching of the eggs, and that Lady Blanche had hastily sent her friend to call Sir Muscovy, the family remaining together until they could bring the babies with them and display their beauty to Phœbe and me.

HOW THE BLUEBIRD BEHAVES

By John Burroughs

IT is sure to be a bright March morning when you first hear the bluebird's note; and it is as if the milder influences up above had found a voice and let a word fall upon your ear, so tender is it and so prophetic, a hope tinged with a regret.

There never was a happier or more devoted husband than the male bluebird. He is the gay champion and escort of the female at all times, and while she is sitting he feeds her regularly. It is very pretty to watch them building their nest. The male is very active in hunting out a place and exploring the boxes and cavities, but seems to have no choice in the matter and is anxious only to please and encourage his mate, who has the practical turn and knows what will do and what will not. After she has suited herself he applauds her immensely, and away the two go in quest of material for the nest, the male acting as guard and flying above and in advance of the female. She brings all the material and does all the work of building, he looking on and encouraging her with gesture and song. He acts also as inspector of her work, but I fear is a very partial one. She enters the nest with her bit of dry grass or straw, and, having adjusted it to her notion, withdraws and waits near by while he goes in and looks it over.

On coming out he exclaims very plainly, "Excellent! excellent!" and away the two go again for more material.

I was much amused one summer day in seeing a bluebird feeding her young one in the shaded street of a large town. She had captured a cicada or harvest-fly, and, after bruising it awhile on the ground, flew with it to a tree and placed it in the beak of the young bird. It was a large morsel, and the mother seemed to have doubts of her chick's ability to dispose of it, for she stood near and watched its efforts with great solicitude. The young bird struggled valiantly with the cicada, but made no headway in swallowing it, when the mother took it from him and flew to the sidewalk, and proceeded to break and bruise it more thoroughly. Then she again placed it in his beak, and seemed to say, "There, try it now," and sympathized so thoroughly with his efforts that she repeated many of his motions and contortions. But the great fly was unyielding, and, indeed, seemed ridiculously disproportioned to the beak that held it. The young bird fluttered and fluttered, and screamed, "I 'm stuck, I 'm stuck!" till the anxious parent again seized the morsel and carried it to an iron railing, where she came down upon it for the space of a minute with all the force and momentum her beak could command. Then she offered it to her young a third time, but with the same result as before, except that this time the bird dropped it; but she reached the ground as soon as the cicada did, and taking it in her beak flew a little distance to a high board fence, where she sat motionless for some moments. While pondering the problem how that fly should be broken, the male bluebird approached her, and said very plainly, and I thought rather curtly, "Give me that bug," but she quickly resented his interference and flew farther away, where she sat apparently quite discouraged when I last saw her.

One day in early May, Ted and I made an expedition to the Shattega, a still, dark, deep stream that loiters silently through the woods not far from my cabin. As we paddled along, we were on the alert for any bit of wild life of bird or beast that might turn up.

There were so many abandoned woodpecker chambers in the small dead trees as we went along that I determined to secure the section of a tree containing a good one to take home and put up for the bluebirds. "Why don't the bluebirds occupy them here?" inquired Ted. "Oh," I replied, "bluebirds do not come so far into the woods as this. They prefer nesting-places in the open, and near human habitations." After carefully scrutinizing several of the trees, we at last saw one that seemed to fill the bill. It was a small dead tree-trunk seven or eight inches in diameter, that leaned out over the water, and from which the top had been broken. The hole, round and firm, was ten or twelve feet above us. After considerable effort I succeeded in breaking the stub off near the ground, and brought it down into the boat. "Just the thing," I said; "surely the bluebirds will prefer this to an artificial box." But, lo and behold, it already had bluebirds in it! We had not heard a sound or seen a feather till the trunk was in our hands, when, on peering into the cavity, we discovered two young bluebirds about half grown. This was a predicament indeed.

Well, the only thing we could do was to stand the tree-trunk up again as well as we could, and as near as we could to where it had stood before. This was no easy thing. But after a time we had it fairly well replaced, one end standing in the mud of the shallow water and the other resting against a tree. This left the hole to the nest about ten feet below and to one side of its former position. Just then we heard the voice of one of the parent birds, and we quickly paddled to the other side of the stream, fifty feet away, to watch her proceedings, saying to each other, "Too bad! too bad!" The mother bird had a large beetle in her beak. She alighted upon a limb a few feet above the former site of her nest, looked down upon us, uttered a note or two, and then dropped down confidently to the point in the vacant air where the entrance to her nest had been but a few moments before. Here she hovered on the wing a second or two, looking for something that was not there, and then returned to the perch she had just left, apparently not a little disturbed. She hammered the beetle rather excitedly upon the limb a few times, as if it were in some way at fault, then dropped down to try for her nest again. Only vacant air there! She hovered and hovered, her blue wings flickering in the checkered light; surely that precious hole *must* be there; but no, again she was baffled, and again she returned to her perch, and mauled the poor beetle till it must have been reduced to a pulp. Then she made a third attempt, then a fourth, and a fifth, and a sixth, till she became very much excited. "What could have happened? am I dreaming? has that beetle hoodooed me?" she seemed to say, and in her dismay she let the bug drop, and looked bewilderedly about her. Then she flew away through the woods, calling. "Going for her mate," I said to Ted "She is in deep trouble, and she wants sympathy and help."

In a few minutes we heard her mate answer, and presently the two birds came hurrying to the spot, both with loaded beaks. They perched upon the familiar limb above the site of the nest, and the mate seemed to say, "My dear, what has happened to you? I can find that nest." And he dived down, and brought up in the empty air just as the mother had done. How he winnowed it with his eager wings! how he seemed to bear on to that blank space! His mate sat regarding him intently, confident, I think, that he would find the clew. But he did not. Baffled and excited, he returned to the perch beside her. Then she tried again, then he rushed down once more, then they both assaulted the place, but it would not give up its secret. They talked, they encouraged each other, and they kept up the search, now one, now the other, now both together. Sometimes they dropped down to within a few feet of the entrance to the nest, and we thought they would surely find it. No, their minds and eyes were intent only upon that square foot of space where the nest had been. Soon they withdrew to a large limb many feet higher up, and seemed to say to themselves, "Well, it is not there, but it must be here somewhere; let us look about." A few minutes elapsed, when we saw the mother bird spring from her perch and go straight as an arrow to the nest. Her maternal eye had proved the quicker. She had found her young. Something like reason and common sense had come to her rescue; she had taken time to look about, and behold! there was that precious doorway. She thrust her head into it, then sent back a call to her mate, then went farther in, then withdrew. "Yes, it is true, they are here, they are here!" Then she went in again, gave them the food in her beak, and then gave place to her mate, who, after similar demonstrations of joy, also gave them his morsel.

Ted and I breathed freer. A burden had been taken from our minds and hearts, and we went cheerfully on our way. We had learned something, too; we had learned that when in the deep woods you think of bluebirds, bluebirds may be nearer you than you think.

One mid-April morning two pairs of bluebirds were in very active and at times violent courtship about my grounds. I could not quite understand the meaning of all the fuss and flutter. Both birds of each pair were very demonstrative, but the female in each case was more so. She followed the male everywhere, lifting and twinkling her wings, and apparently seeking to win him by both word and gesture. If she was not telling him by that cheery, animated, confiding, softly endearing speech of hers, which she poured out incessantly, how much she loved him, what was she saying? She was constantly filled with a desire to perch upon the precise spot where he was sitting, and if he had not moved away I think she would have alighted upon his back. Now and then, when she flitted away from him, he followed her with like gestures and tones and demonstrations of affection, but never with quite the same ardor. The two pairs kept near each other, about the house, the bird boxes, the trees, the posts and vines in the vineyard, filling the ear with their soft, insistent warbles, and the eye with their twinkling azure wings.

Was it this constant presence of rivals on both sides that so stimulated them and kept them up to such a pitch of courtship? Finally, after I had watched them over an hour, the birds began to come into collision. As they met in the vineyard, the two males clinched and fell to the ground, lying there for a moment with wings sprawled out, like birds brought down by a gun. Then they separated, and each returned to his mate, warbling and twinkling his wings. Very soon the females clinched and fell to the ground and fought savagely, rolling over and over each other, clawing and tweaking and locking beaks and hanging on like bull terriers. They did this repeatedly; once one of the males dashed in and separated them, by giving one of the females a sharp tweak and blow. Then the males were at it again, their blue plumage mixing with the green grass and ruffled by the ruddy soil. What a soft, feathery, ineffectual battle it seemed in both cases! — no sound, no blood, no flying feathers, just a sudden mixing up and general disarray of blue wings and tails and ruddy breasts, there on the ground; assault but no visible wounds; thrust of beak and grip of claw, but no feather loosened and but little ruffling; long holding of one down by the other, but no cry of pain or fury. It was the kind of battle that one likes to witness. The birds usually locked beaks, and held their grip half a minute at a time. One of the females would always alight by the struggling males and lift her wings and utter her soft notes, but what she said — whether she was encouraging one of the blue coats or berating the other, or imploring them both to desist, or egging them on — I could not tell. So far as I could understand her speech, it was the same that she had been uttering to her mate all the time.

When my bluebirds dashed at each other with beak and claw, their preliminary utterances had to my ears anything but a hostile sound. Indeed, for the bluebird to make a harsh, discordant sound seems out of the question. Once, when the two males lay upon the ground with outspread wings and locked beaks, a robin flew down by them and for a moment gazed intently at the blue splash upon the grass, and then went his way.

As the birds drifted about the grounds, first the males, then the females rolling on the grass or in the dust in fierce combat, and between times the members of each pair assuring each other of undying interest and attachment, I followed them, apparently quite unnoticed by them. Sometimes they would lie more than a minute upon the ground, each trying to keep his own or to break the other's hold. They seemed so oblivious of everything about them that I wondered if they might not at such times fall an easy prey to cats and hawks. Let me put their watchfulness to the test, I said. So, as the two males clinched again and fell to the ground, I cautiously approached them, hat in hand. When ten feet away and unregarded, I made a sudden dash and covered them with my hat. The struggle continued for a few seconds under there, then all was still. Sudden darkness had fallen upon the field of battle. What did they think had happened? Presently their heads and wings began to brush the inside of my hat. Then all was still again. Then I spoke to them, called to them, exulted over them, but they betrayed no excitement or alarm. Occasionally a head or a body came in gentle contact with the top or the sides of my hat.

But the two females were evidently agitated by the sudden disappearance of their contending lovers, and began uttering their mournful alarm-note. After a minute or two I lifted one side of my hat and out darted one of the birds; then I lifted the hat from the other. One of the females then rushed, apparently with notes of joy and congratulation, to one of the males, who gave her a spiteful tweak and blow. Then the other came and he served her the same. He was evidently a little bewildered, and not certain what had happened or who was responsible for it. Did he think the two females were in some way to blame? But he was soon reconciled to one of them again, as was the other male with the other, yet the two couples did not separate till the males had come into collision once more. Presently, however, they drifted apart, and each pair was soon holding an animated conversation, punctuated by those pretty wing gestures, about the two bird-boxes.

These scenes of love and rivalry had lasted nearly all the forenoon, and matters between the birds apparently remained as they were before — the members of each pair quite satisfied with each other. One pair occupied one of the bird-boxes in the vineyard and reared two broods there during the season, but the other pair drifted away and took up their abode somewhere else.

THE RED-BREASTED NUTHATCH

By Cordelia J. Stanwood

THE red-breasted nuthatch is a quaint-looking, beautifully marked, little bird and well adapted to his work as caretaker of the tree bark. Though he wanders all over North America, this tiny bark surgeon returns to the coniferous forests to build his nest and rear his young. Each spring and autumn the nuthatches call more or less generally throughout the evergreen and mixed growths, and from the trees of the city streets while in migration, but only rarely do they nest in this vicinity in large numbers. One precious tract of ancient woods, bedecked with lichens, overgrown with moss, and, alas, now fast disappearing beneath the axe of the woodsman, always harbors a few red-breasted nuthatches, winter wrens, and golden-crowned kinglets during the breeding season; but it is only occasionally that this bark specialist, the nuthatch, remains to partake of my suet when the snowdrifts lie deep and Jack Frost sketches on the window-panes.

In the year 1912, however, the nuthatches did winter among us; in the spring, the numbers of those that tarried in our midst were augmented by fresh arrivals. The red-breasted nuthatch nested everywhere — in dead stubs and trees in the forest, and even in a dead tree opposite one of the city grammar schools. In April they were so pervaded with the nesting instinct that they bored holes in every dead tree that came within their range.

The nest of the red-breasted nuthatch resembles that of the chickadee and the woodpecker; it is a chamber excavated in a tree. In this locality the bird chooses to fashion his domicile in a dead fir or poplar, the wood of which is soft enough to be easily worked with the beak. A pair of nuthatches spent about eight days hollowing a nest I examined. Both birds worked nearly the same length of time in shaping the nesting chamber. The cavity was fashioned, and the waste wood was removed with the beak; sometimes it was thrown from the door, at other times from the surrounding branches. While the birds were excavating their living-room, they toiled diligently and appeared not to notice my presence. During this stage of nest-building, I sat on a log not far from the nest, and came and went when I chose; but the moment that the birds began to bring shreds of yellow birch bark with which to line the chamber, they became exceedingly wary. Every time that I approached, they ceased all work. No matter how carefully I concealed myself, they were aware of my presence. Lining the nest occupied about five days, After the tiny tenement was entirely fitted up, the parent birds smeared the space around the entrance with pitch; every few days, fresh globules were added.

In due time, eggs were laid. The female brooded the eggs and the faithful mate fed her at the door of the little house and called her away for the rest periods. After the little mother had brooded fourteen wearisome days, both birds began to carry food to the young in the nest.

It was most unsatisfactory to sit on a log, and wonder how many nestlings the birds were feeding, and just how little nuthatches looked! At last I could curb my curiosity no longer. I carefully removed a section of the wood below the nest hole, and found six fragile baby nuthatches about three days old, in the dainty, warm, birch-bark cradle. I avoided keeping the nest open for more than a few seconds for fear of lowering the temperature. The parents fed the young moths, caterpillars and crane flies in large numbers. The last nestling, every inch a nuthatch, left the nest on the eighteenth day. It may be that the young would have occupied this cosy tenement longer had they not been disturbed. The birds had grown so strong and become so active that the dainty, statant cup of shreds of yellow birch bark, that made such an effective cradle for the eggs and the newly-hatched young, had been worn to dust.

While I was observing at this nest, I carried the portion of the trunk containing the young to a studio twice. Although the parent birds always disappeared when I was about the nest, when I returned the young to the woods, they always came and ministered to the offspring in the nest, even when five of them had taken wing many hours before. The parent birds were ever most gentle about the nest and the mother nuthatch most patient as she coaxed one fluffy fledgling after another up a tree trunk to a place of safety, — with crooning notes and a juicy caterpillar.

The red-breasted nuthatch uses all the melodies in his repertoire while ministering to the young in the nest. Besides the common call, *quank!* he has a little song that sounds like a highland fling played on a bagpipe, a trill *pit, pit, pit, pit,* or *pit-ti, pit-ti, pit-ti, pit-ti,* also, a musical twitter.

The calls and the songs of the nuthatch are so inconspicuous that he might spend many hours in the trees of a village street without his presence being discovered, but a bird-lover always hears his nasal *quank! quank!* and cannot refrain from stopping to watch the little gymnast as he walks headforemost down the tree as deftly as he ascends it, or out the underside of a branch with as little effort as he trips along the top of it, all the while dexterously extricating noxious tree vermin from the cracks and crevices in the bark.

Although the red-breasted nuthatch is a bark specialist, he leaves no sources of revenue untapped. Sometimes he gathers insects from the foliage, particularly when the spruce-bud moths are common; occasionally he extricates seeds from the cones, and either eats them or hides them in the crevices of the bark for a day of need; he descends to the ground and forages there, not forgetting to investigate thoroughly each old mossy log and stump.

While the nuthatch is industrious, he loves company, and after his nesting duties are over, he is never too busy to utter his *quank! quank!* to inform his companions of his whereabouts. One autumn I came across a large band of these cheerful gypsies in their favorite forest. They called back and forth constantly. The effect was not unlike that of a pond of hylas in full chorus. If a nuthatch strays from his kind, then he attaches himself to a company of brown creepers, golden-crowned kinglets, and chickadees. To see one of these society-loving birds is to be sure that a troop of foes to insect pests is in the neighborhood.

WOODPECKERS AS WORKMEN

By E. G. Chapin

AMONG American birds probably none — with the exception of robin redbreast — is more widely known and loved than the woodpecker. While the woodpecker may not venture quite so boldly into civilization as does the ubiquitous and jolly robin, he is common enough, at least in some branches of his family, to be found without difficulty in the country stretches, and is handsome, energetic and skilful to a point that repays study. Out of 350 kinds of peckers known to exist, twenty-four species, and a greater number of subspecies, occur in North America. Of these, the hairy and downy are the most common, and, owing to their similarity, are often confused. The red-headed woodpecker, the yellow-bellied sapsucker are well known, while the three-toed log cock (pileated) and the ivory-billed are more rare. Other varieties are known to the student and scientist, — we are here more concerned with the general work done by the woodpeckers, and with their equipment, than with the different kinds possible to identify.

The woodpecker's work is strenuous. First of all, he must take a firm position. This is made possible by the arrangement of the four-toed foot, — two toes forward and two back; and even in the rarer three-toed variety, the back toe is modified and made longer, to serve the same purpose of the usual fore-and-aft distribution, which is that of a clamp. By this strong gripping tool the bird can cling fast in the position it must take in working on tree trunks and large limbs, where ordinary "perching," with the toes curled around, is out of the question. When we consider the force the bird must use to drive his bill into solid wood — green, as well as decaying and dead — the importance of this grip is seen. He is further braced by his tail of twelve feathers, ten of which are stiff enough to act as a prop. The tail is rounded at the end, and, since the bird can move and spread it at will, the tail can be made to fit the tree trunk at any angle necessary to brace the body comfortably. In fact, the feet and tail together make a three-cornered base, allowing the body to swing from the hips in delivering the — relatively — terrific blows. The woodpecker is not unique in the habit of clinging to tree trunks, since nuthatches, brown creepers and titmice also find their pasture on and in the bark, but the woodpecker alone really goes under the surface to get an important item in his diet, namely the boring worm, and he alone digs out of solid wood, instead of building a nest.

His bill is strong and chisel-like, and, according to Forbush, springs from a very thick and hard skull, with a firm but elastic attachment which somewhat breaks the jar of his blows, while the brain is protected by an enveloping cushion of membrane. He drives the bill, with incessant, rapid blows, as a wedge through the bark, striking out small chips, and working with infinite patience until the desired depth is reached, — even to the heart of a tree sometimes, when pursuing a deeply embedded borer. The nostrils are protected by a screen of fine bristles to keep out dust. Even the ability to drill might not always enable the woodpecker to extract a boring grub, for the latter is snug in his tunnel and will brace himself against attack. Here nature has given the bird a further tool in the backward-barbed, extensile tongue, whose structure is amazingly interesting, and admits of its darting some two inches (in certain varieties of peckers) beyond the bill, spearing the prey and dragging it back to be nipped by the strong mandibles. This tongue is supported, we might say steered, by a long, slender bone which branches like a Y at the surface of the skull, the two arms curling under, then up and over, the skull, as the outer end of a wire spring might clutch a knob. This arrangement gives play to the tongue in its darting forth, and also a strong anchorage when the barbs are hooked into a resisting borer.

The various woodpeckers have some little differences in the shape and structure of the bill and tongue, but the general characters are similar. Just how the woodpecker locates his prey when it is invisible is a matter of some dispute. One authority claims that the concussion endured while pecking has affected the bird's hearing; while another assures us that it locates the hidden borer by *listening* to the vibrations it causes in the fibers of the wood. Another theory is that since woodpeckers are commonly seen to trail the wings while hunting, they feel the vibrations. Whatever the method of discovery, the method of work is quick and sure, as with unerring aim the bird drives into the borer's tunnel opposite the point where the worm is lodged. Pictures have been taken showing sections of bark, outside and inside, where the puncture of the bird from the outer surface exactly coincided with the inside spot where the grub lay dormant. The importance of this efficient work on the trees is not confined to the orchard where we so often find the woodpecker at work, but is invaluable in timber lands, particularly among white pines, which are often crippled by the pine weevil. This discerning insect elects the leader or topmost shoot of a vigorous young tree as lodging-place for its eggs, and a juicy pasture for its larvæ, which eat away and destroy the invaluable young stem. As fast as the tree seeks to replace its lost leader by turning up a side branch, the insects destroy that in turn. Since the pine depends for perfect development on the uninterrupted growth of its main stem, when this is riddled the tree is seriously deformed, grows crooked and is ruined for timber purposes.

The woodpecker's careful search for insects, eggs and larvæ, for ants, etc., as well as for the borers within the tree, makes it a natural and perfect guardian of the forest, with whose aid we can never dispense. Though at some seasons the woodpecker takes a certain percentage of vegetable food, this is of wild berries, weed-seed and substances useless to man, and he is never a robber of the garden or orchard. If he is noticed pecking an apple, he should not be condemned without examination of the evidence, which will show the fruit to be wormy, and the worm the desired tidbit. He has, however, one habit which should be noticed in close connection with his *markings*, for while many woodpeckers will tap healthy trees, maples, birches, etc., for sap and a taste of the pulpy inner bark, the occasional punctures made by downy and hairy are *not* considered harmful; the systematic riddling by the yellow-bellied sapsucker *is*. His system is to make a series of punctures that girdle the tree, and to work particularly in the late summer and autumn when the elaborated sap should be feeding down into the roots. The canny tippler knows enough to make an air opening above the point where he wants to drink, thus insuring a free flow of sap. When he has drained one girdle, he begins another higher up, and this process, repeated and thorough, makes an effective check on the downward passage of the life-giving sap, weakening and eventually killing the tree. As many insects are attracted to these sticky sap wounds, and the pecker eats them along with his grog, he does *some* good, and certain naturalists insist that even the sapsucker should be protected. Others admit that he is a plunderer and deserving of execution. The point is that a woodpecker seen taking sap should not be convicted of sin without examining his work and his person to make sure that he is the guilty workman. The sapsucker's holes are grouped with considerable regularity, are a more nearly square shape (with rounded corners) than those of other peckers, and his coat is so marked that a little real observation will identify him. The male downy and hairy have a *small* red patch at the *back* of the head; the females have no red marks at all. Both male and female downy and hairy have unmarked breasts. The male and female sapsuckers have a *large* red patch on the *front* of the head, right down to the bill, and have each a black bib or crescent at the top of the breast, which is yellow-tinged in each case. In addition to this mark, the male sapsucker has a red patch *under* his bill, filling the space within the black crescent, while this spot in the female is white. If these markings and their location are kept in mind, one need not be confused by the general similarity in color scheme which spells "woodpecker," undifferentiated, to the uninformed eye.

The peculiar skill of the woodpeckers in carving nests is told with such closeness of observation in the various passages in Burroughs, that we need not here review this feature of his work, but will trust to the zeal of our readers to discover through John Burroughs's eyes how, when and where this ingenious bird makes his home.

THE BROWN CREEPER

By Cordelia J. Stanwood

ONE of the most interesting birds' nests that I have ever found is that of the brown creeper. The nest of weathered twigs and shredded bark fiber, suspended between a flake of bark and the trunk of a tree, is a wonderful bit of protective coloration. The young birds and the old, likewise, are just the colors of the dead bark, twigs, and leaves. One would suppose that a nest so nearly the color of its surroundings, tucked away under the bark and watched over by such inconspicuous guardians, would be quite safe, but it proves to be no more immune from the depredations of the keen-eyed denizens of the forest than those of other birds. The eggs were destroyed in two nests out of three that I found one summer.

The nest of the brown creeper is most closely related in its construction to that of the vireo. The birds, in starting one nest, fastened spiders' silk to the inside of a flake of bark, and to the tree in parallel loops, six and one fourth inches wide by six inches deep. Later the silk was stretched across from the points of attachment on the bark and the tree, making a sort of hammock. The materials were attached within this deep loop in rough concentric semicircles until there was just space enough, a little to one side of the center, for the wall-pocket-shaped lining.

At another time, I came upon the beginning of a nest that was never completed. In the second instance, the birds fastened fragments of dead wood and weathered twigs to the bark and the tree in the form of an imperfeet hexagon that was flattened laterally, so that it was about three times as long as it was wide. The ends of the hexagon were higher than the center, so that, when the silk was stretched across from the bark to the tree, the hammock took the form of a wide, shallow loop. In this latter style of nest, the material is built up for eight and one half to nine inches before the birds succeed in making a deep enough loop to hold the wall-pocket-shaped lining. Although the creeper builds its nest from the bottom up and from the outside in, as does the cliff swallow, the nest is suspended by spiders' silk between the bark and the tree. While to the casual observer it appears to have the characteristics of the statant, increment nest, it is constructed more after the method of the pensile or pendent type.

The birds construct the nest of materials that they find close at hand. One nest had for its foundation flakes of cedar bark, a few spruce twigs, and a few bits of usnea moss, held together with large knots of spiders' silk. This nest was lined with fine fibers of cedar bark and a few feathers. In a second nest, the foundation was made entirely of spruce twigs bound together with beautiful, large knots of spiders' silk. This nest was likewise lined with cedar-bark fiber and a few feathers. Sometimes the foundation is miscellaneous, and soft shreds of dead wood and silky fibers of yellow birch bark form the lining. Although the foundation of the nest is made of coarse materials, the lining is always so carefully selected, and so finely shredded, that it is as warm and soft as cotton wool. The space between the bark and the tree is not quite wide enough for a lining in the form of a cup; accordingly the bird compromises, models the bottom and one side perfectly, like the large end of an egg, and lets the tree in some cases, and the bark in other instances, serve for the other side of the lining and the nest. Thus the lining is forced to take the form of a wall-pocket, one side being but one half inch deep.

The brown creeper appears to find the best nesting-sites near swamps. On damp land the bark warps off from the firs (and I have found them nesting only in firs) in large flakes or sheets which remain intact at the top or one side, and behind which a creeper can suspend his domicile; but on more elevated land, the bark has a tendency to dry up and burst asunder all over the surface. Commonly the flakes of bark on such trees are not large enough or strong enough to protect a nest.

The brown creepers are very gentle; quite aware that they are being watched, they will go on with their work of nest-building with an observer sitting but three or four yards away. Both birds bring materials, and apparently both birds assist in constructing the nest, for they enter the crevices in the bark at the same time, and remain for a period. When the female works alone the male sings near by. They spend about four days in constructing the nest; they appear to do most of the work in the early part of the day.

I have found the female incubating five and six eggs. The eggs are a pinkish cream-white, wreathed around the crown with brown dots. The first nest that I found was situated three feet above the ground. When I peeped down into the crevice between the bark and the trunk, and saw the six dainty eggs nestling in the little wall-pocket, my enthusiasm was unlimited. As nearly as I have been able to determine, the bird spends twelve or thirteen days in incubation. While the female is brooding, the male feeds her and calls her away for exercise. Both parents feed the young.

While the creeper is common to the eastern part of North America, he is scarcely noticeable in migration unless a person is familiar with his favorite woodlands and follows him there. Here about the middle of April you will hear his wild, sweet song floating down from high spruces and pines, and mingling with those of the winter wren, the red-breasted nuthatch, and the golden-crowned kinglet.

Usually this tiny member of the guild of bark surgeons tarries in this region but a brief period, in the spring and fall. Once in a while one or two remain all winter; occasionally all the year.

A BRAVE LITTLE WIDOWER

By Cordelia J. Stanwood

CARDS BROOK is a jolly little stream. In its winding ways are still, dark reaches where the trout like to hide; but usually its amber waters tumble, rush, bubble, gurgle over large rocks. Near one of these merry places in the brook, just off the highway, amongst a grove of gray birches, two little redstarts chose to rest, one spring after their long journey from South America. They were there before the leaves were out. Often I paused to admire the black-and-flame-colored garb of the male or delight my eye with his marvelous, acrobatic feats as he flew, fell, or whirled through the air, like some bright, wind-tossed, autumn leaf.

But it was not until the thirteenth day of July came that I had an opportunity to look for the nest. That I found it at all is surprising, it proved to be such a good example of protective coloration. The bird had constructed it in the crotch of a gray birch, about twelve feet from the ground where the dark markings of the bark were nearly the color of the nest. To examine the contents of the nest it was necessary to have a platform made and placed beside the tree. While the staging was being adjusted, the female kept her place; but when I climbed to the level of the nest, the bird slid off. A few moments later she returned with food for the young; fed them; and resumed her brooding. The coloring of the little dame resembled a bit of green and yellow foliage, as she settled in the dainty structure. After a time she chirped once, waited awhile, then chirped again. Still the male refused to appear. With a loud *'tchuck*, she flew from the nest and began gathering insects. As she worked, she called so incessantly to her mate that before long the recreant came to her assistance.

Four lively nestlings, either five or six days old, opened their mouths for food when I looked into the nest. Their eyes were narrow slits; the little holes for ears showed plainly. On the feather tract of the back pin feathers were conspicuous, while the quills of the wings were well developed. There was the least indication of a row of quills across the coccyx. Over the entire bird was a thin coat of fine dark-brown down.

Every day I went to the grove to watch the parent birds feed the young with moths, caterpillars, and various insects. The male sang continuously, filling the grove with his "Sis, sis, you wist." The untiring solicitude of the mother bird for the little family was touching.

The fourth day, toward night, the nest seemed very crowded. The following morning, the male visited the nest oftener, appeared more interested, and remained longer than usual. Sometimes he would put a moth in each young bird's mouth, then go the rounds again and poke the morsel well down each tiny throat with his beak. After observing for several hours, I became convinced that what I feared was true, — the female was missing. The fate of the little mother remained a mystery. All the day the father bird sang less than formerly. The young were very sensitive to every sound of his voice. The swallows chattered overhead, the bobolinks caroled near — the young paid not the slightest attention; but let the father bird sing far away or make the faintest chirp, and the nest was on the alert at once. Each bird turned his head in the direction of the sound and stretched until his neck must have been an inch long by actual measurement. When the male neared the nest, each atom was aquiver, with open mouth and fluttering wings, chirping, "Sis-sis-sis-sis" as loudly as it could until it received food, then continuing to chirp until the father bird was out of sight.

Every time the redstart flew away, I was beset with grave fears lest he might grow weary of his task and leave the little ones to perish. Was it possible for the gayly dressed little songster to assume all the cares of a quiet, patient, self-sacrificing mother bird? Thus I questioned as I sat and watched through the long day.

The young would take exercise in turn. Usually the bird at the bottom of the nest would thrust its head high above the rest at the risk of pushing them all out; draw one wing from the tangle of nestlings, then the other, until at length it rested on the backs of the other birds; next it moistened its beak with oil from an oil gland situated on the rump, carefully preened its wing feathers by drawing each one through the beak, and was ready for the first mouthful of food as soon as the father bird came. Each nestling took its place in time at the top, and rested and refreshed itself in the same way. After feeding the young, the father bird carried away the droppings in his beak. Thus the nest was kept perfectly neat.

The young, at this stage, looked like fluffy balls of gray-olive-brown feathers; the crown was lighter than the back, the throat and breast grayer, and the belly whiter. The wing bars were buffy white, the primaries edged with the same color.

Their appetites were insatiable. As the light faded in the grove, they grew more restless. The father bird on the other hand, became more quiet, seldom chirped and never sang. I wondered if the little fellow missed his mate, as the time approached when she was wont to fold the little ones under her wings. Would he take the place of the mother bird on the nest and shield the young through the cool, damp night? After feeding the nestlings between seven o'clock and eight, he flew away. Anxiously I waited until it was quite dark, but he did not return.

Early the next morning, I visited the grove. The nest was empty. The chatter of young birds, however, came from the alders on the brink of the brook. Following the sound, I beheld a pretty tableau. On a branch some four feet above the ground, the father bird was feeding a twittering little redstart. I was greatly relieved to find that the brave little widower had, indeed, assumed the full care of his motherless family.

THE PURPLE MARTIN

By Olive Thorne Miller

SWALLOWS more than any other birds like to make use of our buildings for their own homes. Barn swallows take the beams inside the barns, eaves swallows settle under the eaves outside, and purple martins, the largest of the family, choose bird houses which we put up for them.

It is said that purple martins will not stay anywhere that men have not made homes for them. But I have seen them living in a place not put up for them, though perhaps they thought it was. It was under a terra-cotta covering to a cornice on a business block in the middle of a busy city. The terra cotta was shaped like a large pipe cut in half, the long way. This half cylinder was laid on top of the brick cornice, and that made a little roof, you see. The whole length of that cornice was thus made into one long room, with a brick floor and terra-cotta roof, and an entrance at the end. That room must have had a dozen martin nests, for a flock was all the time sailing about in the air, above the roofs of the houses.

As these birds eat only flying insects, they cannot stay with us when it is too cool for insects to fly abroad. So they leave us very early. When the little ones are out of the nest and can fly well, swallows from all the country around collect in great flocks, and go to some swamp, or lonely place where people do not go much. There the young ones are taught and exercised every day in flying. And some day we shall go out and find them all gone, not a swallow to be seen. They have started for their winter home, which is far south, in tropical countries, where insects never fail; but it is a comfort to think that next summer we shall have them back with us again.

The swallows I have mentioned, barn swallow, eaves swallow, and purple martin, are found all over our country.

Let me tell you a story that shows the purple martin has a good deal of sense. One of these birds built in a box under a window, fixed so that the owner could open it and take out eggs. He took out several, one at a time, and at last he took out one of the birds.

The mate of the stolen bird went off and in a few days came back with another mate. The box was too good to give up, so both the birds went to work to make it safe against the nest robber. They built up a wall of mud before the too handy back door. The egg thief could not get in without breaking down the wall, and he was ashamed to do that. So the birds kept their pleasant home, and reared their family there.

WHY I DID NOT SEE THE GROSBEAK

By Bradford Torrey

I WAS sauntering idly along the path (idleness like this is often the best of ornithological industry), when suddenly I had a vision! Before me, in the leafy top of an oak sapling, sat a blue grosbeak. I knew him on the instant. But I could see only his head and neck, the rest of his body being hidden by the leaves. It was a moment of feverish excitement. Here was a new bird, a bird about which I had felt fifteen years of curiosity; and, more than that, a bird which here and now was quite unexpected, since it was not included in either of the two Florida lists that I had brought with me from home. For perhaps five seconds I had my opera glass on the blue head and the thick-set, dark bill, with its lighter-colored under mandible. Then I heard the clatter of a horse's hoofs, and lifted my eyes. My friend, the owner of the plantation, was coming down the road at a gallop, straight upon me. If I was to see the grosbeak and make sure of him, it must be done at once. I moved to bring him fully into view, and he flew into the thick of a pine tree out of sight. But the tree was not far off, and if Mr. —— would pass me with a nod, the case was still far from hopeless. A bright thought came to me. I ran from the path with a great show of eager absorption, leveled my glass upon the pine tree, and stood fixed. Perhaps Mr. —— would take the hint. Alas! he had too much courtesy to pass his own guest without speaking. "Still after the birds?" he said, as he checked his horse. I responded, as I hope, without any symptom of annoyance. Then, of course, he wished to know what I was looking at, and I told him that a blue grosbeak had just flown into that pine tree, and that I was most distressingly anxious to see more of him. He looked at the pine tree. "I can't see him," he said. No more could I. "It was n't a blue jay, was it?" he asked. And then we talked of one thing and another, I have no idea what, till he rode away to another part of the plantation where a gang of women were at work. By this time the grosbeak had disappeared utterly. Possibly he had gone to a bit of wood on the opposite side of the cane swamp. I scaled a barbed-wire fence and made in that direction, but to no purpose. The grosbeak was gone for good. Probably I should never see another. Could the planter have read my thoughts just then he would perhaps have been angry with himself, and pretty certainly he would have been angry with me. That a Yankee should accept his hospitality, and then load him with curses and call him all manner of names: How should he know that I was so insane a hobbyist as to care more for the sight of a new bird than for all the laws and customs of ordinary politeness? As my feelings cooled, I saw that I was stepping over hills or rows of some strange-looking plants just out of the ground. Peanuts, I guessed;

but to make sure I called to a colored woman who was hoeing not far off. "What are these?" "Pinders," she answered. I knew she meant "goobers," — and now that I once more have a dictionary at my elbow, I learn that the word, like "goober," is, or is supposed to be, of African origin.

I was preparing to surmount the barbed-wire fence again, when the planter returned and halted for another chat. It was evident that he took a genuine and amiable interest in my researches. There were a great many kinds of sparrows in that country, he said, and also of woodpeckers. He knew the ivorybill, but, like other Tallahasseans, he thought I should have to go into Lafayette County (all Florida people say La*fay*-ette) to find it. "That bird calling now is a bee bird," he said, referring to a kingbird; "and we have a bird that is called the French mocking bird; he catches other birds." The last remark was of interest for its bearing upon a point about which I had felt some curiosity, and, I may say, some skepticism, as I had seen many loggerhead shrikes, but had observed no indication that other birds feared them or held any grudge against them. As he rode off he called my attention to a great blue heron just then flying over the swamp. "They are very shy," he said. Then, from farther away, he shouted once more to ask if I heard the mocking bird singing yonder, pointing with his whip in the direction of the singer.

For some time longer I hung about the glade, vainly hoping that the grosbeak would again favor my eyes. Then I crossed more planted fields, — climbing more barbed-wire fences, and stopping on the way to enjoy the sweetly quaint music of a little chorus of white-crowned sparrows, — and skirted once more the muddy shore of the cane swamp, where the yellowlegs and sand-pipers were still feeding. That brought me to the road from which I had made my entry to the place some days before; but being still unable to forego a splendid possibility, I recrossed the plantation, tarried again in the glade, sat again on the wooden fence (if that grosbeak only *would* show himself!) and thence went on, picking a few heads of handsome buffalo clover, the first I had ever seen, and some sprays of pentstemon, till I came again to the six-barred gate and the Quincy road. At that point, as I now remember, the air was full of vultures (carrion crows), a hundred or more, soaring over the fields in some fit of gregariousness. Along the road were white-crowned and white-throated sparrows (it was the 12th of April), orchard orioles, thrashers, summer tanagers, myrtle and palm warblers, cardinal grosbeaks, mocking birds, kingbirds, loggerheads, yellow-throated vireos, and sundry others, but not the blue grosbeak, which would have been worth them all.

Once back at the hotel, I opened my Coues's Key to refresh my memory as to the exact appearance of that bird. "Feathers around the base of bill black," said the book. I had not noticed that. But no matter; the bird was a blue grosbeak, for the sufficient reason that it could not be anything else. A black line between the almost black beak and the dark-blue head would be inconspicuous at the best, and quite naturally would escape a glimpse so hasty as mine had been. And yet, while

I reasoned in this way, I foresaw plainly enough that, as time passed, doubt would get the better of assurance, as it always does, and I should never be certain that I had not been the victim of some illusion. At best, the evidence was worth nothing for others. If only that excellent Mr. ——, for whose kindness I was unfeignedly thankful (and whose pardon I most sincerely beg if I seem to have been a bit too free in this rehearsal of the story), if only Mr. —— could have left me alone for ten minutes longer!

HUMMERS

By Florence Merriam Bailey

CALIFORNIA is the land of flowers and humming birds. Humming birds are there the winged companions of the flowers. In the valleys the airy birds hover about the filmy golden mustard and the sweet-scented primroses; on the blooming hillsides in spring the air is filled with whirring wings and piping voices, as the fairy troops pass and repass at their mad gambols. At one moment the birds are circling methodically around the whorls of the blue sage; at the next, hurtling through the air after a distant companion. The great wild gooseberry bushes with red fuchsia-like flowers are like beehives, swarming with noisy hummers. The whizzing and whirring lead one to the bushes from a distance, and on approaching one is met by the brown spindle-like birds, darting out from the blooming shrubs, gleams of green, gold, and scarlet glancing from their gorgets.

The large brown hummers probably stop in the valley only on their way north, but the little black-chinned ones make their home there, and the big spreading sycamores and the great live oaks are their nesting grounds. In the big oak beside the ranch house I have seen two or three nests at once; and a ring of live oaks in front of the house held a complement of nests. From the hammock under the oak beside the house one could watch the birds at their work. If the front door was left open, the hummers would sometimes fly inside; and as we stepped out they often darted away from the flowers growing under the windows.

California is the place of all places to study humming birds. The only drawback is that there are always too many other birds to watch at the same time; but one sees enough to want to see more. I never saw a humming bird courtship unless — perhaps one performance I saw was part of the wooing. I was sitting on Mountain Billy under the little lover's sycamore when a buzzing and a whirring sounded overhead. On a twig sat a wee green lady and before her was her lover (?), who, with the sound and regularity of a spindle in a machine, swung shuttling from side to side in an arc less than a yard long. He never turned around, or took his eyes off his lady's, but threw himself back at the end of his line by a quick spread of his tail. She sat with her eyes fixed upon him, and as he moved from side to side her long bill followed him in a very droll way. When through with his dance he looked at her intently, as if to see what effect his performance had had upon her. She made some remark, apparently not to his liking, for when he had answered he flew away. She called after him, but as he did not return she stretched herself and flew up on a twig above with an amusing air of relief.

This is all I have ever seen of the courtship; but when it comes to nest building, I have often been an eyewitness to that. One little acquaintance made a nest of yellow down and put it among the green oak leaves, making me think that the laws of protective coloration had no weight with her, but before the eggs were laid she had neatly covered the yellow with flakes of green lichen. I found her one day sitting in the sun with the top of her head as white as though she had been diving into the flour barrel. Here was one of the wonderful cases of "mutual help" in nature. The flowers supply insects and honey to the humming birds, and they, in turn, as they fly from blossom to blossom probing the tubes with the long slender bills that have gradually come to fit the shape of the tubes, brush off the pollen of one blossom to carry it on to the next, so enabling the plants to perfect their flowers as they could not without help. It is said that, in proportion to their numbers, humming birds assist as much as insects in the work of cross-fertilization.

Though this little hummer that I was watching let me come within a few feet of her, when a lizard ran under her bush she craned her neck and looked over her shoulder at him with surprising interest. She doubtless recognized him as one of her egg-eating enemies, on whose account she put her nest at the tip of a twig too slender to serve as a ladder.

Another humming bird who built across the way was still more trustful — with people. I used to sit leaning against the trunk of her oak and watch the nest, which was near the tip of one of the long swinging branches that drooped over the trail. When the tiny worker was at home, a yardstick would almost measure the distance between us. As she sat on the nest she sometimes turned her head to look down at the dog lying beside me, and often hovered over us on going away.

The nest was saddled on a twig and glued to a glossy dark green oak leaf. Like the other nest, it was made of a spongy yellow substance, probably down from the underside of sycamore leaves; and like it, also, the outside was coated with lichen and wound with cobweb. The bird was a rapid worker, buzzing in with her material and then buzzing off after more. Once I saw the cobweb hanging from her needle-like bill, and thought she probably had been tearing down the beautiful suspension bridges the spiders hang from tree to tree.

It was very interesting to see her work. She would light on the rim of the nest, or else drop directly into the bottom of the tiny cup, and place her material with the end of her long bill. It looked like trying to sew at arm's length. She had to draw back her head in order not to reach beyond the nest. How much more convenient it would have been if her bill had been jointed! It seemed better suited to probing flower tubes than making nests. But then, she made nests only in spring, while she fed from flowers all the year round, and so could afford to stretch her neck a trifle one month for the sake of having a good long fly spear during the other eleven. The peculiar feature of her work was her quivering motion in molding. When her material was placed she molded her nest like a potter, twirling around against the sides, sometimes pressing so hard she ruffled up the feathers of her breast. She shaped her cup as if it were a piece of clay. To round the outside, she would sit on the rim and lean over, smoothing the sides with her bill, often with the same peculiar tremulous motion. When working on the outside, at times she almost lost her balance, and fluttered to keep from falling. To turn around in the nest she lifted herself by whirring her wings.

When she found a bit of her green lichen about to fall, she took the loose end in her bill and drew it over the edge of the nest, fastening it securely inside. She looked very wise and motherly as she sat there at work, preparing a home for her brood. After building rapidly she would take a short rest on a twig in the sun, while she plumed her feathers. She made nest making seem very pleasant work.

One day, wanting to experiment, I put a handful of oak blossoms on the nest. They covered the cup and hung down over the sides. When the small builder came, she hovered over it a few seconds before making up her mind how it got there and what she had better do about it. Then she calmly lit on top of it! Part of it went off as she did so, but the rest she appropriated, fastening in the loose ends with the cobweb she had brought.

She often gave a little squeaky call when on the nest, as if talking to herself about her work. When going off for material she would dart away and then, as if it suddenly occurred to her that she did not know where she was going, would stop and stand perfectly still in the air, her vibrating wings sustaining her till she made up her mind, when she would shoot off at an angle. It seemed as if she would be worn out before night, but her eyes were bright and she looked vigorous enough to build half a dozen houses.

"There 's odds in folks," our great-grandmothers used to say; and there certainly is in bird folks; even in the ways of the same one at different times. Now this humming bird was content to build right in front of my eyes, and the hummer down at the little lover's tree, with her first nest, was so indifferent to Billy and me that I took no pains to keep at a distance or disguise the fact that I was watching her. But when her nest was destroyed she suddenly grew old in the ways of the world, and apparently repented having trusted us. In any case, I got a lesson on being too prying. The first nest had not been down long before I found that a second one was being built only a few feet away — by the same bird? I imagined so. The nest was only just begun, and being especially interested to see how such buildings were started, I rode close up to watch the work. A roll of yellow sycamore down was wound around a twig, and the bottom of the nest — the floor — attached to the underside of this beam; with such a solid foundation, the walls could easily be supported.

The small builder came when Billy and I were there. She did not welcome us as old friends, but sat down on her floor and looked at us — and I never saw her there again. Worse than that, she took away her nest, presumably to put it down where she thought inquisitive reporters would not intrude. I was disappointed and grieved, having already planned — on the strength of the first experience — to have the mother hummer's picture taken when she was feeding her young on the nest.

At first I thought this suspicion reflected upon the good sense of humming birds, but after thinking it over concluded that it spoke better for humming birds than for Billy and me. If this were, as I supposed, the same bird who had to brood her young with Billy grazing at the end of her bill, and if she had been present at the unlucky moment when he got the oak branches tangled in the pommel of the saddle, although her branch was not among them, I can but admire her for moving when she found that the Philistines were again upon her, for her new house was hung at the tip of a branch that Billy might easily have swept in passing.

These nests had all been very low, only four or five feet above the ground; but one day I found young in one of the common tree-top nests. I could see it through the branches. Two little heads stuck up above the edge like two small Jacks-in-boxes. Billy made such a noise under the oak when the bird was feeding the youngsters that I took him away where he could not disturb the family, and tied him to an oak covered with poison ivy, for he was especially fond of eating it, and the poison did not affect him.

Before the old hummer flew off, she picked up a tiny white feather that she found in the nest, and wound it around a twig. On her return, in the midst of her feeding, she darted down and set the feather flying; but as it got away from her, she caught it again. The performance was repeated the next time she came with food; but she did it all so solemnly I could not tell whether she were playing or trying to get rid of something that annoyed her.

She fed at the long intervals that are so trying to an observer, for if you are going to sit for hours with your eyes glued to a nest, it really is pleasant to have something happen once in a while! Though the mother bird did not go to the nest often, she sometimes flew by, and once the sound of her wings roused the young, and they called out to her as she passed. When they were awake, it was amusing to see the little midgets stick out their long, thread-like tongues, preen their pin-feathers, and stretch their wings over the nest.

One fine morning when I went to the oak I heard a faint squeak, and saw something fluttering up in the tree. When the mother came, she buzzed about as though not liking the look of things, for her children were out of the nest, and behold! — a horse and rider were under her tree. She tried to coax the unruly nestlings to follow her into the upper stories, but they would not go.

Although not ready to be led, one of the infants soon felt that it would be nice to go alone. When a bird first leaves the nest it goes about very gingerly, but this little fellow now began to feel his strength and the excitement of his freedom. He wiped his tongue on a branch, and then, to my astonishment, his wings began to whirl as if he were getting up steam, and presently they lifted him from his twig, and he went whirring off as softly as a humming-bird moth, among the oak sprays. His nerves were evidently on edge, for he looked around at the sound of falling leaves, started when Billy sneezed, and turned from side to side very apprehensively, in spite of his out-in-the-world, big-boy airs. He may have felt hampered by his unused wings, for, as he sat there waiting for his mother to come, he stroked them out with his bill to get them in better working order. That done, he leaned over, rounded his shoulders, and pecked at a leaf as if he were as much grown up as anybody.

Of all the beautiful humming birds' nests I saw in California, three are particularly noteworthy because of their positions. One cup was set down on what looked like an inverted saucer, in the form of a dark green oak leaf wound with cobweb. That was in the oak beside the ranch-house. Another one was on a branch of eucalyptus, set between two leaves like the knot in a bow of stiff ribbon. To my great satisfaction, the photographer was able to induce the bird to have a sitting while she brooded her eggs. The third nest I imagined belonged to the bird who took up her floor because Billy and I looked at her. If she were, her fate was certainly hard, for her eggs were taken by some one, boy or beast. Her nest was most skillfully supported. It was fastened like the seat of a swing between two twigs no larger than knitting needles, at the end of a long drooping branch. It was a unique pleasure to see the tiny bird sit in her swing and be blown by the wind. Sometimes she went circling about as though riding in a merry-go-round; and at others the wind blew so hard her round boat rose and fell like a little ship at sea.

A WIDOW AND TWINS

By Bradford Torrey

"The fatherless and the widow . . . shall eat and be satisfied." — DEUTERONOMY XIV. 29.

ON the 1st of June, 1890, I formally broke away from ornithological pursuits. For two months, more or less, — till the autumnal migration should set in, — I was determined to have my thoughts upon other matters. There is no more desirable plaything than an outdoor hobby, but a man ought not to be forever in the saddle. Such, at all events, had always been my opinion, so that I long ago promised myself never to become, what some of my aquaintances, perhaps with too much reason, were now beginning to consider me, a naturalist, and nothing else. That would be letting the hobby-horse run away with its owner. For the time being, then, birds should pass unnoticed, or be looked at only when they came in my way. A sensible resolve. But the maker of it was neither Mede nor Persian, as the reader, if he have patience enough, may presently discover for himself.

As I sat upon the piazza, in the heat of the day, busy or half busy with a book, a sound of humming bird's wings now and then fell on my ear, and, as I looked toward the honeysuckle vine, I began after a while to remark that the visitor was invariably a female. I watched her probe the scarlet tubes and dart away, and then returned to my page. She might have a nest somewhere near; but if she had there was small likelihood of my finding it, and, besides, I was just now not concerned with such trifles. On the 24th of June, however, a passing neighbor dropped into the yard. Was I interested in humming birds, he inquired. If so, he could show me a nest. I put down my book, and went with him at once.

The beautiful structure, a model of artistic workmanship, was near the end of one of the lower branches of an apple tree, eight or ten feet from the ground, saddled upon the dropping limb at a point where two offshoots made a good holding place, while an upright twig spread over it a leafy canopy against rain and sun. Had the builders sought my advice as to a location, I could hardly have suggested one better suited to my own convenience. The tree was within a stone's toss of my window, and, better still, the nest was overlooked to excellent advantage from an old bank wall which divided my premises from those of my next-door neighbor. How could I doubt that Providence itself had set me a summer lesson?

At our first visit the discoverer of the nest — from that moment an ornithologist — brought out a step-ladder, and we looked in upon the two tiny white eggs, considerately improving a temporary absence of the owner for that purpose. It was a picture to please not only the eye, but the imagination; and before I could withdraw my gaze the mother bird was back again, whisking about my head so fearlessly that for a moment I stood still, half expecting her to drop into the nest within reach of my hand.

This, as I have said, was on the 24th of June. Six days later, on the afternoon of the 30th, the eggs were found to be hatched, and two lifeless-looking things lay in the bottom of the nest, their heads tucked out of sight, and their bodies almost or quite naked, except for a line of grayish down along the middle of the back.

Meanwhile, I had been returning with interest the visits of the bird to our honeysuckle, and by this time had fairly worn a path to a certain point in the wall, where, comfortably seated in the shade of the hummer's own tree, and armed with opera glass and notebook, I spent some hours daily in playing the spy upon her motherly doings.

For a widow with a house and family upon her hands, she took life easily; at frequent intervals she absented herself altogether, and even when at home she spent no small share of the time in flitting about among the branches of the tree. On such occasions, I often saw her hover against the bole or a patch of leaves, or before a piece of caterpillar or spider web, making quick thrusts with her bill, evidently after bits of something to eat. On quitting the nest, she commonly perched upon one or another of a certain set of dead twigs in different parts of the tree, and at once shook out her feathers and spread her tail, displaying its handsome white markings, indicative of her sex. This was the beginning of a leisurely toilet operation, in the course of which she scratched herself with her feet and dressed her feathers with her bill, all the while darting out her long tongue with lightning-like rapidity, as if to moisten her beak, which at other times she cleansed by rubbing it down with her claws or by wiping it upon a twig. In general she paid little attention to me, though she sometimes hovered directly in front of my face, as if trying to stare me out of countenance. One of the most pleasing features of the show was her method of flying into the nest. She approached it, without exception, from the same quarter, and, after an almost imperceptible hovering motion, shut her wings and dropped upon the eggs.

When the young were hatched I redoubled my attentions. Now I should see her feed them. On the first afternoon I waited a long time for this purpose, the mother conducting herself in her customary manner: now here, now there, preening her plumage, driving away a meddlesome sparrow, probing the florets of a convenient clover head (an unusual resource, I think), or snatching a morsel from some leaf or twig. Suddenly she flew at me, and held herself at a distance of perhaps four feet from my nose. Then she wheeled, and, as I thought, darted out of the orchard. In a few seconds I turned my head, and there she sat in the nest! I owned myself beaten. While I had been gazing toward the meadow, she had probably done exactly what I had wasted the better part of the afternoon in attempting to see.

Twenty-four hours later I was more successful, though the same ruse was again tried upon me. The mother left the nest at my approach, but in three minutes (by the watch) flew in again. She brooded for nine minutes. Then, quite of her own motion, she disappeared for six minutes. On her return she spent four minutes in dressing her feathers, after which she alighted on the edge of the nest, fed the little ones, and took her place upon them. This time she brooded for ten minutes. Then she was away for six minutes, dallied about the tree for two minutes longer, and again flew into the nest. While sitting, she pecked several times in quick succession at a twig within reach, and I could plainly see her mandibles in motion, as if she were swallowing. She brooded for thirteen minutes, absented herself for three minutes, and spent six minutes in her usual cautionary maneuvers before resuming her seat. For the long interval of twenty-two minutes she sat still. Then she vanished for four minutes, and on her return gave the young another luncheon, after a fast of one hour and six minutes.

The feeding process, which I had been so desirous to see, was of a sort to make the spectator shiver. The mother, standing on the edge of the nest, with her tail braced against its side, like a woodpecker or a creeper, took a rigidly erect position, and craned her neck until her bill was in a perpendicular line above the short, wide-open, upraised beak of the little one, who, it must be remembered, was at this time hardly bigger than a humblebee. Then she thrust her bill for its full length down into his throat, a frightful-looking act, followed by a series of murderous gesticulations, which fairly made one observer's blood run cold.

On the day after this (on the 2d of July, that is to say) I climbed into the tree, in the old bird's absence, and stationed myself where my eyes were perhaps fifteen feet from the nest, and a foot or two above its level. At the end of about twenty minutes, the mother, who meantime had made two visits to the tree, flew into place and brooded for seventeen minutes. Then she disappeared again, and on her return, after numberless pretty feints and sidelong approaches, alighted on the wall of the nest, and fed both little ones. The operation, though still sufficiently reckless, looked less like infanticide than before, — a fact due, as I suppose, to my more elevated position, from which the nestlings' throats were better seen. After this she brooded for another seventeen minutes. On the present occasion, as well as on many others, it was noticeable that, while sitting upon the young, she kept up an almost incessant motion, as if seeking to warm them, or perhaps to develop their muscles by a kind of massage treatment. A measure of such hitchings and fidgetings might have meant nothing more than an attempt to secure for herself a comfortable seat; but when they were persisted in for fifteen minutes together, it was difficult not to believe that she had some different end in view. Possibly, as human infants get exercise by dandling on the mother's knee, the baby humming bird gets his by this parental kneading process. Whether brooding or feeding, it must be said that the hummer treated her tiny charges with no particular carefulness, so far as an outsider could judge.

The next day I climbed again into the tree. The mother bird made off at once, and did not resume her seat for almost an hour, though she would undoubtedly have done so earlier but for my presence. Again and again she perched near me, her bill leveled straight at my face. Finally she alighted on the nest, and, after considerable further delay, as if to assure herself that everything was quite safe, fed the two chicks from her throat, as before. "She thrust her bill into their mouths so far" (I quote my notes) "that the tips of their short little beaks were up against the root of her mandibles!"

Only once more, on the 4th of July, I ventured into the apple tree. For more than an hour and a half I waited. Times without number the mother came buzzing into the tree, made the circuit of her favorite perches, dressed her plumage, darted away again, and again returned, till I was almost driven to get down, for her relief. At last she fed the nestlings, who by this time must have been all but starved, as indeed they seemed to be. "The tips of their bills *do* come clean up to the base of the mother's mandibles." So I wrote in my journal; for it is the first duty of a naturalist to verify his own observations.

On the 10th we again brought out the ladder. Though at least eleven days old, the tiny birds — the "widow's mites," as my facetious neighbor called them — were still far from filling the cup. While I stood over it, one of them uttered some pathetic little cries that really went to my heart. His bill, perceptibly longer than on the 5th, was sticking just above the border of the nest. I touched it at the tip, but he did not stir. Craning my neck, I could see his open eye. Poor, helpless things! Yet within three months they would be flying to Central America, or some more distant clime. How little they knew what was before them! As little as I know what is before me.

The violence of the feeding act was now at its height, I think, but it would be impossible to do justice to it by any description. My neighbor, who one day stood beside me looking on, was moved to loud laughter. When the two beaks were tightly joined, and while the old bird's was being gradually withdrawn, they were shaken convulsively, — by the mother's attempts to disgorge, and perhaps by the young fellow's efforts to hasten the operation. It was plain that he let go with reluctance, as a boy sucks the very tip of the spoon to get the last drop of jam; but, as will be mentioned in the course of the narrative, his behavior improved greatly in this respect as he grew older.

On the 12th, just after the little ones had been fed, one of them got his wings for the first time above the wall of the nest, and fluttered them with much spirit. He had spent almost a fortnight in the cradle, and was beginning to think he had been a baby long enough.

From the first I had kept in mind the question whether the feeding of the young by regurgitation, as described briefly by Audubon, and more in detail by Mr. William Brewster,[1] would be continued after the nestlings were fully grown. On the 14th I wrote in my journal: "The method of feeding remains unchanged, and, as it seems, is likely to remain so to the end. It must save the mother much labor in going and coming, and perhaps renders the coöperation of

[1] *The Auk,* vol. VII, p. 206.

the male parent unnecessary.'" This prediction was fulfilled, but with a qualification to be hereafter specified.

Every morning, now, I went to the apple tree uncertain whether the nest would not be found empty. According to Audubon, Nuttall, Mr. Burroughs, and Mrs. Treat, young humming birds stay in the nest only seven days. Mr. Brewster, in his notes already cited, says that the birds on which his observations were made — in the garden of Mr. E. S. Hoar, in Concord — were hatched on the 4th of July,[1] and forsook the nest on the 18th. My birds were already fifteen days old, at least, and, unless they were to prove uncommonly backward specimens, ought to be on the wing forthwith. Nevertheless they were in no haste. Day after day passed. The youngsters looked more and more like old birds, and the mother grew constantly more and more nervous.

On the 18th I found her in a state of unprecedented excitement, squeaking almost incessantly. At first I attributed this to concern at my presence, but after a while it transpired that a young oriole — a blundering, tailless fellow — was the cause of the disturbance. By some accident he had dropped into the leafy treetop, as guiltless of any evil design as one of her own nestlings. How she did buzz about him! In and out among the branches she went, now on this side of him, now on that,

[1] But Mr. Hoar, from whom Mr. Brewster had his dates, informs me that the time of hatching was not certainly known; and from Mr. Brewster's statement about the size of the nestlings, I cannot doubt that they had been out of the shell some days longer than Mr. Hoar then supposed.

and now just over his back; all the time squeaking fiercely, and carrying her tail spread to its utmost. The scene lasted for some minutes. Through it all the two young birds kept perfectly quiet, never once putting up their heads, even when the mother, buzzing and calling, zigzagged directly about the nest. I had seen many birds in the tree, first and last, but none that created anything like such a stir. The mother was literally in a frenzy. She went the round of her perches, but could stay nowhere. Once she dashed out of the tree for an instant, and drove a sparrow away from the tomato patch. Ordinarily his presence there would not have annoyed her in the least, but in her present state of mind she was ready to pounce upon anybody. All of which shows once more how "human-like" birds are. The bewilderment of the oriole was comical. "What on earth can this crazy thing be shooting about my ears in this style for?" I imagined him saying to himself. In fact, as he glanced my way, now and then, with his innocent baby face, I could almost believe that he was appealing to me with some such inquiry.

The next morning ("at 7.32," as my diary is careful to note) one of the twins took his flight. I was standing on the wall, with my glass leveled upon the nest, when I saw him exercising his wings. The action was little more pronounced than had been noticed at intervals during the last three or four days, except that he was more decidedly on his feet. Suddenly, without making use of the rim of the nest, as I should have expected him to do, he was in the air, hovering in the prettiest fashion, and in a moment more had alighted on a leafless twig slightly above the level of the nest, and perhaps a yard from it. Within a minute the mother appeared, buzzing and calling, with answering calls from the youthful adventurer. At once — after a hasty reconnaissance of the man on the wall — she perched beside him, and plunged her bill into his throat. Then she went to the nest, served the other one in the same way, and made off. She had no time to waste at this juncture of affairs.

When she had gone, I stepped up to the trunk of the tree to watch the little fellow more closely. He held his perch, and occupied himself with dressing his plumage, though, as the breeze freshened, he was compelled once in a while to keep his wings in motion to prevent the wind from carrying him away. When the old bird returned, — in just half an hour, — she resented my intrusion (what an oppressor of the widow and the fatherless she must by this time have thought me!) in the most unmistakable manner, coming more than once quite within reach. However, she soon gave over these attempts at intimidation, perched beside the percher, and again put something into his maw. This time she did not feed the nestling. As she took her departure, she told the come-outer — or so I fancied — that there was a man under the tree, a pestilent fellow, and it would be well to get a little out of his reach. At all events, she had scarcely disappeared before the youngster was again on the wing. It was wonderful how much at home he seemed, — poising, backing, soaring, and alighting with all the ease and grace of an old hand.

One only piece of awkwardness I saw him commit: he dropped upon a branch much too large for his tiny feet, and was manifestly uncomfortable. But he did did not stay long, and at his next alighting was well up in the tree, where it was noticeable that he remained ever after.

With so much going on outside, it was hard to remain indoors, and finally I took a chair to the orchard, and gave myself up to watching the drama. The feeding process, though still always by regurgitation, was by this time somewhat different from what it had been when the bills of the young were less fully developed. In my notes of this date I find the following description of it: "Number Two is still in the nest, but uneasy. At 10.25 the mother appeared and fed him.[1] Her beak was thrust into his mouth at right angles, — the change being necessitated, probably, by the greater length of his bill, — and he seemed to be jerking strenuously at it. Then he opened his beak and remained motionless, while the black mandibles of the mother could be seen running down out of sight into his throat."

The other youngster, Number One, as I now called him, stayed in the tree, or at most ventured only into the next one, and was fed at varying intervals, — as often, apparently, as the busy mother could find anything to give him. Would he go back to his cradle for the night? It seemed not improbable, notwithstanding he had shown no sign of such an intention so long as

[1] For convenience, I use the masculine pronoun in speaking of both the young birds; but I knew nothing as to the sex of either of them, though I came finally to believe that one was a male and the other a female.

daylight lasted. At 3.50 the next morning, therefore, I stole out to see. No: Number Two was there alone.

At seven o'clock, when I made my second visit, the mother was in the midst of another day's hard work. Twice within five minutes she brought food to the nestling. Once the little fellow — not so very little now — happened to be facing east, while the old bird alighted, as she had invariably done, on the western side. The youngster, instead of facing about, threw back his head and opened his beak. "Look out, there!" exclaimed my fellow-observer; "you 'll break his neck if you feed him in that way." But she did not mind. Young birds' necks are not so easily broken. Within ten minutes of this time she fed Number One, giving him three doses. They were probably small, however (and small wonder), for he begged hard for more, opening his bill with an appealing air. The action in this case was particularly well seen, and the vehement jerking, while the beaks were glued together, seemed almost enough to pull the young fellow's head off. Within another ten minutes the mother was again ministering to Number Two! Poor little widow! Between her incessant labors of this kind and her overwhelming anxiety whenever any strange bird came near, I began to be seriously alarmed for her. As a member of a strictly American family, she was in a fair way, I thought, to be overtaken by the "most American of diseases," — nervous prostration. It tired me to watch her.

With us, and perhaps with her likewise, it was a question whether Number Two would remain in the nest for the day. He grew more and more restless; as my companion — a learned man — expressed it, he began to "ramp round." Once he actually mounted the rim of the nest, a thing which his more precocious brother had never been seen to do, and stretched forward to pick at a neighboring stem. Late that afternoon the mother fed him five times within an hour, instead of once an hour, or thereabouts, as had been her habit three weeks before. She meant to have him in good condition for the coming event; and he, on his part, was active to the same end, — standing upon the wall of the nest again and again, and exercising his wings till they made a cloud about him. A dread of launching away still kept him back, however, and shortly after seven o'clock I found him comfortably disposed for the night. "He is now on his twenty-first day (at least) in the nest. To-morrow will see him go." So end my day's notes.

At 5.45 the next morning he was still there. At 6.20 I absented myself for a few minutes, and on returning was hailed by my neighbor with the news that the nest was empty. Number Two had flown between 6.25 and 6.30, but, unhappily, neither of us was at hand to give him a cheer. I trust that he and his mother were not hurt in their feelings by the oversight. The whole family (minus the father) was still in the apple tree; the mother full, and more than full, of business, feeding one youngster after the other, as they sat here and there in the upper branches.

Twenty-four hours later, as I stood in the orchard, I heard a hum of wings, and found the mother over my head. Presently she flew into the top of the tree, and the next instant was sitting beside one of the young ones. His hungry mouth was already wide open, but before feeding him she started up from the twig, and circled about him so closely as almost or quite to touch him with her wings. On completing the circle she dropped upon the perch at his side, but immediately rose again, and again flew round him. It was a beautiful act,—beautiful beyond the power of any words of mine to set forth; an expression of maternal ecstasy, I could not doubt, answering to the rapturous caresses and endearments in which mothers of human infants are so frequently seen indulging. Three days afterward, to my delight, I saw it repeated in every particular, as if to confirm my opinion of its significance. The sight repaid all my watchings thrice over, and even now I feel my heart growing warm at the recollection of it. Strange thoughtlessness, is it not, which allows mothers capable of such passionate devotion, tiny, defenseless things, to be slaughtered by the million for the enhancement of woman's charms!

At this point we suddenly became aware that for at least a day or two the old bird had probably been feeding her offspring in two ways, — sometimes by regurgitation, and sometimes by a simple transfer from beak to beak. The manner of our discovery was somewhat laughable. The mother perched beside one of the young birds, put her bill into his, and then apparently fell off the limb head first. We thought she had not finished, and looked to see her return; but she flew away and after a while the truth dawned upon us. Thereafter, unless our observation was at fault, she used whichever method happened to suit her convenience. If she found a choice collection of spiders,[1] for instance, she brought them in her throat (as cedar birds carry cherries), to save trips; if she had only one or two, she retained them between her mandibles. It will be understood, I suppose, that we did not see the food in its passage from one bird to the other, — human eyesight would hardly be equal to work of such nicety; but the two bills were put together so frequently and in so pronounced a manner as to leave us in no practical uncertainty about what was going on. Neither had I any doubt that the change was connected in some way with the increasing age of the fledglings; yet it is to be said that the two methods continued to be used interchangeably to the end, and on the 28th, when Number Two had been out of the nest for seven days, the mother thrust her bill down his throat, and repeated the operation, just as she had done three weeks before.

For at least two days longer, as I believe, the faithful creature continued her loving ministrations, although I failed to detect her in the act. Then, on the 1st of August, as I sat on the piazza, I saw her for the last time. The honeysuckle vine had served her well, and still bore half a dozen scattered blossoms, as if for her especial benefit. She hovered before them, one by one, and in another instant was gone. May the Fates be

[1] Mr. E. H. Eames reports (in *The Auk*, vol. VII, p. 287) that, on dissecting a humming bird, about two days old, he found sixteen young spiders in its throat, and a pultaceous mass of the same in its stomach.

kind to her, and to her children after her, to the latest generation! Our intercourse had lasted for eight weeks, — wanting one day, — and it was fitting that it should end where it had begun, at the sign of the honeysuckle.

The absence of the father bird for all this time, though I have mentioned it but casually, was of course a subject of continual remark. How was it to be explained? My own opinion is, reluctant as I have been to reach it, that such absence or desertion — by whatever name it may be called — is the general habit of the male rubythroat. Upon this point I shall have some things to say in a subsequent paper.

TWO POPULAR WOODPECKERS

By Bradford Torrey

THERE are two birds in Newton, the present summer, that have perhaps attracted more attention than any pair of Massachusetts birds ever attracted before; more, by a good deal, I imagine, than was paid to a pair of crows that, for some inexplicable reason, built a nest and reared a brood of young a year ago in a back yard on Beacon Hill, in Boston. I refer to a pair of red-headed woodpeckers that have a nest (at this moment containing young birds nearly ready to fly) in a tall dead stump standing on the very edge of the sidewalk, like a lamp-post. The road, it should be said, is technically unfinished; one of those "private ways," not yet accepted by the city and therefore legally "dangerous," though in excellent condition and freely traveled. If the birds had intended to hold public receptions daily, — as they have done without intending it, — they could hardly have chosen a more convenient spot. The stump, which is about twenty-five feet in height, stands quite by itself in the middle of a small open space, with a wooded amphitheatrical knoll at its back, while on the other side it is overlooked by the windows of several houses, the nearest almost within stone's throw. So conspicuous is it, indeed, that whenever I go there, as I do once in two or three days, to see how matters are coming on, I am almost sure to see the birds far in advance of my arrival.

They are always there. I heard of them through the kindness of a stranger, on the 26th of June. His letter reached me (in Boston) at two o'clock in the afternoon, and at half past three I was admiring the birds. It cannot be said that they welcomed my attentions. From that day to this they have treated me as an intruder. "You have stayed long enough." "We are not at home to-day." "Come now, old inquisitive, go about your business." Things like these they repeat to me by the half hour. Then, in audible asides, they confide to each other what they think of me. "Watch him," says one at last. "I must be off now after a few grubs." And away she goes, while her mate continues to inform me that I am a busybody, a meddler in other birds' matters, a common nuisance, a duffer, and everything else that is disreputable. All this is unpleasant. I feel as I imagine a baseball umpire feels when the players call him a "gump" and the crowd yells "robber;" but like the umpire, I bear it meekly and hold my ground. A good conscience is a strong support.

In sober truth I have been scrupulously careful of the birds' feelings; or, if not of their feelings, at least of their safety. I began, indeed, by being almost ludicrously careful. The nest was a precious secret, I thought. I must guard it as a miser guards his treasure. So, whenever a foot passenger happened along the highway at my back, I made pretense of being concerned with anything in the world rather than with that lamp-post of a stump. What was Hecuba to me, or I to Hecuba? I pretty soon learned, however, that such precautions were unnecessary. The whole town, or at least the whole neighborhood, was aware of the birds' presence. Every school teacher in the city, one man told me, had been there with his or her pupils to see them. So popular is ornithology in these modern days. He had seen thirty or forty persons about the place at once, he said, all on the same errand. "Look at the bank there," he added. "They have worn it smooth by sitting on it."

I have not been fortunate enough to assist at any such interesting "function," but I have plenty of evidence to prove the truth of what I said just now — that the birds and their nest have become matters of common knowledge. On my third visit, just as I was ready to come away, a boy turned the corner on a bicycle, holding his younger sister in front of him.

"Are they there?" he inquired as he dismounted.

"Who?" said I.

"The red-headed woodpeckers," he answered.

He had known about the nest for some weeks. Oh, yes, everybody knew it. So-and-so found it (I forget the name), and pretty soon it was all over Newtonville. A certain boy, whose wretched name also I have forgotten, had talked about shooting one of the birds; he could get a dollar and a half for it, he professed; but policeman Blank had said that a dollar and a half wouldn't do a boy much good if he got hold of him. He — my informant, a bright-faced, manly fellow of eleven or twelve — had brought his younger sister down to see the birds. He thought they were very handsome. "There!" said he, as one of them perched on a dead tree near by, "Look!" and he knelt behind the little girl till she got the direction. After all, I thought, a boy is almost as pretty as a woodpecker. His father and mother were Canadians, and had told him that birds of this kind were common where they used to live. Then he lifted his sister upon the wheel, jumped up behind her, and away they trundled.

At another time an older boy came along, also on a bicycle, and stopped for a minute's chat. He, too, was in the secret, and had been for a good while. "Pretty nice birds," his verdict was. And at a later visit a man with his dog suddenly appeared. "Handsome, are n't they?" he began, by way of good morning. He had seen one of them as long ago as when snow was on the ground, but he did n't discover the nest. He was looking in the wrong place. Since then he had spent hours in watching the birds, and believed that he could tell the female's voice from the male's. "There!" said he; "that 's the mother's call." He was acquainted with all the birds, and could name them all, he said, simply by their notes; and he told me many things about them. There were grosbeaks here. Did I know them? And tanagers, also. Did I know them? And another bird that he was especially fond of; a beautiful singer, though it never sang after the early part of the season; the indigo bird, its name was. Did I know that?

As will readily be imagined, we had a good session

(one does n't fall in with so congenial a spirit every day in the week), though it ran a little too exclusively to questions and answers, perhaps, for I, too, am a Yankee. He was the man who told me about the throngs of sightseers that came there. The very publicity of the thing had been the birds' salvation, he was inclined to believe. The entire community had taken them under its protection, and with so many windows overlooking the place, and the police on the alert (I had noticed a placard near by, signed by the chief, laying down the law and calling upon all good citizens to help him enforce it), it would have been hard for anybody to meddle with the nest without coming to grief. At all events, the birds had so far escaped molestation, and the young, as I have said, would soon be on the wing. One of them was thrusting its full-grown, wide-awake, eager-looking, mouse-colored head out of the aperture as we talked.

"But why so much excitement over a family of woodpeckers?" some reader may be asking. Rarity, my friend; rarity and brilliant feathers. So far as appears from the latest catalogue of Massachusetts birds, this Newton nest is one of a very small number ever found in the State, and the very first one ever recorded from the eastern half of it. Put that fact with the further one that the birds are among the showiest in North America, real marvels of beauty, — splendid colors, splendidly laid on, — and it is plain to see why a city full of nature lovers should have welcomed this pair with open arms and watched over their welfare as one watches over the most honored of guests. For my part, I should not think it inappropriate if the mayor were to order the firing of a salute and the ringing of bells on the happy morning when the young birds take wing. Tons of gunpowder have been burnt before now with less reason.

BASHFUL DRUMMERS

By Bradford Torrey

He goes but to see a noise that he heard.
SHAKESPEARE.

AT the back of my father's house were woods, to my childish imagination a boundless wilderness. Little by little I ventured into them, and among my earliest recollections of their somber and lonesome depths was a long, thunderous, far-away drumming noise, beginning slowly and increasing in speed till the blows became almost continuous. This, somebody told me, was the drumming of the partridge. Now and then, in open spaces in the path, I came upon shallow circular depressions where the bird had been dusting, an operation in which I had often seen our barnyard fowls complacently engaged. At other times I was startled by the sudden whir of the bird's wings as he sprang up at my feet, and went dashing away through the underbrush. I heard with open-mouthed wonder of men who had been known to shoot a bird thus flying! All in all, the partridge made a great impression upon my boyish mind.

Many years passed, and I became in my own way an ornithologist. One by one I scraped acquaintance with all the common birds of our woods and fields;

but the drumming of the partridge (or of the ruffled grouse, as I now learned to call him) remained a mystery. I read Emerson's description of the "forest-seer:" —

> "He saw the partridge drum in the woods;
> He heard the woodcock's evening hymn;
> He found the tawny thrushes' broods;
> And the shy hawk did wait for him;"

and I thought: "Well, now, I have seen and heard the woodcock at his vespers; I have found the nest of the tawny thrush; the shy hawk has sat still on the branch just over my head; but I have *not* seen the partridge drum in the woods. Why should n't I do that, also?" I made numerous attempts. A bird often drummed in a small wood where I was in the habit of rambling before breakfast. The sound came always from a particular quarter, and probably from a certain stone wall, running over a slight rise of ground near a swamp. The crafty fellow evidently did not mean to be surprised; but I made a careful reconnaissance, and finally hit upon what seemed a feasible point of approach. A rather large bowlder offered a little cover, and, after several failures, I one day spied the bird on the wall. He had drummed only a few minutes before; but his lookout was most likely sharper than mine. At all events, he dropped off the wall on the farther side, and for that time I saw nothing more of him. Nor was I more successful the next time, nor the next. Be as noiseless as I could, the wary creature inevitably took the alarm. To make matters worse, mornings were short and birds were many. One day there were rare visiting warblers to be looked after; another day the gray-cheeked thrushes had dropped in upon us on their way northward, and, if possible, I must hear them sing. Then the pretty blue golden-winged warbler was building her nest, and by some means or other I must find it.

Thus season after season slipped by. Then, in another place, I accidentally passed quite round a drummer. I heard him on the right, and after traveling only a few rods, I heard him on the left. He must be very near me, and not far from the crest of a low hill, over which, as in the former instance, a stone wall ran. He drummed at long intervals, and meanwhile I was straining my eyes and advancing at a snail's pace up the slope. Happily, the ground was carpeted with pine needles, and comparatively free from brush and dead twigs, those snapping nuisances that so often bring all our patience and ingenuity to nought. A section of the wall came into sight, but I got no glimpse of the bird. Presently I went down upon all fours; then lower yet, crawling instead of creeping, till I could look over the brow of the hill. Here I waited, and had begun to fear that I was once more to have my labor for my pains, when all at once I saw the grouse step from one stone to another. "Now for it!" I said to myself. But the drumming did not follow, and anon I lost sight of the drummer. Again I waited, and finally the fellow jumped suddenly upon a top stone, lifted his wings, and commenced the familiar roll call. I could see his wings beating against his sides with quicker and quicker strokes; but an unlucky bush was between us, and hoping to better my position, I moved a little to one side.

Upon this, the bird became aware of my presence, I think. At least I could see him staring straight at me, and a moment later he dropped behind the wall; and though I remained motionless till a cramp took me, I heard nothing more. "If it had not been for that miserable bush!" I muttered. But I need not have quarreled with an innocent bush, as if it, any more than myself, had been given a choice where it should grow. A wiser man would have called to mind the old saw, and made the most of "half a loaf."

Another year passed, and another spring came round. Then, on the same hillside, a bird (probably the same individual) was drumming one April morning, and, as my notebook has it, "I came within one" of taking him in the act. I miscalculated his position, however, which, as it turned out, was not upon the wall, but on a bowlder surrounded by a few small pine trees. The rock proved to be well littered, and clearly was the bird's regular resort. "Very good," said I, "I will catch you yet."

Five days later I returned to the charge, and was rewarded by seeing the fellow drum once; but, as before, intervening brush obscured my view. I crept forward, inch by inch, till the top of the bowlder came into sight, and waited, and waited, and waited. At last I pushed on, and lo, the place was deserted. There is a familiar Scripture text that might have been written on purpose for ornithologists: "Let patience have her perfect work."

This was April 14th. On the 19th I made the experiment again. The drummer was at it as I drew near, and fortune favored me at last. I witnessed the performance three times over. Even now, to be sure, the prospect was not entirely clear, but it was better than ever before, and by this time I had learned to be thankful for small mercies. The grouse kept his place between the acts, moving his head a little one way and another, but apparently doing nothing else.

Of course I had in mind the disputed question as to the method by which the drumming noise is produced. It had seemed to me that whoever would settle this point must do it by attending carefully to the first slow beats. This I now attempted, and after one trial was ready, offhand, to accept a theory which heretofore I had scouted; namely, that the bird makes the sound by striking his wings together over his back. He brought them up, even for the first two or three times, with a quick convulsive movement, and I could almost have made oath that I heard the beat before the wings fell. But fortunately, or unfortunately, I waited till he drummed again; and now I was by no means so positive in my conviction. If an observer wishes to be absolutely sure of a thing, — I have learned this by long experience, — let him look at it once, and forever after shut his eyes! On the whole, I return to my previous opinion, that the sound is made by the downward stroke, though whether against the body or against the air, I will not presume to say.

A man who is a far better ornithologist than I, and who has witnessed this performance under altogether more favorable conditions than I was ever afforded, assures me that his performer *sat down!* My bird took no such ridiculous position. So much, at least, I am sure of.

When he had drummed three times, my partridge quit his bowlder (I was near enough to hear him strike the dry leaves), and after a little walked suddenly into plain sight. We discovered each other at the same instant. I kept motionless, my field glass up. He made sundry nervous movements, especially of his ruff, and then silently walked away.

I could not blame him for his lack of neighborliness. If I had been shot at and hunted with dogs as many times as he probably had been, I too might have become a little shy of strangers. To my thinking, indeed, the grouse is one of our most estimable citizens. A liking for the buds of fruit trees is his only fault (not many of my townsmen have a smaller number, I fancy), and that is one easily overlooked, especially by a man who owns no orchard. Every sportsman tries to shoot him, and every winter does its worst to freeze or starve him; but he continues to flourish. Others may migrate to sunnier climes, or seek safety in the backwoods, but not so the partridge. He was born here, and here he means to stay. What else could be expected of a bird whose notion of a lover's serenade is the beating of a drum?

THE BIRD THAT "PLAYED 'POSSUM"

By John Burroughs

AT one point in the grayest, most shaggy part of the woods, I come suddenly upon a brood of screech owls, full grown, sitting together upon a dry, moss-draped limb, but a few feet from the ground. I pause within four or five yards of them and am looking about me, when my eye lights upon these gray, motionless figures. They sit perfectly upright, some with their backs and some with their breasts toward me, but every head turned squarely in my direction. Their eyes are closed to a mere black line, through this crack they are watching me, evidently thinking themselves unobserved. The spectacle is weird and grotesque, and suggests something impish and uncanny. It is a new effect, the night side of the woods by daylight. After observing them a moment I take a single step toward them, when, quick as thought, their eyes fly wide open, their attitude is changed, they bend, some this way, some that, and, instinct with life and motion, stare wildly around them. Another step, and they all take flight but one, which stoops low on the branch, and with the look of a frightened cat regards me for a few seconds over its shoulder. They fly swiftly and softly, and disperse through the trees.

A winter neighbor of mine, in whom I am interested, and who perhaps lends me his support after his kind, is a little red owl, whose retreat is in the heart of an old apple tree just over the fence. Where he keeps himself in spring and summer, I do not know, but late every fall, and at intervals all winter, his hiding place is discovered by the jays and nuthatches, and proclaimed from the treetops for the space of half an hour or so, with all the powers of voice they can command. Four times during one winter they called me out to behold this little ogre feigning sleep in his den, sometimes in one apple tree, sometimes in another. Whenever I heard their cries, I knew my neighbor was being berated. The birds would take turns at looking in upon him, and uttering their alarm notes. Every jay within hearing would come to the spot, and at once approach the hole in the trunk or limb, and with a kind of breathless eagerness and excitement take a peep at the owl, and then join the outcry. When I approached they would hastily take a final look, and then withdraw and regard my movements intently. After accustoming my eye to the faint light of the cavity for a few moments, I could usually make out the owl at the bottom feigning sleep. Feigning, I say, because this is what he really did, as I first discovered one day when I cut into his retreat with the axe. The loud blows and the falling chips did not disturb him at all. When I reached in a stick and pulled him over on his side, leaving one of his wings spread out, he made no attempt to recover himself, but lay among the chips and fragments of decayed wood, like a part of themselves. Indeed, it took a sharp eye to distinguish him. Not till I had pulled him forth by one wing, rather rudely, did he abandon his trick of simulated sleep or death. Then, like a detected pickpocket, he was suddenly transformed into another creature. His eyes flew wide open, his talons clutched my finger, his ears were depressed, and every motion and look said, "Hands off, at your peril." Finding this game did not work, he soon began to "play 'possum" again. I put a cover over my study wood box and kept him captive for a week. Look in upon him at any time, night or day, and he was apparently wrapped in the profoundest slumber; but the live mice which I put into his box from time to time found his sleep was easily broken; there would be a sudden rustle in the box, a faint squeak, and then silence. After a week of captivity I gave him his freedom in the full sunshine; no trouble for him to see which way and where to go.

Just at dusk in the winter nights, I often hear his soft *bur-r-r-r*, very pleasing and bell-like. What a furtive, woody sound it is in the winter stillness, so unlike the harsh scream of the hawk! But all the ways of the owl are ways of softness and duskiness. His wings are shod with silence, his plumage is edged with down.

Another owl neighbor of mine, with whom I pass the time of day more frequently than with the last, lives farther away. I pass his castle every night on my way to the post-office, and in winter, if the hour is late enough, am pretty sure to see him standing in his doorway, surveying the passers-by and the landscape through narrow slits in his eyes. For four successive winters now have I observed him. As the twilight begins to deepen, he rises up out of his cavity in the apple tree, scarcely faster than the moon rises from behind the hill, and sits in the opening, completely framed by its outlines of gray bark and dead wood, and by his protective coloring virtually invisible to every eye that does not know that he is there. Probably my own is the only eye that has ever penetrated his secret, and mine never would have done so had I not chanced on one occasion to see him leave his retreat and make a raid upon a shrike that was impaling a shrew-mouse upon a thorn in a neighboring tree, and which I was watching. I was first advised of the owl's presence by seeing him approaching swiftly on silent, level wing. The shrike did not see him till the owl was almost within the branches. He then dropped his game, and darted back into the thick cover, uttering a loud, discordant squawk, as one would say, "Scat! scat! scat!" The owl alighted, and was, perhaps, looking about him for the shrike's impaled game, when I drew near. On seeing me, he reversed his movement precipitately, flew straight back to the old tree, and alighted in the entrance to the cavity. As I approached, he did not so much seem to move as to diminish in size, like an object dwindling in the distance; he depressed his plumage, and, with his eye fixed upon me, began slowly to back and sidle into his retreat till he faded from my sight. The shrike wiped his beak upon the branches, cast an eye down at me and at his lost mouse, and then flew away.

A few nights afterward, as I passed that way, I saw the little owl again sitting in his doorway, waiting for the twilight to deepen, and undisturbed by the passers-by; but when I paused to observe him, he saw that he was discovered, and he slunk back into his den as on the former occasion. Ever since, while going that way, I have been on the lookout for him. Dozens of teams and foot passengers pass him late in the day, but he regards them not, nor they him. When I come along and pause to salute him, he opens his eyes a little wider, and, appearing to recognize me, quickly shrinks and fades into the background of his door in a very weird and curious manner. When he is not at his outlook, or when he is, it requires the best powers of the eye to decide the point, as the empty cavity itself is almost an exact image of him. If the whole thing had been carefully studied, it could not have answered its purpose better. The owl stands quite perpendicular, presenting a front of light mottled gray; the eyes are closed to a mere slit, the ear-feathers depressed, the beak buried in the plumage, and the whole attitude is one of silent, motionless waiting and observation. If a mouse should be seen crossing the highway, or scudding over any exposed part of the snowy surface in the twilight, the owl would doubtless swoop down upon it. I think the owl has learned to distinguish me from the rest of the passers-by; at least, when I stop before him, and he sees himself observed, he backs down into his den, as I have said, in a very amusing manner.

OUR GUEST THE MARSH HAWK

By John Burroughs

MOST country boys, I fancy, know the marsh hawk. It is he you see flying low over the fields, beating about bushes and marshes and dipping over the fences, with his attention directed to the ground beneath him. He is a cat on wings. He keeps so low that the birds and mice do not see him till he is fairly upon them. The hen hawk swoops down upon the meadow mouse from his position high in air, or from the top of a dead tree; but the marsh hawk stalks him and comes suddenly upon him from over the fence, or from behind a low bush or tuft of grass. He is nearly as large as the hen hawk, but has a much longer tail. When I was a boy I used to call him the long-tailed hawk. The male is of a bluish slate-color; the female reddish-brown, like the hen hawk, with a white rump.

Unlike the other hawks, they nest on the ground in low, thick marshy places. For several seasons a pair have nested in a bushy marsh a few miles back of me, near the house of a farmer friend of mine, who has a keen eye for the wild life about him. Two years ago he found the nest, but when I got over to see it the next week, it had been robbed, probably by some boys in the neighborhood. The past season, in April or May, by watching the mother bird, he found the nest again. It was in a marshy place, several acres in extent, in the bottom of a valley, and thickly grown with hard-hack, prickly ash, smilax, and other low thorny bushes. My friend took me to the brink of a low hill, and pointed out to me in the marsh below us, as nearly as he could, just where the nest was located. Then we crossed the pasture, entered upon the marsh, and made our way cautiously toward it. The wild, thorny growths, waist-high, had to be carefully dealt with. As we neared the spot, I used my eyes the best I could, but I did not see the hawk till she sprang into the air not ten yards away from us. She went screaming upward, and was soon sailing in a circle far above us. There, on a coarse matting of twigs and weeds, lay five snow-white eggs, a little more than half as large as hens' eggs. My companion said the male hawk would probably soon appear and join the female, but he did not. She kept drifting away to the east, and was soon gone from our sight.

We presently withdrew and secreted ourselves behind the stone wall, in hopes of seeing the mother hawk return. She appeared in the distance, but seemed to know she was being watched, and kept away.

About ten days later we made another visit to the nest. An adventurous young Chicago lady also wanted to see a hawk's nest, and so accompanied us. This time three of the eggs were hatched, and as the mother hawk sprang up, either by accident or intentionally she threw two of the young hawks some feet from the nest. She rose up and screamed angrily. Then, turning toward us, she came like an arrow straight at the young lady, a bright plume in whose hat probably drew her fire. The damsel gathered up her skirts about her and beat a hasty retreat. Hawks were not so pretty as she thought they were. A large hawk launched at one's face from high in the air is calculated to make one a little nervous. It is such a fearful incline down which the bird comes, and she is aiming exactly toward your eye. When within about thirty feet of you, she turns upward with a rushing sound, and, mounting higher, falls toward you again. She is only firing blank cartridges, as it were; but it usually has the desired effect, and beats the enemy off.

After we had inspected the young hawks, a neighbor of my friend offered to conduct us to a quail's nest. Anything in the shape of a nest is always welcome, it is such a mystery, such a center of interest and affection, and, if upon the ground, is usually something so dainty and exquisite amid the natural wreckage and confusion. A ground nest seems so exposed, too, that it always gives a little thrill of pleasurable surprise to see the group of frail eggs resting there behind so slight a barrier. I will walk a long distance any day just to see a song sparrow's nest amid the stubble or under a tuft of grass. It is a jewel in a rosette of jewels, with a frill of weeds or turf. A quail's nest I had never seen, and to be shown one within the hunting ground of this murderous hawk would be a double pleasure. Such a quiet, secluded, grass-grown highway as we moved along was itself a rare treat. Sequestered was the word that the little valley suggested, and peace the feeling the road evoked. The farmer, whose fields lay about us, half grown with weeds and bushes, evidently did not make stir or noise enough to disturb anything. Beside this rustic highway, bounded by old mossy stone walls, and within a stone's throw of the farmer's barn, the quail had made her nest. It was just under the edge of a prostrate thornbush.

"The nest is right there," said the farmer, pausing within ten feet of it, and pointing to the spot with his stick.

In a moment or two we could make out the mottled brown plumage of the sitting bird. Then we approached her cautiously till we bent above her.

She never moved a feather.

Then I put my cane down in the brush behind her. We wanted to see the eggs, yet did not want rudely to disturb the sitting hen.

She would not move.

Then I put down my hand within a few inches of her; still she kept her place. Should we have to lift her off bodily?

Then the young lady put down her hand, probably the prettiest and the whitest hand the quail had ever seen. At least it started her, and off she sprang, uncovering such a crowded nest of eggs as I had never before beheld. Twenty-one of them! a ring or disk of white like a china tea saucer. You could not help saying, How pretty! How cunning! like baby hens' eggs, as if the bird were playing at sitting, as children play at housekeeping.

If I had known how crowded her nest was, I should

not have dared disturb her, for fear she would break some of them. But not an egg suffered harm by her sudden flight. And no harm came to the nest afterward. Every egg hatched, I was told, and the little chicks, hardly bigger than bumblebees, were led away by the mother into the fields.

In about a week I paid another visit to the hawk's nest. The eggs were all hatched, and the mother bird was hovering near. I shall never forget the curious expression of those young hawks sitting there on the ground. The expression was not one of youth, but of extreme age. Such an ancient, infirm look as they had, — the sharp, dark, and shrunken look about the face and eyes, and their feeble, tottering motions! They sat upon their elbows and the hind part of their bodies, and their pale, withered legs and feet extended before them in the most helpless fashion. Their angular bodies were covered with a pale yellowish down, like that of a chicken; their heads had a plucked, seedy appearance; and their long, strong, naked wings hung down by their sides till they touched the ground: power and ferocity in the first rude draft, shorn of everything but its sinister ugliness. Another curious thing was the gradation of the young in size; they tapered down regularly from the first to the fifth, as if there had been, as probably there was, an interval of a day or two between the hatchings.

The two older ones showed some signs of fear on our approach, and one of them threw himself upon his back, and put up his impotent legs, and glared at us with open beak. The two smaller ones regarded us not at all. Neither of the parent birds appeared during our stay.

When I visited the nest again, eight or ten days later, the birds were much grown, but of as marked a difference in size as before, and with the same look of extreme old age, — old age in men of the aquiline type, nose and chin coming together, and eyes large and sunken. They now glared upon us with a wild, savage look, and opened their beaks threateningly.

The next week, when my friend visited the nest, the larger of the hawks fought him savagely. But one of the brood, probably the last to hatch, had made but little growth. It appeared to be on the point of starvation. The mother hawk (for the male seemed to have disappeared) had perhaps found her family too large for her, and was deliberately allowing one of the number to perish; or did the larger and stronger young devour all the food before the weaker member could obtain any? Probably this was the case.

Arthur brought the feeble nestling away, and the same day my little boy got it and brought it home, wrapped in a woolen rag. It was clearly a starved bantling. It cried feebly but would not lift up its head.

We first poured some warm milk down its throat, which soon revived it, so that it would swallow small bits of flesh. In a day or two we had it eating ravenously, and its growth became noticeable. Its voice had the sharp whistling character of that of its parents, and was stilled only when the bird was asleep. We made a pen for it, about a yard square, in one end of the study, covering the floor with several thicknesses of newspapers; and here, upon a bit of brown woolen blanket for a nest, the hawk waxed strong day by day. An uglier-looking pet, tested by all the rules we usually apply to such things, would have been hard to find. There he would sit upon his elbows, his helpless feet out in front of him, his great featherless wings touching the floor, and shrilly cry for more food. For a time we gave him water daily from a stylograph-pen filler, but the water he evidently did not need or relish. Fresh meat, and plenty of it, was his demand. And we soon discovered that he liked game, such as mice, squirrels, birds, much better than butcher's meat.

Then began a lively campaign on the part of my little boy against all the vermin and small game in the neighborhood, to keep the hawk supplied. He trapped and he hunted, he enlisted his mates in service, he even robbed the cats to feed the hawk. His usefulness as a boy of all work was seriously impaired. "Where is J——?" "Gone after a squirrel for his hawk." And often the day would be half gone before his hunt was successful. The premises were very soon cleared of mice, and the vicinity of chipmunks and squirrels. Farther and farther he was compelled to hunt the surrounding farms and woods to keep up with the demands of the hawk. By the time the hawk was ready to fly, it had consumed twenty-one chipmunks, fourteen red squirrels, sixteen mice, and twelve English sparrows, besides a great deal of butcher's meat.

His plumage very soon began to show itself, crowding off tufts of the down. The quills on his great wings sprouted and grew apace. What a ragged, uncanny appearance he presented! but his look of extreme age gradually became modified. What a lover of the sunlight he was! We would put him out upon the grass in the full blaze of the morning sun, and he would spread his wings and bask in it with the most intense enjoyment. In the nest the young must be exposed to the full power of the midday sun during our first heated terms in June and July, the thermometer often going up to ninety-three or ninety-five degrees, so that sunshine seemed to be a need of his nature. He liked the rain equally well, and when put out in a shower would sit down and take it as if every drop did him good.

His legs developed nearly as slowly as his wings. He could not stand steadily upon them till about ten days before he was ready to fly. The talons were limp and feeble. When we came with food, he would hobble along toward us like the worst kind of a cripple, drooping and moving his wings, and treading upon his legs from the foot back to the elbow, the foot remaining closed and useless. Like a baby learning to stand, he made many trials before he succeeded. He would rise up on his trembling legs only to fall back again.

One day, in the summer house, I saw him for the first time stand for a moment squarely upon his legs with the feet fully spread beneath them. He looked about him as if the world suddenly wore a new aspect.

His plumage now grew quite rapidly. One red squirrel a day, chopped fine with an axe, was his ration. He began to hold his game with his foot while he tore it. The study was full of his shed down. His dark-brown mottled plumage began to grow beautiful. The wings drooped a little, but gradually he got control of them, and held them in place.

It was now the 20th of July, and the hawk was about five weeks old. In a day or two he was walking or jumping about the grounds. He chose a position under the edge of a Norway spruce, where he would sit for hours dozing, or looking out upon the landscape. When we brought him game, he would advance to meet us with wings slightly lifted, and uttering a shrill cry. Toss him a mouse or sparrow, and he would seize it with one foot and hop off to his cover, where he would bend above it, spread his plumage, look this way and that, uttering all the time the most exultant and satisfied chuckle.

About this time he began to practice striking with his talons, as an Indian boy might begin practicing with his bow and arrow. He would strike at a dry leaf in the grass, or at a fallen apple, or at some imaginary object. He was learning the use of his weapons. His wings also, — he seemed to feel them sprouting from his shoulders. He would lift them straight up and hold them expanded, and they would seem to quiver with excitement. Every hour in the day he would do this. The pressure was beginning to center there. Then he would strike playfully at a leaf or a bit of wood, and keep his wings lifted.

The next step was to spring into the air and beat his wings. He seemed now to be thinking entirely of his wings. They itched to be put to use.

A day or two later he would leap and fly several feet.

A pile of brush ten or twelve feet below the bank was easily reached. Here he would perch in true hawk fashion, to the bewilderment and scandal of all the robins and catbirds in the vicinity. Here he would dart his eye in all directions, turning his head over and glancing up into the sky.

He was now a lovely creature, fully fledged, and as tame as a kitten. But he was not a bit like a kitten in one respect, — he could not bear to have you stroke or even touch his plumage. He had a horror of your hand, as if it would hopelessly defile him. But he would perch upon it, and allow you to carry him about. If a dog or cat appeared, he was ready to give battle instantly. He rushed up to a little dog one day, and struck him with his foot savagely. He was afraid of strangers, and of any unusual object.

The last week in July he began to fly quite freely, and it was necessary to clip one of his wings. As the clipping embraced only the ends of his primaries, he soon overcame the difficulty, and, by carrying his broad long tail more on that side, flew with considerable ease. He made longer and longer excursions into the surrounding fields and vineyards, and did not always return. On such occasions we would go to find him and fetch him back.

Late one rainy afternoon he flew away into the vineyard, and when, an hour later, I went after him, he could not be found, and we never saw him again. We hoped hunger would soon drive him back, but we have had no clew to him from that day to this.

WHIPPED BY EAGLES

By Dallas Lore Sharp

AS you head into Maurice River Cove from Delaware Bay by boat, the great eagle's nest of Garren's Neck Swamp soon looms into view. It is a famous nest, and an ancient nest; for it has a place in the chart of every boat that sails up the river, and has had for I don't know how many years. From the river side of the long swamp the nest is in sight the year round, but from the land side, and from the house where we lived, the nest could be seen only after the leaves of the swamp had fallen. Then all winter long we could see it towering over the swamp; and often, in the distance, we could see the eagles coming and going or soaring in mighty circles high up in the air above it.

That nest had a strange attraction for me. It was the home of eagles, the monarchs of this wide land of swamp and marsh and river.

Between me and the great nest lay a gloomy gum swamp, wet and wild, untouched by the axe and untraveled, except in winter by the coon hunters. The swamp began just across the road that ran in front of the house; and often at night I would hear the scream of a wildcat in the dark hollows; and once I heard the *pat, pat* of its feet as it went leaping along the road.

Then beyond the swamp and the nest stretched a

vast wild marsh land, where the reeds grew, and the tides came in, and the mud hens lived. And beyond that flowed the river, and beyond the river lay another marsh, and beyond the marsh another swamp. And over all this vast wild world towered the nest of the eagles, like some ancient castle; and over it all — swamp and marsh and river — ruled the eagles, as bold and free as the mighty barons of old.

Is it any wonder that I often found myself gazing away at that nest on the horizon and longing for wings? — for wings with which to soar above the swamp and the bay and the marsh and the river, to circle about and about that lofty aerie, as wild as the eagles and as free? Is it any wonder that I determined some day to stand up in that nest, wings or no wings, while the eagles should scream about me, and away below me should stretch river and marsh and swamp.

To stand up in that nest, to yell and wave my arms with the eagles wheeling and screaming over me, became the very peak of my boy ambitions.

And I did it. I actually had the eggs of those eagles in my hands. I got into the nest; but I am glad even now that I got out of the nest and reached the ground.

It must have been in the spring of my fourteenth year when, at last, I found myself beneath the eagle tree. It was a stark old white oak, almost limbless, and standing out alone on the marsh some distance from the swamp. The eagle's nest capped its very top.

The nest, I knew, must be big; but not until I had climbed up close under it did I realize that it was the size of a small haystack. There was certainly half a cord of wood in it. I think that it must originally have been built by fish hawks.

Holding to the forking top upon which the nest was placed, I reached out, but could not touch the edge from any side.

I had come determined to get up into it, however, at any hazard; and so I set to work. I never thought of how I was to get down; nor had I dreamed, either, of fearing the eagles. A bald eagle is a bully. I should as soon have thought of fearing our hissing old gander at home.

As I could not get out to the edge of the nest and scale the walls, the only possible way up, apparently, was through the nest. The sticks here in the bottom were old and quite rotten. Digging was easy, and I soon had a good beginning.

The structure was somewhat cone-shaped, the smaller end down. It had grown in circumference as it grew in years and in height, probably because at the bottom the building materials had decayed and gradually fallen away, until now there was a decided outward slant from bottom to top. It had grown lopsided, too, there being a big bulge on one side of the nest near the middle.

The smallness of the bottom at first helped me; there was less of the stuff to be pulled out. I easily broke away the dead timbers and pushed aside the tougher sticks. I intended to cut a channel clear to the top and go up through the nest. Already my head and shoulders were well into it.

Now the work became more difficult. The sticks

were newer, some of them being of seasoned oak and hickory, which the birds had taken from cordwood piles.

I had cut my channel up the side of the nest nearly halfway when I came to a forked branch that I could neither break off nor push aside. I soon found that it was not loose, but that it belonged to the oak tree itself. It ran out through the nest horizontally, extending a little more than a foot beyond the rough walls.

Backing down, I saw that this fork was the support of the bulge that had given the nest its lopsided appearance. A few large timbers had been rested across it, small loose pieces had gradually lodged upon these, and thus in time brought about the big bulge.

I pushed off this loose stuff and the few heavy timbers and found that the fork would bear my weight. It now projected a little way from the walls of the nest. I got a firm hold on the forks out at their ends, swung clear, and drew myself up between them. After a lively scramble, I got carefully to my feet, and, clutching the sticks protruding from the side, stood up, with my eyes almost on a level with the rim of the great nest. This was better than cutting a channel, certainly — at least for the ascent, and I was not then thinking of the descent.

I looked over the protruding sticks of the rim. I caught a glimpse of large dull white eggs!

Eggs of shining gold could not have so fascinated me. There were thousands of persons who could have gold eggs if they cared. But the eagles' eggs! Money could not buy such a sight as this.

I was more than ever eager now to get into the nest. Working my fingers among the sticks of the rim for a firm grip, I stuck my toes into the rough wall and began to climb. At some considerable hazard and at the cost of many rents in my clothing, I wriggled up over the edge and into the hollow of the nest where the coveted eggs lay.

The eagles were wheeling and screaming overhead. The weird *cac, cac, cac* of the male came down from far above me; while the female, circling closer, would swoop and shrill her menacing, maniacal half laugh almost in my ears.

Their wild cries thrilled me, and their mighty wings, wheeling so close around me, seemed to catch me in their majestic sweep and almost to carry me in swift, swinging circles through the empty air. An ecstasy of excitement overcame me. I felt no body, no weight of anything. I lost my head completely, and, seizing the eggs, rose to my feet and stood upright in the nest.

The eagles swept nearer. I could feel the wind from their wings. I could see the rolling of their gleaming eyes, and the glint of the sun on their snow-white necks. And as they dipped and turned and careened over me, I came perilously near trying to fly myself.

What a scene lay under me and rolled wide and free to the very edge of the world! The level marsh, the blue, hazy bay, the far-off, unblurred horizon beyond the bending hill of the sea! The wild, free wind from the bay blew in upon my face, the old tree trembled and rocked beneath me, the screaming eagles wove a mazy spell of double circles about me, till I screamed back at them in wild delight.

The sound of my voice seemed to infuriate the birds. The male turned suddenly in his round and swooped directly at me. The movement was instantly understood by his mate, who, thus emboldened, cut under him and hurled herself downward, passing with a vicious grab at my face. I dodged, or she would have hit me.

For the moment I had forgotten where I stood; and, in dodging the eagle, I almost stepped over the edge of the nest. I caught my balance and dropped quickly to my knees, completely unnerved.

Fear like a panic took instant hold on me. Only one desire possessed me — to get down. I crept to the edge and looked over. The sight made me dizzy. Sixty feet of almost empty air! Far down, a few small limbs intervened between me and the ground. But there was nothing by which to descend.

I was dismayed; and my expression, my posture — something, betrayed my confusion to the eagles. They immediately lost all dread of me. While I was looking over, one of them struck me a stinging blow on the head, knocking my cap off into the air.

That started me. I must climb down or be knocked over. If only I had continued with my channel to the top! If only that forked branch by which I ascended were within reach! But how could I back over the flaring rim to my whole length and swing my body under against the inward-slanting nest until my feet could touch the fork? But if I ever got down, that was what I must do; for the eagles gave me no chance to cut a channel now.

Laying the eggs back for the time in the hollow, I began tearing away the rim of the nest in order to clear a place over which to back down.

I was momentarily in danger of being hurled off by the birds; for I could not watch them and work, too. And they were growing bolder with every dash. One of them, driving fearfully from behind, flattened me out on the nest. Had the blow been delivered from the front, I should have been knocked headlong to the ground.

I was afraid to delay longer. A good sized breach was opened in the rim of the nest by this time. And now, if the sticks would not pull out, I might let myself over and reach the fork. Once my feet touched that, I could manage the rest, I knew.

Digging my hands deep into the nest for a firm hold, I began cautiously to back over the rough, stubby rim, reaching with my feet toward the fork.

The eagles seemed to appreciate the opportunity my awkward position offered them. I could not have arranged myself more conveniently to their minds, I am sure. And they made the most of it. I can laugh now; but the memory of it can still make me shiver, too.

I had wriggled over just so that I could bend my body at the waist and bring my legs against the nest when a sharp stub caught in my clothes and held me. I could get neither up nor down. My handhold was of the most precarious kind, and I dared not let go for a moment to get off the snag.

I tried to back out and push off from it, but it seemed to come out with me. It must be broken; and pulling myself up, I dropped with all the force I could put into my body. That loosened, but did not break it. Suddenly, while I was resting between the efforts, the thing gave way.

I was wholly unprepared. All my weight was instantly thrown upon my hands. The jagged sticks cut into my wrists, my grip was pried off, and I fell.

Once, twice, the stubs in the wall of the nest caught and partly stopped me, then broke. I clutched frantically at them, but could not hold. Then, almost before I realized that I was falling, I hung suspended between two limbs — the forks of the white oak branch in the side of the nest.

I had been directly above it when the stub broke, and had fallen through it; and the two branches had caught me right under both of my arms.

For a second I was too dazed to think. Then a swish of wings, a hard blow on the neck, and a shooting pain made my position clear. I was not down yet nor out of danger. The angry birds still had me in reach.

Hanging with one arm, I twisted round until the other arm was free, then seized the branches and swung under, but not before the eagles had given me another raking dab.

Here beneath the branches, close up to the bottom of the nest, I was quite out of the reach of the birds; and through the channel I had cut in my ascent, I climbed quickly down into the tree.

It was now a mere matter of sliding to the ground.

But I was so battered and faint that I nearly tumbled. I was a sorry-looking boy — my clothing torn, my hands bleeding, my head and neck clawed in a dozen places.

But what did I do with the eagles' eggs? Why, I allowed the old eagles to hatch them. What else could I do? or what better?

A GREAT BLUE HERON

By Bradford Torrey

> Why appear you with this ridiculous boldness?
>
> SHAKESPEARE.

THE watcher of birds in the bush soon discovers that they have individual as well as race characteristics. They are not things, but persons, — beings with intellect, affections, and will, — and a strong specific resemblance is found to be consistent with no small measure of personal variation. All robins, we say, look and act alike. But so do all Yankees; yet it is part of every Yankee's birthright to be different from every other Yankee. Nature abhors a copy, it would seem, almost as badly as she abhors a vacuum. Perhaps, if the truth was known, a copy *is* a vacuum.

I walked down the bay shore of Cape Cod one summer morning, and at a certain point climbed the steep cliff to the railway track, meaning to look into a large cranberry meadow where, on previous visits, I had found a few sandpipers and plovers. Near one end of the perfectly level, sand-covered meadow was a little pool, and my first glance in that direction showed me a great blue heron wading about its edge. With as much quietness as possible I stole out of sight, and then hastened up the railway through a cut, till I had the sun at my back and a hill between me and the bird. Then I began a stealthy approach, keeping behind one object after another, and finally going down flat upon the ground (to roll in the soil is an excellent method of cleansing one's garments on Cape Cod) and crawling up to a patch of bayberry bushes, the last practicable cover.

Here let me say that the great blue heron is, as its name implies, a big bird, standing almost as high as an ordinary man, and spreading its wings for nearly or quite six feet. Its character for suspiciousness may be gathered from what different writers have said about it. "He is most jealously vigilant and watchful of man," says Wilson, "so that those who wish to succeed in shooting the heron must approach him entirely unseen, and by stratagem." "Extremely suspicious and shy," says Audubon. "Unless under very favorable circumstances, it is almost hopeless to attempt to approach it. To walk up towards one would be a fruitless adventure." Dr. Brewer's language is to the same effect, — "At all times very vigilant and difficult to approach."

This, then, was the bird which I now had under my field glass, as I lay at full length behind the friendly bayberry bushes. Up to this point, for aught that appeared, he was quite unaware of my espionage. Like all the members of his family that I have ever seen, he possessed so much patience that it required much patience to watch him. For minutes together he stood perfectly still, and his movements, as a rule, were either so slow as to be all but imperceptible, or so rapid as almost to elude the eye. Boys who have killed frogs —

which was pretty certainly my heron's present employment — will need no explanation of his behavior. They know very well that, if the fatal club is to do its work, the slowest kind of preliminary motions must be followed by something like a flash of lightning.

I watched the bird for perhaps half an hour, admiring his handsome blue wings as now and then he spread them, his dainty manner of lifting his long legs, and the occasional flashing stroke of his beak. My range was short (for a field glass, I mean), and, all in all, I voted it "a fine show."

When I wearied of my position I rose and advanced upon the heron in full sight, expecting every moment to see him fly. To my astonishment he held his ground. Down the hillside I went, nearer and nearer, till I came to a barbed-wire fence, which bounded the cranberry field close by the heron's pool. As I worried my way through this abominable obstruction, he stepped into a narrow, shallow ditch and started slowly away. I made rapidly after him, whereupon he got out of the ditch and strode on ahead of me. By this time I was probably within twenty yards of him, so near that, as he twisted his long neck every now and then, and looked at me through his big yellow eyes, I began to wonder whether he might not take it into his head to turn the tables upon me. A stab in the face with that ugly sharp beak would have been no laughing matter; but I did not believe myself in any danger, and quickened my steps, being now highly curious to see how near the fellow I could get. At this he broke into a kind of dog-trot, very comical to witness, and, if I had not previously seen him fly a few yards, I should have supposed him disabled in the wing. Dr. Brewer, by the way, says that this bird is "never known to run, or even to walk briskly;" but such negative assertions are always at the maker's risk.

He picked up his legs at last, for I pressed him closer and closer, till there could not have been more than forty or fifty feet between us; but even then he settled down again beside another pool, only a few rods farther on in the same meadow, and there I left him to pursue his frog hunt unmolested. The ludicrousness of the whole affair was enhanced by the fact, already mentioned, that the ground was perfectly flat, and absolutely without vegetation, except for the long rows of newly planted cranberry vines. As to what could have influenced the bird to treat me thus strangely, I have no means of guessing. As we say of each other's freaks and oddities, it was *his way*, I suppose. He might have behaved otherwise, of course, had I been armed; but of that I felt by no means certain at the time, and my doubts were strengthened by an occurrence which happened a month or so afterward.

I was crossing the beach at Nahant with a friend when we stole upon a pair of golden plovers, birds that both of us were very happy to see. The splendid old-gold spotting of their backs was plain enough; but immature black-bellied plovers are adorned in a similar manner, and it was necessary for us to see the rumps of our birds before we could be sure of their identity. So, after we had scrutinized them as long as we wished, I asked my companion to put them up while I should keep my glass upon their backs and make certain of the color of their rumps as they opened their wings. We were already within a very few paces of them, but they ran before him as he advanced, and in the end he had almost to tread on them.

The golden plover is not so unapproachable as the great blue heron, I suppose, but from what sportsmen tell me about him I am confident that he cannot be in the habit of allowing men to chase him along the beach at a distance of five or six yards. And it is to be added that, in the present instance, my companion had a gun in his hand.

Possibly all these birds would have behaved differently another day, even in what to us might have seemed exactly the same circumstances. Undoubtedly, too, it is easier, as an almost universal rule, to approach one or two birds than a considerable flock. In the larger body there are almost certain to be a few timorous souls, — a few wider-awake and better instructed souls, let us rather say, — who by their outcries and hasty flight will awaken all the others to a sense of possible danger. But it is none the less true, as I have said to begin with, that individual birds have individual ways. And my great blue heron, I am persuaded, was a "character." It would be worth something to know what was passing behind those big yellow eyes as he twisted his neck to look once more at the curious fellow — curious in two senses — who was keeping after him so closely. Was the heron curious, as well as his pursuer? Or was he only a little set in his own way; a little resentful of being imposed upon; a little inclined to withstand the "tyrant of his fields," just for principle's sake, as patriots ought to do? Or was he a young fellow, in whom heredity had mysteriously omitted to load the bump of caution, and upon whom experience had not yet enforced the lesson that if a creature is taller and stronger than you are, it is prudent to assume that he will most likely think it a pleasant bit of sport to kill you? It is nothing to the credit of humankind that the sight of an unsuspicious bird in a marsh or on the beach should have become a subject for wonder.

THE STORY OF AN EGRET WARDEN

By Oscar E Baynard

IF you know nothing of it, the daily life of an egret warden may seem anything but exciting or adventurous. Long days of monotony there certainly are, weeks in which watching the life of the birds and the enjoyment of being in the open are the only events of interest, yet there is always a feeling of alert anticipation that something may happen. It frequently does, often unexpectedly, and is likely to be as serious as it is exciting.

Protecting plumage birds is assuredly no child's play. In spite of the apparently closed markets of New York and New Jersey, plumes are as much in demand as ever before, and as long as they command a price greater than their weight in gold there will always be men willing to risk even death to get them, laws of trespass and closed markets notwithstanding. So long as this condition of affairs continues it will be necessary to protect egrets by armed patrol, and the camp of an egret warden therefore takes on something of the aspect of a small military garrison with its regular watches.

Danger, you ask? Yes, there is, for the plume hunter's calling is not an honorable one, but rather that of the sneak who creeps upon you unawares and shoots you in the dark or in the back when you have relaxed a little in your watchfulness. It is not honorable warfare, but murder for gain. I am warden of a reservation of the Audubon Society where about six thousand pairs of birds breed, and in guarding them from unwelcome visitors I practically lived with the birds for the four months of April, May, June, and July, 1911, during which time I was always armed and on the alert for plume hunters. They killed a warden on one of our South Florida reservations several years ago.

As for myself I have not had any serious trouble here yet, but fear some this year, as the egrets are now in such numbers as to tempt hunters. I shall protect the birds with my life though, if necessary, and I have a "hunch" that I'll win out.

I had one serious scrape in guarding egrets, but not on this reservation. It was at a small colony in a vast cypress swamp that I was protecting "on my own hook," and before I was connected with the Audubon Society. A plume hunter told me boldly that he would get the plumes or "get" me. I told him he would have to "get" me first.

Fortunately I learned when he intended to visit the roost, and as there was only one way to enter the swamp, I went in first and stationed myself near the birds. I had taken with me cooked rations for several days, a hammock, and a mosquito bar. Swinging my hammock between two trees I spent three days and nights there over the water. Soon after I arrived I heard the plume hunter coming and called out to him to go back.

No answer, but I knew he was there, although I never saw him or heard him again for the entire time I stayed. The last morning I was getting tired and climbed a tree to look around. Not higher than twenty feet did I get when there came the crack of a rifle and I tumbled down, luckily catching between the tree and the large cypress "knees," where I remained unconscious for more than three hours. The plume hunter had shot a hole through my army hat just below the ventilators in the side, shaving a narrow pathway of hair off the top of my head and stunning me. When I finally regained consciousness and left the swamp I learned at a negro's cabin close at hand that the hunter had gone by on the run, thinking probably that he had killed me. He left the state and had better stay away if he values his liberty.

Unfortunately my work at this reservation all went for naught. Later on a marauder visited the rookery unexpectedly and killed the entire colony.

Nor is the lawless plume hunter the only menace which an egret warden must face. The swamps in which the birds breed are not healthful habitations for man, and even the completion of this article was delayed several months because of an almost fatal attack of fever. There is a fascination about the life, though, to one who loves the open as I do, and the work is a noble one which I am proud to be connected with. The Audubon Society has so many calls on its treasury that I have been guarding this reservation for no remuneration other than my living expenses, making what outside money I can with my pen and camera, and gathering material for a book on the birds of Florida, as I am a collecting naturalist.

The Audubon Society has been protecting the egret for several years now, and has printed and distributed thousands of pamphlets describing the cruelties of the plume trade which are fairly well known to readers of "Country Life in America." Through the efforts of the Society the legislatures of New York and New Jersey have passed very stringent laws regarding the sale of heron plumes. These are not as well enforced as one might wish, but with ten wardens protecting the larger breeding colonies it looks now as if the egret will be saved from utter destruction and that the remnant of American and snowy egrets will increase and spread over the South again as in days gone by.

Probably the largest rookery of egrets in the United States is that of which I am warden. It is located on Bird Island, about one mile out in Orange Lake in Central Florida, which has been a "roost" or breeding place of birds for more than forty years, and I have been told by old settlers that long ago the greater portion were egrets, but that as soon as any great number gathered here the ever-vigilant plume hunter swooped down and left a trail of death behind. This island of less than forty acres rises dark and green out of the water, and about one third of the northern end is densely overgrown with willow trees and alder bushes. At times during the spring and summer months the dark foliage is almost hidden under a cover of white birds — herons, ibises, and egrets — together with many others of less conspicuous plumage. Knowledge of the location of this island was brought to the attention of the National Association of Audubon societies a few years ago, and the island was finally bought by the association, thus assuring a protected breeding place for these birds for all time. Here the much sought after and persecuted egret is making an encouraging stand. Happily, this reservation is easily guarded against invasion, as an island in open water in sight of a town and railroad is more readily watched than a "rookery" in some lonely and out of the way cypress swamp. The people living in the vicinity, too, are intelligent and sympathetic regarding bird protection, which is of distinct assistance.

In 1909, when I first became warden of this island reservation, there were only four pairs of egrets here. The following year there were about thirty pairs, and in 1911 nearly two hundred pairs successfully reared their young, showing how quickly these birds respond to protection. In a few years at this rate of increase egrets will again be seen all over the state, exciting the wonder and admiration of the thousands of winter visitors from the North.

There are about 30,000 fish crows that use this island as a "roost" every night, as do thousands of blackbirds and jackdaws, making in all fully 100,000 birds sleeping on the island. By ten o'clock this vast winged army is asleep and it seems incredible that there can be such quiet. It gets on one's nerves. This lasts for perhaps an hour, when a dead limb breaks under the weight of too many birds. The din that ensues for the half hour before quiet is restored would almost awaken the dead.

With the first streak of dawn the birds awake, the ibises usually being first to leave in search of food, closely followed by the egrets. The crows are usually last, and they hunt around for eggs before going. These black pests have eaten thousands of eggs in the rookery and I shall try to discourage their visits to the roost this year.

Egrets always nest in colonies. They mate in early March and in a few weeks begin building their nests, which consist of closely built platforms of sticks and twigs. The American egret always places its nest exposed to the sun, and when in bushes will invariably be seen in the top, never down under the limbs like the nest of the snowy egret and the smaller herons. This is due to the habit of the egret to drop down directly to the nest when there are eggs or small young. When the young are older, however, the parent always alights on a perch overlooking the nest and remains there for several minutes before feeding the young.

Egret eggs are from three to five in number and of a light greenish color. The large egret begins to shed its plumes almost as soon as the young are hatched, and by the time the young are able to fly it is "plumeless." The snowy egret, on the contrary, does not shed its plumes so soon; I have seen many of them with young large enough to fly, and still wearing their plumes. This leads me to believe that they carry them until they molt. A plume hunter once told me that in shooting the "long whites," the plumer's name for the American egrets, he has shot the plumes from their backs without seriously injuring the birds and that they would return at once to their nests and pay no more attention to him, seeming to know that he would not shoot them again.

I spent several entire nights on the island in my photographic blind to make notes on the breeding birds, and found that the American egret would come home as late as 9.30 p.m., but when coming in late never offered to feed the young. As the young were very large at this time I judged that their demands were so great that the parent birds could not spare enough food during the day for themselves and so stayed late to satisfy their own wants. At six weeks of age the young would roost on the nest and the parents a foot or more away on a higher branch, not covering them when a rain came up at night.

Spending as I did an average of eight hours a day for two months with these birds, they became very tame and fearless and I was enabled to see and learn a great deal about their habits and conduct and to photograph them at close range in some very interesting positions. One nasty, cloudy day I was watching a nest of snowy egrets with baby young when it began to rain hard. I was within five feet of the nest when the female came back and hovered about them, all the time watching me nervously, showing that her maternal instinct was stronger than her fear of man. This instinct has been the undoing of the egret, for the merciless plume hunter has taken advantage of it.

I partially tamed a young American egret — Billy White we named him. I would take him in from the island late in the evening, keep him at camp all night and early in the morning return him to his nest. I never fed him and he never acted as if he wanted to be fed. His mother's actions when I returned him to the nest were good to see. She would stop feeding her other little one and take on over the prodigal in a way that was almost human. She would feed him several times more than I thought was good for him, paying no attention whatever to the other young bird, and this neglected one would move away with a full-grown grouch that was worth seeing; a grouch that lasted for more than an hour after his mother's departure. Billy became quite tame and when I stopped taking him to camp and when he could almost fly would come running down the path to meet me in the morning, acting like a puppy that is glad to see his master. He kept this up even after he could fly.

Naturally, with such an army of birds on this reservation, the food question is one of vital importance. However, there are more than fifteen large lakes, prairies, and marshes within a radius of eighteen miles of the reservation, and to those the birds go many times daily for food. Many, of course, fall victims to the guns of prowling negroes or worthless whites, and fail to return; and the frequent sight of young starving birds forever put to rest any doubts I might have had on the subject of young egrets being able to care for themselves.

In one nest four young egrets about six weeks old that I had been photographing were left parentless and I had the opportunity, and a sad one, of seeing their end. One had expired before I reached the nest and was lying with its head hanging over the edge, while the other three were staggering about; soon one of them stretched himself out and died. The remaining two tried many times to attract the attention of passing egrets and even ibises on the way to feed their own young. It was a sad and pitiful sight to see this pair of young starving egrets with open bills and weak voices imploring the passing birds to feed them — a sickening sight which I could not watch to the end. This recalls a scene on a larger scale which I witnessed only a few years ago at an egret rookery in a cypress swamp where the plume hunters had killed every parent and where I counted 172 nests all containing from 3 to 5 dead or dying young birds. The crows and vultures had already begun their gruesome feast. The hunters, as usual, had shot day after day along the lines of flight to the various feeding grounds, and finally in the rookery itself they had shot the parent birds as they were about to feed their hungry offspring.

Julian Dimock tells a pathetic little story of a tender-hearted boy who went plume hunting for the first time. The first day he and his brother shot a few birds. The next day the little birds were hungry and called so plaintively for frogs and fish that his heart melted. "I couldn't stand it, hearing those hungry little birds," he said, with tears in his eyes, "and I needed the money awful bad. John and I went 'gator hunting and worked a month to make a day's wages of plume hunting, but I couldn't stand the little birds."

It is difficult sometimes to believe that we are living in an enlightened age, when such cruelties exist, and all for the lust for gold which results from the whim of some women to wear egret plumes in their hats. When such scenes pass through my mind I renew my vow that nothing like it shall ever happen on Bird Island. The birds here are more to me than friends, and if a plume hunter ever leaves this island alive it will be because the hunter "gets" me first.

HOW THE MOTHER BIRD SAVED HER BABY

By Dallas Lore Sharp

ONE of the most interesting instances of variation of the mother instinct in the same species of birds, which has ever come under my observation, occurred in the summer of 1912 in the rookeries of the Three-Arch Rocks Reservation off the coast of Oregon.

We had gone out to the Reservation in order to study and photograph its wild life, and were making our slow way toward the top of the outer rock. Up the sheer south face of the cliff we had climbed, through rookery after rookery of nesting birds, until we reached the edge of the blade-like back, or top, that ran up to the peak. Scrambling over this edge we found ourselves in the midst of a great colony of nesting murres — hundreds of them — covering the steep rocky part of the top.

As our heads appeared above the rim, many of the colony took wing and whirred over us out to sea, but most of them sat close, each bird upon her egg or over her chick, loath to leave, and so expose to us her hidden treasure.

The top of the rock was somewhat cone-shaped, and in order to reach the peak and the colonies on the west side, we had to make our way through this rookery of the murres. The first step among them, and the whole colony was gone, with a rush of wings and feet that sent several of the top-shaped eggs rolling, and several of the young birds toppling, over the cliff to the pounding waves and ledges far below.

We stopped instantly. We had not come to frighten and kill. Our climb up had been very disturbing to the birds and had been attended with some loss of both eggs and young. This we could not help; and we had been too much concerned for our own lives really to notice what was happening. But here on the top, with the climb beneath us, the sight of a young murre going over the rim, clawing and clinging with beak and nails and unfledged wings, down from jutting point to shelf, to ledge, down, down — the sight of it made one dizzy and sick.

We stopped, but the colony had bolted, leaving scores of eggs and scores of downy young squealing and running together for shelter, like so many beetles under a lifted board.

But the birds had not every one bolted, for here sat two of the colony among the broken rocks. These two had not been frightened off. That both of them were greatly alarmed anyone could see from their open beaks, their rolling eyes, their tense bodies on tiptoe for flight. Yet here they sat, their wings out like props, or more like gripping hands, as if they were trying to hold themselves down to the rocks against their wild desire to fly.

And so they were in truth, for under their extended wings I saw little black feet moving. Those two mother murres were not going to forsake their babies

— no, not even for fear of these approaching monsters, which had never been seen clambering over their rocks before!

One of the monsters stood stock still a moment for the other one, the photographer, to come up. Then both of them took a step nearer. It was very interesting. I had often come slowly up to quails on their nests, and to other birds. Once I crept upon a killdeer in a bare field until my fingers were almost touching her. She did not move because she thought I did *not* see her, it being her trick thus to hide within her own feathers, colored as they are to blend with the pebbly fields where she lays her eggs. So the brown quail also blends with its brown grass nest. But those murres, though colored in harmony with the rocks, were still, not because they hoped I did not see them. I did see them. They knew it. Every bird in the great colony had known it, and had gone — with the exception of these two.

What was different about these two? They had their young ones to protect. But so had every bird in the great colony its young one, or its egg, to protect; yet all the others had gone. Did these two have more love than the others, and with it, or because of it, more courage, more intelligence?

We took another step toward them, and one of the two birds sprang into the air, knocking her baby over and over with the stroke of her wing, coming within an inch of hurling it across the rim to be battered on the ledges below. The other bird raised her wings to follow, then clapped them back over her baby. Fear is the most contagious thing in the world; and that flap of fear by the other bird thrilled her, too, but as she had withstood the stampede of the colony, so she caught herself again and held on.

She was now alone on the bare top of the rock, with ten thousand circling birds screaming to her in the air above, and with two men creeping up to her with a big black camera which clicked ominously. She let the multitude scream, and with threatening beak watched the two men come on. A motherless baby, spying her, ran down the rock squealing for his life. She spread her wing, put her bill behind him and shoved him quickly in out of sight with her own baby. The man with the camera saw the act, for I heard his machine click, and I heard him say something under his breath that you would hardly expect a mere man and a game warden to say. But most men have a good deal of the mother in them; and the old bird had acted with such decision, such courage, such swift, compelling instinct, that any man, short of the wildest savage, would have felt his heart sicken at the sight.

Just how compelling might that mother-instinct be? I wondered. Just how much would that mother-love stand?

I had dropped to my knees, and on all fours had crept up within about three feet of the bird. She still had a chance for flight. Would she allow us to crawl any nearer? Slowly, very slowly, I stretched forward on my hands, like a measuring worm, until my body lay flat on the rocks, and my fingers were within three inches of her. But her wings were twitching; a wild light danced in her eyes; and her head turned itself toward the sea.

For a whole minute I did not stir. Then the wings again began to tighten about the babies; the wild light in the eyes died down; the long sharp beak turned once more toward me. Then slowly, very slowly, I raised my hand, and gently touched her feathers with the tip of one finger — with two fingers — with my whole hand, while the loud camera click-clacked, click-clacked hardly four feet away!

It was a thrilling moment. I was not killing anything. I had no high-powered rifle in my hands, coming up against the wind toward an unsuspecting creature hundreds of yards away. This was no wounded leopard charging me; no mother bear defending with her giant might a captured cub. It was only a mother bird, the size of a wild duck, with swift wings at her command, hiding under those wings her own and another's young, and her own boundless fear!

For the second time in my life I had taken captive with my bare hands a free wild bird. No, I had not taken her captive. She had made herself a captive; she had taken herself in the strong net of her mother-love.

And now her terror seemed quite gone. At the first touch of my hand she felt, I think, the love restraining it, and without fear or fret allowed me to push my hand under her and pull out the two downy babies. But she reached after them with her bill to tuck them back out of sight, and when I did not let them go, she sidled toward me quacking softly, — a language that I perfectly understood, and was quick to answer.

I gave them back, fuzzy, and black and white. She

got them under her, stood up over them, pushed her wings down hard around them, her stout tail down hard behind them, and together with them she pushed in an abandoned egg which was close at hand. Her own baby, some one else's baby, and some one else's forsaken egg! She could cover no more; she had not feathers enough. But she had heart enough; and into her mother's heart she had already tucked every motherless egg and nestling of the thousands of frightened birds that were screaming and wheeling in the air high over her head.

TURTLE EGGS FOR AGASSIZ

By Dallas Lore Sharp

I TOOK down, recently, from the shelves of a great public library, the four volumes of Agassiz's "Contributions to the Natural History of the United States." I doubt if anybody but the charwoman, with her duster, had touched those volumes for twenty-five years. They are a monumental work, the fruit of vast and heroic labors, with colored plates on stone, showing the turtles of the United States, and their life history. The work was published more than half a century ago, but it looked old beyond its years — massive, heavy, weathered, as if dug from the rocks; and I soon turned with a sigh from the weary learning of its plates and diagrams to look at the preface.

Then, reading down through the catalogue of human names and of thanks for help received, I came to a sentence beginning: —

"In New England I have myself collected largely; but I have also received valuable contributions from the late Rev. Zadoc Thompson of Burlington; . . . from Mr. D. Henry Thoreau of Concord; . . . and from Mr. J. W. P. Jenks of Middleboro." And then it hastens on with the thanks in order to get to the turtles, as if turtles were the one and only thing of real importance in all the world.

Turtles are important — interesting; so is the late Rev. Zadoc Thompson of Burlington. Indeed any reverend gentleman who would catch turtles for Agassiz must have been interesting. If Agassiz had only put a chapter into his turtle book about him! and as for the Mr. Jenks of Middleboro (at the end of the quotation) I know that he was interesting; for years later he was an old college professor of mine. He told me some of the particulars of his turtle contributions, particulars which Agassiz should have found a place for in his big book. The preface says merely that this gentleman sent turtles to Cambridge by the thousands — brief and scanty recognition. For that is not the only thing this gentleman did. On one occasion he sent, not turtles, but turtle *eggs* to Cambridge — *brought* them, I should say; and all there is to show for it, so far as I could discover, is a small drawing of a bit of one of the eggs!

Of course, Agassiz wanted to make that drawing, and had to have a *fresh* turtle egg to draw it from. He had to have it, and he got it. A great man, when he wants a certain turtle egg, at a certain time, always gets it, for he gets some one else to get it for him. I am glad he got it. But what makes me sad and impatient is that he did not think it worth while to tell us about the getting of it.

It would seem, naturally, that there could be nothing unusual or interesting about the getting of turtle eggs when you want them. Nothing at all, if you should chance to want the eggs as you chance to find them. So with anything else. But if you want turtle eggs *when* you want them, and are bound to have them, then you must — get Mr. Jenks or somebody else to get them for you.

Agassiz wanted those turtle eggs when he wanted them — not a minute over three hours from the minute they were laid. Yet even that does not seem exacting, hardly more difficult than the getting of hens' eggs only three hours old. Just so, provided the professor could have had his private turtle coop in Harvard College Yard; and provided he could have made his turtles lay. But turtles will not respond, like hens, to meat scraps and the warm mash. The professor's problem was not to get from a mud turtle's nest in the back yard to his work table in the laboratory; but to get from the laboratory in Cambridge to some pond when the turtles were laying, and back to the laboratory within the limited time. And this might have called for nice and discriminating work — as it did.

Agassiz had been engaged for a long time upon his "Contributions." He had brought the great work nearly to a finish. It was, indeed, finished but for one small yet very important bit of observation: he had carried the turtle egg through every stage of its development with the single exception of one—the very earliest. That beginning stage had brought the "Contributions" to a halt. To get eggs that were fresh enough to show the incubation at this period had been impossible.

There were several ways that Agassiz might have proceeded; he might have got a leave of absence for the spring term, taken his laboratory to some pond inhabited by turtles, and there camped until he should catch the reptile digging out her nest. But there were difficulties in all of that — as those who are college professors and naturalists know. As this was quite out of the question, he did the easiest thing — asked Mr. Jenks of Middleboro to get him the eggs. Mr. Jenks got them. Agassiz knew all about his getting them; and I say the strange and irritating thing is, that Agassiz did not think it worth while to tell us about it, at least in the preface to his monumental work.

It was many years later that Mr. Jenks, then a gray-haired college professor, told me how he got those eggs to Agassiz.

"I was principal of an academy during my younger years," he began, "and was busy one day with my classes, when a large man suddenly filled the doorway of the room, smiled to the four corners of the room, and called out with a big, quick voice that he was Professor Agassiz.

"Of course he was. I knew it, even before he had had time to shout it to me across the room.

"Would I get him some turtle eggs? he called. Yes, I would. And would I get them to Cambridge within three hours from the time they were laid? Yes, I would. And I did. And it was worth the doing. But I did it only once.

"When I promised Agassiz those eggs, I knew where I was going to get them. I had got turtle eggs there before — at a particular patch of sandy shore along a pond, a few miles distant from the academy.

"Three hours was the limit. From the railroad station to Boston was thirty-five miles; from the pond to the station was perhaps three or four miles; from Boston to Cambridge we called about three miles. Forty miles in round numbers! We figured it all out before he returned, and got the trip down to two hours, —record time:—driving from the pond to the station; from the station by express train to Boston; from Boston by cab to Cambridge. This left an easy hour for accidents and delays.

"Cab and car and carriage we reckoned into our time-table; but what we didn't figure on was the turtle." And he paused abruptly.

"Young man," he went on, his shaggy brows and spectacles hardly hiding the twinkle in the eyes that were bent severely upon me, "young man, when *you* go after turtle eggs, take into account the turtle. No! No! that's bad advice. Youth never reckons on the turtle—and youth seldom ought to. Only old age does that; and old age would never have got those turtle eggs to Agassiz.

"It was in the early spring that Agassiz came to the academy, long before there was any likelihood of the turtles laying. But I was eager for the quest, and so fearful of failure that I started out to watch at the pond, fully two weeks ahead of the time that the turtles might be expected to lay. I remember the date clearly: it was May 14th.

"A little before dawn — along near three o'clock — I would drive over to the pond, hitch my horse near by, settle myself quietly among some thick cedars close to the sandy shore, and there I would wait, my kettle of sand ready, my eye covering the whole sleeping pond. Here among the cedars I would eat my breakfast, and then get back in good season to open the academy for the morning session.

"And so the watch began.

"I soon came to know individually the dozen or more turtles that kept to my side of the pond. Shortly after the cold mist would lift and melt away, they would stick up their heads through the quiet water; and as the sun slanted down over the ragged rim of treetops, the slow things would float into the warm lighted spots, or crawl out and doze comfortably on the hummocks and snags.

"What fragrant mornings those were! How fresh and new and unbreathed! The pond odors, the woods odors, the odors of the plowed fields — of water lily, and wild grape, and the dew-laid soil! I can taste them yet, and hear them yet — the still, large sounds of the waking day — the pickerel breaking the quiet with his swirl; the kingfisher dropping anchor; the stir of feet and wings among the trees. And then the thought of the great book being held up for me! Those were rare mornings!

"But there began to be a good many of them, for the turtles showed no desire to lay. They sprawled in the sun, and never one came out upon the sand as if she intended to help on the great professor's book. The story of her eggs was of small concern to her; her contribution to the 'Natural History of the United States' could wait.

"And it did wait. I began my watch on the 14th

of May; June 1st found me still among the cedars, still waiting, as I had waited every morning, Sundays and rainy days alike. June 1st was a perfect morning, but every turtle slid out upon her log, as if egg laying might be a matter strictly of next year.

"I began to grow uneasy, — not impatient yet, for a naturalist learns his lesson of patience early, and for all his years; but I began to fear lest, by some subtile sense, my presence might somehow be known to the creatures; that they might have gone to some other place to lay, while I was away at the schoolroom.

"I watched on to the end of the first week, on to the end of the second week in June, seeing the mists rise and vanish every morning, and along with them vanish, more and more, the poetry of my early morning vigil. Poetry and rheumatism cannot long dwell together in the same clump of cedars, and I had begun to feel the rheumatism. A month of morning mists wrapping me around had at last soaked through to my bones. But Agassiz was waiting, and the world was waiting, for those turtle eggs; and I would wait. It was all I could do, for there is no use bringing a china nest egg to a turtle; she is not open to any such delicate suggestion.

"Then came a mid-June Sunday morning, with dawn breaking a little after three: a warm, wide-awake dawn, with the level mist lifted from the level surface of the pond a full hour higher than I had seen it any morning before.

"This was the day. I knew it. I have heard persons say that they can hear the grass grow; that they know by some extra sense when danger is nigh. For a month I had been watching, had been brooding over this pond, and now I knew. I felt a stirring of the pulse of things that the cold-hearted turtles could no more escape than could the clods and I.

"Leaving my horse unhitched, as if he, too, understood, I slipped eagerly into my covert for a look at the pond. As I did so, a large pickerel plowed a furrow out through the spatter-docks, and in his wake rose the head of a large painted turtle. Swinging slowly round, the creature headed straight for the shore, and, without a pause, scrambled out on the sand.

"She was nothing unusual for a turtle, but her manner was unusual and the gait at which she moved; for there was method in it and fixed purpose. On she came, shuffling over the sand toward the higher open fields, with a hurried, determined see-saw that was taking her somewhere in particular, and that was bound to get her there on time.

"I held my breath. Had she been a dinosaurian making Mesozoic footprints, I could not have been more fearful. For footprints in the Mesozoic mud, or in the sands of time, were as nothing to me when compared with fresh turtle eggs in the sands of this pond.

"But over the strip of sand, without a stop, she paddled, and up a narrow cow path into the high grass along a fence. Then up the narrow cow path, on all fours, just like another turtle, I paddled, and into the high wet grass along the fence.

"I kept well within sound of her, for she moved recklessly, leaving a wide trail of flattened grass behind.

I wanted to stand up, — and I don't believe I could have turned her back with a rail, — but I was afraid if she saw me that she might return indefinitely to the pond; so on I went, flat to the ground, squeezing through the lower rails of the fence, as if the field beyond were a melon patch. It was nothing of the kind, only a wild, uncomfortable pasture, full of dewberry vines, and very discouraging. They were excessively wet vines and briery. I pulled my coat sleeves as far over my fists as I could get them, and with the tin pail of sand swinging from between my teeth to avoid noise, I stumped fiercely, but silently, on after the turtle.

"She was laying her course, I thought, straight down the length of this dreadful pasture, when, not far from the fence, she suddenly hove to, warped herself short about, and came back, barely clearing me. I warped about, too, and in her wake bore down across the corner of the pasture, across the powdery public road, and on to a fence along a field of young corn.

"I was somewhat wet by this time, but not so wet as I had been before wallowing through the deep, dry dust of the road. Hurrying up behind a large tree by the fence, I peered down the corn rows and saw the turtle stop, and begin to paw about in the loose, soft soil. She was going to lay!

"I held on to the tree and watched, as she tried this place, and that place, and the other place. But *the* place, evidently, was hard to find. What could a female turtle do with a whole field of possible nests to choose from? Then at last she found it, and, whirling about, she backed quickly at it and, tail first, began to bury herself before my staring eyes.

"Those were not the supreme moments of my life; perhaps those moments came later that day; but those certainly were among the slowest, most dreadfully mixed of moments that I ever experienced. They were hours long. There she was, her shell just showing, like some old hulk in the sand alongshore. And how long would she stay there? and how should I know if she had laid an egg?

"I could still wait. And so I waited, when, over the freshly awakened fields, floated four mellow strokes from the distant town clock.

"Four o'clock! Why there was no train until seven! No train for three hours! The eggs would spoil! Then with a rush it came over me that this was Sunday morning, and there was no regular seven o'clock train, — none till after nine.

"I think I should have fainted had not the turtle just then begun crawling off. I was weak and dizzy; but there, there in the sand, were the eggs! and Agassiz! and the great book! Why, I cleared the fence — and the forty miles that lay between me and Cambridge — at a single jump! He should have them, trains or no. Those eggs should go to Agassiz by seven o'clock, if I had to gallop every mile of the way. Forty miles! Any horse could cover it in three hours, if he had to; and, upsetting the astonished turtle, I scooped out her long white eggs.

"On a bed of sand in the bottom of the pail I laid them, with what care my trembling fingers allowed;

filled in between them with more sand; so with layer after layer to the rim; and covering all smoothly with more sand, I ran back for my horse.

"That horse knew, as well as I, that the turtles had laid, and that he was to get those eggs to Agassiz. He turned out of that field into the road on two wheels, a thing he had not done for twenty years, doubling me up before the dashboard, the pail of eggs miraculously lodged between my knees.

"I let him out. If only he could keep this pace all the way to Cambridge! — or even halfway there, I should have time to finish the trip on foot. I shouted him on, holding to the dasher with one hand, holding the pail of eggs with the other, not daring to get off my knees, though the bang on them, as we pounded down the wood road, was terrific. But nothing must happen to the eggs; they must not be jarred, or even turned over in the sand before they came to Agassiz.

"In order to get out on the pike it was necessary to drive back away from Boston toward the town. We had nearly covered the distance, and were rounding a turn from the woods into the open fields, when, ahead of me, at the station it seemed, I heard the quick, sharp whistle of a locomotive.

"What did it mean? Then followed the *puff, puff, puff,* of a starting train. But what train? Which way going? And jumping to my feet for a longer view, I pulled into a side road that paralleled the track, and headed hard for the station.

"We reeled along. The station was still out of sight, but from behind the bushes that shut it from view, rose the smoke of a moving engine. It was perhaps a mile away, but we were approaching, head on, and, topping a little hill, I swept down upon a freight train, the black smoke pouring from the stack, as the mighty creature pulled itself together for its swift run down the rails.

"My horse was on the gallop, following the track, and going straight toward the coming train. The sight of it almost maddened me — the bare thought of it, on the road to Boston! On I went; on it came, a half — a quarter of a mile between us, when suddenly my road shot out along an unfenced field with only a level stretch of sod between me and the engine.

"With a pull that lifted the horse from his feet, I swung him into the field and sent him straight as an arrow for the track. That train should carry me and my eggs to Boston!

"The engineer pulled the whistle. He saw me stand up in the rig, saw my hat blow off, saw me wave my arms, saw the tin pail swing in my teeth, and he jerked out a succession of sharp Halts! But it was he who should halt, not I; and on we went, the horse with a flounder landing the carriage on the top of the track.

"The train was already grinding to a stop; but before it was near a standstill, I had backed off the track, jumped out, and, running down the rails with the astonished engineers gaping at me, had swung aboard the cab.

"They offered no resistance; they hadn't had time. Nor did they have the disposition, for I looked strange, not to say dangerous. Hatless, dew-soaked, smeared with yellow mud, and holding, as if it were a baby or a bomb, a little tin pail of sand!

" 'Crazy,' the fireman muttered, looking to the engineer for his cue.

"I had been crazy, perhaps, but I was not crazy now.

" 'Throw her wide open,' I commanded. 'Wide open! These are fresh turtle eggs for Professor Agassiz of Cambridge. He must have them before breakfast.'

"Then they knew I was crazy, and, evidently thinking it best to humor me, threw the throttle wide open, and away we went.

"I kissed my hand to the horse, grazing unconcernedly in the open field, and gave a smile to my crew. That was all I could give them, and hold myself and the eggs together. But the smile was enough. And they smiled through their smut at me, though one of them held fast to his shovel, while the other kept his hand upon a big ugly wrench. Neither of them spoke to me, but above the roar of the swaying engine I caught enough of their broken talk to understand that they were driving under a full head of steam, with the intention of handing me over to the Boston police, as perhaps the safest way of disposing of me.

"I was only afraid that they would try it at the next station. But that station whizzed past without a bit of slack, and the next, and the next; when it came over me that this was the through freight, which should have passed in the night, and was making up lost time.

"Only the fear of the shovel and the wrench kept me

from shaking hands with both men at this discovery. But I beamed at them; and they at me. I was enjoying it. The unwonted jar beneath my feet was wrinkling my diaphragm with spasms of delight. And the fireman beamed at the engineer, with a look that said, 'See the lunatic grin; he likes it!'

"He did like it. How the iron wheels sang to me as they took the rails! How the rushing wind in my ears sang to me! From my stand on the fireman's side of the cab I could catch a glimpse of the track just ahead of the engine, where the ties seemed to leap into the throat of the mile-devouring monster. The joy of it! of seeing space swallowed by the mile!

"I shifted the eggs from hand to hand and thought of my horse, of Agassiz, of the great book, of my great luck,—luck,—luck,—until the multitudinous tongues of the thundering train were all chiming 'luck! luck! luck!' They knew! they understood! This beast of fire and tireless wheels was doing its best to get the eggs to Agassiz!

"We swung out past the Blue Hills, and yonder flashed the morning sun from the towering dome of the State House. I might have leaped from the cab and run the rest of the way on foot, had I not caught the eye of the engineer watching me narrowly. I was not in Boston yet, nor in Cambridge either. I was an escaped lunatic, who had held up a train, and forced it to carry me from Middleboro to Boston.

"Perhaps I had overdone the lunacy business. Suppose these two men should take it into their heads to turn me over to the police, whether I would or no? I could never explain the case in time to get the eggs to Agassiz. I looked at my watch. There were still a few minutes left in which I might explain to these men, who, all at once, had become my captors. But how explain? Nothing could avail against my actions, my appearance, and my little pail of sand.

"I had not thought of my appearance before. Here I was, face and clothes caked with yellow mud, my hair wild and matted, my hat gone, and in my full-grown hands a tiny tin pail of sand, as if I had been digging all night with a tiny tin shovel on the shore! And thus to appear in the decent streets of Boston of a Sunday morning!

"I began to *feel* like a lunatic. The situation was serious, or might be, and rather desperately funny at its best. I must in some way have shown my near fears, for both men watched me more sharply.

"Suddenly, as we were nearing the outer freight yard, the train slowed down and came to a stop. I was ready to jump, but still I had no chance. They had nothing to do, apparently, but to guard me. I looked at my watch again. What time we had made! It was only six o'clock, — a whole hour left in which to get to Cambridge!

"But I didn't like this delay. Five minutes — ten — went by.

" 'Gentlemen,' I began, but was cut short by an express train coming past. We were moving again, on — into a siding — on to the main track — on with a bump and a crash and a succession of crashes, running the length of the train — on, on at a turtle's pace, but on, — when the fireman, quickly jumping for the bell-rope, left the way to the step free, and —

"I never touched the step, but landed in the soft sand at the side of the track, and made a line for the freight-yard fence.

"There was no hue or cry. I glanced over my shoulder to see if they were after me. Evidently their hands were full, or they did n't know I had gone.

"But I had gone; and was ready to drop over the high board fence, when it occurred to me that I might drop into a policeman's arms. Hanging my pail in a splint on top of a post, I peered cautiously over — a very wise thing to do before you jump a high board fence. There, crossing the open square toward the station, was a big, burly fellow with a club — looking for me.

"I flattened for a moment, when some one in the freight yard yelled at me. I preferred the policeman; grabbing my pail, I slid softly over to the street. The policeman moved on past the corner of the station out of sight. The square was free, and yonder stood a cab.

"Time was flying now. Here was the last lap. The cabman saw me coming, and squared away. I waved a dollar bill at him, but he only stared the more. A dollar can cover a good deal, but I was too much for one dollar. I pulled out another, thrust them both at him, and dodged into the cab, calling, 'Cambridge!'

"He would have taken me straight to the police station, had I not said, 'Harvard College. Professor Agassiz's house! I've got eggs for Agassiz,' pushing another dollar up at him through the hole.

"It was nearly half past six.

" 'Let him go!' I ordered. 'Here's another dollar if you make Agassiz's house in twenty minutes. Let him out; never mind the police!'

"He evidently knew the police, or there were none around at that time on a Sunday morning. We went down the sleeping streets, as I had gone down the wood roads from the pond two hours before, but with the rattle and crash now of a fire brigade. Whirling a corner into Cambridge Street, we took the bridge at a gallop, the driver shouting out something in Hibernian to a pair of waving arms and a belt and brass buttons.

"Across the bridge with a rattle and jolt that put the eggs in jeopardy, and on over the cobblestones, we went. Half standing, to lessen the jar, I held the pail in one hand and held myself in the other, not daring to let go even to look at my watch.

"But I was afraid to look at the watch. I was afraid to see how near to seven o'clock it might be. The sweat was dropping down my nose, so close was I running to the limit of my time.

"Suddenly there was a lurch, and I dived forward, ramming my head into the front of the cab, coming up with a rebound that landed me across the small of my back on the seat, and sent half of my pail of eggs helter-skelter over the floor.

"We had stopped. Here was Agassiz's house; and without taking time to pick up the eggs that were scattered, I jumped out with my pail and pounded at the door.

"No one was astir in the house. But I would stir

some one. And I did. Right in the midst of the racket the door opened. It was the maid.

"'Agassiz!' I gasped. 'I want Professor Agassiz, quick!' And I pushed by her into the hall.

"'Go 'way, sir. I'll call the police. Professor Agassiz is in bed. Go 'way, sir!'

"'Call him — Agassiz — instantly, or I'll call him myself.'

"But I did n't; for just then a door overhead was flung open, a great white-robed figure appeared on the dim landing above, and a quick loud voice called excitedly, —

"'Let him in! Let him in. I know him. He has my turtle eggs!'

"And the apparition, slipperless, and clad in anything but an academic gown, came sailing down the stairs.

"The maid fled. The great man, his arms extended, laid hold of me with both hands, and dragging me and my precious pail into his study, with a swift, clean stroke laid open one of the eggs, as the watch in my trembling hands ticked its way to seven — as if nothing unusual were happening to the history of the world.'"

IN THE TOADFISH'S SHOE

By Dallas Lore Sharp

I WAS winding up my summer vacation with a little fishing party all by myself, on a wharf whose piles stood deep in the swirling waters from Buzzards Bay. My heavy-leaded line hummed taut in the swift current; my legs hung limp above the water; my back rested comfortably against a great timber that was warm in the September sun. Exciting? Of course not. Fishing is fishing — any kind of fishing is fishing to me. But the kind I am most used to, and the kind I like best, is from the edge of a wharf, where my feet dangle over, where my "throw-out" line hums taut over my finger, in a tide that runs swift and deep and dark below me.

For what may you not catch in such dark waters? And when there are no "bites," you can sit and wait; and I think that sitting and waiting with my back against a big warm timber is just as much fun now as it used to be when I was a boy.

But after all it is fish that you want when you go fishing; and it is exciting, moreover, just to sit as I was sitting on the wharf, with all the nerves of your body concentrated in the tip of your right forefinger, under the pressure of your line. For how do you know but that the next instant you may get a bite? And how do you know what the fish may be?

When you whip a trout stream for trout — why, you expect trout; when you troll a pond for pickerel, you expect pickerel; but when you sit on a wharf with your line far out in big, deep waters — why, you can expect almost anything — except shoes!

Shoes? Yes, old shoes!

As I sat there on the wharf of Buzzards Bay, there was suddenly a sharp tug at my line. A short quick snap, and I hooked him, and began quickly hauling him in.

How heavily he came! How dead and stupid! Even a flounder or a cod would show more fight than this; and very naturally, for on the end of my line hung an old shoe!

"Well," I thought, "I have fished for soles, and down on the Savannah I have fished for 'gators, but I never fished for shoes before." And taking hold of my big fish (for it must have been a No. 12 shoe), I was about to feel for the hook when I heard a strange grunting noise inside, and nearly tumbled overboard at sight of two big eyes and a monstrous head filling the whole inside of the shoe!

"In the name of Davy Jones!" I yelled, flinging line and shoe and *thing* (whatever it might be) far behind me, "I 've caught the Old Man of the Sea with his shoe on!" And, scrambling to my feet, I hurried across the wharf to see if it really were a fish that now lay flapping close beside the shoe.

It was really a fish; but it was also a hobgoblin,

nightmare, and ooze-croaker! — if you know what that is!

I had never seen a live toadfish before, and it is small wonder that I sighed with relief to see that he had unhooked himself; for he looked not only uncanny, but also dangerous! He was slimy all over, with a tremendous head and a more tremendous mouth (if that could be), with jaws studded on the inside with rows of sharp teeth, and fringed on the outside with folds of loose skin and tentacles. Great glaring eyes stared at me, with ragged bits of skin hanging in a ring about them.

Ugly? Oh, worse than ugly. Two thirds of the monster was head; the rest, a weak, shapeless, slimy something with fins and tail, giving the creature the appearance of one whose brain had grown at the expense of the rest of his body, making him only a kind of living head.

I looked at him. He looked at me, and croaked.

"I don't understand you," said I, and he croaked again. "But you are alive," said I; "and God made you, and therefore you ought not to look so ugly to me," and he flapped in the burning sun and croaked again.

Stooping quickly, I seized him, crowded him back into the old shoe, and dipped him under water. He gasped with new life and croaked again.

"Now," said I, "I begin to understand you. That croak means that you are glad to taste salt water again;" and he croaked again, and I dipped him in again.

Then I looked him over thoughtfully. He was about fifteen inches long, brown in color, and coarsely marbled with a darker hue, which ran along the fins in irregular wavy lines.

"You are odd, certainly, and peculiar, and altogether homely," said I; "but really you are not very ugly. Ugly? No, you are *not* ugly. How could anybody be ugly with a countenance so wise and learned? — so thoughtful and meditative?" And the toadfish croaked and croaked again. And I dipped him again, and understood him better, and liked him better all the time.

Then I took him in his shoe to the edge of the wharf.

"I am glad to have made your acquaintance, sir," said I. "If I come this way next summer, I shall look you up; for I want to know more about you. Good-bye." And I heard him croak "Good-bye," as he and his shoe went sailing out and dropped with a splash into the deep dark water of the Bay.

I meant what I said, and the next summer, along the shores of the Bay I hunted him up. He was not in an old shoe this time, but under certain rather large stones that lay just below ebb-tide mark, so that they were usually, though not always, covered with water. Here I found him keeping house; and as I was about to keep house myself, my heart really warmed to him.

I was understanding him more and more, and so I was liking him better and better. Ugly? Wait until I tell you what the dear fellow was doing.

He was keeping house, and he was keeping it all alone! Now listen, for this is what I learned that summer about the strange habits of Mrs. Toadfish, and the handsome behavior of her husband.

It is along in June that the toadfish of our New England bays begin to look round for their summer homes. As far as we now know, it is the female who makes the choice and leaves her future mate to find her and her home. A rock is usually chosen, always in shallow water, and sometimes so far up on the shore that at low tide it is left high and almost dry. The rock may vary in size from one as small as your hat up to the very largest.

Having selected the place for her nest, she digs a pathway down under the rock, and from beneath scoops out a hollow quite large enough to swim round in. This completes the nest, or more properly burrow, in which her little toadfish babies are to be reared.

She now begins to lay the eggs, but not in the sand, as one would suppose; she deliberately pastes them on the under surface of the rock. Just how she does this no one knows.

The eggs are covered with a clear, sticky paste which hardens in contact with water, and is the means by which the mother sticks them fast to the rock. This she must do while swimming on her back, fastening one egg at a time, each close beside its neighbor in regular order, till all the cleared surface of the rock is covered with hundreds of beautiful amber eggs, like drops of pure, clear honey.

The eggs are about the size of buckshot; and, curiously enough, when they hatch, the young come out with their heads all turned in the same direction. Does the mother know which is the head end of the egg? Or has some strange power drawn them around? Or do they turn themselves for some reason?

It will be noticed, in lifting up the rocks, that the heads of the fish are always turned toward the entrance to their nest, through which the light and fresh water come; and it is quite easy to see that these two important things have much to do with the direction in which the little fish are turned.

After Mrs. Fish had finished laying her eggs, her maternal cares are over. She leaves both eggs and cares to the keeping of Mr. Fish, swims off, and crawls into a tin can — or old shoe! — to meditate in sober satisfaction for the rest of the summer.

So it was *she* that I caught, and not the gallant Mr. Toadfish at all! I am glad of it. I have a deal of sympathy and downright admiration for Mr. Fish. He behaves most handsomely.

However, Mrs. Fish is very wise, and could not leave her treasures in better keeping. If ever there was a faithful parent, it is a Father Toadfish. For three weeks he guards the eggs before they hatch out, and then they are only half hatched; for it has taken the little fish all this time to get out on the top side of the eggs, to which they are still attached by their middles, so that they can move only their heads and tails.

They continue to wiggle in this fashion for some weeks, until the yolk of the egg is absorbed, and they have grown to be nearly half an inch long. They are then free from the rock and swim off, looking as much like their parents as children can, and every bit as ugly.

Ugly? Did I say ugly? Is a baby ever ugly to its mother? Or a baby toadfish to its father? No. You cannot love a baby and at the same time see it ugly. You cannot love the out of doors with all your *mind* as well as with all your heart, and ever see it ugly.

All this time the father has been guarding the little toadfish; and if, during the whole period, he goes out to get a meal, I have not been able to find when it is, for I always find him at home, minding the babies.

The toadfish lives entirely unmolested by enemies, so far as I can learn; and his appearance easily explains the reason of it. I know of nothing that would willingly enter a croaking, snapping, slimy toadfish's nest to eat him; and it takes some courage to put one's hand into his dark hole and pull him out.

His principal diet seems to be shrimp, worms and all kinds of small fish. Yet he may be said to have no principal diet; for, no matter what you are fishing for, or what kind of bait you are using, if there is a toadfish in the vicinity you are sure to catch him. If fishing along a wharf in September, you may catch the fish, and an old shoe along with him — with *her*, perhaps I should say.

And if you do, please notice how wise and thoughtful the face, how beautifully marbled the skin, how courageous the big strong jaw!

Ugly? Not if you will put yourself in the toadfish's shoe.

AS THE BEE FLIES

By Elisabeth Woodbridge

JONATHAN had taken me to see the "bee tree" down in the "old John Lane lot." Judging from the name, the spot must have been a clearing at one time, but now it is one of the oldest pieces of woodland in the locality. The bee tree, a huge chestnut, cut down thirty years ago for its store of honey, is sinking back into the forest floor, but we could still see its hollow heart and charred sides where the fire had been made to smoke out the bees.

"Jonathan," I said, "I'd like to find some wild honey. It sounds so good."

"No better than tame honey," said Jonathan.

"It sounds better. I'm sure it would be different scooped out of a tree like this than done up neatly in pound squares."

"Tastes just the same," persisted Jonathan prosaically.

"Well, anyway, I want to find a bee tree. Let's go bee hunting!"

"What's the use? You don't know a honeybee from a bumblebee."

"Well, you do, of course," I answered, tactfully.

Jonathan, mollified, became gracious. "I never

went bee hunting, but I've heard the old fellows tell how it's done. But it takes all day."

"So much the better," I said.

And that night I looked through our books to find out what I could about bees. Over the fireplace in what was once the "best parlor" is a long, low cupboard with glass doors. Here Bibles, albums, and a few other books have always been stored, and from this I pulled down a fat, gilt-lettered volume called "The Household Friend." This book has something to say about almost everything, and, sure enough, it had an article on bees. But "The Household Friend" had obviously never gone bee hunting, and the only real information I got was that bees had four wings and six legs.

"So has a fly," said Jonathan, when I came to him with this nugget of wisdom.

The neighbors gave suggestions. "You want to go when the yellertop's in bloom," said one.

"Yellowtop?" I questioned, stupidly enough.

"Yes. Yellertop — 't's in bloom now!" with a comprehensive wave of the hand.

"Oh, you mean goldenrod!"

"Well, I guess you call it that. Yellertop we call it. You find one o' them old back fields where the yellertop's come in, 'n' you'll see bees 'nough."

Another friend told us that when we had caught our bee we must drop honey on her back. This would send her to the hive to get her friends to groom her off, and they would all return with her to see where the honey came from. This sounded improbable, but we were in no position to criticize our information.

As to the main points of procedure all advisers agreed. We were to put honey in an open box, catch a bee in it, and when she had loaded up with honey, let her go, watch her flight and locate the direction of her home. When she returned with friends for more honey, we were to shut them in, carry the box on in the line of flight, and let them go again. We were to keep this up until we reached the bee tree. It sounded simple.

We got our box — two boxes, to be sure of our resources — baited them with chunks of comb, and took along little window panes for covers. Then we packed up luncheon and set out for an abandoned pasture in our woods where we remembered the "yellertop" grew thick. Our New England fall mornings are cool, and as we walked up the shady wood road Jonathan predicted that it would be no use to hunt bees. "They'll be so stiff they can't crawl. Look at that lizard, now!" He stooped and touched a little red newt lying among the pebbles of the roadway. The little fellow seemed dead, but when Jonathan held him in the hollow of his hand for a few moments he gradually thawed out, began to wriggle and finally dropped through between his fingers and scampered under a stone. "See!" said Jonathan. "We'll have to thaw out every bee just that way."

But I had confidence that the sun would take the place of Jonathan's hand, and refused to give up my hunt. From the main log road we turned off into a path, once a well-trodden way to the old ox pastures, but now almost overgrown, and pushed on through brier and sweet fern and huckleberry and young birch, down across a little brook, and up again to the "old Sharon lot," a long field framed in big woods and grown up to sumac and brambles and goldenrod. It was warmer here, in the steady sunshine, sheltered from the crisp wind by the tree walls around us, and we began to look about hopefully for bees. At first Jonathan's gloomy prognostications seemed justified — there was not a bee in sight. A few wasps were stirring, trailing their long legs as they flew. Then one or two "yellow jackets" appeared, and some black-and-white hornets. But as the field grew warmer it grew populous, bumblebees hummed, and finally some little soft brown bees arrived — surely the ones we wanted. Cautiously Jonathan approached one, held his box under the goldenrod clump, brought the glass down slowly from above — and the bee was ours. She was a gentle little thing, and did not seem to resent her treatment at all, but dropped down on to the honeycomb and fell to work. Jonathan had providently cut a three-forked stick, and he now stuck this into the ground and set the box on the forks so that it was about on a level with the goldenrod tops. Then he carefully drew off the glass, and we sat down to watch.

"Should n't you think she must have had enough?" I said, after a while. "Oh! there she comes now!"

Our bee appeared on the edge of the box, staggering heavily. She rubbed her legs, rubbed her wings, shook herself, girded up her loins, as it were, and brushed the hair out of her eyes, and finally rose, turning on herself in a close spiral which widened into larger and larger circles above the box, and at length, after two or three wide sweeps where we nearly lost track of her, she darted off in a "bee-line" for a tall chestnut tree on a knoll to the westward.

"Will she come back?" we wondered. Five minutes — ten — fifteen — it seemed an hour.

"She must have been a drone," said Jonathan.

"Or maybe she was n't a honeybee at all," I suggested, gloomily. "She might be just another kind of hornet — no, look! There she is!"

I could hardly have been more thrilled if my fairy godmother had appeared on the goldenrod stalk and waved her wand at me. To think that the bee really did play the game! I knelt and peered in over the side of the box. Yes, there she was, all six feet in the honey, pumping away with might and main through her little red tongue, or proboscis, or whatever it was. We sank back among the weeds and waited for her to go. As she rose, in the same spirals, and disappeared westward, Jonathan said, "If she does n't bring another one back with her this time, we 'll try dropping honey on her back. You wait here and be a landmark for the bee while I try to catch another one in the other box."

I settled down comfortably under the yellowtop, and instantly I realized what a pleasant thing it is to be a landmark. For one thing, when you sit down in a field you get a very different point of view from that when you stand. Goldenrod is different looked at from beneath, with sky beyond it; sky is different seen through waving masses of yellow. Moreover, when you sit still outdoors, the life of things comes to you; when you are moving yourself, it evades you.

Down among the weeds where I sat, the sun was hot, but the breeze was cool, and it brought to me, now the scent of wild grapes from an old stone wall, now the spicy fragrance of little yellow apples on a gnarled old tree in the fence corner, now the sharp tang of the goldenrod itself. The air was full of the hum of bees, and soon I began to distinguish their different tones — the deep, rich drone of the bumblebees, the higher sing-song of the honeybees, the snarl of the yellow-jacket, the jerky, nasal twang of the black-and-white hornet. They began to come close around me; two bumblebees hung on a frond of goldenrod so close to my face that I could see the pollen dust on their fur. Crickets and grasshoppers chirped and thrilled beside me. All the little creatures seemed to have accepted me — all but one black-and-white hornet, who left his proper pursuits, whatever they may have been, to investigate me. He buzzed all around me in an insistent, ill-bred way that was annoying. He examined my neck and hair with unnecessary thoroughness, flew away, returned to begin all over again, flew away and returned once more; but at last even he gave up the matter and went off about his business.

Butterflies came fluttering past me: — big, rust-colored ones pointed in black; pale russet and silver ones; dancing little yellow ones; big black ones with blue-green spots, rather shabby and languid, as at the end of a gay season. Darning needles darted back and forth, with their javelin-like flight, or mounted high by sudden steps, or lighted near me, with that absolute rigidity that is the positive negation of movement. A flying grasshopper creeping along through the tangle at my feet rose and hung flutteringly over one spot, for no apparent reason, and then, for no better reason, dropped suddenly and was still. A big cicada with green head and rustling wings worked his way clumsily among a pile of last year's goldenrod stalks, freed himself, and whirred away with the harsh, strident buzz that dominates every other sound while it lasts, and when it ceases makes the world seem wonderfully quiet.

Our bee had gone and come twice before Jonathan returned. "Has n't she brought anybody yet? Well, here goes!" He took a slender stem of goldenrod, smeared it with honey, and gently lodged a drop on the bee's back, just where she could not by any possible antics get it off for herself. When the little thing flew she fairly reeled under her burden, tumbled down on to a leaf, recovered herself, and at last flew off on her old line.

"Now, let's go and cook luncheon," said Jonathan, "and leave her to work it out."

"But how can I move? I 'm a landmark."

"Oh, leave your handkerchief. Anything white will do."

So I tied my handkerchief to a goldenrod stalk, and we went back to the brook. We made a fire on a flat stone, under which we could hear the brook running, broiled our chops on long, forked sticks, broiled some "beefsteak" mushrooms that we had found on a chestnut stump, and ended with water from the spring under the giant birch tree. Blue jays came noisily to investigate us; a yellow-hammer floated softly down to the branch overhead, gave a little purring cluck of surprise, and flew off again, with a flare of tawny-yellow wings. In the warmth of the Indian summer noon the shade of the woods was pleasant, and I let Jonathan go back to the bees while I lay on a dry slope above the brook and watched the slim, tall chestnuts swaying in the wind. It is almost like being at sea to lie in the woods and look up at the trees. Their waving tops seem infinitely far away, but the sky beyond seems very near, and one can almost feel the earth go round.

As I lay there I heard a snapping of twigs and rustling of leaves. It was the wrong direction for Jonathan, and I turned gently, expecting nothing smaller than a deer — for deer are growing plentiful now in old New England — and met the shameless face of a jerky little red squirrel! He clung to a chestnut trunk and examined me, twitching all over the while, then whisked himself upside down and looked at me from that standpoint, mounted to a branch, clung to the under side and looked again, pretended fright and vanished behind the limb, only to peer over it the next moment to see what I looked like from there — all the time clucking and burring like an alarm clock under a pillow.

The rude thing had broken the spell of quiet, and I got up, remembering the bees, and wandered back to the sunny field, now palpitating with waves of heat. Jonathan was nowhere to be seen, but as I approached the box I discovered him beside it flat on his back among the weeds.

"Sh-h-h," he warned, "don't frighten them. There were a lot of them when I got here and I've been watching their line. They all go straight for that chestnut."

"What are you lying down for?" I asked.

"I had to. I nearly twisted my neck off following their circles. I'm no owl."

I sat down near by and we watched a few more go while others began to arrive.

"That dab of honey did the work," said Jonathan. "We might as well begin to follow up their line now."

Waiting till there were a dozen or more in the box, he gently slid on the glass cover, laid a paper over it to darken it, and we set out. Ten minutes' walking brought us past the big chestnut and out to a little clearing. Jonathan set the box down on a big rock where it would show up well, laid a handkerchief beside it, drew off the glass, and crouched. A bunch of excited bees burst out and away, without noticing their change of place. "They 'll never find their way back there," said Jonathan regretfully; "they 'll go straight back to the Sharon lot."

But there were others in the box, still feeding, who had not been disturbed by the move, and these he touched with honey drops. They staggered off, one by one, orienting themselves properly as they rose, and taking the same old line off to the westward. This was disappointing. We had hoped to see them turn back, showing that we had passed their home tree. However, there was nothing to do but sit and wait for them. In six minutes they began to come back, in twos and threes — evidently the honey drops on their shoulders had told the hive a sufficiently alluring story. Again we waited until the box was well filled with them, then closed it and went on westward. Two more moves brought us to a half-cleared ridge from which we could see out across country. To the westward, and sadly near, was the end of the big woods and the beginning of pastures and farm land.

Jonathan scrutinized the farms dotting the slopes. "See that bunch of red barns with a white house?" he said. "That's Bill Morehead's. He keeps bees. Bet we've got bees from his hive and they'll lead us plumb into his back yard."

It did begin to seem probable, and we took up our box in some depression of spirits. Two more stops, and the bees still perversely flying westward, and we emerged in pastures.

"Here's our last stop," said Jonathan. "If they don't go back into that edge we've just left, they're Morehead's. There isn't another bit of woods big enough to hold a bee tree for seven miles to the west of us."

There was no rock to set the box on, so we lay down on the turf; Jonathan set the box on his chest, and partly slid the cover. He had by this time learned the trick of making the bees, even the excited ones, come out singly. We watched each one as she escaped circle above us, circle, circle against the clear blue of the afternoon sky, then dart off — alas! — westward. As the last one flew we sat up, disconsolately, and gazed across the pasture.

"Tame bees!" muttered Jonathan, in a tone of grief

and disgust. "Tame bees, down there in my old woodlots. It 's trespass!"

"You might claim some of Morehead's honey," I suggested, "since you 've been feeding his bees. But, then," I reflected, "it would n't be wild honey, and what I wanted was wild honey."

We rose dejectedly, and Jonathan picked up the box. "Are n't you going to leave it for the bees?" I asked. "They 'll be so disappointed when they come back."

"They are n't the only ones to be disappointed," he remarked grimly. "Here, we 'll have mushrooms for supper, anyway." And he stooped to collect a big puffball.

We walked home, our spirits gradually rising. After all, it is hard to stay depressed under a blue fall sky, with a crisp wind blowing in your face and the sense of completeness that comes of a long day out of doors. And as we climbed the last long hill to the home farm we could not help feeling cheerful.

"Bee hunting is fun," I said, "even if they are tame bees."

"It 's the best excuse for being a loafer that I 've found yet," said Jonathan; "I wonder the tramps don't all go into the business."

"And some day," I pursued hopefully, "we 'll go again and find really wild bees and really wild honey."

"It would taste just the same, you know," jeered Jonathan.

And I was so content with life that I let him have the last word.

THE BUSY BEE

By Elizabeth G. Chapin

IN attempting to give a short sketch of bees and bee-keeping, we hope chiefly to stimulate such of our readers as have never taken up this interesting study to do so.

Three varieties of bees constitute a swarm: the queen or mother, drones or males, and worker bees, the latter *not* a neuter sex, but considered as undeveloped female bees. While worker bees do occasionally lay unfertilized eggs, we may say, speaking generally of the bee community, that the queen mother lays the eggs which produce the swarm, and lays two varieties of eggs, fertilized ones which hatch into worker bees, and unfertilized, which hatch into drones. The normal span for hatching a complete bee is twenty-one days, of which three are spent in the egg stage, six in the larval, and twelve sealed up in a cell. During the larval stage the embryos are fed (generally by young workers) on a mixture of pollen and honey, partially digested in the stomach of the worker into chyle, a milky substance, and regurgitated. At the end of the larval stage, or about nine or ten days from the egg, the cells are capped by the workers, those cells which contain drone larvæ having a more convex or bulging cap — like wax bullets — than is given to the worker grubs.

But when, in obedience to nature's plan for continuing the swarm, young queens must be provided, the worker bees exercise a peculiar magic and *develop* a worker larva or grub into a royal child, providing it with a larger cell — occupying about the space of three ordinary cells — and looking, according to that veteran bee keeper, Mr. Root of Ohio, — "like a big peanut." This royal cell is stocked with a special rich food, "royal jelly," which so stimulates and nourishes the candidate for queen that she hatches possessed of abilities which insure her function as egg layer or mother of the swarm.

Young bees of all varieties spend their first few days alike, eating honey, then pollen, and gaining strength before trying to fly. For about two weeks their tint is whitish, coloration becoming deeper with maturity. In stature drones stand between the queen and the workers, have a blunter, squarer form both at head and abdomen. They cannot gather nectar from flowers, have no pollen baskets on their legs, are fed by the workers, do not labor, do not fight (though they have a loud and rather terrifying hum), do not sting, and exist in what seem to be superfluous numbers, evidently that the queen may not lack opportunity when she desires to meet a partner. The drones have but one use in life, the fecundation of the queen; and when in her apparently haphazard nuptial flight she meets and selects her mate, he perishes in her embrace. In the late summer such drones as are found in the hive are murdered by the workers, who sting them to death, thus ridding the swarm of their maintenance when they are no longer potentially useful.

The queen in infancy differs little in appearance from the workers, but is precocious in learning to fly. Her first real activity is to explore the hive for other queen cells, which she at once destroys by tearing them down. If other queens hatch earlier than she, a fight between rivals is pretty certain to take place, and the royal aspirant who proves most deft in using her sting, will slay other pretenders and reign alone. When five or six days old the queen will be seen crawling about the entrance to the hive and trying her wings in short preliminary flights. All bees, when leaving the hive, appear to take observations of their surroundings, but the queen is particularly careful to know her home's location before risking any long flight. Her wedding journey, or quest, as it might better be called, is thought by experienced observers to occur, on an average, about ten days from her first appearance. She sometimes mates with a drone in her own neighborhood, returning in fifteen or twenty minutes, but has been known to go as far as two miles to meet and choose her consort. After her return to the hive she begins laying and continues this function for the remainder of her life, which may last three or even four years. Beekeepers rarely find a queen a profitable mother of swarms after her third year. She can lay fertilized eggs, or workers, only *after* mating, while unfertilized eggs resulting in drones, may be laid by a virgin queen, or apparently at will by a mated queen. In late life, when the fertilizing principle seems to show exhaustion, mated queens are likely to lay a good many drone eggs. It is estimated that a vigorous queen will lay three thousand eggs in a day. Of these, the workers live but about six weeks, or a few months at the farthest, and hence if a queen dies or is killed, and leaves the swarm motherless, it is quickly deprived of new members to take the place of those that wear out in working, becomes demoralized, and fails as a honey-making organization. Fortunately, new queens are constantly being developed, but if there is no natural heir to the royal duties, a queen must be introduced by the beekeeper from some other colony.

The worker bees in the hive never mate, though occasionally cases are known where workers lay unfertilized eggs, all drone producers. The worker in early life acts in the hive as nurse to the larvæ; as cleaner, patcher, and polisher; as comb builder (it is interesting to know that each of the myriad six-sided wax cells is not the work of one bee, but a community product); and as porter and packer of pollen and honey brought in by foraging bees. Young workers fly when about one week old, and take to pollen gathering at about two weeks. Pollen is gathered in little baskets on the workers' back legs, is kicked off in the hive, gathered by younger workers and packed in cells by "butting" it in with the bee's head. The honey-gathering impulse follows shortly after, and the worker is at its prime when about a month old, diminishing in value with age by reason of the wearing and fraying of its wings in constant flight; and if it is not killed in the course of its short life by cold or damp, or snapped up by natural enemies, tree toads, etc., the worker, when it can no longer fly strongly, crawls off to die.

Honey is not exactly "gathered" by workers, but produced from the nectar they glean from flowers and swallow into a special honey stomach or reservoir, which is *not* the stomach of the bee's individual alimentary system. Nectar thus swallowed is in some fashion modified and regurgitated into the comb cell, where it is further submitted to a working over or ripening process, which lasts well into the evening, when the bees have finished bringing in fresh supplies.

Worker bees also make wax, a product of honey, and a fatty substance, but not animal fat in the usual sense, secreting it in scales under the abdomen. The more generous the honey flow and the greater the honey stores, the more copious must be the supply of wax to provide comb for storing. From ten to twelve pounds of honey enter into the composition of one pound of wax; hence it will be seen that the modern appliances for making artificial comb or foundation, pressed out of wax by machinery, have increased the potential honey yield by eliminating one process.

Having now in mind the three kinds of citizens in a hive and their respective functions, let us turn for a moment to the bee community or swarm. While the mother bee is called queen, and is the source of life for the hive, she is not queen in a political sense, the swarm being a perfect democracy, each member working voluntarily for the well-being of the whole body. Whether or not the queen gives the signal for swarming has been a matter of some dispute, but beekeepers now incline toward the belief that the workers decide when and where to move, sending out scouts in advance to locate a suitable cavity for a new home. Swarming is thought to be due at least in part to natural conditions, when a crowded hive and full store of honey suggest to the insatiable workers the advantage of new spheres for their industry. Beekeepers learn to know the symptoms,—restlessness and interrupted working habits on the part of the bee,—weather conditions, etc., indicative of swarming; and watching for the critical moment, try to arrest the flight of the bees at some near-by convenient point, as the low branch of a tree, from which transfer to a new hive can readily be made. The various methods and devices of professional beekeepers we need not discuss here—the main point is, that he who would not see his honey- and presumably money-makers escape beyond recall, must learn to provide fresh quarters so furnished with empty comb that the energetic new tenants will at once find work to do, and rest contented, the workers building and stocking new honey comb, the queen continuing to produce new brood for future swarms.

Beekeeping by amateurs probably will never prove the get-rich-quick scheme it is sometimes painted. Occasional newspaper articles—inspired by the visit of some reporter to a bee appliance agency—would have us believe that all we need do is to buy an outfit, install it in the back yard or on the roof of the apartment house, and let the bees do the rest, while we complacently do the resting and have money in the bank at the year's end. But beekeeping, like any other business, takes time and care, and one great point of its advantage—when done on a small scale—lies in the very fact that it does require care of a nature so different from ordinary business that it is a fascinating diversion and no heavy task. The writer knows of a university professor living in a city — but also near a large public garden — who installed bees in his back yard chiefly for scientific observation, and was rewarded for his painstaking care with enough honey for his own table, plus a snug little sum for charity from the proceeds of sales to delighted neighbors.

Beekeeping on a moderate scale can profitably be added to the farming proclivities of the suburban dweller who has enough space on the back lot to allow the bees to pass to and fro without disputing right of way with human neighbors. On farms, a few hives under the orchard trees will serve the double purpose of supplying a luxury and of perfecting fertilization in the fruit blossoms and improving the fruit crop. True, the grass about the hives must be kept short — in large apiaries sheep are sometimes used as convenient grass croppers — or the bees will get lost as in a forest in trying to return to the entrance of the hive. Attention must be given to proper shade, and if trees do not provide it, vine-covered trellises or board or thatch shade must be supplied. Some water supply is necessary, and of course there is much to study in the construction and placing of hives. But all this information is obtainable and no great amount of money need be sunk in the venture, particularly where the would-be keeper can do his or her own carpentry. Mr. Root, the well-known authority, declares that not more than twenty-five dollars should be expended until the "plant" is bringing in some return. He furthermore urges that amateurs will do well to content themselves with a small outfit which they can hope to manage successfully, getting honey for the home table and perhaps a small yearly money return, rather than to risk capital in attempting beekeeping as a livelihood. A hive installed as part of the nature study course for school children is truly a live interest, and can be no less so for any older students who can find place and pasturage to maintain an example of these wonder-working colonists.

OUR WASP

By George W. Peckham and Elizabeth G. Peckham

ON the morning of the third of August, at a little after ten o'clock, we saw one of these hunters [*Sphex ichneumonea* Linn.] start to dig a nest on the side of a stony hill. After making some progress in the work she flew off and selected a second place, where she dug so persistently that we felt confident that this was to be her final resting place; but when the hole was two and one half inches deep, it too was deserted. Again our wasp chose a spot and began to burrow. She worked very rapidly, and at twenty minutes before twelve, the hole was three inches deep. At high noon she flew away, and was gone forty minutes. The day was excessively hot, about 98° Fahr., and we ourselves were only deterred from taking a noonday rest by our fixed determination not to leave the place until we had seen all that there was to be seen in the maneuvers of ichneumonea. On returning she appeared very much excited, fairly quivering with vitality as she resumed her work. She came up backwards, carrying the earth with her mouth and anterior legs, and went back from the opening some little distance, when it was dropped, and she at once went in again. While in the burrow we could hear her humming, just as the Pelopæi do when, head downward in the wet mud, they gather their loads for nest building. In five or six trips a little mass of earth would accumulate, and then she would lie quite flat on the heap and kick the particles away in all directions. As the work progressed the earth was carried farther and farther away before it was placed on the ground, and as she backed in different directions the material brought out was well spread about from the down-hill side of the nest. Sometimes she would spend several moments in smoothing the débris all around, so that the opening presented much the appearance of an immense ant hill, only the particles were much larger. During the first hour that we watched her she frequently turned directly toward us, and, sometimes remaining on the ground and sometimes rising on her wings to a level with our faces, appeared to be eyeing us intently for four or five seconds. Her attitude was comical, and she seemed to be saying, "Well, what are you hanging around here for?"

As the afternoon wore on she worked more calmly and her fidgety and excited manner disappeared; the excavation progressed steadily until half past three. At that time she came out and walked slowly about in front of her nest and all around it. Then she rose and circled just above it, gradually widening her flight, now going farther afield and now flying in and out among the plants and bushes in the immediate vicinity. The detailed survey of every little object near her nest was remarkable; and not until her tour of observation had carried her five times entirely around the spot did she appear satisfied and fly away. All her actions showed that she was studying the locality and getting her bearings before taking her departure. A fact that impressed us very much was that with the two nests that she had begun and then deserted she had taken no such precaution, but simply came up and flew off. Had she made up her mind, if we may be allowed to use the term, that the localities were in some way unsuitable and that hence she had no occasion to return to them? Had she decided, in the last instance, that she would return and so must get her bearings?

When she flew away we naturally supposed that she had gone in search of her prey, and we were on the *qui vive* to observe every step in her actions when she came home. Alas! when she came back half an hour later, she was empty-handed. She dug for four minutes, then flew off and was gone two minutes, then returned and worked for thirty-five minutes. Another two minutes' excursion, and then she settled down to work in good earnest and brought up load after load of earth until the shadows grew long. We noticed that on these later trips she flew directly away, depending upon her first careful study of the surroundings to find her way back. At fifteen minutes after five the patient worker came to the surface, and made a second study, this time not so detailed, of the environment. She flew this way and that, in and out among the plants, high and low, far and near, and at last, satisfied, rose in circles, higher and higher, and disappeared from view. We waited for her return with all the patience at our command, from fifteen minutes after five until fifteen minutes before seven. We felt sure that when she came back she would bring her victim with her, and when we saw her approaching we threw ourselves prone on the ground, eagerly expecting to see the end of the drama; but her search had been unsuccessful, — she carried nothing. In the realms of wasp life, disappointments are not uncommon, and this time she had us to share her chagrin, for we felt as tired and discouraged as she perhaps did herself. When we saw her entering without any provision for her future offspring, we were at a loss what to do next; and it may be that this state of mind was shared by her also, for she at once began to fill in the entrance to her nest. We now thought it time to act, and decided to capture her, to keep her over night in one of our wasp cages, and to try to induce her to return to her duty on the following day. We therefore secured her in a large bottle, carried her to the cottage, and having made every possible arrangement for her comfort, left her for the night.

On the next morning, at half after eight o'clock, we took Lady Sphex down to her home, and placed the mouth of the bottle so that when she came out she had to enter the nest. This she did, remaining below, however, only a moment. When she came up to the surface she stood still and looked about for a few seconds, and then flew away. It surprised us that having been absent from the place for so many hours, she made no study of the locality as she had done before. We thought it a very unpromising sign, and had great fears that she was deserting the place and that we should see her no more. One would need to watch a wasp through the long hours of a broiling hot day to appreciate the joy that we felt when at nine o'clock we saw her coming back. She had no difficulty in finding her nest, nor did she feel any hesitation as to what ought to be done next, but fell to work at once at carrying out more dirt. The weather, although still hot, had become cloudy and so threatening that we expected a downpour of rain every minute, but this seemed to make no difference to her. Load after load was brought up, until, at the end of an hour, everything seemed completed to her satisfaction. She came to the entrance and flew about, now this way, and now that, repeating the locality study in the most thorough manner, and then went away. At the expiration of an hour we saw her approaching with a large light green meadow grasshopper, which was held in the mouth and supported by the forelegs, which were folded under. On arriving, the prey was placed, head first, near the entrance, while the wasp went in, probably to reassure herself that all was right. Soon she appeared at the door of the nest and remained motionless for some moments, gazing intently at her treasure. Then seizing it (we thought by an antenna) she dragged it head first into the tunnel.

The laying of the egg did not detain her long. She was up in a moment and began at once to throw earth into the nest. After a little she went in herself, and we could plainly hear her humming as she pushed the loose material down with her head. When she resumed the work outside we interrupted her to catch a little fly that we had already driven off several times just as it was about to enter the nest. The Sphex was disturbed and flew away, and this gave us an opportunity to open the burrow.

We had not supposed that the digging up of her nest would much disturb our Sphex, since her connection with it was so nearly at an end; but in this we were mistaken. When we returned to the garden about half an hour after we had done the deed, we heard her loud and anxious humming from a distance. She was searching far and near for her treasure house, returning every few minutes to the right spot, although the upturned earth had entirely changed its appearance. She seemed unable to believe her eyes, and her persistent refusal to accept the fact that her nest had been destroyed was pathetic. She lingered about the garden all through the day, and made so many visits to us, getting under our umbrellas and thrusting her tremendous personality into our very faces, that we wondered if she were trying to question us as to the whereabouts of her property. Later we learned that we had wronged her more deeply than we knew. Had we not interfered she would have excavated several cells to the side of the main tunnel, storing a grasshopper in each. Who knows but perhaps our Golden Digger, standing among the ruins of her home, or peering under our umbrella, said to herself: "Men are poor things; I don't know why the world thinks so much of them"?

ANTS THAT GO HUNTING

By Thomas Belt

As I returned to the boat, I crossed a column of the army or foraging ants, many of them dragging along the legs and mangled bodies of insects that they had captured in their foray. I afterwards often encountered these ants in the forests. Whilst the leaf-cutting ants are entirely vegetable feeders, the foraging ants are hunters, and live solely on insects or other prey; and it is a curious analogy that, like the hunting races of mankind, they have to change their hunting grounds when one is exhausted, and move on to another. In Nicaragua they are generally called "Army Ants." One of the smaller species (*Eciton predator*) used occasionally to visit our house, swarm over the floors and walls, searching every cranny, and driving out the cockroaches and spiders, many of which were caught, pulled or bitten to pieces, and carried off. The individuals of this species are of various sizes; the smallest measuring one and a quarter lines, and the largest three lines, or a quarter of an inch.

I saw many large armies of this, or a closely allied species, in the forest. My attention was generally first called to them by the twittering of some small birds, belonging to several different species, that follow the ants in the woods. On approaching to ascertain the cause of the disturbance, a dense body of the ants, three or four yards wide, and so numerous as to blacken the ground, would be seen moving rapidly in one direction, examining every cranny and underneath every fallen leaf. On the flanks, and in advance of the main body, smaller columns would be pushed out. These smaller columns would generally first flush the cockroaches, grasshoppers, and spiders. The pursued insects would rapidly make off, but many, in their confusion and terror, would bound right into the midst of the main body of ants. A grasshopper, finding itself in the midst of its enemies, would give vigorous leaps, with perhaps two or three of the ants clinging to its legs. Then it would stop a moment to rest, and that moment would be fatal, for the tiny foes would swarm over the prey, and after a few more ineffectual struggles it would succumb to its fate, and soon be bitten to pieces and carried off to the rear. The greatest catch of the ants was, however, when they got amongst some fallen brushwood. The cockroaches, spiders, and other insects, instead of running right away, would ascend the fallen branches and remain there, whilst the host of ants were occupying all the ground below. By and by up would come some of the ants, following every branch, and driving before them their prey to the ends of the small twigs, when nothing remained for them but to leap, and they would alight in the very throng of their foes, with the result of being certainly caught and pulled to pieces. Many of the spiders would escape by hanging suspended by a thread of silk from the branches, safe from the foes that swarmed both above and below.

I noticed that spiders were generally most intelligent in escaping, and did not, like the cockroaches and the other insects, take shelter in the first hiding place they found, only to be driven out again, or perhaps caught by the advancing army of ants. I have often seen large spiders making off many yards in advance, and apparently determined to put a good distance between themselves and their foe. I once saw one of the false spiders, or harvestmen (*Phalangidæ*), standing in the midst of an army of ants, and with the greatest circumspection and coolness lifting, one after the other, its long legs, which supported its body above their reach. Sometimes as many as five out of its eight legs would be lifted at once, and whenever an ant approached one of those on which it stood, there was always a clear space within reach to put down another, so as to be able to hold up the threatened one out of danger.

I was much more surprised with the behavior of a green, leaflike locust. This insect stood immovably amongst a host of ants, many of which ran over its legs, without ever discovering there was food within their reach. So fixed was its instinctive knowledge that its safety depended on its immovability, that it allowed me to pick it up and replace it amongst the ants without making a single effort to escape. This species closely resembles a green leaf, and the other senses, which in the Ecitons appear to be more acute than that of sight, must have been completely deceived. It might easily have escaped from the ants by using its wings, but it would only have fallen into as great a danger, for the numerous birds that accompany the army ants are ever on the outlook for any insect that may fly up, and the heavy flying locusts, grasshoppers, and cockroaches have no chance of escape. Several species of ant thrushes always accompany the army ants in the forest. They do not, however, feed on the ants, but on the insects they disturb. Besides the ant thrushes, trogons, creepers, and a variety of other birds are often seen on the branches of trees above where an ant army is foraging below, pursuing and catching the insects that fly up.

The insects caught by the ants are dismembered, and their too bulky bodies bitten to pieces and carried off to the rear. Behind the army there are always small columns engaged on this duty. I have followed up these columns often; generally they led to dense masses of impenetrable brushwood, but twice they led me to cracks in the ground, down which the ants dragged their prey. These habitations are only temporary, for in a few days not an ant would be seen in the neighborhood; all would have moved off to fresh hunting grounds.

Another much larger species of foraging ant (*Eciton hamata*) hunts sometimes in dense armies, sometimes in columns, according to the prey it may be after. When in columns, I found that it was generally, if not always, in search of the nests of another ant (*Hypoclinea* sp.), which rear their young in holes in rotten trunks of fallen timber, and are very common in cleared places. The Ecitons hunt about in columns, which branch off in various directions. When a fallen log is reached, the column spreads out over it, searching through all the holes and cracks. The workers are of various sizes, and the smallest are here of use, for they squeeze themselves into the narrowest holes, and search out their prey in the furthest ramifications of the nests. When a nest of the *Hypoclinea* is attacked, the ants rush out, carrying the larvæ and pupæ in their jaws, only to be immediately despoiled of them by the Ecitons, which are running about in every direction with great swiftness. Whenever they come across a *Hypoclinea* carrying a larva or pupa, they capture the burden so quickly that I could never ascertain exactly how it was done.

As soon as an Eciton gets hold of its prey, it rushes off back along the advancing column, which is composed of two sets, one hurrying forward, the other returning laden with their booty, but all and always in the greatest haste and apparent hurry. About the nest which they are harrying everything is confusion, Ecitons run here and there and everywhere in the greatest haste and disorder; but the result of all this apparent confusion is that scarcely a single *Hypoclinea* gets away with a pupa or larva. I never saw the Ecitons injure the Hypoclineas themselves, they were always contented with despoiling them of their young. The ant that is attacked is a very cowardly species, and never shows fight. I often found it running about sipping at the glands of leaves, or milking aphides, leaf-hoppers, or scale-insects that it found unattended by other ants. On the approach of another, though of a much smaller, species, it would immediately run away. Probably this cowardly and unantly disposition has caused it to become the prey of the Eciton. At any rate, I never saw the Ecitons attack the nest of other species.

The moving columns of Ecitons are composed almost entirely of workers of different sizes, but at intervals of two or three yards there are larger and lighter-colored individuals that will often stop, and sometimes run a little backward, halting and touching some of the ants with their antennæ. They look like officers giving orders and directing the march of the column.

This species is often met with in the forest, not in quest of one particular form of prey, but hunting, like *Eciton predator*, only spread out over a much greater space of ground. Crickets, grasshoppers, scorpions, centipedes, wood lice, cockroaches, and spiders are driven out from below the fallen leaves and branches. Many of them are caught by the ants; others that get away are picked up by the numerous birds that accompany the ants, as vultures follow the armies of the East. The ants send off exploring parties up the trees, which hunt for nests of wasps, bees, and probably birds. If they find any, they soon communicate the intelligence to the army below, and a column is sent up immediately to take possession of the prize. I have seen them pulling out the larvæ and pupæ from the cells of a large wasp's nest, whilst the wasps hovered about, powerless, before the multitude of the invaders, to render any protection to their young.

I have no doubt that many birds have acquired instincts to combat or avoid the great danger to which their young are exposed by the attacks of these and other ants. Trogons, parrots, toucans, mot-mots, and many other birds build in holes of trees or in the ground, and these, with their heads ever turned to the only entrance, are in the best possible position to pick off singly the scouts when they approach, thus effectually preventing them from carrying to the main army intelligence about the nest. Some of these birds, and especially the toucans, have bills beautifully adapted for picking up the ants before they reach the nest. Many of the smaller birds build on the branches of the bull's-horn thorn, which is always thickly covered with small stinging honey-eating ants, that would not allow the Ecitons to ascend these trees.

Amongst the mammalia the opossums can convey their young out of danger in their pouches, and the females of many of the tree rats and mice have a hard callosity near the teats, to which the young cling with their milk teeth, and can be dragged away by the mother to a place of safety.

The eyes in the Ecitons are very small, in some of the species imperfect, and in others entirely absent; in this they differ greatly from those ants which hunt singly and which have the eyes greatly developed. The imperfection of eyesight in the Ecitons is an advantage to the community and to their particular mode of hunting. It keeps them together and prevents individual ants from starting off alone after objects that, if their eyesight were better, they might discover at a distance. The Ecitons and most other ants follow each other by scent, and, I believe, they can communicate the presence of danger, of booty, or other intelligence, to a distance by the different intensity or qualities of the odors given off. I one day saw a column of *Eciton hamata* running along the foot of a nearly perpendicular tramway cutting, the side of which was about six feet high. At one point I noticed a sort of assembly of about a dozen individuals that appeared in consultation. Suddenly one ant left the conclave, and ran with great speed up the perpendicular face of the cutting without stopping. It was followed by others which, however, did not keep straight on like the first, but ran a short way, then returned, then again followed a little farther than the first time. They were evidently scenting the trail of the pioneer, and making it permanently recognizable. These ants followed the exact line taken by the first one, although it was far out of sight. Wherever it had made a slight détour they did so likewise. I scraped with my knife a small portion of the clay on the trail, and the ants were completely at fault for a time which way to go. Those ascending and those descending stopped at the scraped portion, and made short circuits until they hit the scented trail again, when all their hesitation vanished, and they ran up and down it with the greatest confidence. On gaining the top of the cutting, the ants entered some brushwood suitable for hunting. In a very short space of time the information was communicated to the ants below, and a dense column rushed up to search for their prey.

The Ecitons are singular amongst the ants in this respect, that they have no fixed habitations, but move on from one place to another, as they exhaust the hunting grounds around them. I think *Eciton hamata* does not stay more than four or five days in one place. I have sometimes come across the migratory columns. They may easily be known by all the common workers moving in one direction, many of them carrying the larvæ and pupæ carefully in their jaws. Here and there one of the light-colored officers moves backwards and forwards directing the columns. Such a column is of enormous length, and contains many thousands, if not millions of individuals. I have sometimes followed them up for two or three hundred yards without getting to the end.

They make their temporary habitations in hollow trees, and sometimes underneath large fallen trunks that offer suitable hollows. A nest that I came across in the latter situation was open at one side. The ants were clustered together in a dense mass, like a great swarm of bees, hanging from the roof, but reaching to the ground below. Their innumerable long legs looked like brown threads binding together the mass, which must have been at least a cubic yard in bulk, and contained hundreds of thousands of individuals, although many columns were outside, some bringing in the pupæ of ants, others the legs and dissected bodies of various insects. I was surprised to see in this living nest tubular passages leading down to the center of the mass, kept open just as if it had been formed of inorganic materials. Down these holes the ants who were bringing in booty passed with their prey. I thrust a long stick down to the center of the cluster, and brought out clinging to it many ants holding larvæ and pupæ, which probably were kept warm by the crowding together of the ants. Besides the common dark-colored workers and light-colored officers, I saw here many still larger individuals with enormous jaws. These they go about holding wide open in a threatening manner and I found, contrary to my expectation, that they could give a severe bite with them, and that it was difficult to withdraw the jaws from the skin again.

One day, when watching a small column of these ants, I placed a little stone on one of the ants to secure it. The next that approached, as soon as it discovered the situation of the prisoner, ran backwards in an agitated manner, and communicated the intelligence to the others. They rushed to the rescue; some bit at the stone and tried to move it, others seized the captive by the legs, and tugged with such force that I thought the legs would be pulled off, but they persevered until they freed it. I next covered one up with a piece of clay, leaving only the ends of its antennæ projecting. It was soon discovered by its fellows, which set to work immediately, and, by biting off pieces of the clay, soon liberated it. Another time I found a very few of them passing along at intervals. I confined one of these under a piece of clay, at a little distance from the line, with his head projecting. Several ants passed it, but at last one discovered it and tried to pull it out, but could not. It immediately set off at a great rate, and I thought it had deserted its comrade, but it had only gone for assistance, for in a short time about a dozen ants came hurrying up, evidently fully informed of the circumstances of the case, for they made directly for their imprisoned comrade, and soon set him free. I do not see how this action could be instinctive. It was sympathetic help, such as man only among the higher mammalia shows. The excitement and ardor with which they carried on their unflagging exertions for the rescue of their comrade could not have been greater if they had been human beings, and this to meet a danger that can be only of the rarest occurrence. Amongst the ants of Central America I place the Eciton as the first in intelligence, and as such at the head of the Articulata. Wasps and bees come next to ants, and then others of the Hymenoptera. Between ants and the lower forms of insects there is a greater difference in reasoning powers than there is between man and the lowest mammalian. A recent writer has argued that of all animals ants approach nearest to man in their social condition. Perhaps if we could learn their wonderful language we should find that even in their mental condition they also rank next to humanity.

I shall relate two more instances of the use of a reasoning faculty in these ants. I once saw a wide column trying to pass along a crumbling, nearly perpendicular, slope. They would have got very slowly over it, and many of them would have fallen, but a number, having secured their hold and reaching to each other, remained stationary, and over them the main column passed. Another time they were crossing a watercourse along a small branch, not thicker than a goose quill. They widened this natural bridge to three times its width by a number of ants clinging to it and to each other on each side, over which the column passed three or four deep. Except for this expedient they would have had to pass over in single file, and treble the time would have been consumed. Can it not be contended that such insects are able to determine by reasoning powers which is the best way of doing a thing, and that their actions are guided by thought and reflection?

OLIVER GOLDSMITH'S SPIDER

By Oliver Goldsmith

OF all the solitary insects I have ever remarked, the spider is the most sagacious; and its actions, to me, who have attentively considered them, seem almost to exceed belief. This insect is formed by nature for a state of war, not only upon other insects, but upon each other. For this state nature seems perfectly well to have formed it. Its head and breast are covered with a strong natural coat of mail, which is impenetrable to the attempts of every other insect, and its belly is enveloped in a soft pliant skin, which eludes the sting even of a wasp. Its legs are terminated by strong claws, not unlike those of a lobster, and their vast length, like spears, serves to keep every assailant at a distance.

Not worse furnished for observation than for an attack or a defense, it has several eyes, large, transparent, and covered with a horny substance, which, however, does not impede its vision. Besides this, it is furnished with a forceps above the mouth, which serves to kill or secure the prey already caught in its claws or its net.

Such are the implements of war with which the body is immediately furnished; but its net to entangle the enemy seems what it chiefly trusts to, and what it takes most pains to render as complete as possible. Nature has furnished the body of this little creature with a glutinous liquid, which it spins into thread, coarser or finer as it chooses. In order to fix its thread, when it begins to weave it emits a small drop of its liquid against the wall, which, hardening by degrees, serves to hold the thread very firmly. Then receding from the first point, as it recedes the thread lengthens; and, when the spider has come to the place where the other end of the thread should be fixed, gathering up with its claws the thread which would otherwise be too slack, it is stretched tightly, and fixed in the same manner to the wall as before.

In this manner, it spins and fixes several threads parallel to each other, which, so to speak, serve as the warp to the intended web. To form the woof, it spins in the same manner its thread, transversely fixing one end to the first thread that was spun, and which is always the strongest of the whole web, and the other to the wall. All these threads, being newly spun, are glutinous, and therefore stick to each other wherever they happen to touch; and, in those parts of the web most exposed to be torn, our natural artist strengthens them by doubling the threads sometimes sixfold.

Thus far naturalists have gone in the description of this animal; what follows is the result of my own observation upon that species of the insect called a house spider. I perceived, about four years ago, a large spider in one corner of my room, making its web; and, though the maid frequently leveled her fatal broom against the labors of the little animal, I had the good fortune then to prevent its destruction; and, I may say, it more than paid me by the entertainment it afforded.

In three days the web was, with incredible diligence, completed; nor could I avoid thinking that the insect seemed to exult in its new abode. It frequently traversed it round, examined the strength of every part of it, retired into its hole, and came out very frequently. The first enemy, however, it had to encounter, was another and a much larger spider, which, having no web of its own, and having probably exhausted all its stock in former labors of this kind, came to invade the property of its neighbor. Soon, then, a terrible encounter ensued, in which the invader seemed to have the victory, and the laborious spider was obliged to take refuge in its hole. Upon this I perceived the victor using every art to draw the enemy from his stronghold. He seemed to go off, but quickly returned; and when he found all arts vain, began to demolish the new web without mercy. This brought on another battle, and, contrary to my expectations, the laborious spider became conqueror, and fairly killed his antagonist.

Now, then, in peaceable possession of what was justly its own, it waited three days with the utmost patience, repairing the breaches of its web, and taking no sustenance that I could perceive. At last, however, a large blue fly fell into the snare, and struggled hard to get loose. The spider gave it leave to entangle itself as much as possible, but it seemed to be too strong for the cobweb. I must own I was greatly surprised when I saw the spider immediately sally out, and in less than a minute weave a new net round its captive, by which the motion of its wings was stopped; and when it was fairly hampered in this manner, it was seized, and dragged into the hole.

In this manner it lived, in a precarious state, and nature seemed to have fitted it for such a life, for upon a single fly it subsisted for more than a week. I once put a wasp into the net; but when the spider came out in order to seize it as usual, upon perceiving what kind of an enemy it had to deal with, it instantly broke all the bands that held it fast, and contributed all that lay in its power to disengage so formidable an antagonist. When the wasp was at liberty, I expected the spider would have set about repairing the breaches that were made in its net, but those it seems were irreparable; wherefore the cobweb was now entirely forsaken, and a new one begun, which was completed in the usual time.

I had now a mind to try how many cobwebs a single spider could furnish; wherefore I destroyed this, and the insect set about another. When I destroyed the other also, its whole stock seemed entirely exhausted, and it could spin no more. The arts it made use of to support itself, now deprived of its great means of subsistence, were indeed surprising. I have seen it roll up its legs like a ball, and lie motionless for hours together, but cautiously watching all the time; when a fly happened to approach sufficiently near, it would dart out all at once, and often seize its prey.

Of this life, however, it soon began to grow weary, and resolved to invade the possession of some other spider, since it could not make a web of its own. It formed an attack upon a neighboring fortification with great vigor, and at first was as vigorously repulsed. Not daunted, however, with one defeat, in this manner it continued to lay siege to another's web for three days, and at length, having killed the defendant, actually took possession. When smaller flies happen to fall into the snare, the spider does not sally out at once, but very patiently waits till it is sure of them; for, upon its immediately approaching, the terror of its appearance might give the captive strength sufficient to get loose: the manner then is to wait patiently till, by ineffectual and impotent struggles, the captive has wasted all its strength, and then it becomes a certain and an easy conquest.

The insect I am now describing lived three years; every year it changed its skin and got a new set of legs. At first it dreaded my approach to its web, but at last it became so familiar as to take a fly out of my hand, and, upon my touching any part of the web, would immediately leave its hole, prepared for either a defense or an attack.

To complete this description, it may be observed that the male spiders are much smaller than the female, and that the latter are oviparous. When they come to lay, they spread a part of their web under the eggs, and then roll them up carefully, as we roll things up in a cloth, and thus hatch them in their hole. If disturbed in their holes, they never attempt to escape without carrying this young brood in their forceps away with them, and thus frequently are sacrificed to their parental affection.

As soon as ever the young ones leave their artificial covering, they begin to spin, and almost sensibly seem to grow bigger. If they have the good fortune, when even but a day old, to catch a fly, they fall to with good appetites; but they live sometimes three or four days without any sort of sustenance, and yet continue to grow larger, so as every day to double their former size. As they grow old, however, they do not still continue to increase, but their legs only continue to grow longer, and when a spider becomes entirely stiff with age, and unable to seize its prey, it dies at length of hunger.

THE WISDOM OF NATURE

By Albert H. Pratt

THE poets tell us that birds are here to cheer us with their songs, to please the eye with their graceful flight and plumage, and to set us a good example by their industry and their devotion to their young. They tell us that the sky is blue and the foliage green because these colors rest the eye, and that the beauty of the flowers is to please the sight of man. From the poet's point of view this is all that is necessary to justify the existence of the birds and flowers and the wonderful color effects of nature.

Recently, however, there has been a tendency to recognize that Nature works for a purpose, and that it is advisable to discover her plan and make it serve our ends by coöperating with her. The changed attitude toward the birds is evidence of this. We are now beginning to realize that the birds are here not only to be our cheerful little companions, but to maintain the balance of nature by keeping in check the hordes of insects, noxious weeds, and destructive rodents that would otherwise render agriculture impossible.

The discovery of the birds' place in the great scheme of nature leads us to a search for a purpose in other things, whether animal or vegetable. Everything has its own work to do. Each species of bird, for instance, is adapted for the work required of it. The swift-flying insectivorous birds clear the upper air of the small insects; others that nest in the underbrush keep the lower foliage clear of worms and caterpillars; others keep the hedgerows and the fields free from weed seeds; and still others, such as the owl, fly at night, acting as the farmer's night watchman, searching out the mice, rats, gophers, and other rodents that would otherwise multiply in great numbers and devastate the farmer's fields.

With this in mind, we naturally pass from the birds to the flowers, and are ready to find a reason for their form, their color, and their perfume. There are many explanations of these matters, but the most reasonable is that based on the assumption that in all that has reference to the organization of a plant or an animal, Nature works solely for its welfare and preservation, not primarily for the use it may be to the welfare and preservation of other plants or animals, — although, by understanding, man may make Nature serve that end for him.[1]

Let us assume that the beautiful forms and hues and the sweet odors of the flowers are given them for some purpose needful to themselves; that they are an indispensable part of Nature's arrangement for the preservation of the individual and for this purpose alone. In looking over a mass of flowers, one may be attracted by the fact that they are almost always regular and geometrical in form. This regularity of shape catches the eye at once, and it is evident that by means of it a

[1] This theory of the coloration of flowers was first formulated by Wilson Flagg.

flower becomes more conspicuous by contrast with the herbage around. To be conspicuous, to call attention to itself, is necessary to the continuance of almost all species of flowers. The insects must be summoned. They must be enticed within reach so that they may come in close contact with the flowers, become covered with the pollen, and then fly to another blossom and, by fertilizing it, continue the species. How wonderfully equipped the flowers are to accomplish this result that is so necessary to themselves!

A bee emerging from the hive goes abroad in search of honey. What signpost does he look for to guide him on his way to the blossoms? At first he perceives the sweet-scented odor that serves, not to guide him direct to the flower, but to detain him in its neighborhood. While hesitating in this captivating fragrance, his sight is suddenly attracted by the flower, its brilliancy of color and regularity of form throwing it out in sharp contrast against the dark-green background of the foliage. Straightway the bee finds the blossom, and guided by its form, unerringly reaches the nectary containing the much-desired sweet juices. While engaged in sipping these, the wings and body become covered with the pollen. When the nectary is exhausted, away flies the bee on its search for more, all unconscious of its services in scattering the precious powder. Another time it is not the odor that attracts, but the bee goes straight to a magnificent cluster of mountain laurel, which summons the insect by its very brilliancy and has no need of the aid of scent.

Thus we find that Nature has given a marked odor,

good or bad, to the less conspicuous flowers that are hidden away under the foliage, or the color of which does not contrast sufficiently to bring it into evidence, and little or none to those whose brilliancy or conspicuousness renders such an aid unnecessary. For instance, the panicled andromeda, whose drooping blossoms are hard to find, is given the delicious odor of cinnamon. The more elegant and showy flowers, on the other hand, are deprived of fragrance, such as the mountain laurel, previously mentioned, while the less showy and white flowers of the azalea are very fragrant. A solitary flower is commonly more beautiful than flowers that grow in clusters, which are rendered conspicuous by their grouping. There seems to be a rivalry between the different plants, each trying to outdo the others in displaying the greatest attraction to the fertilizing insect. The dandelion placed upon the green background of the lawn needs no other contrast besides that of its own yellow disk to render it a conspicuous object. The pansy, on the other hand, not being able to compete with the dandelion through sheer brilliancy, compensates itself by assuming a beautiful union of three colors, yellow, white, and purple, and constantly turns its face to the sun, not because it receives any direct benefit from its rays, but to be more conspicuous by the reflected light to the insect advancing in the direction of the sun's rays. The combination of these three colors can be seen at a greater distance than any one of the colors alone.

As the most gaudy flowers have the least odor, so white flowers are generally sweeter than those of the same family which are highly colored. The white lily and the white tulip are the most fragrant of their respective groups, while some of the most powerful odors are emitted by the greenish flowers, like those of the mignonette or the skunk cabbage. These flowers of inconspicuous and greenish hue seldom grow in a solitary blossom, but usually in dense clusters or upon trees, where they are rendered apparent to the insect in search of them.

That Nature has adapted the color of the flowers to their situation is apparent when we find that flowers that grow in the shade of the woods are mostly white, while those that stand out in the open field often have darker hues which would be indistinguishable under the shade of the forest. This can be noted in the blossoms of the fruit trees. White forms a more conspicuous contrast with green than with the naked branches of the trees. Those trees, therefore, that produce their blossoms before the leaves unfold are usually pink or crimson — such as those of the peach; while the white blossoms of the pear and cherry do not appear until the foliage is out and open at the same time with it. The blossoms of the apple tree are crimson before they are open, for at the time the leaves are not yet expanded, but the blossoms grow white when the flowers are fully open, having then a fully developed background of green leaves. The necessity for a green background is apparent in the case of the water lily. From one position water appears white, and there would be no contrast, but the lilies always bloom on a thick green carpet of broad-backed flat leaves.

Honey is placed in the flowers, not for the sake of the bees or other insects in order to supply them with the food they most desire, but to entice them to the blossoms and cause them to perform an act of special benefit to the flower or the plant. The honey being placed there, Nature then forms the bee with the instruments for obtaining it and an instinct that guides him to it.

Where a plant does not need the aid of insects in order to maintain itself, it does not contain a supply of honey. The grasses, for instance, are entirely independent of the services of insects for promoting their fertilization. Nature takes care of this by causing them to grow in dense masses, elevating flowers on long and slender stems which are blown to and fro by the wind, and thus are constantly brought in contact with one another. The flowers of the grass, therefore, do not attract by their form, their color, or their odor. To have a nectary filled with honey would be useless, and therefore Nature, which never carries anything superfluous, has omitted it.

In the spring and early summer, when the insects are comparatively few, most of the flowers are aided with a fragrance. The flowers, however, that bloom in the late summer and in the autumn, at a time when the insects are more numerous, have less fragrance. Many plants that flower in the autumn, when the insects abound, are defended from their attacks by a rank, herbaceous smell that emanates from their leaves, and a similar flavor from their taste; while the gaudy flowers of the same plant invite the bee to their blossoms —

such as, for instance, the thorn apple. Plants which have a medicated leaf are more common in the late summer when the grasshoppers and locusts come in swarms. Nature cares for the grasses which are devoured both by insects and quadrupeds by providing them with a means of multiplying by their roots, which are secure from attack by growing underground. This security, however, is only from the flying insects, and not from the grub. To care for the latter, Nature has provided the robins and blackbirds. Sometimes Nature gives a sweet smell to the whole plant instead of confining it to the flower, as in the case of the mint, the sweetbrier, and the myrtle. These odors not only attract the insects that are necessary, but defend the plants from the grazing animals and the herbivorous insects. Nature does not entice an insect or any other creature to a plant if the habit of the insect or animal be to devour it, except in the case of fruits.

When the plant is of such a nature that it would be destroyed by the loss of its foliage, the new growth is invariably protected by thorns or by a poisonous quality of its sap, or strong odor, or acrid taste. Hence the apple, the hawthorn, the pear, and the rose, whose foliage and tender branches are agreeable to animals, are protected in their wild state by thorns. The peach, the plum, and the cherry are without thorns, and are protected from the ravages of the insects and animals by a bitter and poisonous principle in their sap. Other trees, like the willow and kindred tribes, are not so well protected in these ways, but as a compensation they have a sort of vitality that enables them to recover from the effect of severe browsing at any season of the year.

Thus Nature in her wisdom gives each species the equipment necessary to enable it to maintain itself in the great struggle for existence.

WEEDS: GOOD, BAD, AND INDIFFERENT

By E. Thayles Emmons

"WEEDS have this virtue: they are not easily discouraged; they never lose heart entirely; they die game. If they cannot have the best, they will take up with the poorest; if fortune is unkind to them to-day, they hope for better luck to-morrow; if they cannot lord it over a cornhill, they will sit humbly at its foot and accept what comes; in all cases they make the most of their opportunities." — *John Burroughs.*

In the first place, what is a weed? Everybody knows the old definition that says a weed is only a plant out of place. The scientist claims that a weed is any plant injurious to agriculture, although this seemingly throws into the category of weeds a long list of beautiful plants that are perfectly proper and desirable, — each in its own place.

Carry the pestiferous dandelion to some isolated portion of the globe where it never before has been seen (we don't imagine such a place exists, however), and it might be cherished as a most beautiful flower. We know it, nevertheless, as one of our worst weeds, and can never forgive it for sprinkling our lawns and garden patches with its bright yellow blossoms. The viper's bugloss is considered in some localities a most pernicious weed; and yet we know other places where it is found so rarely that the local botanists have marked the station of every growing plant, and flower lovers prize it for their gardens.

This serves to illustrate the point that there is, perhaps, no real distinction between weeds and flowers. It is largely a question of scarcity or abundance. Abundant flowers become weeds, and rare weeds become flowers. Many of the flowers we find in our gardens are, after all, but weeds, imported, perhaps, from Europe, — which, by the way, is the source of many of our troublesome plants. From our gardens they spread out into the adjacent fields, and are soon firmly established in such numbers as to be detrimental to the farmer and his crops.

To the farmers, weeds have an immense economic importance, and it frequently is the case that a crop shortage is caused by the growth of weeds. If all weeds could be eliminated from the growing crops, the latter might possibly be increased one third; and yet they are so persistent and so hardy that "all the king's horses and all the king's men" would be powerless to control them.

Weeds, as every one must understand, are injurious to crops because they take from the soil the valuable nutrient material which otherwise would be left for the more useful plants; at least a part of the depletion of our soils must be attributed to the growth of weeds. When weeds grow in rank profusion they choke out the crops, and at once become the agriculturist's enemies. Other weeds gain their undesirable reputation from the fact that they are poisonous to man, or otherwise obnoxious. The poison ivy and the thistle illustrate weeds of this type. The ivy is a somewhat "pretty" plant, though man fears it; and the big "bull" thistle is beautiful enough when in blossom to become a house plant were it not for the needle-like spikes that make all living creatures avoid it.

Such weeds as the pigweed, "pusley," burdock, nettle, etc., can be placed in the class of undesirables at once. The homely dock, with its ugly leaves and long root, is also a plant enemy; and, sad to relate, there is no more obnoxious weed than the common field daisy. We doubt if there is any other weed so detrimental to a crop of growing grass, or one that spreads to such vast areas of meadowland, unless, possibly, it be the wild carrot, which certainly is a close second to the daisy in both beauty and undesirability.

However, not all weeds possess nothing but bad traits. In his book on "Weeds of the Farm and Garden," L. H. Pammell concedes that many weeds are useful, and says: —

"Digitalis is obtained from foxglove; hyoscyamine from black henbane; daturin from Jimson weed. Many weeds, like tansy and hemp, have medicinal properties. Others serve culinary purposes, as when the roots of chicory are used as substitutes for coffee. Lamb's quarter, dandelion, and the shoots of pokeweed are used as spring greens. The roots of tanweed were formerly used in the process of tanning. The tubers of the cultivated artichoke are used as food, and the Indian used the wild artichoke in the same manner.

Sweet clover is an excellent bee plant, a good forage plant, and a satisfactory soil renovator."

Among the weeds used for spring greens might also be included the marsh marigold or American cowslip, the milkweed, mustard, and cress. Mint serves as one of our chiefest household delicacies, and there are any number of herbs — catnip, for instance — that form part of every household's winter supply of tonics. Lobelia may be used in preparing a very effective cough sirup, and is there a man who has grown up in a rural community and has not, at some period in his lifetime, been compelled to drink thoroughwort tea? It did him good, too, no doubt of it. Perhaps it had little or no effect upon his physical system, but at least it taught him how to endure some of the bitter things of life later on.

Harold C. Long, author of an English work on common weeds, also reminds us that all of our cultivated crops have been derived from wild plants, and that it is not at all improbable that certain so-called "weeds" of to-day may become valuable cultivated plants of the future, "though they still will be weeds," he says, "if found growing in the wrong place."

This author also concedes artistic value to certain "weeds" which makes them desirable as garden flowers. Many of our most common garden flowers are but derivatives of wild forms which in their native lands are counted as "weeds." Cornflowers of various colors are forms of the corn blue bottle; Shirley poppies were derived from the wild red poppy, and soon revert to their weed type if not carefully cultivated; meadow saffron is also grown in many English gardens because of its beauty, although it ranks as a poisonous weed; there are many other examples.

If I should attempt to divide the weeds into the three classes of good, bad, and indifferent, I am positive the agriculturists would not agree with me save in a few rare instances. Weeds which I find rare and harmless in my locality would be most certain to be over-abundant and harmful somewhere else. However, if I were to prepare a list of this sort along lines in accordance with my own observations, it would look something like this: —

GOOD WEEDS — Tansy, catnip, lobelia, artichoke, sweet clover, marsh marigold, horse-radish, asparagus, fuller's teazle, sweet flag, cat-tail, mint, caraway, wintergreen, mandrake, violets, strawberry, boneset.

BAD WEEDS — Canada thistle, bull thistle, purslane, nettle, poison ivy, pigweed, buckhorn, plantain, white daisy, ox-eyed daisy, wild parsnip, wild carrot, dandelion, burdock, milkweed, ragweed, goldenrod, dock, sow thistle, chickweed, smartweed, cowbane, hawkweed, mallow, cocklebur, sorrel, wild garlic.

INDIFFERENT WEEDS — Bouncing Bet, mullein, touch-me-not, toadflax, viper's bugloss, houseleek, four o'clock, ragged robin, purple aster, bloodroot, buttercup, blue flag, everlasting.

In closing may I again resort to Burroughs, who finds it pleasant to remember that there is nothing that grows so persistently, so lastingly, and so universally as grass. "And in human nature, too," he concludes, "weeds are by no means in the ascendant, troublesome as they are. The good green grass of love and truthfulness and common sense is more universal, and crowds the idle weeds to the wall."

MAKING FRIENDS WITH THE VIOLETS

By Alice Lounsberry

AFTER we had started, grandmother said: "It's likely we shall find several kinds of violets to-day. They are not all purple with round, heart-shaped leaves, as my little city girl supposes. There are besides white violets, yellow violets, and purple ones with leaves queerly cut all about their edges. They all begin to open when the windflowers and dog's-tooth violets unfold."

I said I should be happy if I could only find a purple one. White or yellow violets were strange to me. First we walked along by the side of the stream where the grass grows tall. All the way I was looking for violets. Suddenly I spied a little white one. It was almost under my foot. It was such a wee thing that I thought at first it could not be a violet at all, yet its leaves were the same round, heart shape as those of the purple violet. Fine, brown lines ran through the blossom's white leaves, and it had a sweet scent, almost as tiny as itself.

"I used to call it the little sweet white violet," grandmother said. "I think it has the sweetest scent of them all."

She started to walk on, but I stayed with the tiny

violets until I had to run to catch up with her. Then she called me and asked: "What color is the ground here, child?"

I was so excited that I called out, "Green," although it really was purple with violets.

"Here are our city friends," said grandmother, "long-stemmed purple violets, with rounded, heart-shaped leaves. They are the so-called common blue violets, although you and I think they are purple." Here, in the high grass, many of them grew very tall, for they had to lift their buds up high enough for the sunshine to kiss them open. We each picked a bunch of these violets. It could do them no harm, grandmother said, because, like pansies in the garden, the more they were picked the better they would bloom.

All through the grass we saw small, white flowers with three-pointed leaflets, which grew on slender stems. The blossoms, I noticed, had five petals, as I have learned to call flower leaves, and in shape they reminded me of a beautiful wild rose, only they were not nearly so large.

"Do not pick them," grandmother said. "They fade very quickly, while if left here each little blossom will turn into a wild strawberry."

"Then I can pick and eat them," I cried.

Before going on to the woods we went into the swampy field, and just after we left the wet place, where we can keep our feet dry only by stepping on big tufts of grass, grandmother stooped down and said: "Here is our other white violet, out bright and early."

Its blossoms were almost as large as those of the purple or common blue violet, and its leaves were rounded and heart-shaped. They grew from the sides of its stems. Any one would have known it was a violet. I thought it a little strange seeing it so white, although its upper petals were tinged a little with purple. It is called Canada violet, and surely it is much larger than the first little white one we had found. Grandmother said that it grew taller than most wild violets.

In the woods we found two other kinds of violets. One was tall and its deep purple face was very much like the purple or common blue violet; only its leaves, instead of being rounded, were jagged all about the edges. They looked as though they had been cut with scissors. Grandmother thought it was properly called early blue violet, and that I should find it most often in the woods.

We did not see the violet with leaves somewhat the shape of a bird's foot, called bird's-foot violet. It grows in more sandy places than our woods, and although I have searched again since then, I have never found it yet, nor been quite sure I saw the little marks of birds' feet the violet was named after. Even when I do find the bird's-foot violet, grandmother says I must not pick it, as it is one of the family that is growing rarer every year.

After the early blue violet, I held in my hand four different kinds of these flowers. Then grandmother reminded me there was still the yellow one which should be in bloom. She found it first. The pale yellow blossom was small and looked, with its fine brown lines, somewhat like the sweet white violet. It had no fragranee. One thing about it that I could not help noticing was that its leaves grew out from the sides of the tall stem which held the flowers. They did not come up straight from the ground as did those of all the others we had found except the Canada violet. These leaves, besides, were covered with a thick down, and I wondered if the plant was chilly and needed something to keep it warm, as the hepaticas need their fuzz. Its name is downy yellow violet.

It seemed strange to me that all these violets should look enough alike for any child to know they were violets, and still be so different. Yet grandmother says there are many more kinds of them, and that I must be sharp-eyed to learn the names of all those even that grow about our home. In the book that I am soon to have for pressing flowers, I shall put in one of each sort that I find. Perhaps I will do this on rainy days and holidays, when Tommy pastes stamps in his album.

While grandmother and I looked at the downy yellow violet, I thought I should like to dig one up from the ground and plant it at home. So I found a sharp stone and dug down in a circle around its roots. I was careful not to hurt it, and when I lifted it grandmother quickly wrapped its roots and earth in some dried leaves. It was easy then to carry it home, and we planted it in a little fig basket, the same one that we had used in March for making a bird's nest basket, and put it on the window seat, where it is shady, and it can have cool, fresh air like that in the wood.

When Tommy came to see us again, he was surprised

to hear many of the things grandmother had to tell us about violets. He did n't know for one thing that the purple ones were favorite flowers of Napoleon.

Just why grandmother thinks them so much more modest than other flowers, and why the poets have written about their being modest, neither Tommy nor I could understand. I said I loved the violet best, but that I thought the white hepatica had a more modest look than any violet. Tommy thought the yellow violet looked downright pert. He asked grandmother if Napoleon was a modest man, and if he loved modest people. When she answered, "No; oh dear, no," it only made things more confusing.

But she said that we should love flowers for their own sake, and have our own impressions about them, no matter what other people thought or wrote about them.

When I went to bed that night, I felt that I had learned a great deal about violets. It all seemed very mysterious to me then, and with the white and yellow ones I still felt strange. In the morning, I thought, I will run out and pay them another visit.

WHY TOMMY LIKES THE COLUMBINE

By Alice Lounsberry

TOMMY thinks that the wild columbine is the most beautiful flower in the whole of America, and that it would be much better for a national one than the Mayflower, which welcomed the Pilgrims, or the goldenrod, which grows in every State in the Union. He says it is a flower that has true glory.

It is red and yellow, and nods over from the end of a slender stem, somewhat as if it were a bell. Then the flower's leaves, or petals, as I should say, are curiously folded together in the shape of horns of plenty, and the way their ends come together makes some people think of an eagle's five talons. This means power. The flower's full face is like a star with five rays, and when its center is seen in another position, it looks as if a ring of five turtle doves were there. These birds are emblems of peace, and grandmother says this is why columba, or columbine, was chosen as a name for this plant, and that peace and power should be part of America.

It is a little like hunting for animals or faces in puzzle pictures to see all these signs, but it is on their account that Tommy thinks columbine would make such a fine national flower. Its leaves, besides, are very, very pretty. They are fine and graceful, like ferns. Then what Tommy likes about columbine is that it is so wild. It chooses to grow in the wildest places, usually by rocks, and to reach it we have often to take a high climb. Sometimes we call it rock bells. Tommy's father hopes it will never be chosen as a national flower, because he thinks that if all the people knew it as such, they would pick it until it would disappear in one season. Already it is a vanishing wild flower, like the arbutus and Dutchman's breeches. It is vanishing because, although every year it should make and sow its own seed, often each flower in a little group of plants is picked and then no seeds are sown, and the next year there are fewer blossoms.

The first day this spring that Tommy and his dog went to the well-known places where columbine grows, they found hardly any plants, and those they did find had a sickly, stunted look. This his father thinks is because they were too much picked last year. Next year perhaps they will not come up at all.

Tommy had a hard tramp with Peter that day, in high, rocky places, and sometimes over trees that had been struck by lightning. In the night there had been a great storm, and the sun had not yet come out very brightly. That day also Tommy heard hundreds of noises; not the kind that people hear in the city, though, — screeching, rumbling noises, — but noises insects make shaking their wings, and tall plants flapping, and birds chirping. Peter loves the woods best on such days and climbs to the highest places with his master. Sometimes they meet no one whom they know; but

Tommy does n't mind that, for he talks as much to flowers and to birds as he does to people. When he came to see grandmother in the afternoon he told us about this long walk he and Peter had had, and then said:—

"There 's a bunk of columbine not too high nor too rough for you to reach; and it 's there, anywhere, that you can see its full glory."

Grandmother said she would like to see it blooming at its best, and that there was no time like the present. So we started, Tommy being the guide. What we had not expected was that he would take us into our own woods, for they are flat with only the Bloodroot Ridge and Old Adam for a rock. About there now there are but a few columbines. We went on over the ridge, and soon Tommy bent down and crawled under some bushes. He held them up for grandmother to pass through, and I slipped under next. Before this Tommy had shown me these bushes. They were maple-leaved arrowwoods, and higher than grandmother's head. Besides, they were in bloom. Very many of their tiny white leaves grew together in flat bunches, and the leaves had almost exactly the same look as those of a young maple tree. They are beautiful wild shrubs, and are called arrowwoods because their twigs are so straight, being without a bend or curve. The Indians used them to make their arrows.

I had always thought that these arrowwoods grew solidly in a clump together; but after we had slipped through, I saw they made only part of a circle, and inside — well, it was just columbine's glory. The arrowwood bushes had hidden these columbines so completely that perhaps for a long time not a single one of their flowers had been picked. Every year they had grown thicker together. Grandmother noticed at once that the blossoms here were almost twice as large as those near the top of Old Adam.

"This is enchanting," she said. "Tommy, you are right: columbine's glory is here in this hidden place."

We all stood quite still, not venturing to move lest we should tread on the flowers. Then came a ruby-throated humming bird, darting in and out among them, and looking as though he would whisper a word or two to each. Tommy said:

"He steals their sweetness. He sips the nectar that is in the flowers. See, he can poise himself on his wings and sip and sip; but that old bumblebee must alight on the flowers before trying to taste their sweets. His weight bears them down, and even then he cannot reach the nectar like rubythroat with his long-pointed bill. It seems as though this humming bird should be columbine's mate, although near by, perhaps, he has one of his own fledglings."

The butterflies amid columbine's glory could not keep still a minute, and when the wind came through the arrowwoods, the whole company nodded and swayed their flowers and rocked to and fro together. After a while they were still again, with only the ruby-throated humming bird, the butterfly, and the heavy bee visiting them in turn.

"We are invaders," grandmother said.

"I 'm the only boy that knows this bunk," Tommy replied, "and I 've known it now for two years. It 's hidden by the bluff on one side and the arrowwoods on the other. There 's just, I think, a dozen boys who 'd give their best jackknives to know this place."

Grandmother asked him how he had found it, and then he told us. "It was when Peter was a puppy. He was just beginning to learn things, and had a way of poking into places of his own accord. One day he slipped right under the arrowwoods where we came through. I thought he 'd be out again soon; but even when I gave him a call, he stayed under. Then I parted the bushes to see where he could be, and he was just looking at columbine's glory as hard as possible. In the autumn then father came up here and set out some other arrowwoods, which now make the screen so thick. He says if the flowers should vanish there will still be this secret place to show its full beauty."

"Even Philip Todd does not know I have this bunk," Tommy added. "I don't tell it because if these flowers were picked by all the people that pass through the woods, they 'd soon have the same look of old soldiers without arms or legs that those have about Old Adam. Nearly every one loves to pick flowers; but when some people see a columbine it seems as though they must take the whole clump and carry the earth away as well.

"Father met a school teacher in these woods one day. She had come out from the city, because she heard this was a good place for finding wild flowers. In her hand she had the largest bunch of columbine that father had ever seen, and she had picked it all from around Old

Adam. She said she was going to distribute it among her class the next day. Father then told her the harm she had done, and she was truly sorry. She said she did n't know that there were some wild flowers which should n't be picked. I thought that was worse than not knowing the queer things they ask in arithmetic."

Grandmother laughed. "Let us hope," she said, "that the school teacher has learned her lesson, and that in future Tommy will know his."

OUR COMMON FERNS

By E. Thayles Emmons

"Pokin' 'round 'mid ferns and mosses
Like a hoptoad or a snail,
Somehow seems to lighten crosses
Where my heart would elsewhere fail."

HOW can I best introduce my readers to my very dear friends, the ferns? I do not mean the rare ferns of the distant cañon or inaccessible mountain side, but rather the more common species that fringe our woodland pathways, peep down from the rocky places where every new nook reveals some new plant mystery, and grow in rankest and most disorderly profusion in our neighboring glens.

The average person who does not make a study of nature's wonders, and who in walking through wood and field sees and yet does not see, can scarcely be expected to know, for instance, that it is quite possible to count twenty or twenty-five different kinds of ferns in the course of one stroll. Such people *see* flowers, ferns, shrubs, etc., and enjoy them to a certain extent, but are content to know them generically, merely, without seeking more specific classification. I prefer, however, to have a more intimate acquaintance with these forms of plant life and believe that a much keener enjoyment of a woodland tramp comes from such knowledge, even though it be slight.

Come with me, then, and let us together take our way across the meadows, through the woods, and to the top of the tree-thatched hill which even from a distance promises to show us so many plant mysteries. Let us not shut our eyes entirely to the flowers and the trees, nor our ears to the bird melodies that everywhere flood the air, but let us give especial thought and attention to the fern family and make a careful record of our observations.

We find our way to the meadows by a rustic lane that at once suggests cows and sheep, and, indeed, here we find them browsing, some of them knee-deep in the swampy lowlands that border the beaten pathway, and here we discover our first fern. It is the very common *Onoclea sensibilis*, or sensitive fern. It is a coarse, unattractive plant, and we are somewhat at a loss to know why it was ever dubbed "sensitive," until informed that it is quite sensitive to early frosts. The plants that border the open lane are small and show no fertile fronds, but later on we explore a moist, shady thicket at the edge of a wood, where this same fern grows two or three feet high, with plenty of the fruited stalks dotted with "berries" either green or dark brown, according to the stage of their development.

In the same thicket, too, we come upon specimens of the cinnamon fern, and also the marsh fern, the common species which everybody should know. The cinnamon fern may nearly always be determined by the little tufts of wool to be found at the base of each pinna; the marsh fern, whether in open field or in swampy woods, is mounted on a stilt, as it were, this very long stalk serving as one means of identification to the amateur. The arrangement of the fruit dots, the shape of the fronds, the character of the pinnæ, etc., of course, serve the expert as means of positive identification after the general appearance of the fern has been noted, and these things we study as each new plant is located.

Here, too, is the interrupted fern, so called because of its peculiarity of bearing fruited pinnæ in the midst of its bright, green leaves. In general appearance and in the absence of the fertile fronds this closely resembles the cinnamon fern, yet it is noticeable that there are no tufts of cotton at the base of the pinnæ as in the *cinnamomea.* Down here by the brook are plenty of the large, vaselike clusters of the well-known ostrich fern which is so easily transplanted, and which is so commonly used for decorative purposes about surburban residences. Its fronds resemble ostrich plumes, hence its name.

Next comes the woodland path, gradually ascending through a tangle of second-growth maple and beech trees to the pasture uplands further on. There are plenty of new ferns here. The well-known maidenhair is abundant everywhere, the long beech fern grows in profusion, and the pretty lady fern is all about us. The little brook still keeps its sluggish way beside the path, and along its moist banks we find quantities of both the bulblet and the fragile bladder ferns. Here, too, is the pretty little oak fern that is as dainty as any we have come upon, and on all sides the hardy Christmas fern is to be found.

As we reach the edge of the thicket, we come upon a

mammoth clump of ferns, in which the sensitive, the lady, the marsh and the *cinnamomea* are conspicuous. Under favorable conditions the ferns have attained gigantic proportions, the *cinnamomea* being five or six feet in height. This interesting group occupies us for a short time, and then we climb over the stone fence and find ourselves in the steep pasture lands. In the soft, moist soil bordering the brooklet we chance upon one of the finer specimens of the ternate grape fern, which, although common enough, is somewhat difficult to find because of its small size, and because of the fact that it grows deep down in the grass, its long rootstalk extending nearly a foot into the ground. Sometimes this fern is found in exceedingly dry soil, which is responsible for its stunted growth.

Climbing the pasture lands through a tangle of weeds and berry bushes we break our way through a miniature forest of the bracken or common brake, and here, too, with the blazing sun full upon us we make our first real fern discovery of the afternoon. Carefully hidden away in the parched and brown grass we discover a large station of the rare adder's tongue, *Ophioglossum vulgatum.* This little plant looks not at all like a fern, and is better classed, perhaps, as a fern ally; nevertheless we decide to place a specimen in our fern collection for the afternoon. We should never have discovered it had we not chanced to sit down upon a hummock of dry moss to rest after the climb up the hill; here, wholly concealed in the grass right at our feet, was *Ophioglossum,* which consists of a single ovate leaf with a long fleshy spike bearing the fruit. We collect several specimens, and then cross another fence into a denser wood that grows on the side of the hill. We note at once a thicket of glorious plants of the royal or flowering fern and soon find plenty of the beautiful spinulose wood fern, also the marginal shield fern and the silver-leaved spleenwort. Maidenhair is everywhere, and there are occasional specimens of the rattlesnake fern. In the edges of the wood among the loose rocks are clumps of sweet-smelling dicksonia, the hay-scented fern, and we amuse ourselves by seeing how large a specimen we can find. As the woodland path begins to penetrate the darker depths of the mountain side we find quantities of the New York fern, and, later, as we come to a rocky glen we are delighted to see numerous colonies of the polypody, "the cheerful community of the polypody," Thoreau says. They cling to the sides of the cliffs and peer down upon us as we pass. The tops of the bowlders are covered with them, and we are able to get a fine photograph of an especially accessible group. A little higher up we begin to find the rusty *Woodsia ilvensis* and get another splendid picture. It is now getting very rocky, and we begin to look for the rarer rock ferns. The fragile bladder fern continues to be abundant, and there is still plenty of the polypody and woodsia, but other varieties seem to have been left behind.

The bridle path we have been following grows less and less interesting with respect to fern life, and we are soon tempted to climb an exceedingly steep but grassy bank composed of shale rock and loose soil. We are rewarded for our trouble when we come upon clumps of not only the obtuse, or blunt-lobed, woodsia, but also the ebony spleenwort, a rare species and a delight to the collector. We attempt a few photographs of the *ebeneum*, which is a slender fern only a few inches long, and then make our way carefully back to more stable paths.

Somewhat later, when we have reached the summit of the hill, we are again delighted to find a station of another rock fern, *Asplenium trichomanes*, or maidenhair spleenwort. This fern greatly resembles the *ebeneum*, but grows in the loose earth on the sides and in the crevices of rocks. It is a dainty little plant and, fortunately, we are enabled to get a good photograph of one group which shows not only the spleenwort, but also plants of the fragile bladder fern and the rusty woodsia, growing together in graceful neighborliness.

We sit for a time in the midst of our pretty little fern friends, until the realization comes that we are some few miles from home, and that it is already mid-afternoon. There is an easy path homeward, and we take it, hoping to make new discoveries by the wayside. It is not until we have reached lower levels, however, that we find anything not previously noted. Then we come upon specimens of the crested shield fern, and also find some of the mammoth Goldie's fern, nearly six feet high with fronds more than a foot broad. Our specimen case will not permit us to collect an entire frond, so we content ourselves with selecting a suitable section well covered with fruit dots; also we pluck a sterile frond at the base of the plant, and then commence the search for the narrow-leaved spleenwort which almost invariably grows somewhere in the vicinity of *goldianum*. We soon find plenty of the *angustifolium* near by, and also discover specimens of the Boott's shield fern, which closely resembles some of the many forms of the spinulose wood fern, but which under microscopic examination reveals characteristics that permit of its being classed separately.

Our last treasure of the afternoon we discover as we are about to leave the woods. It is a station of the Braun's holly fern, an unusually handsome member of the fern family, whose fronds are shaped like the broad Roman daggers of ancient days. Its stalks are covered with long, hairy chaff, and we have in our hand a fern that in no manner resembles any other, and can always be identified at a glance. This fern is rarely encountered, and makes a big addition to our already large collection.

Leaving the woods we find nothing between ourselves and home save a few cultivated meadows which promise nothing and yield nothing in the way of fern life, although we are ever on the alert for specimens of the exceedingly rare moonwort and even for the *Botrychium simplex* or grape fern.

At home again, we find that in a little more than five hours, and by walking less than five miles, we have been able to make the acquaintance of more than thirty different members of the fern family. Some of the rarer ones we have in our specimen cases; and in our cameras there are negatives of some of the other varieties. Is it not fascinating? Have I made it sound real? I trust so. Try it yourself some day.

SNOWFLAKES UNDER A MICROSCOPE

By Elizabeth G. Chapin

WHEN you see a bank of snow, does it ever occur to you that every bit of that thick blanket is formed of millions and millions of loveliest jewels? Probably most of us have noticed that snowflakes look different at different times; in a cold, dry, blizzardy storm, we see that they are tiny and hard, and sometimes they drop down on the window sill like so many little pills, and yet another time they are like broad, fluffy feathers. All this is familiar, but how many of us think to put a microscope over one of these dainty visitors to see how it is formed? Once we begin to look and observe, we understand the interest and enthusiasm of an expert in Jericho, Vermont, — Mr. Wilson A. Bentley, a government Weather Bureau observer, — who has a collection of photographs of snow crystals numbering quite one thousand, with no duplicates!

Mr. Bentley began to keep record of his short-lived "specimens" before 1885, by drawing what he could see under the microscope, making one hundred drawings each winter for three years. Then he learned to use a camera with a microscope attachment, producing microphotographs, or magnified photographs, showing every detail of the shape and pattern of the snow crystals.

A snowflake may be one crystal, or a collection of crystals; usually it is the latter. The crystals have two chief divisions as to form, columnar — that is, shaped like a column — and tabular, or shaped like a tablet or lozenge, having six sides, and a diameter from one thirtieth to one third of an inch.

The tablet shape is often developed into a six-pointed star, called stellar, or, more elaborate still, into fern-stellar, where each star point is like a beautiful fern. Occasionally the columnar crystals are very fine and thin, and are then called needilar, or needleshaped. Sleet takes this form.

The condition of the atmosphere influences the development of the various forms. A cold, still atmosphere produces the more elaborate stellar forms, while a driving wind is likely to prevent perfectly geometrical formation or to cause fractures in the crystals. The more solid columnar shapes and some small tabular ones are less likely to show a variety in their development, because, being heavier than the stellar or branched forms, they are not whirled and modified by the wind so constantly as are the softer and frailer flakes. Sometimes the tabular crystals show lovely and intricate patterns apparently under their surface. These are thought to be due to "minute inclusions of air," or, roughly speaking, to little air bubbles that have been forced into the crystal, perhaps by the rush of the air, forming tubes which are distributed with geometric regularity to every point and angle, and are more wonderfully etched by the action of the atmosphere than a bit of crystal might be by the tool of an artist.

Mr. Bentley tells us that there is some connection (not altogether understood as yet) between the size and form of the crystals and the temperature and density of the air, and that about four fifths of the perfect forms are born within the west and north quadrants of great storms, particularly in those that spread over a wide area. "The first great lesson of the study of crystals," says Mr. Bentley, "is their obedience to law, their conformity to conditions which from time to time are reproduced in the cloud strata where crystals have their birth. . . . The extent and character of a storm may be read from its crystals."

A word about examining the crystals. This is an excellent stormy-day occupation, either indoors or on the porch. If you work indoors, it must be in a cold room with the window open, or else the flakes will melt. Have a piece of dark cloth or velveteen spread flat on a board, and catch the crystals upon it. Use a broom splint to lift the specimen, and if it needs to be arranged or flattened, a common goose or hen feather is the heaviest tool the delicate flake will bear. If you have only a reading glass for a magnifier, that will show you a good deal. A more powerful glass, such as botanists use, is better, and if you buy a new microscope, one having three legs (and costing from one dollar to about seven) is very convenient, for you can stand it over the specimen and have your hands free. After taking a good look, deciding in your mind which of the classes of crystal the specimen belongs to, and noticing the shape as accurately as possible, go into a warmer room (where your hands will not be so cold) and try to make a drawing of what you remember. Even if your drawing is not accurate, it will help to fix in your mind the various forms, and will sharpen your eye to new varieties.

Another way to keep a record is to make paper cut-out forms with scissors. The schools teach the use of scissors in place of the pencil, and no doubt many of you are familiar with their use. With them, cutting through a folded paper, you can make at least a rough record of the type of crystal you have in mind. As long ago as 1863, before scissor-cutting was dreamed of for the schoolroom, a lady in Portland, Maine, tried this method for keeping an album of the snow crystals she examined. Her cuttings look very crude compared with the wonderful microphotographs Mr. Bentley has made, yet they are interesting both as a record of what she saw, and because they are an example of early interest in a little known form of nature study. Her collection was shown to Mr. Agassiz, who was so impressed with what was — for that time — a unique and original experiment, that he suggested her publishing it. This she did, under the title "A Snow Album" for which she wrote a preface, telling some interesting facts about the formation of snowflakes, and how their beauty had suggested the making of this series of paper stars.

OUR FRIEND THE INDIAN CHIEF

By John Muir

AHOONA, one of the head men of the tribe, paid Mr. Young a visit and presented him with porpoise meat and berries and much interesting information. He naturally expected a return visit, and when we called at his house, a mile or two down the fiord, he said his wives were out in the rain gathering fresh berries to complete a feast prepared for us. We remained, however, only a few minutes, for I was not aware of this arrangement or of Mr. Young's promise until after leaving the house. Anxiety to get around Cape Wimbledon was the cause of my haste, fearing the storm might increase. On account of this ignorance, no apologies were offered him, and the upshot was that the good Hoona became very angry. We succeeded, however, in the evening of the same day, in explaining our haste, and by sincere apologies and presents made peace.

After a hard struggle we got around Wimbledon and into the next fiord to the northward (Klunastucksana — Dundas Bay). A cold, drenching rain was falling, darkening but not altogether hiding its extraordinary beauty, made up of lovely reaches and side fiords, feathery headlands and islands, beautiful every one and charmingly collocated. But how it rained, and how cold it was, and how weary we were pulling most of the time against the wind! The branches of this bay are so deep and so numerous that, with the rain and low clouds concealing the mountain landmarks, we could hardly make out the main trends. While grouping and gazing among the islands through the misty rain and clouds, we discovered wisps of smoke at the foot of a sheltering rock in front of a mountain, where a choir of cascades were chanting their rain songs. Gladly we made for this camp, which proved to belong to a rare old Hoona subchief, so tall and wide and dignified in demeanor he looked grand even in the sloppy weather, and every inch a chief in spite of his bare legs and the old shirt and draggled, ragged blanket in which he was dressed. He was given to much handshaking, gripping hard, holding on and looking you gravely in the face while most emphatically speaking in Thlinkit, not a word of which we understood until interpreter John came to our help. He turned from one to the other of us, declaring, as John interpreted, that our presence did him good like food and fire, that he would welcome white men, especially teachers, and that he and all his people compared to ourselves were only children. When Mr. Young informed him that a missionary was about to be sent to his people, he said he would call them all together four times and explain that a teacher and preacher were coming and that they therefore must put away all foolishness and prepare their hearts to receive them and their words. He then introduced his three children, one a naked lad five or six years old who, as he fondly assured us, would soon

OLD CHIEF AND TOTEM POLE, WRANGELL, ALASKA

be a chief, and later to his wife, an intelligent-looking woman, of whom he seemed proud. When we arrived she was out at the foot of the cascade mountain gathering salmonberries. She came in dripping and loaded. A few of the fine berries saved for the children she presented, proudly and fondly beginning with the youngest, whose only clothing was a nose-ring and a string of beads. She was lightly appareled in a cotton gown and a bit of blanket, thoroughly bedraggled, but after unloading her berries she retired with a dry calico gown around the corner of a rock and soon returned fresh as a daisy and with becoming dignity took her place by the fireside. Soon two other berry-laden women came in, seemingly enjoying the rain like the bushes and trees. They put on little clothing so that they may be the more easily dried, and as for the children, a thin shirt of sheeting is the most they encumber themselves with, and get wet and half dry without seeming to notice it while we shiver with two or three dry coats. They seem to prefer being naked. The men also wear but little in wet weather. When they go out for all day they put on a single blanket, but in choring around camp, getting firewood, cooking, or looking after their precious canvas, they seldom wear anything, braving wind and rain in utter nakedness to avoid the bother of drying clothes. It is a rare sight to see the children bringing in big chunks of firewood on their shoulders, balancing in crossing bowlders with firmly set bowlegs and bulging back muscles.

We gave Ka-hood-oo-shough, the old chief, some tobacco, rice, and coffee, and pitched our tent near his hut among tall grass. Soon after our arrival the Taylor Bay subchief came in from the opposite direction from ours, telling us that he came through a cut-off passage not on our chart. As stated above, we took pains to conciliate him and soothe his hurt feelings. Our words and gifts, he said, had warmed his sore heart and made him glad and comfortable.

The view down the bay among the islands was, I thought, the finest of this kind of scenery that I had yet observed.

The weather continued cold and rainy. Nevertheless Mr. Young and I and our crew, together with one of the Hoonas, an old man who acted as guide, left camp to explore one of the upper arms of the bay, where we were told there was a large glacier. We managed to push the canoe several miles up the stream that drains the glacier to a point where the swift current was divided among rocks and the banks were overhung with alders and willows. I left the canoe and pushed up the right bank past a magnificent waterfall some twelve hundred feet high, and over the shoulder of a mountain, until I secured a good view of the lower part of the glacier. It is probably a lobe of the Taylor Bay or Brady Glacier.

On our return to camp, thoroughly drenched and cold, the old chief came to visit us, apparently as wet and cold as ourselves.

"I have been thinking of you all day," he said, "and pitying you, knowing how miserable you were, and as soon as I saw your canoe coming back I was ashamed to think that I had been sitting warm and dry at my fire while you were out in the storm; therefore I made haste to strip off my dry clothing and put on these wet rags to share your misery and show how much I love you."

I had another talk with Ka-hood-oo-shough the next day.

"I am not able," he said, "to tell you how much good your words have done me. Your words are good, and they are strong words. Some of my people are foolish, and when they make their salmon traps they do not take care to tie the poles firmly together, and when the big rain floods come the traps break and are washed away because the people who made them are foolish people. But your words are strong words, and when storms come to try them, they will stand the storms."

There was much handshaking as we took our leave and assurances of eternal friendship. The grand old man stood on the shore watching us and waving farewell until we were out of sight.

A BREACH IN THE BANK

By Dallas Lore Sharp

THE February freshet had come. We had been expecting it, but no one along Maurice River had ever seen so wild and warm and ominous a spring storm as this. So sudden and complete a break-up of winter no one could remember; not so high a tide, so rain-thick and driving a south wind. It had begun the night before, and now, along near noon, the river and meadows were a tumult of white waters, with the gale so strong that one could hardly hold his own on the drawbridge that groaned from pier to pier in the grip of the maddened storm.

It was into the teeth of this gale that a small boy dressed in large yellow "oilskins" made his slow way out along the narrow bank of the river toward the sluices that controlled the tides of the great meadows.

The boy was *in* the large yellow oilskins, not dressed, no, for he was simply inside of them, his feet and hands and the top of his head having managed to work their way out. It seems, at least, that his head was partly out, for on the top of the oilskins, sat a large black sou'wester. And in the arms of the oilskins lay an old army musket, so big and long that it seemed to be walking away with the oilskins, as the oilskins seemed to be walking away with the boy.

I can feel the kick of that old musket yet, and the

prick of the dried sand burs among which she knocked me. I can hear the rough rasping of the chafing legs of those oilskins too, though I was not the boy this time inside of them. But I knew the boy who was, a real boy; and I know that he made his careful way along the trembling river bank out into the sunken meadows, meadows that later on I saw the river burst into and claim—and it still claims them, as I saw only last summer, when after thirty years of absence I once more stood at the end of that bank looking over a watery waste which was once the richest of farm lands.

Never, it seemed, had the village known such wind and rain and such a tide. It was a strange, wild scene from the drawbridge — wharves obliterated, river white with flying spume and tossing ice cakes, the great bridge swaying and shrieking in the wind, and over everything the blur of the swirling rain.

The little figure in yellow oilskins was not the only one that had gone along the bank since morning, for a party of men had carefully inspected every foot of the bank to the last sluice, for fear that there might be a weak spot somewhere. Let a breach occur with such a tide as this and it could never be stopped.

And now, somewhat past noon, the men were again upon the bank. As they neared Five-Forks sluice, the central and largest of the water gates, they heard a smothered *boom* above the scream of the wind in their ears. They were startled; but it was only the sound of a gun somewhere off in the meadow. It was the gun of the boy in the oilskins.

Late that afternoon Doctor "Sam," driving home

along the flooded road of the low back swamp, caught sight, as he came out in view of the river, of a little figure in yellow oilskins away out on the meadow.

The doctor stopped his horse and hallooed. But the boy did not hear. The rain on his coat, the wind and the river in his ears drowned every other sound.

The dusk was falling, and as the doctor looked out over the wild scene, he put his hands to his mouth and called again. The yellow figure had been blotted out by the rain. There was no response, and the doctor drove on.

Meanwhile the boy in the yellow oilskins was splashing slowly back along the narrow, slippery clay bank. He was wet, but he was warm, and he loved the roar of the wind and the beat of the driving rain.

As the mist and rain were fast mixing with the dusk of the twilight, he quickened his steps. His path in places was hardly a foot wide, covered with rose and elder bushes mostly, but bare in spots where holes and low worn stretches had been recently built up with cubes of the tough blue mud of the flats.

The tide was already even with the top of the bank and was still rising. It leaped and hit at his feet as he picked his way along. The cakes of white ice crunched and heeled up against the bank with here and there one flung fairly across his path. The tossing water frequently splashed across. Twice he jumped places where the tide was running over down into the meadows below.

How quickly the night had come. It was dark when he reached Five-Forks sluice — the middle point in the long, high bank. While still some distance off he heard the sullen roar of the big sluice, through which the swollen river was trying to force its way.

He paused to listen a moment. He knew the peculiar voice of every one of these gateways, as he knew every foot of the river bank.

There was nothing wrong with the sullen roar. But how deep and threatening! He could *feel* the sound even better than he could hear it, far down below him. He started forward, to pass on, when he half felt, through the long, regular throbbing of the sluice, a shorter, a faster, closer quiver, as of a small running stream in the bank very near his feet.

Dropping quickly to his knees, he laid his ear to the wet earth. A cold, black hand seemed to seize upon him. He heard the purr of running water!

It must be down about three feet. He could distinctly feel it tearing through.

Without rising he scrambled down the meadow side of the bank to see the size of the breach. He could hear nothing of it for the boiling at the gates of the sluice. It was so dark he could scarcely see. But near the bottom the mud suddenly caved beneath his feet, and a rush of cold water caught at his knees.

The hole was greater than he feared.

Crawling back to the top of the bank, he leaned out over the river side. A large cake of ice hung in water in front of him. He pushed it aside and, bending until his face barely cleared the surface of the river, he discovered a small sucking eddy, whose swirling hole he knew ran into the breach.

He edged farther out and reached down under the water and touched the upper rim of the hole. How large might it be? Swinging round, he dug his fingers into the bank and lowered himself feet first until he stood in the hole. It was the size of a small bucket, but he could almost feel it going beneath his feet, and a sudden terror took hold upon him.

He was only a boy, and the dark night, the wild river, the vast, sweeping storm, the roar and tremor and tumult flattened him for a moment to the ridge of the bank in a panic of fear!

But he heard the water running, he felt the bank going directly beneath where he lay, and getting to his feet he started for the village. A single hasty step and, but for the piles of the sluice, he would have plunged into the river.

He must feel his way; but he never could do it in time to save the bank. The breach must be stopped at once. He must stop it and keep it stopped until the next patrol brought help.

Feeling his way back, he dropped again upon his hands and knees above the breach to think for a moment. The cake of ice hung as before in the eddy. Catching it, he tipped it and thrust it down across the mouth of the hole, but it slipped from his cold fingers and dived away. He pushed down the butt of his musket, turned it flat, but it was not broad enough to cover the opening. Then he lowered himself again, and stood in it, wedging the musket in between his boots; but he could feel the water still tearing through at the sides, and eating all the faster.

He clambered back to the top of the bank, put his hand to his mouth and shouted. The only answer was the scream of the wind and the cry of a brant passing overhead.

Then the boy laughed. "Easy enough," he muttered, and, picking up the musket, he leaned once more out over the river and thrust the steel barrel of the gun hard into the mud just below the hole. Then, stepping easily down, he sat squarely into the breach, the gun like a stake in front of him sticking up between his knees.

Then he laughed again, as he caught his breath, for he had squeezed into the hole like a stopper into a bottle, his big oilskins filling the breach completely.

The water stood above the middle of his breast, and the tide was still rising. Darkness had now settled, but the ghostly ice cakes, tipping, slipping toward him, were spectral white. He had to shove them back as now and then one rose before his face. The sky was black, and the deep water below him was blacker. And how cold it was!

Doctor Sam had been stopped by the flooded roads on his way home, and lights shone in the windows as he entered the village. He turned a little out of his way and halted in front of a small cottage near the bridge.

"Is Joe here?" he asked.

"No," answered the mother; "he went down the meadow for muskrats and has not returned yet. He 's probably over with the men at the store."

Doctor Sam drove on to the store.

There was no boy in yellow oilskins in the store.

Doctor Sam picked up a lighted lantern.

"Come on," he said, "I 'm wet, but I want a look at those sluices," and started for the river, followed immediately by the men, whom he led in single file out along the bank.

Swinging his lantern low, he pushed into the teeth of the gale at a pace that left the line of lights straggling far behind.

"What a night!" he growled. "If I had a boy of my own —" and he threw the light as far as he could over the seething river and then down over the flooded meadow.

Ahead he heard the roar of Five-Forks sluice, and swung his lantern high, as if to signal it, so like the rush of a coming train was the sound of the waters.

But the little engineer in yellow oilskins could not see the signal. He had almost ceased to watch. With his arm cramped about his gun, he was still at his post; but the ice cakes floated in and touched him; the water no longer felt cold.

On this side, then on that, out over the swollen river, down into the tossing meadow flared the lantern as the doctor worked his way along.

Above the great sluice be paused a moment, then bent his head to the wind and started on, when his foot touched something soft that yielded strangely, sending a shiver over him, and his light fell upon a bunch of four dead muskrats lying in the path.

Along the meadow side flashed the lantern, up and over the river side, and Doctor Sam, reaching quickly

IN A TWINKLING HE WAS IN THE WATER

down, drew a limp little form in yellow oilskins out of the water, as the men behind him came up.

A gurgle, a hiss, a small whirlpool sucking at the surface, — and the tide was again tearing through the breach that the boy had filled.

The men sprang quickly to their task, and did it well, while Doctor Sam, shielding the limp little form from the wind, forced a vial of something between the white lips, saying over to himself as he watched the closed eyes open, "If I had a boy of my own — If I had a boy —"

. . . .

No, Doctor Sam never had a boy of his own; but he always felt, I think, that the boy of those yellow oilskins was somehow pretty nearly his.

. . . .

After a long, cold winter how I love the spatter on my face of the first February rain! The little trout brook below me foams and sometimes overruns the road, and as its small noise ascends the hill, I can hear — the wind on a great river, the wash of waves against a narrow bank, and the muffled roar of quaking sluices as when a February freshet is on.

BREAKING THE JAM AT GRAY ROCK

By Kate Douglas Wiggin

THE men ran hither and thither like ants, gathering their tools. There were some old-fashioned pick-poles, straight, heavy levers without any "dog," and there were modern pickpoles and peaveys, for every river has its favorite equipment in these things. There was no dynamite in those days to make the stubborn jams yield, and the dog warp was in general use. Horses or oxen, sometimes a line of men, stood on the riverbank. A long rope was attached by means of a steel spike to one log after another, and it was dragged from the tangled mass. Sometimes, after unloading the top logs, those at the bottom would rise and make the task easier; sometimes the work would go on for hours with no perceptible progress, and Mr. Wiley would have opportunity to tell bystanders of a "turrible jam" on the Kennebec that had cost the Lumber Company ten thousand dollars to break.

There would be great arguments on shore, among the villagers as well as among the experts, as to the particular log which might be a key to the position. The boss would study the problem from various standpoints, and the drivers themselves would pass from heated discussion into long consultations.

"They're paid by the day," Old Kennebec would philosophize to the doctor; "an' when they're consultin' they don't hev to be doggin', which is a turrible sight harder work."

Rose had created a small sensation, on one occasion, by pointing out to the under boss the key log in a jam. She was past mistress of the pretty game of jackstraws, much in vogue at that time. The delicate little lengths of polished wood or bone were shaken together and emptied on the table. Each jackstraw had one of its ends fashioned in the shape of some sort of implement,— a rake, a hoe, spade, fork, or mallet. All the pieces were intertwined by the shaking process, and they lay as they fell, in a hopeless tangle. The task consisted in taking a tiny pickpole, scarcely bigger than a match, and with the bit of curved wire on the end lifting off the jackstraws one by one without stirring the pile or making it tremble. When this occurred, you gave place to your opponent, who relinquished his turn to you when ill fortune descended upon him, the game, which was a kind of river-driving and jam-picking in miniature, being decided by the number of pieces captured and their value. No wonder that the under boss asked Rose's advice as to the key log. She had a fairy's hand, and her cunning at deciding the pieces to be moved, and her skill at extricating and lifting them from the heap, were looked upon in Edgewood as little less than supernatural.

The afternoon proved a lively one. In the first place, one of the younger men slipped into the water between two logs, part of a lot chained together waiting to be let out of the boom. The weight of the mass higher up and the force of the current wedged him in rather tightly, and when he had been "pried" out he declared that he felt like an apple after it had been squeezed in the cider mill, so he drove home, and Rufus Waterman took his place.

Two hours' hard work followed this incident, and at the end of that time the "bung" that reached from the shore to Waterman's Ledge (the rock where Pretty Quick met his fate) was broken up, and the logs that composed it were started down river. There remained now only the great side-jam at Gray Rock. This had been allowed to grow, gathering logs as they drifted past, thus making higher water and a stronger current on the other side of the rock, and allowing an easier passage for the logs at that point.

All was excitement now, for, this particular piece of work accomplished, the boom above the falls would be "turned out," and the river would once more be clear and clean at the Edgewood bridge.

Small boys, perching on the rocks with their heels hanging, hands and mouths full of red Astrakhan apples, cheered their favorites to the echo, while the drivers shouted to one another and watched the signs and signals of the boss, who could communicate with them only in that way, so great was the roar of the water.

The jam refused to yield to ordinary measures. It was a difficult problem, for the rocky river bed held many a snare and pitfall. There was a certain ledge under the water, so artfully placed that every log striking under its projecting edges would wedge itself firmly there, attracting others by its evil example.

"That galoot-boss ought to hev shoved his crew down to that jam this mornin'," grumbled Old Kennebec to Alcestis Crambry, who was always his most loyal and attentive listener. "But he wouldn't take no advice, not if Pharaoh nor Boaz nor Herod nor Nicodemus come right out o' the Bible an' give it to him. The logs air con*tra*ry to-day. Sometimes they'll go along as easy as an old shoe, an' other times they'll do nothin' but bung, bung, bung! There's a log nestlin' down in the middle o' that jam that I've be'n watchin' for a week, It's a cur'ous one, to begin with; an' then it has a mark on it that you can reco'nize it by. Did ye ever hear tell o' George the Third, King of England, Alcestis, or ain't he known over to the crambry medders? Well, once upon a time men used to go through the forests over here an' slash a mark on the trunks o' the biggest trees. That was the royal sign, as you might say, an' meant that the tree was to be taken over to England to make masts an' yardarms for the King's ships. What made me think of it now is that the King's mark was an arrer, an' it's an arrer that's on that there log I'm showin' ye. Well, sir, I seen it fust at Milliken's Mills a Monday. It was in trouble then, an' it's be'n in trouble ever sence. That's allers the way; there'll be one pesky, crooked, con*tra*ry, consarnèd log that can't go anywheres without gittin' into difficulties. You can yank it out an' set it afloat, an' before you hardly git your doggin' iron off of it, it'll be snarled up agin in some new place. From the time it 's chopped down to the day it gets to Saco, it costs the Comp'ny 'bout ten times its pesky valler as lumber. Now they 've sent over to Benson's for a team of horses, an' I bate ye they can't git 'em. I wish I was the boss on this river, Alcestis."

"I wish I was," echoed the boy.

"Well, your head-fillin' ain't the right kind for a boss, Alcestis, an' you 'd better stick to dry land. You set right down here while I go back a piece an' git the pipe out o' my coat pocket. I guess nothin' ain't goin' to happen for a few minutes."

The surmise about the horses, unlike most of Old Kennebec's, proved to be true. Benson's pair had gone to Portland with a load of hay; accordingly the tackle was brought, the rope was adjusted to a log, and five of the drivers, standing on the river bank, attempted to drag it from its intrenched position. It refused to yield the fraction of an inch. Rufus and Stephen joined the five men, and the augmented crew of seven were putting all their strength on the rope when a cry went up from the watchers on the bridge. The "dog" had loosened suddenly, and the men were flung violently to the ground. For a second they were stunned both by the surprise and by the shock of the blow, but in the same moment the cry of the crowd swelled louder. Alcestis Crambry had stolen, all unnoticed, to the rope, and had attempted to use his feeble powers for the common good. When the blow came he fell backward, and, making no effort to control the situation, slid over the bank and into the water.

The other Crambrys, not realizing the danger, laughed audibly, but there was no jeering from the bridge.

Stephen had seen Alcestis slip, and in the fraction of a moment had taken off his boots and was coasting down the slippery rocks behind him; in a twinkling he was in the water, almost as soon as the boy himself.

"Doggoned idjut!" exclaimed Old Kennebec, tearfully. "Wuth the hull fool family! If I hed n't 'a' be'n so old, I 'd 'a' jumped in myself, for you can't drownd a Wiley, not without you tie nail kags to their head an' feet an' drop 'em in the falls."

Alcestis, who had neither brains, courage, nor experience, had, better still, the luck that follows the witless. He was carried swiftly down the current; but, only fifty feet away, a long, slender log, wedged between two low rocks on the shore, jutted out over the water, almost touching its surface. The boy's clothes were admirably adapted to the situation, being full of enormous rents. In some way the end of the log caught in the rags of Alcestis's coat and held him just seconds enough to enable Stephen to swim to him, to seize him by the nape of the neck, to lift him on the log, and thence to the shore. If was a particularly bad place for a landing, and there was nothing to do but to lower ropes and drag the drenched men to the high ground above.

Alcestis came to his senses in ten or fifteen minutes, and seemed as bright as usual, with a kind of added swagger at being the central figure in a dramatic situation.

"I wonder you hed n't stove your brains out, when

you landed so turrible suddent on that rock at the foot of the bank," said Mr. Wiley to him.

"I should, but I took good care to light on my head," responded Alcestis; a cryptic remark which so puzzled Old Kennebec that he mused over it for some hours.

A LITTLE GIRL ON THE ISLES OF SHOALS

By Celia Thaxter

I WELL remember my first sight of White Island, where we took up our abode on leaving the mainland. I was scarcely five years old; but from the upper windows of our dwelling in Portsmouth, I had been shown the clustered masts of ships lying at the wharves along the Piscataqua River, faintly outlined against the sky, and, baby as I was, even then I was drawn, with a vague longing, seaward. How delightful was that long, first sail to the Isles of Shoals! How pleasant the unaccustomed sound of the incessant ripple against the boat side, the sight of the wide water and limitless sky, the warmth of the broad sunshine that made us blink like young sandpipers as we sat in triumph, perched among the household goods with which the little craft was laden! It was at sunset in autumn that we were set ashore on that loneliest, lovely rock, where the lighthouse looked down on us like some tall, black-capped giant, and filled me with awe and wonder. At its base a few goats were grouped on the rock, standing out dark against the red sky as I looked up at them. The stars were beginning to twinkle; the wind blew cold, charged with the sea's sweetness; the sound of many waters half bewildered me. Some one began to light the lamps in the tower. Rich red and golden, they swung round in mid-air; everything was strange and fascinating and new. We entered the quaint little old stone cottage that was for six years our home. How curious it seemed, with its low, whitewashed ceiling and deep window seats, showing the great thickness of the walls made to withstand the breakers, with whose force we soon grew acquainted! A blissful home the little house became to the children who entered it that quiet evening and slept for the first time lulled by the murmur of the encircling sea. I do not think a happier triad ever existed than we were, living in that profound isolation. It takes so little to make a healthy child happy; and we never wearied of our few resources. True, the winters seemed as long as a whole year to our little minds, but they were pleasant, nevertheless. Into the deep window seats we climbed, and with pennies (for which we had no other use) made round holes in the thick frost, breathing on them till they were warm, and peeped out at the bright, fierce, windy weather, watching the vessels scudding over the intensely dark-blue sea, all "feather-white" where the short waves broke hissing in the cold, and the sea-fowl soaring aloft or tossing on the water; or, in calmer days, we saw how the stealthy Star-Islander paddled among the ledges, or lay for hours stretched on the wet seaweed with his gun, watching for wild fowl. Sometimes the round head of a seal moved about among the kelp-covered rocks. A few are seen every winter, and are occasionally shot; but they are shyer and more alert even than the birds.

THE LIGHTHOUSE, WHITE ISLAND, ISLES OF SHOALS

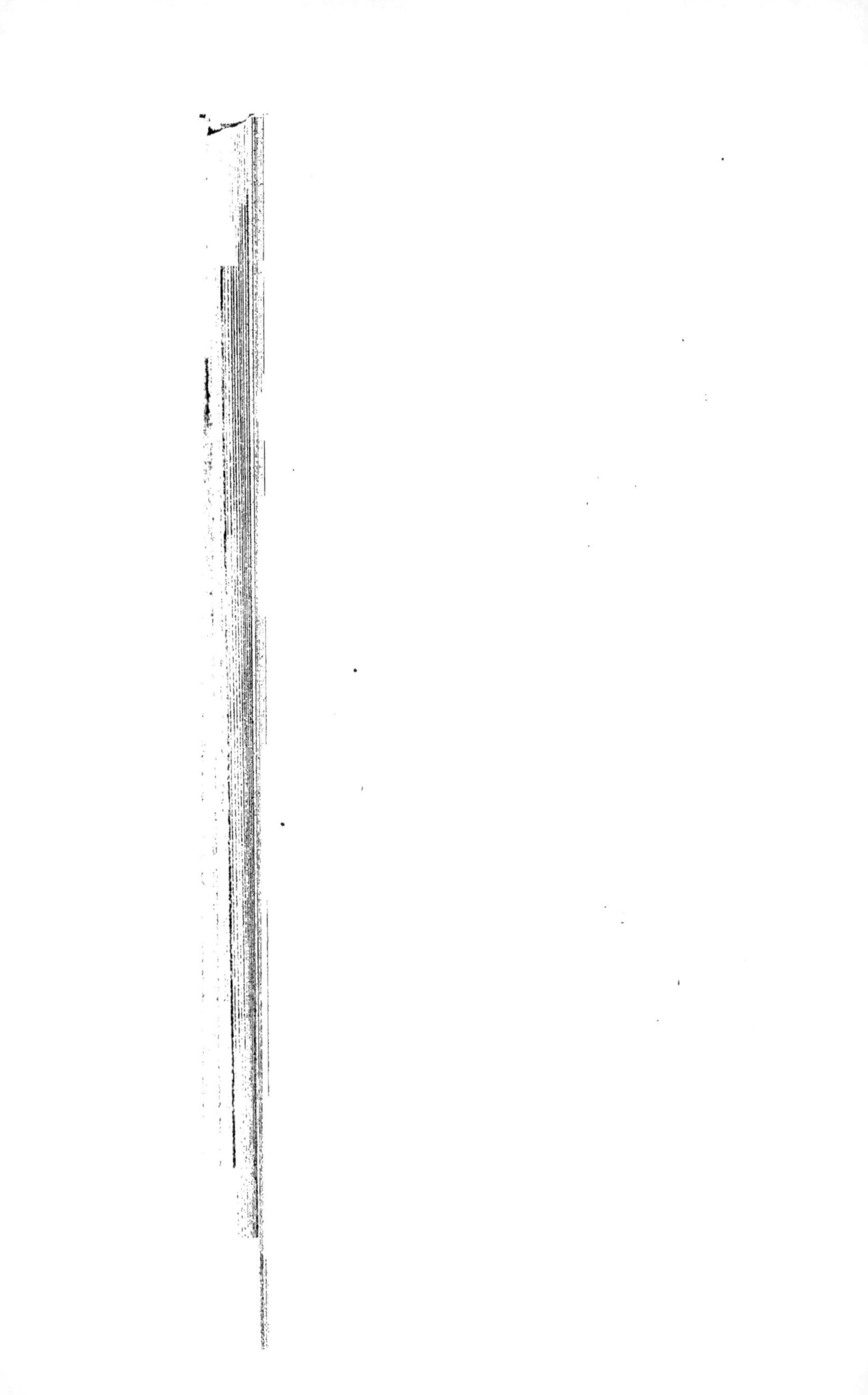

We were forced to lay in stores of all sorts in the autumn, as if we were fitting out a ship for an Arctic expedition. The lower story of the lighthouse was hung with mutton and beef, and the storeroom packed with provisions.

In the long, covered walk that bridged the gorge between the lighthouse and the house, we played in stormy days; and every evening it was a fresh excitement to watch the lighting of the lamps, and think how far the lighthouse sent its rays, and how many hearts it gladdened with assurance of safety. As I grew older I was allowed to kindle the lamps sometimes myself. That was indeed a pleasure. So little a creature as I might do that much for the great world! But by the fireside our best pleasure lay, — with plants and singing birds and books and playthings and loving care and kindness the cold and stormy season wore itself at last away, and died into the summer calm. We hardly saw a human face besides our own all winter; but with the spring came manifold life to our lonely dwelling, — human life among other forms. Our neighbors from Star rowed across; the pilot boat from Portsmouth steered over, and brought us letters, newspapers, magazines, and told us the news of months. The faint echoes from the far-off world hardly touched us little ones. We listened to the talk of our elders. "Winfield Scott and Santa Anna!" "The war in Mexico!" "The famine in Ireland!" It all meant nothing to us. We heard the reading aloud of details of the famine, and saw tears in the eyes of the reader, and were vaguely sorry; but the fate of Red Riding-Hood was much more near and dreadful to us. We waited for the spring with an eager longing; the advent of the growing grass, the birds and flowers and insect life, the soft skies and softer winds, the everlasting beauty of the thousand tender tints that clothed the world, — these things brought us unspeakable bliss. To the heart of Nature one must needs be drawn in such a life; and very soon I learned how richly she repays in deep refreshment the reverent love of her worshiper. With the first warm days we built our little mountains of wet gravel on the beach, and danced after the sandpipers at the edge of the foam, shouted to the gossiping kittiwakes that fluttered above, or watched the pranks of the burgomaster gull, or cried to the crying loons. The gannet's long, white wings stretched overhead, perhaps, or the dusky shag made a sudden shadow in mid-air, or we startled on some lonely ledge the great blue heron that flew off, trailing legs and wings, storklike, against the clouds. Or, in the sunshine on the bare rocks, we cut from the broad, brown leaves of the slippery, varnished kelps, grotesque shapes of man and bird and beast that withered in the wind and blew away; or we fashioned rude boats from bits of driftwood, manned them with a weird crew of kelpies, and set them adrift on the great deep, to float we cared not whither.

We played with the empty limpet-shells; they were mottled gray and brown, like the song sparrow's breast. We launched fleets of purple mussel shells on the still pools in the rocks, left by the tide, — pools that were like bits of fallen rainbow with the wealth of the sea, with tints of delicate seaweeds, crimson and green and ruddy brown and violet; where wandered the pearly æolis with rosy spines and fairy horns; and the large, round sea-urchins, like a boss upon a shield, were fastened here and there on the rock at the bottom, putting out from their green, prickly spikes transparent tentacles to seek their invisible food. Rosy and lilac starfish clung to the sides; in some dark nook, perhaps, a holothure unfolded its perfect ferns, a lovely, warm buff color, delicate as frostwork; little forests of coralline moss grew up in stillness, gold-colored shells crept about, and now and then flashed the silver-darting fins of slender minnows. The dimmest recesses were haunts of sea anemones that opened wide their starry flowers to the flowing tide, or drew themselves together, and hung in large, half-transparent drops, like clusters of some strange, amber-colored fruit, along the crevices as the water ebbed away. Sometimes we were cruel enough to capture a female lobster hiding in a deep cleft, with her millions of mottled eggs; or we laughed to see the hermit crabs challenge each other, and come out and fight a deadly battle till the stronger overcame, and, turning the weaker topsy-turvy, possessed himself of his ampler cockleshell, and scuttled off with it triumphant. Or, pulling all together, we dragged up the long kelps, or devil's-aprons; their roots were almost always fastened about large, living mussels; these we unclasped, carrying the mussels home to be cooked; fried in crumbs or batter, they were as good as oysters. We picked out from the kelp roots a kind of starfish which we called sea spider; the moment we touched it an extraordinary process began. One by one it disjointed all its sections, — whether from fear or anger we knew not, but it threw itself away, bit by bit, until nothing was left of it save the little, round body whence the legs had sprung!

With crab and limpet, with grasshopper and cricket, we were friends and neighbors, and we were never tired of watching the land spiders that possessed the place. Their webs covered every windowpane to the lighthouse top, and they rebuilt them as fast as they were swept down. One variety lived among the round gray stones on the beach, just above high-water mark, and spun no webs at all. Large and black, they speckled the light stones, swarming in the hot sun; at the first footfall they vanished beneath the pebbles.

All the cracks in the rocks were draped with swinging veils like the windowpanes. How often have we marveled at them, after a fog or a heavy fall of dew, in the early morning, when every slender thread was strung with glittering drops, — the whole symmetrical web a wonder of shining jewels trembling in the breeze! Tennyson's lines,

> "The cobweb woven across the cannon's throat
> Shall shake its threaded tears in the wind no more,"

always bring back to my mind the memory of those delicate, spangled draperies, more beautiful than any mortal loom could weave, that curtained the rocks at White Island and "shook their threaded tears" in every wind.

Sometimes we saw the bats wheel through the summer dusk, and in profoundly silent evenings heard, from the lighthouse top, their shrill, small cries, their voices sharper and finer than needle-points. One day I found one clinging to the under side of a shutter, — a soft, dun-colored, downy lump. I took it in my hand, and in an instant it changed to a hideous little demon, and its fierce white teeth met in the palm of my hand. So much fury in so small a beast I never encountered, and I was glad enough to give him his liberty without more ado.

A kind of sandhopper about an inch long, that infested the beach, was a great source of amusement. Lifting the stranded seaweed that marked the high-water line, we always startled a gray and brown cloud of them from beneath it, leaping away, like tiny kangaroos, out of sight. In storms these were driven into the house, forcing their way through every crack and cranny till they strewed the floors, — the sea so encircled us! Dying immediately upon leaving the water from which they fled, they turned from a clear brown, or what Mr. Kingsley would call a "pellucid gray," to bright brick-color, like a boiled lobster, and many a time I have swept them up in ruddy heaps; they looked like bits of coral.

I remember in the spring kneeling on the ground to seek the first blades of grass that pricked through the soil, and bringing them into the house to study and wonder over. Better than a shop full of toys they were to me! Whence came their color? How did they draw their sweet, refreshing tint from the brown earth, or the limpid air, or the white light? Chemistry was not at hand to answer me, and all her wisdom would not have dispelled the wonder. Later the little scarlet pimpernel charmed me. It seemed more than a flower; it was like a human thing. I knew it by its homely name of poor-man's weatherglass. It was so much wiser than I, for, when the sky was yet without a cloud, softly it clasped its small red petals together, folding its golden heart in safety from the shower that was sure to come! How could it know so much? Here is a question science cannot answer. The pimpernel grows everywhere about the islands, in every cleft and cranny where a suspicion of sustenance for its slender root can lodge; and it is one of the most exquisite of flowers, so rich in color, so quaint and dainty in its method of growth. I never knew its silent warning fail. I wondered much how every flower knew what to do and to be; why the morning-glory did n't forget sometimes and bear a cluster of elder bloom, or the elder hang out pennons of gold and purple like the iris, or the goldenrod suddenly blaze out a scarlet plume, the color of the pimpernel, was a mystery to my childish thought. And why did the sweet wild primrose wait till after sunset to unclose its pale yellow buds; why did it unlock its treasure of rich perfume to the night alone? Few flowers bloomed for me upon the lonesome rock; but I made the most of all I had, and neither knew of nor desired more. Ah, how beautiful they were! Tiny stars of crimson sorrel threaded on their long brown stems; the blackberry blossoms in bridal white; the surprise of the blue-eyed grass; the crowfoot flowers, like drops of yellow gold spilt about among the short grass and over the moss; the rich, blue-purple beach-pea, the sweet, spiked germander, and the homely, delightful yarrow that grows thickly on all the islands. Sometimes its broad clusters of dull white bloom are stained a lovely reddish-purple, as if with the light of sunset. I never saw it colored so elsewhere. Quantities of slender, wide-spreading mustard bushes grew about the house; their delicate flowers were like fragrant golden clouds. Dandelions, buttercups, and clover were not denied to us; though we had no daisies nor violets nor wild roses, no asters, but gorgeous spikes of goldenrod, and wonderful wild morning-glories, whose long, pale, ivory buds I used to find in the twilight, glimmering among the dark leaves, waiting for the touch of dawn to unfold and become each an exquisite incarnate blush,—the perfect color of a South Sea shell. They ran wild, knotting and twisting about the rocks, and smothering the loose bowlders in the gorges with lush green leaves and pink blossoms.

Many a summer morning have I crept out of the still house before anyone was awake, and, wrapping myself closely from the chill wind of dawn, climbed to the top of the high cliff called the Head to watch the sunrise. Pale grew the lighthouse flame before the broadening day as, nestled in a crevice at the cliff's edge, I watched the shadows draw away and morning break. Facing the east and south, with all the Atlantic before me, what happiness was mine as the deepening rose color flushed the delicate cloudflocks that dappled the sky, where the gulls soared, rosy too, while the calm sea blushed beneath. Or perhaps it was a cloudless sunrise with a sky of orange-red, and the sea-line silver-blue against it, peaceful as heaven. Infinite variety of beauty always awaited me, and filled me with an absorbing, unreasoning joy such as makes the song sparrow sing, — a sense of perfect bliss. Coming back in the sunshine, the morning-glories would lift up their faces, all awake, to my adoring gaze. Like countless rosy trumpets sometimes I thought they were, tossed everywhere about the rocks, turned up to the sky, or drooping toward the ground, or looking east, west, north, south, in silent loveliness. It seemed as if they had gathered the peace of the golden morning in their still depths even as my heart had gathered it.

In some of those matchless summer mornings when I went out to milk the little dun cow, it was hardly possible to go farther than the doorstep, for pure wonder, as I looked abroad at the sea lying still, like a vast, round mirror, the tide drawn away from the rich brown rocks, a sail or two asleep in the calm, not a sound abroad except a few bird voices; dew lying like jewel dust sifted over everything, — diamond and ruby, sapphire, topaz, and amethyst, flashing out of the emerald deeps of the tufted grass or from the bending tops. Looking over to the mainland, I could dimly discern in the level sunshine the depths of glowing green woods faintly revealed in the distance, fold beyond fold of hill and valley thickly clothed with the summer's splendor. But my handful of grass was more precious to me than miles of green fields, and I was led to consider every blade where there were so few. Not long ago I had watched them piercing the ground toward the light; now, how strong in their slender grace were these stems, how perfect the poise of the heavy heads that waved with such harmony of movement in the faintest breeze! And I noticed at midday when the dew was dry, where the tall, blossoming spears stood in graceful companies that, before they grew purple, brown, and ripe, when they began to blossom, they put out first a downy ring of pollen in tiny, yellow rays, held by an almost invisible thread, which stood out like an aureole from each slow-waving head, — a fairylike effect. On Seavey's Island (united to ours by a narrow beach covered at high tide with contending waves) grew one single root of fern, the only one within the circle of my little world. It was safe in a deep cleft, but I was in perpetual anxiety lest my little cow, going there daily to pasture, should leave her cropping of the grass and eat it up some day. Poor little cow! One night she did not come home to be milked as usual, and on going to seek her we found she had caught one foot in a crevice and twisted her hoof entirely off! That was a calamity; for we were forced to summon our neighbors and have her killed on the spot.

I had a scrap of garden, literally not more than a yard square, wherein grew only African marigolds, rich in color as barbaric gold. I knew nothing of John Keats at that time, — poor Keats, "who told Severn that he thought his intensest pleasure in life had been to watch the growth of flowers," — but I am sure he never felt their beauty more devoutly than the little, half-savage being who knelt, like a fire worshiper, to watch the unfolding of those golden disks. When, later, the "brave new world" of poets was opened to me, with what power those glowing lines of his went straight to my heart,

> "Open afresh your rounds of starry folds,
> Ye ardent marigolds!"

All flowers had for me such human interest, they were so dear and precious, I hardly liked to gather them, and when they were withered, I carried them all to one place and laid them tenderly together, and never liked to pass the spot where they were hidden.

Once or twice every year came the black, lumbering old "oil-schooner" that brought supplies for the lighthouse, and the inspector, who gravely examined everything, to see if all was in order. He left stacks of clear red and white glass chimneys for the lamps, and several doeskins for polishing the great, silver-lined copper reflectors, large bundles of wicks, and various pairs of scissors for trimming them, heavy black casks of ill-perfumed whale oil, and other things, which were all stowed in the round, dimly-lighted rooms of the tower. Very awestruck, we children always crept into the corners, and whispered and watched the intruders till they embarked in their ancient, clumsy vessel, and, hoisting their dark, weather-stained sails, bore slowly away again. About ten years ago that old white lighthouse was taken away, and a new, perpendicular brick tower built in its place. The lantern, with its fifteen lamps, ten golden and five red, gave place to Fresnel's powerful single burner, or, rather, three burners in one, inclosed in its case of prisms. The old lighthouse was by far the more picturesque; but perhaps the new one is more effective, the light being, undoubtedly, more powerful.

Often, in pleasant days, the head of the family sailed away to visit the other islands, sometimes taking the children with him, oftener going alone, frequently not returning till after dark. The landing at White Island is so dangerous that the greatest care is requisite, if there is any sea running, to get ashore in safety. Two long and very solid timbers about three feet apart are laid from the boathouse to low-water mark, and between those timbers the boat's bow must be accurately steered; if she goes to the right or the left, woe to her crew unless the sea is calm! Safely lodged in the slip, as it is called, she is drawn up into the boathouse by a capstan, and fastened securely. The lighthouse gave no ray to the dark rock below it; sending its beams far out to sea, it left us at its foot in greater darkness for its lofty light. So when the boat was out late, in soft, moonless summer nights, I used to light a lantern, and, going down to the water's edge, take my station between the timbers of the slip, and, with the lantern at my feet, sit waiting in the darkness, quite content, knowing my little star was watched for, and that the safety of the boat depended in a great measure upon it. How sweet the summer wind blew, how softly plashed the water round me, how refreshing was the odor of the sparkling brine! High above, the lighthouse rays streamed out into the humid dark, and the cottage windows were ruddy from the glow within. I felt so much a part of the Lord's universe, I was no more afraid of the dark than the waves or winds; but I was glad to hear at last the creaking of the mast and the rattling of the rowlocks as the boat approached; and, while yet she was far off, the lighthouse touched her one large sail into sight, so that I knew she was nearing me, and shouted, listening for the reply that came so blithely back to me over the water.

HOW CAPE COD TRAVELS

By Henry David Thoreau

THE lighthouse, known to mariners as the Cape Cod or Highland Light, is one of our "primary seacoast lights," and is usually the first seen by those approaching the entrance of Massachusetts Bay from Europe. It is forty-three miles from Cape Ann Light, and forty-one from Boston Light. It stands about twenty rods from the edge of the bank, which is here formed of clay. I borrowed the plane and square, level and dividers, of a carpenter who was shingling a barn near by, and, using one of those shingles made of a mast, contrived a rude sort of quadrant, with pins for sights and pivots, and got the angle of elevation of the bank opposite the lighthouse, and with a couple of codlines the length of its slope, and so measured its height on the shingle. It rises one hundred and ten feet above its immediate base, or about one hundred and twenty-three feet above mean low water. Graham, who has carefully surveyed the extremity of the Cape, makes it one hundred and thirty feet. The mixed sand and clay lay at an angle of forty degrees with the horizon, where I measured it, but the clay is generally much steeper. No cow nor hen ever gets down it. Half a mile farther south the bank is fifteen or twenty-five feet higher, and that appeared to be the highest land in North Truro. Even this vast clay bank is fast wearing away. Small streams of water trickling down it at intervals of two or three rods, have left the intermediate clay in the form of steep Gothic roofs fifty feet high or more, the ridges as sharp and rugged-looking as rocks; and in one place the bank is curiously eaten out in the form of a large semicircular crater.

According to the lighthouse keeper, the Cape is wasting here on both sides, though most on the eastern. In some places it had lost many rods within the last year, and, erelong, the lighthouse must be moved. We calculated, *from his data,* how soon the Cape would be quite worn away at this point, "for," said he, "I can remember sixty years back." We were even more surprised at this last announcement — that is, at the slow waste of life and energy in our informant, for we had taken him to be not more than forty — than at the rapid wasting of the Cape, and we thought that he stood a fair chance to outlive the former.

Between this October and June of the next year, I found that the bank had lost about forty feet in one place, opposite the lighthouse, and it was cracked more than forty feet farther from the edge at the last date, the shore being strewn with the recent rubbish. But I judged that generally it was not wearing away here at the rate of more than six feet annually. Any conclusions drawn from the observations of a few years, or one generation only, are likely to prove false, and the Cape may balk expectation by its dura-

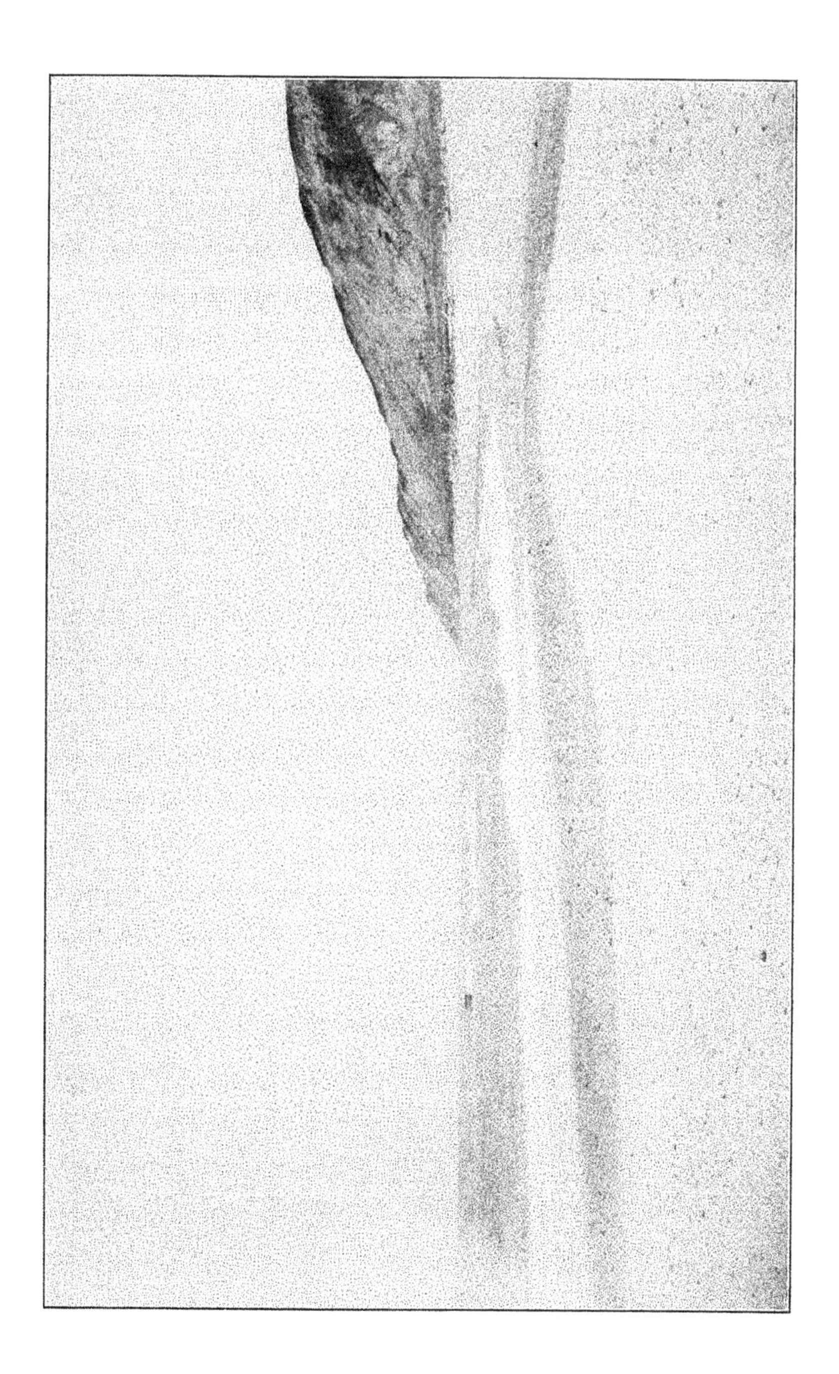

bility. In some places even a wrecker's footpath down the bank lasts several years. One old inhabitant told us that when the lighthouse was built, in 1798, it was calculated that it would stand forty-five years, allowing the bank to waste one length of fence each year, "but," said he, "there it is" (or rather another near the same site, about twenty rods from the edge of the bank).

The sea is not gaining on the Cape everywhere, for one man told me of a vessel wrecked long ago on the north of Provincetown whose "*bones*" (this was his word) are still visible many rods within the present line of the beach, half buried in sand. Perchance they lie alongside the *timbers* of a whale. The general statement of the inhabitants is, that the Cape is wasting on both sides, but extending itself on particular points on the south and west, as at Chatham and Monomoy Beaches, and at Billingsgate, Long, and Race Points. James Freeman stated in his day that above three miles had been added to Monomoy Beach during the previous fifty years, and it is said to be still extending as fast as ever. A writer in the "Massachusetts Magazine," in the last century, tells us that "when the English first settled upon the Cape, there was an island off Chatham, at three leagues' distance, called Webb's Island, containing twenty acres, covered with red cedar or savin. The inhabitants of Nantucket used to carry wood from it;" but he adds that in his day a large rock alone marked the spot, and the water was six fathoms deep there. The entrance to Nauset Harbor, which was once in Eastham, has now traveled south into Orleans. The islands in Wellfleet Harbor once formed a continuous beach, though now small vessels pass between them. And so of many other parts of this coast.

Perhaps what the ocean takes from one part of the Cape it gives to another, — robs Peter to pay Paul. On the eastern side the sea appears to be everywhere encroaching on the land. Not only the land is undermined, and its ruins carried off by currents, but the sand is blown from the beach directly up the steep bank, where it is one hundred and fifty feet high, and covers the original surface there many feet deep. If you sit on the edge you will have ocular demonstration of this by soon getting your eyes full. Thus the bank preserves its height as fast as it is worn away. This sand is steadily traveling westward at a rapid rate, "more than a hundred yards," says one writer, within the memory of inhabitants now living; so that in some places peat meadows are buried deep under the sand, and the peat is cut through it; and in one place a large peat meadow has made its appearance on the shore in the bank covered many feet deep, and peat has been cut there. This accounts for that great pebble of peat which we saw in the surf. The old oysterman had told us that many years ago he lost a "crittur" by her being mired in a swamp near the Atlantic side east of his house, and twenty years ago he lost the swamp itself entirely, but has since seen signs of it appearing on the beach. He also said that he had seen cedar stumps "as big as cartwheels"(!) on the bottom of the Bay, three miles off Billingsgate

Point, when leaning over the side of his boat in pleasant weather, and that that was dry land not long ago. Another told us that a log canoe known to have been buried many years before on the Bay side at East Harbor in Truro, where the Cape is extremely narrow, appeared at length on the Atlantic side, the Cape having rolled over it, and an old woman said,— "Now, you see it is true what I told you, that the Cape is moving."

The bars along the coast shift with every storm, and in many places there is occasionally none at all. We ourselves observed the effect of a single storm with a high tide in the night, in July, 1855. It moved the sand on the beach opposite the lighthouse to the depth of six feet, and three rods in width as far as we could see north and south, and carried it bodily off no one knows exactly where, laying bare in one place a large rock five feet high which was invisible before, and narrowing the beach to that extent. There is usually, as I have said, no bathing on the back side of the Cape, on account of the undertow, but when we were there last, the sea had, three months before, cast up a bar near this lighthouse, two miles long and ten rods wide, over which the tide did not flow, leaving a narrow cove, then a quarter of a mile long, between it and the shore, which afforded excellent bathing. This cove had from time to time been closed up as the bar traveled northward, in one instance imprisoning four or five hundred whiting and cod, which died there, and the water as often turned fresh and finally gave place to sand. This bar, the inhabitants assured us, might be wholly removed, and the water six feet deep there in two or three days.

The lighthouse keeper said that when the wind "blowed strong on to the shore," the waves ate fast into the bank, but when it "blowed off" they took no sand away; for in the former case the wind heaped up the surface of the water next to the beach, and to preserve its equilibrium a strong undertow immediately set back again into the sea, which carried with it the sand and whatever else was in the way, and left the beach hard to walk on; but in the latter case the undertow set on, and carried the sand with it, so that it was particularly difficult for shipwrecked men to get to land when the wind blew on to the shore, but easier when it blew off. This undertow, meeting the next surface wave on the bar which itself has made, forms part of the dam over which the latter breaks, as over an upright wall. The sea thus plays with the land, holding a sandbar in its mouth awhile before it swallows it, as a cat plays with a mouse; but the fatal gripe is sure to come at last. The sea sends its rapacious east wind to rob the land, but before the former has got far with its prey, the land sends its honest west wind to recover some of its own.

THE SANDS OF CAPE COD

By Henry David Thoreau

FROM that elevation we could overlook the operations of the inhabitants almost as completely as if the roofs had been taken off. They were busily covering the wickerwork flakes about their houses with salted fish, and we now saw that the back yards were improved for this purpose as much as the front; where one man's fish ended another's began. In almost every yard we detected some little building from which these treasures were being trundled forth and systematically spread, and we saw that there was an art as well as a knack even in spreading fish, and that a division of labor was profitably practiced. One man was withdrawing his fishes a few inches beyond the nose of his neighbor's cow, which had stretched her neck over a paling to get at them. It seemed a quite domestic employment, like drying clothes, and indeed in some parts of the county the women take part in it.

I noticed in several places on the Cape a sort of clothes-*flakes*. They spread brush on the ground, and fence it round, and then lay their clothes on it, to keep them from the sand. This is a Cape Cod clothes-yard.

The sand is the great enemy here. The tops of

some of the hills were inclosed and a board put up forbidding all persons entering the inclosure, lest their feet should disturb the sand, and set it a-blowing or a-sliding. The inhabitants are obliged to get leave from the authorities to cut wood behind the town for fish flakes, bean poles, pea brush, and the like, though, as we were told, they may transplant trees from one part of the township to another without leave. The sand drifts like snow, and sometimes the lower story of a house is concealed by it, though it is kept off by a wall. The houses were formerly built on piles, in order that the driving sand might pass under them. We saw a few old ones here still standing on their piles, but they were boarded up now, being protected by their younger neighbors. There was a school-house, just under the hill on which we sat, filled with sand up to the tops of the desks, and of course the master and scholars had fled. Perhaps they had imprudently left the windows open one day, or neglected to mend a broken pane. Yet in one place was advertised "Fine sand for sale here," — I could hardly believe my eyes, — probably some of the street sifted, — a good instance of the fact that a man confers a value on the most worthless thing by mixing himself with it, according to which rule we must have conferred a value on the whole back side of Cape Cod; — but I thought that if they could have advertised "Fat Soil," or perhaps "Fine sand got rid of," aye, and "Shoes emptied here," it would have been more alluring. As we looked down on the town, I thought that I saw one man, who probably lived beyond the extremity of the planking, steering and tacking for it in a sort of snowshoes, but I may have been mistaken. In some pictures of Provincetown the persons of the inhabitants are not drawn below the ankles, so much being supposed to be buried in the sand. Nevertheless, natives of Provincetown assured me that they could walk in the middle of the road without trouble, even in slippers, for they had learned how to put their feet down and lift them up without taking in any sand. One man said that he should be surprised if he found half a dozen grains of sand in his pumps at night, and stated, moreover, that the young ladies had a dexterous way of emptying their shoes at each step, which it would take a stranger a long time to learn. The tires of the stage wheels were about five inches wide; and the wagon tires generally on the Cape are an inch or two wider, as the sand is an inch or two deeper than elsewhere. I saw a baby's wagon with tires six inches wide to keep it near the surface. The more tired the wheels, the less tired the horses. Yet all the time that we were in Provincetown, which was two days and nights, we saw only one horse and cart, and they were conveying a coffin. They did not try such experiments there on common occasions. The next summer I saw only the two-wheeled horse cart which conveyed me thirty rods into the harbor on my way to the steamer. Yet we read that there were two horses and two yoke of oxen here in 1791, and we were told that there were several more when we were there, besides the stage team. In Barber's "Historical Collections," it is said, "so rarely are wheel carriages seen in the place that they are a matter of some curiosity to the younger part of the community. A lad who understood navigating the ocean much better than land travel, on seeing a man driving a wagon in the street, expressed his surprise at his being able to drive so straight without the assistance of a rudder.'" There was no rattle of carts, and there would have been no rattle if there had been any carts. Some saddle horses that passed the hotel in the evening merely made the sand fly with a rustling sound like a writer sanding his paper copiously, but there was no sound of their tread. No doubt there are more horses and carts there at present. A sleigh is never seen, or at least is a great novelty on the Cape, the snow being either absorbed by the sand or blown into drifts.

Nevertheless, the inhabitants of the Cape generally do not complain of their "soil," but will tell you that it is good enough for them to dry their fish on.

Nothwithstanding all this sand, we counted three meetinghouses, and four schoolhouses nearly as large, on this street, though some had a tight board fence about them to preserve the plot within level and hard. Similar fences, even within a foot of many of the houses, gave the town a less cheerful and hospitable appearance than it would otherwise have had. They told us that, on the whole, the sand had made no progress for the last ten years, the cows being no longer permitted to go at large, and every means being taken to stop the sandy tide.

In 1727, Provincetown was "invested with peculiar

privileges," for its encouragement. Once or twice it was nearly abandoned; but now lots on the street fetch a high price, though titles to them were first obtained by possession and improvement, and they are still transferred by quitclaim deeds merely, the township being the property of the State. But though lots were so valuable on the street, you might in many places throw a stone over them to where a man could still obtain land or sand by squatting on or improving it.

Stones are very rare on the Cape. I saw a very few small stones used for pavements and for bank walls, in one or two places in my walk, but they are so scarce, that, as I was informed, vessels have been forbidden to take them from the beach for ballast, and therefore their crews used to land at night and steal them. I did not hear of a rod of regular stone wall below Orleans. Yet I saw one man underpinning a new house in Eastham with some "rocks," as he called them, which he said a neighbor had collected with great pains in the course of years, and finally made over to him. This I thought was a gift worthy of being recorded, — equal to a transfer of California "rocks," almost. Another man who was assisting him, and who seemed to be a close observer of nature, hinted to me the locality of a rock in that neighborhood which was "forty-two paces in circumference and fifteen feet high," for he saw that I was a stranger, and, probably, would not carry it off. Yet I suspect that the locality of the few large rocks on the forearm of the Cape is well known to the inhabitants generally.

I even met with one man who had got a smattering of mineralogy, but where he picked it up I could not guess. I thought that he would meet with some interesting geological nuts for him to crack, if he should ever visit the mainland, — Cohasset or Marblehead, for instance.

The well stones at the Highland Light were brought from Hingham, but the wells and cellars of the Cape are generally built of brick, which also are imported. The cellars, as well as the wells, are made in a circular form, to prevent the sand from pressing in the wall. The former are only from nine to twelve feet in diameter, and are said to be very cheap, since a single tier of brick will suffice for a cellar of even larger dimensions. Of course, if you live in the sand, you will not require a large cellar to hold your roots. In Provincetown, when formerly they suffered the sand to drive under their houses, obliterating all rudiment of a cellar, they did not raise a vegetable to put into one. One farmer in Wellfleet, who raised fifty bushels of potatoes, showed me his cellar under a corner of his house, not more than nine feet in diameter, looking like a cistern; but he had another of the same size under his barn.

You need dig only a few feet almost anywhere near the shore of the Cape to find fresh water. But that which we tasted was invariably poor, though the inhabitants called it good, as if they were comparing it with salt water. In the account of Truro, it is said, "Wells dug near the shore are dry at low water, or rather at what is called young flood, but are replenished with the flowing of the tide," — the salt water, which is the lowest in the sand, apparently forcing the fresh up. When you express your surprise at the greenness of a Provincetown garden on the beach, in a dry season, they will sometimes tell you that the tide forces the moisture up to them. It is an interesting fact that low sandbars in the midst of the ocean, perhaps even those which are laid bare only at low tide, are reservoirs of fresh water, at which the thirsty mariner can supply himself. They appear, like huge sponges, to hold the rain and dew which fall on them, and which, by capillary attraction, are prevented from mingling with the surrounding brine.

THE GRAND CAÑON OF ARIZONA

By Charles S. Olcott

I ARRIVED at the cañon on a cold night in January, 1903, alone. There were few guests at the hotel, which was a capacious log cabin, with long, single-storied frame structures projecting in various directions, to serve the purposes of sleeping rooms and kitchens. It had a primitive look, far more in keeping with the solitude of its surroundings than the present comfortable hotel. An old guide (I hoped he might be John Hance) sat by the fire talking with a group of loungers, and I sauntered near enough to hear the conversation, expecting to listen to some good tale of the cañon. But the talk was commonplace. Presently an Indian came in accompanied by a young squaw. He was said to be a hundred years old — a fact no doubt easily proved by the layers of dirt on his face and hands, if one could count them like the rings on a tree. He proved to be only a lazy old beggar and quite unromantic. The hotel management did not provide Indian dances and other forms of amusement then as now and I was obliged to spend a dull evening. I read the guidebooks and reached the conclusion that the cañon was not worth visiting if one did not go "down the trail" to the bottom of it. So I inquired at the desk when the party would start in the morning, and was dismayed to be told that there would be none unless somebody wanted to go. I was told to put my name on the "list" and no doubt others would see it and we might "get up" a party. I therefore boldly signed my name at the top of a white sheet of paper, feeling much like a decoy, and awaited results. Again and again during the lonesome evening I sauntered over to the desk, but not one of the few guests had shown the slightest interest. At ten o'clock my autograph still headed an invisible list, as lonely as the man for whom it stood, and I went to bed, vowing to myself that if I could get only one companion, besides the guide, I would go down the trail.

It was still dark when I heard the strident voice of a Japanese porter calling through the corridor, "Brek-foos! Brek-foos!" and I rose quickly. The dawn was just breaking as I stepped out into the chill air and walked to the edge of the great chasm. Before me rolled a sea of vapor. It was as though a massive curtain of clouds had been let down from the sky to protect the cañon in the night. The spectacle was not to be exhibited until the proper hour arrived. The great white ocean stretched away to the north as far as the eye could reach, filling every nook and corner of the vast depression. In the east the rosy tints of the morning brightened the sky. Suddenly a ray of light illumined what appeared to be a rock, far out in the filmy ocean, and the black mass blazed with the ruddy hue. The tip of another great butte suddenly projected itself and caught another ray of light. One by one the rugged domes of the great rock temples of Brahma and Buddha and Zoroaster and Isis, as they are called, peeped into view as the mists gradually disappeared, catching the morning sunbeams at a thousand different angles, and throwing back a kaleidoscope of purples, blues, reds, and yellows, until at last the whole superb cañon was revealed in a burst of color, over which the amethyst reigned supreme.

How long I should have stood enraptured before this scene of superlative grandeur, so marvelously unfolded to the sight, I do not know, had not the more prosaic call of "Brek-foos!" long since forgotten, again resounded to bring me back to human levels. I returned to the hotel and entered the breakfast room, with an appetite well sharpened by the crisp wintry air, first taking a furtive glance at the "list," where my name still presided in solitary dignity. It was still early and I was seated at the head of a long table, where there were as yet only two or three other guests. I felt sure that the day would be a busy one, particularly if I should find that one companion with whom I was determined to attempt the trail. It would be well to lay in a good supply of fuel, and accordingly I asked the waiter to get me a good beefsteak and a cup of coffee. He suggested griddle cakes in addition, as appropriate for a cold morning, and I assented. Then suddenly remembering that country hotels have a way of serving microscopic portions in what a distinguished author has described as "bird bathtubs," I called over my shoulder to bring me some ham and eggs also. "George" disappeared with a grin. When he returned, holding aloft a huge and well-loaded tray, that darkey's face was a vision of delight. His eyes sparkled and his thick lips had expanded into an upturned crescent, wherein two rows of gleaming ivory stood in military array, every one determined to be seen. He laid before me a porter-house steak, large enough for my entire family, an immense elliptical piece of ham sliced from rim to rim off the thigh of a huge porker, three fried eggs, a small mountain of buckwheat cakes, and a pot of coffee, remarking, as he made room for the generous repast, "Ah reckon you-all 's powerful hungry dis mawnin', boss!"

By this time the table was well filled. There is no formality at such places and we were soon chatting together like old acquaintances. I resolved to open up the subject of the trail and asked my neighbor at the right whether he intended to take the trip. He said "No," rather indifferently, I thought, and I expressed my surprise. I had read the guidebooks to good purpose and was soon expatiating on the wonders of the trail, declaring that I could not understand why people should come from all parts of the world to see the cañon and miss the finest sight of all, the view from below. (Somebody said that in the guidebook.) They were all listening now. Some one asked if it was not dangerous. "Not in the least," I replied; "no lives have ever been lost and there has never been an accident" (the guidebook said that, too) — "and, besides," I continued, knowingly, "it 's lots of fun." Just here a maiden lady of uncertain age, cadaverous cheeks, and a high, squeaky voice, piped out, — "I believe I'll go." I remembered my vow about the *one* companion and suddenly felt a strange, sickly feeling of irresolution. But it was only for a moment. A little girl of twelve was tugging at her father's coat-tails — "Papa, can't I go?" Papa conferred with Mamma, who agreed that Bessie might go if Papa went too. I was making progress. A masculine voice from the other end of the table then broke in with a few more questions, and its owner, a man from Minnesota, whom we afterward called the "Major," was the next recruit. I had suddenly gained an unwonted influence. The guests were evidently inspired with a feeling of respect for a man who would order such a regal breakfast! After the meal was over, a lady approached and prefacing her request with the flattering remark that I "looked respectable," said that her daughter, a young lady of twenty, was anxious to go down the trail; she would consent if I would agree to see that no harm befell her. I thought I might as well be a chaperon as a cicerone, since I had had no experience as either, and promptly assured the mother of my willingness to accept the charge. It was a vain promise. The young lady was the first to mount her mule and fell into line behind the guide; before I could secure my animal others had taken their places and I found myself three mules astern, with no possibility of passing to the front or of exchanging a word with my "charge." I fancied a slight gleam of mischievous triumph in her eyes as she looked back, seeming to say, "I can take care of myself, quite well, thank you, Mr. Chaperon!" After a slight delay, I secured my mule and taking the bridle firmly in my hand said, "Get up, Sam." The animal deliberately turned his head and looked back at me with a sardonic smile in his mulish eye that said clearly — "You imagine that *you* are guiding me, don't you? Just wait and see!"

There were seven of us, including the guide, as we started down the long and crooked path. The guide rode a white horse, but the rest of the party were mounted, like myself, on big, sturdy mules — none of your little, lazy burros, as most people imagine. At first the trail seemed to descend at a frightful angle, and the path seemed — oh, so narrow! I could put out my left hand against a perpendicular wall of rock and look down on the right into what seemed to be the bottomless pit. I noticed that the trail was covered with snow and ice. Suppose any of the mules should slip? Had we not embarked upon a foolhardy undertaking? And if there should be an accident, all the blame would justly fall upon my head. How silly of me to be so anxious to go! And how reckless to urge all these other poor innocents into such a trap!

Fortunately such notions lasted only a few minutes. The mules were sharp-shod and did not slip. They went down every day, nearly, and knew their business. They were born in the cañon. They would have been terribly frightened in Broadway, but here they were at home and followed the familiar path with a firm tread. I threw the bridle over the pommel of the saddle and gave Sam my implicit trust. He knew a great deal more about the job than I did. From that moment I had no further thought of danger.

I came to have a high respect for that mule. Most people respect a mule only because of the possibility that his hind legs may suddenly fly out at a tangent and hit something. I respected Sam because I knew his legs would do nothing of the kind. He needed all of them under him and he knew it. He never swerved a hair's breadth nearer the outer edge of the path than was absolutely necessary. The trail descends in a series of zigzag lines and sharp angles like the teeth of a saw. Sam would march straight down to one of these angles; then, with the precipice yawning thousands of feet below, he would slowly squirm around until his head was pointed down the next segment and then with great deliberation resume his journey. The guide thought him too deliberate and once came back to give me a small willow switch. I was riding on a narrow shelf of rock, less than a yard wide, where I could look down into a chasm thousands of feet deep. "That mule is too slow," he said; "you must whip him up." I took the switch and thanked him. But I wouldn't have used it then for a million dollars!

It was a glorious ride. The trail itself was the only sign of human handiwork. Everything else in sight was as Nature made it — a wild, untouched ruggedness near at hand and a softer, gentler aspect in the distance, where the exposed strata of all the geologic ages caught the sunshine at millions of angles, each reflecting its own particular hue and all blending together in a rich harmony of color; where the bright blue sky and the fleecy clouds came down to join their earthly brethren in a revelry of rainbow tints

THE TRAIL, GRAND CAÑON OF ARIZONA

and the sun overhead, despite the snow about the rim, was smiling his happiest summer benison upon the deep valley.

We came, presently, to a place called Jacob's Ladder, where the path ceased to be an inclined plane and became a series of huge steps, each about as high as an ordinary table. Here we all dismounted, for the mules could not safely descend with such burdens. It was comical to watch them. My Sam would stand on each step for several minutes, gazing about as though enjoying the scenery. Then, as if struck by a sudden notion, he would drop his fore legs to the next step, and with hind legs still at the higher elevation, pause in further contemplation. At length it would occur to this deliberate animal that his hind legs, after all, really belonged on the same level with the other two, and he would suddenly drop them down and again become rapt in thought. This performance was repeated on every step for the entire descent of more than one hundred feet.

After traveling about three hours, during which we had descended three thousand feet below the rim, we came to Indian Garden, where an Indian family once found a fertile spot on which they could practice farming in their own crude way. Here we came to some tents belonging to a camping-party, and I found the solution of a problem that had puzzled me earlier in the day. Standing on the rim and looking across the cañon I had seen what appeared to be a newspaper lying on the grass. I knew it must be three or four miles from where I stood, and that a newspaper would be invisible at that distance, yet I could not imagine how any natural object could appear white and rectangular so far away. Presently I saw some tiny objects moving slowly like a string of black ants, and realized that these must be some early trail party. We met them at Indian Garden. They proved to be prospectors and the "newspaper" was in reality the group of tents.

We had now left the steep zigzag path, and riding straight forward over a great plateau, we came to the brink of some granite cliffs, where we could at last see the Colorado River, thundering through the gorge thirteen hundred feet below. And what a river it is! From the rim we could only catch an occasional glimpse, looking like a narrow silver ribbon, threading in and out among a multitude of strangely fashioned domes and turrets. Here we saw something of its true character, though still too far away to feel its real power — a boiling, turbulent, angry, and useless stream dashing wildly through a barren valley of rock and sand, its waters capable of generating millions of horse power, but too inaccessible to be harnessed, and its surface violently resisting the slightest attempt at navigation; a veritable anarchist of a river! For more than a thousand miles it rushes through a deep cañon toward the sea, falling forty-two hundred feet between its source and mouth and for five hundred miles of its course tumbling in a series of five hundred and twenty cataracts and rapids — an average of slightly more than one to every mile.

Think of the courage of brave Major Powell and his

men, who descended this terrible river for the first time, and you have a subject for contemplation as sublime as the cañon itself. In the spring of 1869, when John W. Powell started on his famous expedition, the Grand Cañon was totally unknown. Hunters and prospectors had seen enough to bring back wonderful stories. Parties had ventured into the gorge in boats and had never been heard of again. The Indians warned him that the cañon was sacred to the gods, who would consider any attempt to enter it an act of disobedience to their wishes and contempt for their authority, and vengeance would surely follow. The incessant roar of the waters told of many cataracts and it was currently reported that the river was lost underground for several hundred miles. Undaunted by these fearful tales, Major Powell, who had seen service in the Civil War, leaving an arm on the battlefield of Shiloh, determined, nevertheless, to descend the river. He had long been a student of botany, zoölogy, and mineralogy and had devoted two years to a study of the geology of the region.

With nine other men as his companions, he started from Green River City, Wyoming, on the 24th of May, with one light boat of pine and three heavy ones built of oak. Nothing could be more modest than his report to the Government, yet it is an account of thrilling adventures and hair-breadth escapes, day by day, almost too marvelous for belief. Yet there is not the slightest doubt of its authenticity in every detail. At times the swift current carried them along with the speed of an express train, the waves breaking and rolling over the boats, which, but for the water-tight compartments, must have been swamped at the outset.

When a threatening roar gave warning of another cataract they would pull for the shore and prepare to make a portage. The boats were unloaded and the stores of provisions, instruments, etc., carried down to some convenient point below the falls. Then the boats were let down, one by one. The bow line would be taken below and made fast. Then with five or six men holding back on the stern line with all their strength, the boat would be allowed to go down as far as they could hold it, when the line would be cast off, the boat would leap over the falls, and be caught by the lower rope. Again and again, day after day throughout the entire summer, this hard work was continued. In the early evenings and mornings Major Powell, with a companion or two, would climb to the top of the high cliffs, towering to a height of perhaps two thousand or three thousand feet above the river, to make his observations, frequently getting into dangerons positions where a man with two arms would have difficulty in clinging to the rocks, and where any one but a man of iron nerve would have met instant death.

Day by day they faced what seemed certain destruction, dashing through rapids, spinning about in whirlpools, capsizing in the breakers, and clinging to the upturned boats until rescued or thrown up on some rocky islet, breaking their oars, losing or spoiling their rations until they were nearly gone, and toiling incessantly every waking hour. One of the boats was completely wrecked before they had crossed the Arizona line, and one man, who barely escaped death in this accident, left the party on July 5, declaring that he had seen danger enough. The remaining eight, whether from loyalty to their chief or because it seemed impossible to climb to the top of the chasm, continued to brave the perils of the river until August 27, when they had reached a point well below the mouth of the Bright Angel River. Here the danger seemed more appalling than at any previous time. Lateral streams had washed great bowlders into the river, forming a dam over which the water fell eighteen or twenty feet; then appeared a rapid for two or three hundred yards on one side, the walls of the cañon projecting sharply into the river on the other; then a second fall so great that its height could not be determined, and beyond this more rapids, filled with huge rocks for one or two hundred yards, and at the bottom a great rock jutting halfway across the river, having a sloping side up which the tumbling waters dashed in huge breakers. After spending the afternoon clambering among the rocks to survey the river and coolly calculating his chances, the dauntless Powell announced his intention to proceed. But there were three men whose courage was not equal to this latest demand, and they firmly declined the risk.

On the morning of the 28th, after a breakfast that seemed like a funeral, the three deserters — one can scarcely find the heart to blame them — climbed a crag to see their former comrades depart. One boat is left behind. The other two push out into the stream and in less than a minute have safely run the dangerous rapids, which seemed bad enough from above, but were in reality less difficult than many others previously experienced. A succession of rapids and falls are safely run, but after dinner they find themselves in another bad place. The river is tumbling down over the rocks in whirlpools and great waves and the angry waters are lashed into white foam. There is no possibility of a portage and both boats must go over the falls. Away they go, dashing and plunging, striking the rocks and rolling over and over until they reach the calmer waters below, when as if by a miracle it is found that every man in the party is uninjured and both the boats are safe. By noon of the next day they have emerged from the Grand Cañon into a valley where low mountains can be seen in the distance. The river flows in silent majesty, the sky is bright overhead, the birds pour forth the music of a joyous welcome, the toil and pain are over, the gloomy shadows have disappeared, and their joy is exquisite as they realize that the first passage of the long and terrible river has been safely accomplished and all are alive and well.

But what of the three who left them? If only they could have known that safety and joy were little more than a day ahead! They successfully climbed the steep cañon walls, only to encounter a band of Indians who were looking for cattle thieves or other plunderers. They could give no other account of their presence except to say they had come down the river. This, to the Indian mind, was so obviously an impossibility that the truth seemed an audacious lie and the three unfortunate men were murdered.

We were obliged to content ourselves with a view of the river from this height, though I had expected to descend to the river's edge and felt correspondingly disappointed. We had started too late for so long a trip and now it was time to turn back. Looking back at the solid and apparently perpendicular rock, nearly a mile high, it seemed impossible that anyone could ascend to the top. It is only when one looks out from the bottom of this vast chasm at the huge walls on every side that he begins to realize its awfulness. We are mere specks in the bottom of a gigantic mold wherein some great mountain range might have been cast. There are great mountains all about us and yet we are not on a mountain but in a vast hole. The surface of the earth is above us. A great gash has been cut into it, two hundred miles long, twelve to fifteen miles wide, and a mile deep, and we are in the depths of that frightful abyss with — to all appearance — no possible means of escape. Perpendicular cliffs of enormous height, which not even a mountain sheep could climb, hem us in on every side. The shadows are growing deep and it seems that the day must be nearly done. Yet we remount our mules and slowly retrace our steps over the steep ascent. It seems as though the strain would break the backs of the animals. As we approached the summit of the path someone remarked, "I should think these mules would be so tired they would be ready to drop."

"Wait and see," said the guide. A few minutes later we reached the top and dismounted, feeling pretty stiff from the exertion. The mules were unsaddled and turned loose. Away they scampered like a lot of schoolboys at recess, kicking their heels high in the air and racing madly across the field. "I guess they're not as tired as we are," said the Major, as he painfully tried to straighten up. Just then the little girl of twelve came up to me. "There is one thing," she said, "that has been puzzling me all day. How in the world did you find out so quickly that your mule's name was Sam?" "Name ain't Sam," interrupted the guide, bluntly. "Name's Teddy — Teddy Roosevelt."

Some years ago I had occasion to attend a steropticon lecture on the Grand Cañon. The speaker was enthusiastic and his pictures excellent. But he fired off all his ammunition of adjectives with the first slide. For an hour and a half we sat listening to an endless repetition of "grand," "magnificent," "sublime," "awe-inspiring," etc. As we walked home a young lad in our party, who was evidently studying rhetoric in school, was heard to inquire, "Mother, would n't you call that an example of tautology?" I fear I should merit the same criticism if I were to undertake a description of the cañon. Yet we may profitably stand, for a few moments, on Hopi Point, a promontory that projects far out from the rim, and try to measure it with our eyes.

That great wall on the opposite side is just thirteen miles away. The strip of white at its upper edge, which in my photograph measures less than a quarter of an inch, is a stratum of limestone five hundred feet thick. Here and there we catch glimpses of the river. It is five miles away, and forty-six hundred feet — nearly a perpendicular mile — below the level upon which we are standing. We look to the east and then to the west, but we see only a small part of the chasm. It melts away in the distance like a ship at sea. From end to end it is two hundred and seventeen miles. It is not one cañon, but thousands. Every river that runs into the Colorado has cut out its own cañon, and each of these has its countless tributaries. It has been estimated that if all the cañons were placed end to end in a straight line they would stretch twenty thousand miles.

If this mighty gash in the earth's surface were only a great valley with gently sloping sides and a level floor, it would still be impressive and inspiring, though not so picturesque. But its floor is filled with a multitude of temples and castles and amphitheaters of stupendous size, all sculptured into strange shapes by the erosion of the waters. Any one of these, if it could be transported to the level plains of the Middle West or set up on the Atlantic Coast, would be an object of wonder which hundreds of thousands would visit. Away off in the distance is the Temple of Shiva, towering seventy-six hundred and fifty feet above the sea and fifty-two hundred and fourteen feet (nearly a mile) above the river. Take it to the White Mountains and set it down in the Crawford Notch. From its summit you would look down upon the old Tip-Top House of Mount Washington, eight hundred feet below. Much nearer, and a little to the right, is the "Pyramid of Cheops," a much smaller butte but rising fifty-three hundred and fifty feet above the sea-level. If the "Great Pyramid of Cheops" in Egypt were to be placed by its side it would scarcely be visible from where we stand, for it would be lost in the mass of rocky formations. Mr. G. Wharton James, who has spent many years of his life in the study of the cañon, says that he gazed upon it from a certain point every year for twenty years and often daily for weeks at a time. He continues, "Such is the marvelousness of distance that never until two days ago did I discover that a giant detached mountain fully eight thousand feet high and with a base ten miles square . . . stood in the direct line of my sight, and as it were, immediately before me." He discovered it only because of a peculiarity of the light. It had always appeared as a part of the great north wall, though separated from it by a cañon fully eight miles wide.

How are we to realize these enormous depths? Those isolated peaks and mountains, of which there are hundreds, are really only details in the vast stretch of the cañon. Not one of them reaches above the level of the plain on the north side. Tourists who have traveled much are familiar with the great cathedrals of Europe. Let us drop a few of them into the cañon. First, St. Peter's, the greatest cathedral in the world. We lower it to the level of the river, and it disappears behind the granite cliff. Let the stately Duomo of Milan follow. Its beautiful minarets and multitude of statues are lost in the distance, and though we place it on the top of St. Peter's, it, too, is out of sight behind the cliffs. We must have something larger, so we place on top of Milan the great cathedral of Cologne, five hundred and one feet high, and the tips of its two great spires barely appear above the point from which we watched the swiftly rolling river. Now let us poise on the top of Cologne's spires, two great Gothic cathedrals of France, Notre Dame and Amiens, one above the other, then add St. Paul's of London, the three great towers of Lincoln, the triple spires of Lichfield, Canterbury with its great central tower, and the single spire, four hundred and four feet high, of Salisbury. We are still far from the top. These units of measurement are too small. Let us add the tallest office building in the world, seven hundred and fifty feet high, and then the Eiffel Tower, of nine hundred and eighty-six feet. We shall still need the Washington Monument, and if my calculations are correct, an extension ladder seventy-five feet long on top of that, to enable us to reach the top of the northern wall. One might amuse himself indefinitely with such comparisons. Perhaps they are futile, but it is only by some such method that one can form the faintest conception of the colossal dimensions of this, the greatest chasm in the world.

Still more bewildering is the attempt to measure the cañon in periods of time. There were two great periods in its history — first, the period of upheaval, and second, that of erosion. When the geologic movement was in process which created the continent, with the Rocky Mountains for its backbone, this entire region became a plateau, vastly higher than at present, with its greatest elevation far to the north. Then the rivers began to carry the rains and snows to the sea, carving channels for themselves through the rocky surface. The steep decline caused the waters to flow with swiftness. The little streamlets united to form larger ones, and these in turn joined their waters in still greater streams. The larger the stream and the swifter the flow, the faster the channel would be carved. The softer rocks gave slight resistance, but when the granite or harder formations were encountered, the streams would eddy and whirl about in search of new channels, the hard rocks forming a temporary dam. In this way the hundreds of buttes were formed. The Green River and the Grand unite to form the Colorado, the entire course of this great waterway stretching for two thousand miles. The two streams carry down a mighty flood — in former ages it was far mightier than now — which in its swift descent has ground the rocks into sand and silt and with resistless force carried them down to the sea. Those great buttes and strangely sculptured temples, each a formidable mountain, were not thrown up by volcanic forces, but have been carved out of the solid earth by the erosion of the waters. That river five miles away, of which we see only glimpses here and there, was the tool with which the Great Sculptor carved all this wondrous chasm. Major Powell has calculated that the amount of rock thus ground to pieces and carried away would be equivalent to a mass two hundred thousand square miles in area and a full mile in thickness. Think of excavating a mile deep the entire territory of New England, New York, New Jersey, Pennsylvania, Delaware, Maryland, and West Virginia, and dumping it all into the Atlantic. Then think that this is the task the Colorado River and other geologic forces have accomplished, and pause to wonder how long it took to complete the process! If the Egyptian kings who built the pyramids had come here for material they would have seen the chasm substantially as we see it!

The geologic story of the cañon's origin is too far beyond our comprehension. Let us turn to the Indian account. A great chief lost his wife and refused to be comforted. An Indian God, Ta-vwoats, came to him and offered to conduct him to a happier land where he might see her, if he would promise to cease mourning. Then Ta-vwoats made a trail through the mountains to the happy land and there the chief saw his wife. This trail was the cañon of the Colorado. The deity made the chief promise that he would reveal the path to no man, lest all might wish to go at once to heaven, and in order to block the way still more effectually he rolled a mad surging river through the gorges so swift and strong that it would destroy anyone who dared attempt to enter heaven by that route.

I have often been asked which is the greater wonder, the Grand Cañon of the Colorado River or the Yellowstone National Park. The question is unanswerable. One might as well attempt to say whether the sea is more beautiful than the sky. If mere size is meant, the Grand Cañon is vastly greater. If all the geysers of the Yellowstone were placed down in the bottom of the Grand Cañon at the level of the river, and all were to play at once, the effect would be unnoticed from Hopi Point. The cañon of the Yellowstone River, impressive as it is, would be lost in one of the side cañons of the Colorado.

The Grand Cañon and the Yellowstone are creations of a totally different kind.

The Yellowstone is a garden of wonders. The Grand Cañon is a sublime spectacle.

The Yellowstone is a variety of interesting units. The Grand Cañon is a unit of infinite variety.

The Yellowstone contains a collection of individual marvels, each wondrous in structure and many of them exquisite in beauty. The Grand Cañon is one vast masterpiece of unimagined architecture, limitless grandeur, and ever-changing but splendidly harmonious brilliancy of color.

The Yellowstone fills the mind with wonder and amazement at all the varied resources of Nature. The Grand Cañon fills the soul with awe and reverence as one stands in silence upon the brink and humbly reflects upon the infinite power of God.

GLIMPSES OF THE YELLOWSTONE

By Charles S. Olcott

THE Yellowstone National Park is Nature's jewel casket, in which she has kept her choicest gems for countless generations. Securely sheltered by ranges of rugged mountains they have long been safe from human depredations. The red man doubtless knew of them, but superstition came to the aid of Nature and held him awestruck at a safe distance. The first white man who came within sight of these wonders a century ago could find no one to believe his tales, and for a generation or two the regions of hot springs and boiling geysers which he described was sneeringly termed "Colter's Hell." Only within the last half-century have the generality of mankind been permitted to view these precious jewels, and even then jealous Nature, it would seem, did not consent to reveal her treasures until fully assured that they would have the protection of no less powerful a guardianship than that of the National Government.

On the 18th of September, 1870, a party of explorers, headed by General Henry D. Washburn, then Surveyor-General of Montana, emerged from the forest into an open plain and suddenly found themselves not one hundred yards away from a huge column of boiling water, from which great rolling clouds of snow-white vapor rose high into the air against the blue sky. It was "Old Faithful" in action. Then and there they resolved that this whole region of wonders should be made into a public park for the benefit of all the people, and renouncing any thought of securing the lands for personal gain, these broad-minded men used their influence to have the National Congress assume the permanent guardianship of the place. And now that protection is fully assured these jewels of Nature may be seen by you and me.

Those who have traveled much will tell you that Nature is prodigal of her riches, and, indeed, this would seem to be true to one who has spent a summer among the snow-clad peaks of the Alps, or dreamed away the days amid the blue lakes of northern Italy, or wandered about in the green forests of the Adirondacks, where every towering spruce, every fragrant balsam, every dainty wild flower and every mossy log is a thing of beauty. But these are Nature's full-dress garments, just as the broad-spreading wheat-fields of the Dakotas are her work-a-day clothes. Her "jewels" are safely locked up in places more difficult of access, where they may be seen by only a favored few; and one of these safe-deposit boxes, so to speak, is the Yellowstone National Park.

The first collection of these natural gems is at Mammoth Hot Springs, and here my camera, as if by instinct, led me quickly to the daintiest in form and most delicate in colorings of them all, a beautiful formation known as Hymen Terrace. A series of steps, covering a circular area of perhaps one hundred feet in diameter, has been formed by the overflow of a hot spring. The terraces consist of a series of semicircular and irregular curves or scallops, like a combination of hundreds of richly carved pulpits, wrought in a soft, white substance resembling coral. Little pools of glistening water reflect the sunlight from the tops of the steps, while a gently flowing stream spreads imperceptibly over about one half the surface, sprinkling it with millions of diamonds as the altar of Hymen ought to be. The pools are greens and blues of many shades, varying with the depth of the water. The sides of the steps are pure white in the places where the water has ceased to flow, but beneath the thin stream they range in color from a rich cream to a deep brown, with all the intermediate shades harmoniously blended. From the highest pools, and especially from the largest one at the very summit of the mound, rise filmy veils of steam, softening the exquisite tints into a rich harmony of color against the azure of the sky.

The Terrace of Hymen is the most exquisite of the formations, but there are others much larger and more magnificent. Minerva Terrace gave me a foreground for a charming picture. Beyond its richly colored steps and sparkling pools were the splendid summits of the Gallatin Range, towering more than ten thousand feet above the level of the sea and seeming, in the clear mountain air, to be much nearer than they really are. Hovering above their peaks were piles upon piles of foamy clouds, through which could be seen a background of the bluest of skies, while down below were the gray stone buildings with their bright red roofs that form the headquarters of the army guarding the park.

Jupiter Terrace, the most imposing of all these formations, extends a quarter of a mile along the edge of a brilliantly colored mound, rising about three hundred feet above the plain upon which Fort Yellowstone is built. Pulpit Terrace, on its eastern slope, reproduces upon a larger scale the rich carvings and exquisite tints of Hymen, though without the symmetry of structure. The springs at its summit are among the most strikingly beautiful of these unique formations which I like to call the "jewels" of Nature. Two large pools of steaming water lie side by side, apparently identical in structure, and separated only by a narrow ridge of lime. The one on the left is a clear turquoise blue, while its neighbor is distinctly Nile green. Surrounding these springs are several smaller pools, one a rich orange color, another light brown, and a third brown of a much darker hue. The edges of all are tinted in yellow, brown, and gold of varied shades. The pools are apparently all a part of the same spring or group of springs, and subject to the same conditions of light; yet I noticed at least five distinct colors in as many pools. The water itself is colorless and the different hues must be imparted by the colorings of the lime deposits, influenced by the varying depth and temperature of the water.

What is known as "the formation" of the Mammoth Hot Springs covers perhaps fifty or sixty acres on the slope of Terrace Mountain. It is a heavy

JUPITER TERRACE, MAMMOTH HOT SPRINGS, YELLOWSTONE NATIONAL PARK

deposit of lime or travertine, essentially the same as the stalagmites and stalactites which one sees in certain caverns. When dry it is white and soft like chalk. The colorings of the terraces are of vegetable origin, caused by a thin, velvety growth, botanically classed as algæ, which flourishes only in warm water. The heat of rocks far beneath the surface warms the water of the springs, which, passing through a bed of limestone, brings to the surface a deposit of pure calcium carbonate. Wherever the flow of water remains warm the algæ appear and tint the growing formation with as many shades of brown as there are varying temperatures of the water. When the water is diverted, as is likely to happen from one season to the next, the algæ die and the surfaces become a chalky white.

Leaving the Hot Springs, the road passes through the Golden Gate, where, on one side, a perpendicular wall of rock rises to a height of two hundred feet or more, and on the other are the wooded slopes and rocky summit of Bunsen Peak — a beautiful cañon, where the view suggests the greater glories of Swiss mountain scenery, but for that very reason is not to be mentioned here among the rare gems of the park. Nor shall I include the "Hoodoos," which, though distinctly unusual, are far from beautiful. An area of many acres is covered with huge fragments of massive rocks, piled in disorderly confusion, as though some Cyclops, in a fit of ugly temper, had torn away the whole side of a mountain and scattered the pieces. Through these rocks project the whitened trunks of thousands of dead trees, — a sort of ghostly nightmare through which we were glad to pass as quickly as possible. We stopped for lunch at the Norris Geyser Basin, and here saw some miniature geysers, as a kind of preparation for the greater ones beyond. The "Constant," true to its name, throws up a pretty little white fountain so often that it seems to prepare for a new eruption almost before the previous one has subsided. The "Minute Man" is always on duty and pops up his little spray of hot water, fifteen feet high, every minute or two. The "Monarch," near by, is much larger, but not at all pretty. It throws up a stream of black, muddy water seventy-five to one hundred feet high about every forty minutes.

Some of these geysers are steady old fellows who have found their appointed task in life and have settled down to perform it with commendable regularity. The Norris Basin, however, seems to be the favorite playground of the youngsters, — a frisky lot of geysers of no fixed habits and a playful disposition to burst out in unexpected places. Such is the "New Crater," which asserted itself with a great commotion in 1891, bursting forth with the violence of an earthquake. Another erratic young fellow is the "Fountain Geyser," — in the Lower Basin. In July, 1899, he was seized with a fit of the "sulks" and for three months refused to play at all. In October he decided to resume operations and behaved quite well for ten years, when he suddenly took a notion to abandon his crater for the apartments of his neighbor next door. Apparently the furnishings of his new abode did not suit him, for he began at once to throw them out with great violence, hurling huge masses of rock with volcanic force to a height of two hundred feet. Amid terrific rumblings and the hissing of escaping steam, this angry outburst continued for several days, and did not wholly cease for nearly two months. Since then the "Fountain" has settled down to the ordinary daily occupation of a self-respecting geyser. When I saw him he was as calm and serene as a summer's day, and to all appearances had never been guilty of mischief, nor even exhibited a ruffled temper in all his life. Indeed, had I not known his history (inconceivable in one of the gentler sex), I should have personified this geyser in the feminine gender, because of his exquisite beauty. A great jewel seemed to be set into the surface of the earth. Its smooth upper face, about thirty feet in diameter, was level with the ground upon which we stood. Its color, at first glance, seemed to be a rich turquoise blue, but as we looked into the clear, transparent depths there seemed to be a hundred other shades of blue, all blending harmoniously. In the farthest corner, beneath a shelf or mound of geyserite, appeared the opening of a fathomless cave. All around its edges, and continuing in wavy lines of delicate tracery around the bottom of the bowl, were marvelous patterns of exquisite lacework, every angle seeming to catch and throw back its own particular ray of bluish light. There was not a ripple to disturb the surface, not a bubble to foretell the violent eruption which a few hours would bring forth, and only a thin film of vapor to suggest faintly the extraordinary character of this beautiful pool.

Only a few hundred feet away is another curious phenomenon in this region of surprises. It is a caldron of boiling mud, measuring forty or fifty feet in diameter, known as the "Mammoth Paint Pots," where a mass of clay is kept in a state of continuous commotion. Millions of bubbles rise to the surface and explode, sputtering like a thick mess of porridge kept at the boiling point. The color is a creamy white where the ebullition is greatest, but thick masses thrown up around the edges and allowed to cool have assumed a delicate shade of pink. A smaller but more beautiful formation of the same kind is seen near the Thumb Station on the Yellowstone Lake.

As we proceeded, Nature's jewels seemed to increase in number and magnificence. Turquoise Spring, a sheet of water one hundred feet wide, has all the beauty of the "Fountain Geyser" in the latter's quiet state, with an added reputation for tranquillity, for it is not a geyser at all. Near by is Prismatic Lake, about four hundred feet long and two hundred and fifty feet wide. Its center is a very deep blue, changing to green of varying shades, and finally, in the shallowest parts, to yellow, orange, and brown. It is a great spring from the center of which the water flows in delicate, wavy ringlets. The mineral deposits have formed countless scallops, like miniature terraces, a few inches high, sculpturing a wonderful pattern in hues of reds, purples, and browns, delicately imposed upon a background of gray. A thin veil of rising steam was carried away by the wind just enough to reveal the wonderful colorings to our eyes, while the sun added to the bewildering beauty of the spectacle by changing the vapor into a million prisms reflecting all the colors of the rainbow.

In this connection I must not fail to mention the Morning-Glory Spring, where the action of a geyser has carved out a deep bowl, twenty feet in diameter. It would seem as though Nature had sunk a gigantic morning-glory into the earth, leaving its rim flush with the surface and yet retaining, clearly visible beneath the smooth surface of the transparent water, all the delicate shades of the original flower.

The Sapphire Spring, not far away, is another of the little gems of the region. It is a small, pulsating spring, and the jewel itself is not less remarkable than its extraordinary setting, resembling coral. The constant flow of the waters from a center to all directions has caused the formation of a series of irregular concentric circles, broken into little knobs or mounds, from which the vicinity takes its name of the "Biscuit Basin."

As we approached the Upper Geyser Region, the number and variety of these highly colored pools, hot springs, geysers, and strange formations increased steadily, until at last we stood in the presence of "Old Faithful," the crown jewel of the collection, the Koh-i-noor of Nature's casket.

A strong breeze from the north was blowing as I stood before the geyser for the first time, and for that reason, I decided to place my camera directly to the west. A small cloud of steam was rising, which seemed gradually to increase in volume. Then, as I watched, a small spray of water would shoot up occasionally above the rim of the crater. Then a puff of steam and another spray, breaking into globules as the wind carried it away. Then silence. Suddenly a large, full stream shot up a distance of twenty or thirty feet and fell back again, and the crater remained quiet for at least five minutes. Is that all? I thought. Does its boasted regularity only mean that while it plays once in sixty-five minutes, yet the height of some of the eruptions may be only trifling? I began to feel doubtful, not to say disappointed. The column of steam seemed smaller, and I wondered if I should have to wait another hour for a real eruption, when suddenly the lazily drifting cloud became a giant, like the genie in the "Arabian Nights." Up into the air shot a huge column of water, followed instantly by another still higher, then another, until in a moment or two there towered above the earth a gigantic column of boiling water one hundred and fifty feet high. Straight as a flagstaff it seemed on the left, while to the right rolled the waving folds of a huge white banner, obscuring the blue of the sky in one great mass of snowy vapor. For several minutes the puffs of steam rolled up, and the fountain continued to play. Then, little by little, its form grew less, its force weakened, and at last there was only the little lazy pillar of vapor outlined against the distant hills.

Again and again during the day I watched it with an ever-increasing sense of fascination, which reached its climax in the evening, when the eruption was lighted by the powerful searchlight on the hotel. As the great clouds of steam rolled up, the strong light seemed to impart a vast variety of colors, ranging from rich cream to yellow, orange, brown, and purple, blended harmoniously but ever changing like the rich silk robes of some Oriental potentate, — a spectacle of bewildering beauty, defying the power of pen to describe or brush to paint.

There are other geysers greater than "Old Faithful." "The Giant" plays to a height of two hundred and fifty feet, and the "Grand" and "Beehive" nearly as high; the "Grotto" has a more fantastic crater; the "Castle" has the largest cone, and with its beautifully colored "Castle Well" is more unique; and the "Riverside," which plays a stream diagonally across the Firehole River, makes a more striking scenic display. But all of these play at irregular intervals and with far less frequency, varying from a few hours to ten or twelve days between eruptions. On the other hand, the regularity with which "Old Faithful" sends his straight, magnificent column to the skies is fascinating beyond description. Every sixty-five or seventy minutes, never varying more than five minutes, day and night, in all seasons and every kind of weather, "Old Faithful" has steadily performed his task since first discovered in 1870 until the present time, and no man can tell for how many centuries before.

> "O! Fountain of the Wilderness! Eternal Mystery!
> Whence came thy wondrous power?
> For ages, — long before the eye of Man
> Found access to thy charm, thou'st played
> Thy stream of marvelous beauty.
> In midnight dark no less than glorious day,

> In wintry storms as well as summer's calm,
> Oblivious to the praise of men,
> Each hour to Heaven thou hast raised
> Thine offering pure, of dazzling white.
> Thine Maker's eye alone has seen
> The tribute of thy faithfulness.
> And thou hast been content to play thy part
> In Nature's solitude."

Not alone as the guardian of Nature's jewels is the Yellowstone National Park remarkable. Even if the wonderful geysers, hot springs, and many-colored pools were taken away, — locked up in a strong box and hidden from sight as jewels often are, — the more familiar phases of natural scenery, such as mountains, rivers, lakes, and waterfalls, would make it one of the wonder places of America. On the eastern boundary is the great Absaroka Range, with peaks rising over 10,000 feet. In the northwest corner is the Gallatin Range, dominated by the Electric Peak, 11,155 feet high, covered with snow, and so charged with electricity as to make the surveyor's transit almost useless. The Yellowstone and Gardiner rivers, which join at the northern boundary, are separated within the park by a range of mountains of which the highest is Mount Washburne (10,350 feet), named for the leader of the expedition of 1870. Farther south, and midway between the Upper Geyser Basin and the Yellowstone Lake, is the Continental Divide. The road passes between two small lakes, one of which discharges its waters into the Atlantic Ocean by way of the Yellowstone, the Missouri, and the Gulf of Mexico, while the other flows into the Pacific through Snake River and the Columbia. From a point a few miles to the east Lake Shoshone may be seen far below, and seeming to tower directly above it, but really fifty miles away, just beyond the southern boundary of the park, are the three sentinels of the Teton Range, the highest 13,741 feet above the sea. The entire park is in the heart of the Rocky Mountains, its lowest level being over 6000 feet elevation.

The park is full of lakes and streams varying in size from the hundreds of little pools and brooks, hidden away among the rocks, to the great Yellowstone Lake, twenty miles in width, and the picturesque river of the same name. Here and there are beautiful cascades which one would go miles to see anywhere else, but the surfeited travelers give them only a careless glance as the stages pass without stopping. The Kepler Cascades tumble over the rocks in a series of falls of more than a hundred feet, making a charming veil of white lace against a dark background of rocks and pines. The Gibbon Falls, eighty feet high, are nearly as attractive, while the little Rustic Falls, of sixty feet, in Golden Gate Cañon, are really quite delightful. These, and many others, are passed in comparative indifference, for the traveler has already seen many wonderful sights and knows that greater ones are yet in store. His anticipations are realized with good measure running over, when at last he catches his first glimpse of the great Cañon of the Yellowstone.

With us this glimpse came at the Upper Falls, where the Yellowstone River suddenly drops one hundred and twelve feet, suggesting the American Fall at

Niagara, though the volume of water is not so great. It is more beautiful, however, because of the wildness of the scenery. Lower down, the river takes another drop, falling to the very bottom of the cañon. Here the cataract is more than twice the height of Niagara, and though lacking the width of the stream that makes the latter so impressive, is in every respect far more beautiful.

One must stand near the edge of the rocks at Inspiration Point to grasp the full majesty of the scene. We are now three miles below the Great Falls. The Upper Fall, which at close range is a great, beautiful white sheet of water, rolling with imperial force over a rocky precipice, seems only a trifling detail in the vast picture — a mere touch of dazzling white where all else is in color. At the bottom is the blue of the river, broken here and there into foamy white waves. Pines and mosses contribute touches of green. The rocky cliffs are yellow and gold, deepening into orange. In the distance a great rock of crimson stands like a fortress, with arched doorway, through which is seen a vista of green fields. But this is an optical illusion, as a strong glass will reveal. The doorway is only a pointed fir, which the distance has softened into the shadow of a pointed arch. Medieval castles rear their buttressed fronts on inaccessible slopes. Cathedral spires, as majestic as those of Cologne and numerous as the minarets of Milan, stand out in bold relief. Away down below is an eagle's nest, into which we can look and see the birds, yet it is perched upon a pinnacle so high that if one were to stand at the level of the river and look up, it would tower above him higher than the tallest building in the world.

Not a sign of the handiwork of man appears in any direction. The gorgeous spectacle, revealing in all the hues of the rainbow, is just as Nature made it — let the geologist say, if he can, how many thousands of years ago. And above all this splendid panorama, unequaled save by the glory of the sunset sky, is that same rich blue which Nature employs to add the final touch of loveliness to all her greatest works, and yet reserves enough to beautify the more familiar scenes at home.

HOW JOHN MUIR FRIGHTENED THE INDIANS

By John Muir

ONE night when a heavy rainstorm was blowing, I unwittingly caused a lot of wondering excitement among the whites as well as the superstitious Indians. Being anxious to see how the Alaska trees behave in storms and hear the songs they sing, I stole quietly away through the gray drenching blast to the hill back of the town, without being observed. Night was falling when I set out, and it was pitch dark when I reached the top. The glad, rejoicing storm in glorious voice was singing through the woods, noble compensation for mere body discomfort. But I wanted a fire, a big one, to see as well as hear how the storm and trees were behaving. After long, patient groping I found a little dry punk in a hollow trunk and carefully stored it beside my matchbox and an inch or two of candle in an inside pocket that the rain had not yet reached; then, wiping some dead twigs and whittling them into thin shavings, stored them with the punk. I then made a little conical bark hut about a foot high, and, carefully leaning over it and sheltering it as much as possible from the driving rain, I wiped and stored a lot of dead twigs, lighted the candle, and set it in the hut, carefully added pinches of punk and shavings, and at length got a little blaze, by the light of which I gradually added larger shavings, then twigs all set on end astride the inner flame, making the little hut higher and wider. Soon I had light enough to enable me to select the best dead branches and large sections of bark, which were set on end, gradually increasing the height and corresponding light of the hut fire. A considerable area was thus well lighted, from which I gathered abundance of wood, and kept adding to the fire until it had a strong, hot heart and sent up a pillar of flame thirty or forty feet high, illuminating a wide circle in spite of the rain, and casting a red glare into the flying clouds. Of all the thousands of camp fires I have elsewhere built none was just like this one, rejoicing in triumphant strength and beauty in the heart of the rain-laden gale. It was wonderful, — the illumined rain and clouds mingled together and the trees glowing against the jet background, the colors of the mossy, lichened trunks with sparkling streams pouring down the furrows of the bark, and the gray-bearded old patriarchs bowing low and chanting in passionate worship!

My fire was in all its glory about midnight, and, having made a bark shed to shelter me from the rain and partially dry my clothing, I had nothing to do but look and listen and join the trees in their hymns and prayers.

Neither the great white heart of the fire nor the quivering enthusiastic flames shooting aloft like auroral lances could be seen from the village on account of the trees in front of it and its being back a little way over the brow of the hill; but the light in the clouds made a great show, a portentous sign in the stormy heavens unlike anything ever before seen or heard of in Wrangell. Some wakeful Indians, happening to see it about midnight, in great alarm aroused the collector of customs and begged him to go to the missionaries and get them to pray away the frightful omen, and inquired anxiously whether white men had ever seen anything like that sky fire, which instead of being quenched by the rain was burning brighter and brighter. The collector said he had heard of such strange fires, and this one he thought might perhaps be what the white man called a "volcano, or an *ignis fatuus*." When Mr. Young was called from his bed to pray, he, too, confoundedly astonished and at a loss for any sort of explanation, confessed that he had never seen anything like it in the sky or anywhere else in such cold wet weather, but that it was probably some sort of spontaneous combustion "that the white man called St. Elmo's fire, or Will-o'-the-wisp." These explanations, though not convincingly clear, perhaps served to veil their own astonishment and in some measure to diminish the superstitious fears of the natives; but from what I heard, the few whites who happened to see the strange light wondered about as wildly as the Indians.

I have enjoyed thousands of camp fires in all sorts of weather and places, warm-hearted, short-flamed, friendly little beauties glowing in the dark on open spots in high Sierra gardens, daisies and lilies circled about them, gazing like enchanted children; and large fires in silver fir forests, with spires of flame towering like the trees about them, and sending up multitudes of starry sparks to enrich the sky; and still greater fires on the mountains in winter, changing camp climate to summer, and making the frosty snow look like beds of white flowers, and oftentimes mingling their swarms of swift-flying sparks with falling snow crystals when the clouds were in bloom. But this Wrangell camp fire, my first in Alaska, I shall always remember for its triumphant storm-defying grandeur, and the wondrous beauty of the psalm-singing, lichen-painted trees which it brought to light.

THE MISSIONARY AND THE MOUNTAIN

By John Muir

AT a distance of about seven or eight miles to the northeastward of the landing, there is an outstanding group of mountains crowning a spur from the main chain of the Coast Range, whose highest point rises about eight thousand feet above the sea, the height to be overcome in climbing this peak is about seven thousand feet. Though the time was short I determined to climb it, because of the advantageous position it occupied for general views of the peaks and glaciers of the east side of the great range.

Although it was now twenty minutes past three and the days were getting short, I thought that by rapid climbing I could reach the summit before sunset, in time to get a general view and a few pencil sketches, and make my way back to the steamer in the night. Mr. Young, one of the missionaries, asked permission to accompany me, saying that he was a good walker and climber and would not delay me or cause any trouble. I strongly advised him not to go, explaining that it involved a walk, coming and going, of fourteen or sixteen miles, and a climb through brush and bowlders of seven thousand feet, a fair day's work for a seasoned mountaineer to be done in less than half a day and part of a night. But he insisted that he was a strong walker, could do a mountaineer's day's work in half a day, and would not hinder me in any way.

"Well, I have warned you," I said, "and will not assume responsibility for any trouble that may arise."

He proved to be a stout walker, and we made rapid progress across a brushy timbered flat and up the mountain slopes, open in some places, and in others thatched with dwarf firs, resting a minute here and there to refresh ourselves with huckleberries, which grew in abundance in open spots. About half an hour before sunset, when we were near a cluster of crumbling pinnacles that formed the summit, I had ceased to feel anxiety about the mountaineering strength and skill of my companion, and pushed rapidly on. In passing around the shoulder of the highest pinnacle, where the rock was rapidly disintegrating and the danger of slipping was great, I shouted in a warning voice, "Be very careful here, this is dangerous."

Mr. Young was perhaps a dozen or two yards behind me, but out of sight. I afterward reproached myself for not stopping and lending him a steadying hand, and showing him the slight footsteps I had made by kicking out little blocks of the crumbling surface, instead of simply warning him to be careful. Only a few seconds after giving this warning, I was startled by a scream for help, and hurrying back, found the missionary face downward, his arms outstretched, clutching little crumbling knobs on the brink of the gully that plunges down a thousand feet or more to a small residual glacier. I managed to get below him, touched one of his feet, and tried to encourage him by saying, "I am below you. You are in no danger. You can't slip past me and I will soon get you out of this."

He then told me that both of his arms were dislocated. It was almost impossible to find available footholds on the treacherous rock, and I was at my wit's end to know how to get him rolled or dragged to a place where I could get about him, find out how much he was hurt, and a way back down the mountain. After narrowly scanning the cliff and making footholds, I managed to roll and lift him a few yards to a place where the slope was less steep, and there I attempted to set his arms. I found, however, that this was impossible in such a place. I therefore tied his arms to his sides with my suspenders and necktie, to prevent as much as possible inflammation from movement. I then left him, telling him to lie still, that I would be back in a few minutes, and that he was now safe from slipping. I hastily examined the ground and saw no way of getting him down except by the steep glacier gully. After scrambling to an outstanding point that commands a view of it from top to bottom, to make sure that it was not interrupted by sheer precipices, I concluded that with great care and the digging of slight footholds he could be slid down to the glacier, where I could lay him on his back and perhaps be able to set his arms. Accordingly, I cheered him up, telling him I had found a way, but that it would require lots of time and patience. Digging a footstep in the sand or crumbling rock five or six feet beneath him, I reached up, took hold of him by one of his feet, and gently slid him down on his back, placed his heels in the step, then descended another five or six feet, dug heel notches, and slid him down to them. Thus the whole distance was made by a succession of narrow steps at very short intervals, and the glacier was reached perhaps about midnight. Here I took off one of my boots, tied a handkerchief around his wrist for a good hold, placed my heel in his armpit, and succeeded in getting one of his arms into place, but my utmost strength was insufficient to reduce the dislocation of the other. I therefore bound it closely to his side, and asked him if in his exhausted and trembling condition he was still able to walk.

"Yes," he bravely replied.

So, with a steadying arm around him and many stops for rest, I marched him slowly down in the starlight on the comparatively smooth, unfissured surface of the little glacier to the terminal moraine, a distance of perhaps a mile, crossed the moraine, bathed his head at one of the outlet streams, and after many rests reached a dry place and made a brush fire. I then went ahead looking for an open way through the bushes to where larger wood could be had, made a good lasting fire of resiny silver-fir roots, and a leafy bed beside it. I now told him I would run down the mountain, hasten back with help from the boat, and carry him down in comfort. But he would not hear of my leaving him.

"No, no," he said, "I can walk down. Don't leave me."

I reminded him of the roughness of the way, his

nerve-shaken condition, and assured him I would not be gone long. But he insisted on trying, saying on no account whatever must I leave him. I therefore concluded to try to get him to the ship by short walks from one fire and resting place to another. While he was resting I went ahead, looking for the best way through the brush and rocks, then returning, got him on his feet and made him lean on my shoulder while I steadied him to prevent his falling. This slow, staggering struggle from fire to fire lasted until long after sunrise. When at last we reached the ship and stood at the foot of the narrow single plank without side rails that reached from the bank to the deck at a considerable angle, I briefly explained to Mr. Young's companions, who stood looking down at us, that he had been hurt in an accident, and required one of them to assist me in getting him aboard. But strange to say, instead of coming down to help, they made haste to reproach him for having gone on a "wild-goose chase" with Muir.

"These foolish adventures are well enough for Mr. Muir," they said, "but you, Mr. Young, have a work to do; you have a family; you have a church, and you have no right to risk your life on treacherous peaks and precipices.'"

The captain, Nat Lane, son of Senator Joseph Lane, had been swearing in angry impatience for being compelled to make so late a start and thus encounter a dangerous wind in a narrow gorge, and was threatening to put the missionaries ashore to seek their lost companion, while he went on down the river about his business. But when he heard my call for help, he hastened forward, and elbowed the divines away from the end of the gangplank, shouting in angry irreverence, "Oh, blank! This is no time for preaching! Don't you see the man is hurt?"

He ran down to our help, and while I steadied my trembling companion from behind, the captain kindly led him up the plank into the saloon, and made him drink a large glass of brandy. Then, with a man holding down his shoulders, we succeeded in getting the bone into its socket, notwithstanding the inflammation and contraction of the muscles and ligaments. Mr. Young was then put to bed, and he slept all the way back to Wrangell.

In his mission lectures in the East, Mr. Young oftentimes told this story. I made no record of it in my notebook and never intended to write a word about it; but after a miserable, sensational caricature of the story had appeared in a respectable magazine, I thought it but fair to my brave companion that it should be told just as it happened.

DOWN IN A CREVASSE

By John Tyndall

LUBBOCK and I decided to ascend the Jungfrau. The proprietor of the hotel keeps guides for this excursion, but his charges are so high as to be almost prohibitory. I, however, needed no guide in addition to my faithful Bennen; but simply a porter of sufficient strength and skill to follow where he led. In the village of Laax, Bennen found such a porter — a young man named Bielander, who had the reputation of being both courageous and strong. He was the only son of his mother, and she was a widow.

This young man and a second porter we sent on with our provisions to the Grotto of the Faulberg, where we were to spend the night. Between the Aeggischhorn and this cave the glacier presents no difficulty which the most ordinary caution cannot overcome, and the thought of danger in connection with it never occurred to us. An hour and a half after the departure of our porters we slowly wended our way to the lake of Märjelin, which we skirted, and were soon upon the ice. The middle of the glacier was almost as smooth as a carriage-road, cut here and there by musical brooks produced by the superficial ablation. To Lubbock the scene opened out with the freshness of a new revelation, as, previously to this year, he had never been among the glaciers of the Alps. To me, though not new, the region had lost no trace of the interest with which I first viewed it. We moved briskly along the frozen incline, until, after a couple of hours' march, we saw a solitary human being standing on the lateral moraine of the glacier, near the point where we were to quit it for the cave of Faulberg.

At first this man excited no attention. He stood and watched us, but did not come toward us, until finally our curiosity was aroused by observing that he was one of our own two men. The glacier here is always cut by crevasses, which, while they present no real difficulty, require care. We approached our porter, but he never moved; and when we came up to him he looked stupid, and did not speak until he was spoken to. Bennen addressed him in the patois of the place, and he answered in the same patois. His answer must have been more than usually obscure, for Bennen misunderstood the most important part of it. "My God!" he exclaimed, turning to us, "Walters is killed!" Walters was the guide at the Aeggischhorn with whom, in the present instance, we had nothing to do. "No, not Walters," responded the man; "it is my comrade that is killed." Bennen looked at him with a wild, bewildered stare. "How killed?" he exclaimed. "Lost in a crevasse," was the reply. We were all so stunned that for some moments we did not quite seize the import of the terrible statement. Bennen at length tossed his arms in the air, exclaiming, "Jesu Maria! what am I to do?" With the swiftness that some ascribe to dreams, I surrounded the fact with imaginary adjuncts, one of which was that the man had been drawn dead from the crevasse, and was now a corpse in the cave of the Faulberg; for I took it for granted that, had he been still entombed, his comrade would have run or called for our aid. Several times in succession the porter affirmed that the missing man was certainly dead. "How does he know that he is dead?" Lubbock demanded. "A man is sometimes rendered insensible by a fall without being killed." This question was repeated in German, but met with the same dogmatic response. "Where is the man?" I asked. "There," replied the porter, stretching his arm toward the glacier. "In the crevasse?" A stolid "Ja!" was the answer. It was with difficulty that I quelled an imprecation. "Lead the way to the place, you blockhead," and he led the way.

We were soon beside a wide and jagged cleft which resembled a kind of cave more than an ordinary crevasse. This cleft had been spanned by a snow bridge, now broken, and to the edge of which footsteps could be traced. The glacier at the place was considerably torn, but simple patience was the only thing needed to unravel its complexity. This quality our porter lacked, and hoping to make shorter work of it, he attempted to cross the bridge. It gave way, and he went down, carrying an immense load of débris along with him. We looked into the hole, at one end of which the vision was cut short by darkness, while immediately under the broken bridge it was crammed with snow and shattered icicles. We saw nothing more.

A CREVASSE IN A GLACIER

We listened with strained attention, and from the depths of the glacier issued a low moan. Its repetition assured us that it was no delusion — the man was still alive. Bennen from the first had been extremely excited. When he heard the moaning he became almost frantic. He attempted to get into the crevasse, but was obliged to recoil. It was quite plain that a second life was in danger, for my guide seemed to have lost all self-control. I placed my hand heavily upon his shoulder, and admonished him that upon his coolness depended the life of his friend.

A first-rate rope accompanied the party, but unhappily it was with the man in the crevasse. Coats, waistcoats, and braces were instantly taken off and knotted together. I watched Bennen while this work was going on; his hands trembled with excitement, and his knots were evidently insecure. The last junction complete, he exclaimed, "Now let me down!" "Not until each of these knots has been tested; not an inch!" Two of them gave way, and Lubbock's waistcoat also proved too tender for the strain. The débris was about forty feet from the surface of the glacier, but two intermediate prominences afforded a kind of footing. Bennen was dropped down upon one of these; I followed, being let down by Lubbock and the other porter. Bennen then descended the remaining distance, and was followed by me. More could not find room.

The shape and size of the cavity were such as to produce a kind of resonance, which rendered it difficult to fix the precise spot from which the sound issued;

but the moaning continued, becoming to all appearance gradually feebler. Fearing to wound the man, the ice rubbish was cautiously rooted away; it rang curiously as it fell into the adjacent gloom. A layer two or three feet thick was thus removed; and finally, from the frozen mass, and so bloodless as to be almost as white as the surrounding snow, issued a single human hand. The fingers moved. Round it we rooted, cleared the arm, and reached the knapsack, which we cut away. We also regained our rope. The man's head was then laid bare, and my brandy flask was immediately at his lips. He tried to speak, but his words jumbled themselves to a dull moan. Bennen's feelings got the better of him at intervals; he wrought like a hero, but at times he needed guidance and stern admonition. The arms once free, we passed the rope underneath them, and tried to draw the man out. But the ice fragments round him had regelated so as to form a solid case. Thrice we essayed to draw him up, thrice we failed; he had literally to be hewn out of the ice, and not until his last foot was extricated were we able to lift him. By pulling him from above, and pushing him from below, the man was at length raised to the surface of the glacier.

For an hour we had been in the crevasse in shirt-sleeves — the porter had been in it for two hours — and the dripping ice had drenched us. Bennen, moreover, had worked with the energy of madness, and now the reaction came. He shook as if he would fall to pieces; but brandy and some dry covering revived him. The rescued man was helpless, unable to stand, unable to utter an articulate sentence. Bennen proposed to carry him down the glacier toward home. Had this been attempted, the man would certainly have died upon the ice. Bennen thought he could carry him for two hours; but the guide underrated his own exhaustion and overrated the vitality of the porter. "It cannot be thought of," I said; "to the cave of Faulberg, where we must tend him as well as we can." We got him to the side of the glacier, where Bennen took him on his back; in ten minutes he sank under his load. It was now my turn, so I took the man on my back and plodded on with him as far as I was able. Helping each other thus by turns, we reached the mountain grot.

The sun had set, and the crown of the Jungfrau was embedded in amber light. Thinking that the Märjelin See might be reached before darkness, I proposed starting in search of help. Bennen protested against my going alone, and I thought I noticed moisture in Lubbock's eyes. Such an occasion brings out a man's feeling if he have any. I gave them both my blessing and made for the glacier. But my anxiety to get quickly clear of the crevasses defeated its own object. Thrice I found myself in difficulty, and the light was visibly departing. The conviction deepened that persistence would be folly, and the most impressive moment of my existence was that on which I stopped at the brink of a profound fissure and looked upon the mountains and the sky. The serenity was perfect — not a cloud, not a breeze, not a sound, while the last hues of sunset spread over the solemn west.

I returned; warm wine was given to our patient, and all our dry clothes were wrapped around him. Hot-water bottles were placed at his feet, and his back was briskly rubbed. He continued to groan a long time; but finally both this and the trembling ceased. Bennen watched him solemnly, and at length muttered in anguish, "Sir, he is dead!" I leaned over the man and found him breathing gently; I felt his pulse — it was beating tranquilly. "Not dead, dear old Bennen; he will be able to crawl home with us in the morning." The prediction was justified by the event; and two days afterwards we saw him at Laax, minus a bit of his ear, with a bruise upon his cheek, and a few scars upon his hand, but without a broken bone or serious injury of any kind.

The self-denying conduct of the second porter made us forget his stupidity — it may have been stupefaction. As I lay there wet, through the long hours of that dismal night, I almost registered a vow never to tread upon a glacier again. But, like the forces in the physical world, human emotions vary with the distance from their origin, and a year afterwards I was again upon the ice.

SEEING AN ECLIPSE IN JAPAN

By Mabel Loomis Todd

FRIDAY, the seventh of August, dawned portentously, with a strong south wind and drifting clouds. It was very warm, and bright at intervals. By evening rain set in, and all night torrents of water fell on the roof with a noise like shot. Saturday brought more south wind, occasional rain, moving cloud. Once in a while spots of blue shone through — increasing the nerve tension. The Astronomer, cheerful, energetic, showed no sign that nature's vagaries and threats were disturbing him, but, constantly busy with final details, passed from one instrument to another, clear, methodical, definite. Working of apparatus was perfect; motions were made with automatic precision, all within the time limit, all without human intervention except to press a key at the start which sent electric currents through its mysterious, ramifying nerves.

Saturday toward evening the rain suddenly ceased; a fresh feeling in the wind disclosed a change to the hopeful west, bringing a superb sunset, — shreds of rose and salmon and lavender glowed against a yellow background.

During the two days' rain none of our usually multitudinous callers had appeared; but by the light of sunset a dozen or more came together, — guests of distinction in the town as well as the village officer and leading citizens.

Another elaborate speech was made, explaining that in the storm their hearts had failed them; they could not look at this fine apparatus, remembering our patient preparation, when a chance of cloud on Sunday might ruin everything; but that now in the light of a bright sunset they came joyfully, bringing congratulations upon the weather from the fishermen, who were said to know all signs of the sky; and with hopeful portents from a book of prophecy and a local oracle, interrogated at a neighboring shrine. This cheering oracle we believed the more readily as telegrams from Sapporo and from the Central Meteorological Observatory at Tokyo announced "Clear to-morrow!" In truth all promised happily.

Stars enough came out in the evening for final tests of the instruments, and everything was in readiness.

Directions for observing the eclipse had been written by the Astronomer, translated into Japanese, printed and distributed to inhabitants all along the pathway of anticipated darkness, and some school-teachers in the village were to ascend a fairly accessible hill near by with implements for drawing the corona, and with a photographic instrument lent from our camp.

Sunday dawned through a heavy shower. Sunshine succeeded: cloud followed blue sky, northwest wind almost supplanted a damp breeze from the south full of scudding vapor. And still the hours rolled on toward two o'clock and "first contact."

The Astronomer had arranged the program of each person with exactness long before. He still kept calmly at work, giving final directions, the multitude of details resolutely kept in mind with a philosophy as imperturbable as if skies were clear, and cloudless totality a celestial certainty. Vagaries of the western horizon, the moods of wind and prevailing drift of cirrus and cumulus had no farther power to annoy or distract. Time was too precious. It remained for the unofficial member of the party to alternate between such hope and despair that nervous prostration seemed imminent. She watched the attempt at clearing, a matter of but a few hours, and still hoped it would come in time.

At one o'clock half the sky was blue — two o'clock, and the moon had already bitten a small piece out of the sun's bright edge, still partly obscured by a dimly drifting mass of cloud. Half after two, and a large part of the town was ranged along the fence inclosing our apparatus, once in a while looking at the narrowing crescent, but generally at our instruments, the sober faces in curious contrast to sooty decorations from their bits of smoked glass.

And then perceptible darkness crept onward — everything grew quiet. The moon was stealing her silent way across the sun till his crescent grew thin and wan.

The Ainu suppose an eclipse is caused by the fainting or dying of the sun god, toward whom, as he grows black in the face, they whisk drops of water from god sticks or mustache lifters as they would in the case of a fainting person.

But no one spoke.

Shortly before totality, to occur just after three, Esashi time, Chief and I went over to the little lighthouse and mounted to its summit, — an ideal vantage ground for a spectacle beyond anything else it has ever been my fortune to witness.

A camera was propped up beside me, with a plate ready for exposure upon sampans and junks near by, to test the photographic power of coronal light. Black disks, carefully prepared upon white paper, had been distributed to a number of persons, and several others were ready on the little platform, for drawing coronal streamers.

By this time the light was very cold and gray, like stormy winter twilight. The Alger rested motionless on a solid sea. A man in a scarlet blanket at work in a junk made a single spot of color.

Grayer and grayer grew the day, narrower and narrower the crescent of shining sunlight. The sea faded to leaden nothingness.

Armies of crows which had pretended entire indifference, gazing abroad upon the scene, or fighting and flapping on gables and flagpoles with unabated energy, at last succumbed and flew off in a body, friends and enemies together, in heavy haste to a dense pine forest on the mountain side.

The Alger became invisible — sampans and junks faded together into colorlessness; but grass and verdure turned suddenly vivid yellow-green. A penetrating chill fell across the land, as if a door had been opened into a long-closed vault. It was a moment of appalling suspense; something was being waited for — the very air was portentous.

The circling sea gulls disappeared with strange cries. One white butterfly fluttered by vaguely. Then an instantaneous darkness leaped upon the world. Unearthly night enveloped all.

With an indescribable outflashing at the same instant the corona burst forth in mysterious radiance. But dimly seen through thin cloud, it was nevertheless beautiful beyond description, a celestial flame from some unimaginable heaven. Simultaneously the whole northwestern sky, nearly to the zenith, was flooded with lurid and startlingly brilliant orange, across which drifted clouds slightly darker, like flecks of liquid flame, or huge ejecta from some vast volcanic Hades. The west and southwest gleamed in shining lemon yellow.

Least like a sunset, it was too somber and terrible. The pale, broken circle of coronal light still glowed on with thrilling peacefulness, while Nature held her breath for another stage in this majestic spectacle.

Well might it have been a prelude to the shriveling and disappearance of the whole world, — weird to horror, and beautiful to heartbreak, heaven and hell in the same sky.

Absolute silence reigned. No human being spoke. No bird twittered. Even sighing of the surf breathed into utter repose, and not a ripple stirred the leaden sea.

One human being seemed so small, so helpless, so slight a part of all this strangeness and mystery! It was as if the hand of Deity had been visibly laid upon space and worlds, to allow one momentary glimpse of the awfulness of creation.

Hours might have passed — time was annihilated; and yet when the tiniest globule of sunlight, a drop, a needle shaft, a pinhole, reappeared, even before it had become the slenderest possible crescent, the fair corona and all color in sky and cloud withdrew, and a natural aspect of stormy twilight returned. Then the two minutes and a half in memory seemed but a few seconds, — a breath, the briefest tale ever told.

Lightning Source UK Ltd.
Milton Keynes UK
UKHW02n1116120218
317657UK00005B/855/P

9 780483 527874